I0822410

THE ANCIENT REALMS COLLECTION

BOOKS 1-6

A.J. FLOWERS

ISBN: 978-1-953393-00-5

Cover by J Caleb Design

CONTENTS

MISGUIDED KNIGHT OF THE ONYX ORDER

THE LAST ORACLE

THE AWAKENING

FLAWLESS

STRANDED

THE LUNAR CLASH

17 BONUS STORIES

Welcome to Ancient Realms! This is a complete collection of 6 Ancient Realms Collection novelettes.

Viking magic is real, not all knights are honorable, and Ancient Magic comes with a price in these incredible epic fantasy tales.

These tales don't have a happy ending... dark, gritty, fantasy at its finest.

PREFACE

The Ancient Realms Collection is a series of ancient legends, dark myths, and tragic tales come to life. I began writing short books as an outlet for my "heart stories," as authors call them, in-between the novels I wrote for the mass market readership. These stories span the early years of my growth as an author and you'll see a progression of skill throughout the stories which are listed in the order they were written, however they have been edited for content and prose while keeping true to their original style. These are tales from my soul and don't have happy endings, but they are an expression of love and sacrifice that emboldens every dark fairytale to exist in the history books.

I sincerely hope you enjoy this collection as much as I've enjoyed writing it over the course of two years. Now grab your sword, your magical artifacts, and hold on for the wild ride!

Grim Fantasy at its Best

MISGUIDED KNIGHT OF THE ONYX ORDER

Book 1 in the Ancient Realms Collection

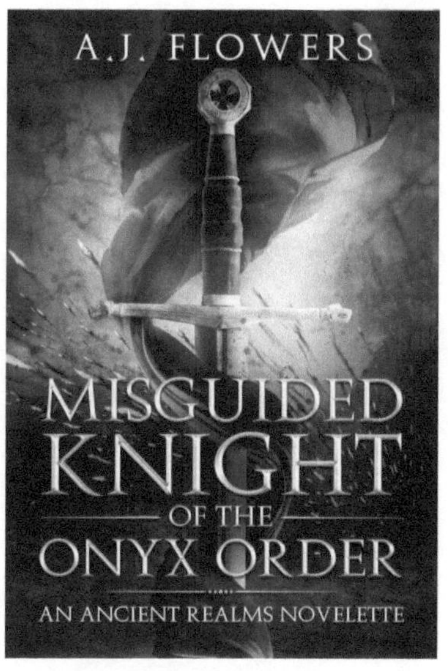

ONE
HOME FROM WAR

Lance, a Knight of the Onyx Order, would have enjoyed the first night home from a successful raid across the border. He'd returned with blood stuck in the crevices of his armor, enough to grant him entry into the brothel of tributes.

Two topless women greeted him as he approached. They wrapped themselves around his neck and begged him to remove his armor. Women were few and rare among the Onyx, with procreation reserved only for the most brutish of knights. Lance should have been pleased to have been given entry to their gates once again. He'd always taken the prize with a sense of duty. But this time, when the scent of sweat and musk wafted from the women's skin, he knew this was no prize at all. He lingered on their gaze, looking to see what souls might lie beneath their pasty flesh. It frightened him when they seemed empty, glinting his own reflection back at him in their cloudy eyes.

Lance had to admit that a change had spread across his stone-cold bones ever since his return. As a rabble of bloodied knights shoved past him, gathering the women's attention, he slunk back into the shadows and left.

He'd always savored his return home, but now he couldn't stand the drab Onyx barracks or the dry humor shared among the knights. A yearning plagued him and wouldn't let him go.

Lance dragged one armored boot in front of the other until the slabs of the onyx streets thinned, overgrown by vines and weeds. The clench in his stomach eased the further he got from his home. Desperate for relief, he plunged into the *otherness* of the foliage. He looked up through the branches, basking in the trickling light that fed through his lashes. The air felt less heavy here, less worn with sin and greed—things he'd never cared about before.

As Lance continued into the forest that separated his land from the next, he found himself stripping his armor. Buckles unlatched and chainmail clung to his damp chest. But he managed to get it all off, every single black bit, until all he had was his vulnerable skin to tickle against the leaves. He suddenly hated that armor, hoped that the forest floor would devour it and suck the dried blood from its crevices.

Lance continued on, searching for something he didn't know how to find. He checked behind every tree, under every rock, delving deeper into the woods than he'd ever gone before on his own. But even this place couldn't seem to offer anything but shadow.

Just when Lance was about to give up, a white flash caught his eye. He shielded his face, expecting a thunderous boom from a squall to follow, but none came. Curious, he brushed aside branches and neared the source. Light pulsed from it like a beacon, calling him to ease the craving in his broken soul. When he was close enough to distinguish the form, he gasped upon seeing a woman staring back at him with eyes brighter than the sun.

She looked through him as if he wasn't even there. He approached, slowly, calling upon his shadows to camouflage him.

This was a shieldmaiden, although he'd never seen one without her helm. Unlike the Onyx, the Pearl Order were entirely comprised of women, and his most hated enemy. She was a goddess of light and brilliance, where he commanded secrecy and shadow. He'd killed so many of her kind, swallowing their screams into darkness, but now he couldn't imagine why he'd ever done such terrible things to such a beautiful creature.

As if the shieldmaiden realized a sliver of shadow had encroached on her domain, her gaze snapped to him and cast unbearable rays into his night-accustomed gaze.

Lance grimaced, but didn't flinch away. He forced himself to go rigid and endure her punishment. Even when white-hot heat bled over her arching cheekbones and she drew a slim sword from its sheath, he didn't move.

Her sword came at him and Lance held her gaze as she struck.

Lance was no stranger to pain. He embraced the sensation as it stabbed through his left shoulder and his muscles seized around the blade. But he watched her, seeing the confusion and doubt swirling in her eyes.

His trembling hand lifted to trace her lips. She'd missed his heart. A shieldmaiden never missed.

TWO
SHIELDMAIDEN

The beacon who'd lured Lance into the woods had a name, a shieldmaiden called Evie. He didn't understand why she'd spared him, nor why she beckoned him to return every night hence.

But he slipped out into the darkness even so, speeding away from the barracks and barreling into the forest to meet his Evie. Before he could peel away his armor, she would teach him to spar, offer him her lightness and speed in favor of familiar brute strength. Like a child learning anew, he'd falter and stumble, only to laugh—*actually laugh*—and snatch her into his arms to discover other, more pleasant things she could teach.

With love he'd found rhythm and ease. His time with tributes was a sorry comparison to the sparking union with Evie. She'd make Lance tremble and his body sing.

Tonight's dance left him breathless and quaking.

"Lance," Evie breathed his name and bade him to stop.

She cast a wary glance to their gear piled haphazardly atop mossy stones. "We push our luck too far. We'll be discovered if we don't leave the realms tonight."

Lance knew her words were true, but he couldn't fathom putting Evie in danger. The Queen was a jealous creature. She watched him closer every day, as if she sensed the darkness leaving one of her finest knights. He'd hid behind his helmet, both needing it and hating the stench of death it wrapped around his face. But the knights were the Queen's protection, her playthings. If he ran, she'd come after him.

"You wouldn't be safe," he explained, caressing Evie's cheek. He encouraged her brilliant gaze to meet his. It was less painful now, and he got lost in the entangling swirls and streaks she left across his vision.

She frowned, her beautiful lips curling in ways they shouldn't. "Then I won't be safe," she insisted stubbornly.

Lance took her mouth with his, for there was no point in arguing. After their final kiss he said, "Tomorrow then, when the moon is full to guide our way."

THE FULL MOON came and Lance hoped it would be enough. The Onyx hated light, especially when it encroached on their city. Perhaps it'd be enough to slip away unnoticed with the provisions they'd need to make it far enough to leave all the realms behind.

Lance hefted the supplies on his shoulder and made his way through the streets. No one braved the moonlight tonight. Hope filled him that this could work. Evie had doused him with her light and love ever since the last full moon. She'd taught him how to appreciate a night like tonight.

Cries and moans bounced off slabs. Dark souls cried to their Queen to douse the moon's gaze. Lance didn't join their plea.

When the moonlight cast shadows everywhere he went, Lance lifted into a jog through the cobbled streets, and became unsettled by the echo of his feet. It could have been the way the sounds were transformed by the pillars of onyx, but it sounded too much as if he were being followed.

When he crossed the boundary of green, Lance should have felt more at ease. But an even worse sense of dread scented the air. A twig snapped and Lance's heart thundered in his chest. Adrenaline shot through his limbs and Lance bolted.

Huffs of breaths followed him as he sped through the forest. He cursed himself for being followed, but he pumped his muscles with renewed speed, determined to get to Evie first. He catapulted through vines and limbs that hindered his way. Terrible shrieks sounded across his armor as the forest fought him.

Lance finally reached the clearing, dropped his pack and stumbled onto soft grass that sank with his weight. Moonlight shed down with full force onto the familiar mossy spot, and for a moment, Lance thought the naked form was Evie lighting her beacon to guide him into her arms. But when shadows gulped down the moonlight and onyx eyes sparkled, he reeled back and snarled at the Queen.

The Queen perversed the light, making it bend and twine around her perfect body. Too perfect, like a sculpture or a carving. Even her skin gleamed and revealed specks and veins as if her transformation into living onyx was nearly complete.

"My knight," she said, her eyelids drooping. "I believe you've been lusting in misguided ways. Why don't I remind you what tasting Onyx is like?"

To taste the Queen was the highest honor among the knights of the Onyx Order. Unlike the tributes, her metallic gaze held a powerful soul, but it was a vile and terrible thing. When disgust lit his face rather than delight, the Queen shot to her feet and hissed. "You deny me?" Her face twisted with rage, straining against the movement as if her features were too engraved to accept the snarl.

"Where is she?" Lance demanded.

The Queen's face eased into a more familiar grin and her onyx eyes glittered with miserable pleasure. "Right where I want her."

Lance's heart slammed into his chest at the Queen's words. Was Evie safe? Was she even alive? As if the clearing had exploded with Evie's light, his vision went white and a guttural roar exploded from his chest. He flung out his sword and dove for the Queen.

A legion of Onyx that had been his echoing footsteps launched from the foliage. They might have enjoyed watching the Queen perform. Instead, they pinned Lance down and poised to strike.

The Queen raised a hand, signaling they keep him alive.

"Fear not, misguided knight," the Queen said, grazing a claw across Lance's cheek, "you'll redeem yourself at the Trial of Blades."

THREE
TRIAL OF BLADES

A night in the dungeons sent Lance mad with impatience. When the day eventually came and silent guards took him to the arena, he could barely contain his rage.

The Trial of Blades had drawn an impressive audience. Lance's sword rattled in his gauntlet to hear their excited murmurings. Hadn't he fought for their pitiful lives? Hadn't he murdered and spread darkness across innocent lands to feed their greed?

The arena threatened to blind him as it reflected sunlight off crystal sand. It was one of the only places in the land of Onyx that wasn't mired in shadow. The Queen wished to see the gore of the games in all its glory.

Lance searched through the brilliance for his Evie. Five gleaming shieldmaidens blended with the arena's glow. Each bore identical sets of pearlescent armor, complete with the iconic helms to cover their faces. Four were imposters, likely Onyx knights from Lance's very barracks. But one, he knew, would be his Evie.

Here bore the cruelty of the Queen's games. Lance had his own set of imposter knights to be pitched against the other team. Only one shieldmaiden would survive, and only one knight. To win Evie's freedom, he would have to figure out which one was her, or risk becoming her executioner.

The tension in the arena sprang to a taut string. His imposter knights shifted as if itching to strike the back of his neck. But the Trial of Blades was one of the Onyx's favorite games. Breaking the rules meant death, but victory meant any wish granted. An Onyx would likely wish for unlimited time with the tributes, or a dose of the Queen's dark powers to wipe out entire armies in her honor. Lance gritted his teeth. If he were to win, he'd simply ask for him and Evie to leave. Out of all the wishes she'd granted, would she grant such a simple request?

The Queen raised her voice to greet the crowd. She was instantly met with a delighted cheer. Lance glowered at the creature he'd once pledged loyalty. He scoured her bannered stand for any hint of an opening to strike. Could he throw his sword from this distance? Could he reach her before the archers took him out?

As if she sensed his eyes on her, the Queen straightened, the motion puffing her midnight dress out at the shoulders like silken vambraces.

Before Lance had time to react, the Queen clapped her hands and set the game into motion.

Crossbows stretched, warning him that any hesitation would qualify them to take his life. He roared and launched himself with the other four dark imposters.

White sand kicked up a fog as the players closed the distance. Then a screech of metal bit the air as Lance's sword landed against another's.

His heart thundered as he tested the blows. He'd sparred with Evie so many times. Yet, a shieldmaiden's armor forced the strikes in familiar ways; was it her? Was it an imposter?

The shieldmaiden didn't give him time to analyze their movements. Parry—Parry—Strike!

Lance swirled close to his opponent and his sword followed the motions, landing on an opening in the pearlescent armor. He wanted to wait, to be sure he knew what kind of soul lay beneath his blade. But his hairs stood on their ends, telling him there was a crossbow aimed at his neck.

Lance's vision wavered when he had no choice but to shove his blade deep. One out of five it was his Evie. Odds he had to hope would hold in his favor.

His opponent gasped, then gurgled before going silent and slumping over Lance's blade.

Before Lance had a chance to swallow the rising bile in his throat, a dark imposter-knight slammed into him, knocking the wind out of his chest. Lance gasped for breath and scrambled against the knight.

Lance was about to return the blow, only to see the knight collapsing to the ground, revealing a gash where an arm had once been.

The realization that a shieldmaiden had amputated one of his imposters lifted his spirits. Evie was a fine fighter, but not so brutal. She preferred speed and precision, like a needle straight to the heart.

Lance spotted the shieldmaiden with a bloodied blade poised over the knight's arm. Lance dove with his sword raised high to strike. And like Lance expected of a burly man dressed in shieldmaiden's armor, he didn't try to dodge. The imposter braced his sword on his elbow and took Lance's blow. The clash rang through the air and the crowd echoed with an excited gasp.

While his opponent's teeth clattered and his fingers went limp with numbness, Lance went through trained motions for the maneuver. Evie had taught him how to use strength against strength. Even though his own fingers complained with a thousand zaps, he didn't need them. He used his legs to heave his sword through the crack in the armor at his opponent's hip. It slid in with a sickening squelch and Lance was rewarded with a man's groan.

The air shifted as another blow came towards Lance's head. His fingers were too numb to block, so Lance dove, rolling on the ground like Evie had taught him.

But he'd practiced in the forest without his armor. This time painful jabs speared through his chest with the motion. Grunting and slow, he righted himself only to find all three shieldmaidens poised with their blades at his face. Like an omen, the imposter knights laid facedown in the sand, pooling blood and soaking the crystalline grains red.

"Brave knight," the Queen said. Her voice carried across the arena and caressed Lance's ears in unwanted ways. "You've done well, but how will you fare against three?"

Lance held his breath as he surveyed the trio. Each silver blade was stained with red.

"Perhaps the bitch is dead," the Queen snapped. "You should kill them all."

Lance knew she was just trying to goad him into breaking the rules. Even now, as the last black knight standing, he still had to prevail before he took off his helm. The Queen's wicked gleam in her eyes said she hoped Evie was alive just to taste her misery at wondering if she'd killed her lover.

Lance strained to see beyond the shieldmaiden's visors. At this distance, he should be able to see Evie's glow. But as he inspected each helm, all he saw was darkness and malice. His heart sank and he had to bite his cheek to keep his wits. Surely Evie was still alive. She had to be.

The Queen offered a cruel laugh as she stroked a taut crossbow aimed at his face. "Fine, keep your silence." Her smile faded as she jerked her chin.

A cascade of trumpets sounded and the shieldmaidens lunged for Lance all at once. The crossbows lowered. If Evie was among this trio, he was proud of her to be so brave. Any hesitation and she'd be dead.

Lance fended off the blows, rolling to grab the severed arm's sword. His body retained his skill, even if his heart had faltered. Each strike was swept clean with his dual blades—all except one. A blur pierced his guard and grazed his cheek like a kiss.

Like a game of cups, Lance locked onto the shieldmaiden who'd stabbed true. She'd retreated to the center of her two imposters. Lance followed her movements and fed his newfound elation into his muscles. He sped to her side and struck both shieldmaidens through their visors. The swords *pinged* on the other side of the helms, having gone straight through.

Victory at last. Heaving for breath, Lance ripped off his helm. The Queen gasped with delight as if she'd known he'd win all along. "My brave knight!" she cried.

Lance snarled and snapped a blade in her direction. Blood flung off with heavy droplets onto the sand. "I'll never be your knight," he growled.

With a pounding heart Lance faced the surviving shieldmaiden. Carefully, he peeled away her helm. Shadows fell from her eyes and her brilliance blasted across his face. Lance's heart constricted, realizing that Evie had prevailed such an impossible trial even with the Queen's interference.

Evie grabbed him and kissed him hard. When she pulled away, she smiled, her glory coming over her in heated waves. Her bleached hair stuck to her head in sweat-soaked streaks and her brilliant eyes burned with love and rage. He'd never found her more beautiful.

FOUR
TRIAL OF FAITH

"Do you think the Queen will honor the decree?" Evie whispered in the pitch black of the dungeons. Even though they'd won the day, the Queen wouldn't grant their wish. Another trial, she'd demanded, and then they'd been cast into darkness and cages. Evie's eyes glowed, giving them enough light to see the grimy bars that held them agonizingly apart.

"She won't let us go," Evie insisted. "We should chop her into a thousand pieces."

Lance chuckled with a humorless laugh. "Nothing can kill the Queen."

Evie snorted as if she knew something he didn't.

With a sigh, Lance relaxed against the muddy prison wall. His muscles tingled from exertion and his wounds stung, reminiscent of sparring sessions with Evie. His body ached to follow his pain with pleasure, to wrap himself in Evie's sun-kissed smell and lose himself in her. But they had no trees to shelter such love and hide it away. The Queen had sent them far underground to breathe the dirt of the dead. Lance's nostrils flared at the stench.

"She'll honor it," he said, even though the word "honor" was as foreign to the Queen as Evie's brilliance. "The Onyx watched the games today," Lance added. Surely with so many witnesses the Queen would have to honor the decree and grant them their wish of exile.

"Games," Evie sneered at the term. "Such a strange people, these Onyx."

Lance smirked. She said the word as if he wasn't Onyx himself. He caught her eye and a thrill fluttered in his chest. "You were brave today," he said, his voice going low and husky. He reached through the sticky bars, slick with the earth's sweat, and found her cheek. "I only survived because of the skills you taught me. Your speed and your cunning." He stroked his thumb over her ever-heated skin. "Like a needle."

Evie pressed her hand over his until his skin burned and Lance had to grit his teeth to endure her pleasure and her rage. "We'll show the Queen the power of our union," Evie promised.

"Yes," he agreed. "We will."

WITH THE APEX of the sun came their reprieve from darkness and death. The court gathered around towering pillars of onyx in the audience chamber. Excitement filled the stale air. No one had ever won the games and asked for such an absurd prize. What would the Queen do?

Lance ached to hold Evie's hand. Instead, his knees pushed into unforgiving slate before the throne and his fingers went numb in his chains as if he'd taken a blow. The sun struggled through stained glass, uselessly trying to shine on the Queen. She billowed with shadow and her eyes glittered darker than Lance had ever seen.

Lance knew such display of her powers cost the Queen. She was always patiently conserving her store for the next big clash with the realms. If he'd won a Trial of Blades a single day before he'd met Evie, he would have asked for a taste of that power. Instead the Queen reveled in it as if she had too much sin to spare. She seemed loose, uncontrolled, and wicked. She glared at Lance as if all she wanted to do was gobble him up into her void and make him disappear forever.

When the Queen finally moved, the audience of nobles, knights, and onyx merchants went silent. They swayed together and watched Lance and Evie as if they would implode by the Queen's whispered command.

"Tell me," the Queen hissed, her voice a spectacular grating of inhuman sounds, "why should I allow you exile?"

Lance opened his mouth to speak, but nothing came out. He was awe-struck with the Queen's darkness. He only saw her like this on the battlefield, far away from him and close to her prey. To see her like this up close was a sight to behold. Mesmerized, he didn't know if he should be terrified or reverent.

Evie's voice pierced the darkness and shook Lance from the Queen's spell. "You made a decree."

The Queen snapped her shadows onto Evie. They hissed and shrieked around the shieldmaiden bound in onyx chains. Evie only straightened and glowed a bit brighter. "Do you deny, before all who have witnessed our victory, to grant our wish of exile?"

The audience chamber filled with murmurs. The Queen snapped to her feet and sent them into silence. Instead of launching herself off the platform, she offered Evie a cruel grin. "Ah, but as my people know, my decree was made to the Onyx." Her dark gaze fled to the backs of the chamber as she addressed the crowd. "What say you, my people? Has the trial been passed?" She swept her palms outward and shadows spiraled up the massive columns. "These two warriors, a shieldmaiden of Pearl, and Lance, a betrayer to the Onyx who has lain with our enemy. What justice is there in exile?"

The people's voices rose and fell like heaving tides.

"I am not cruel," the Queen said as her dark eyes glittered with delight. "You shall have one more chance to earn your exile." Her fingers swept down Evie's collarbone, sizzling at the contact of midnight dark against her pearl skin. "You wish to be together? Then prove to me you are worthy of such treachery." Her lips stretched over her teeth in a terrifying grin. "Let there be a Trial of Faith."

THE ENTIRE KINGDOM gathered for the Trial of Faith. The Queen had transformed the arena. The pristine sand had been melted and the air smelled of ash. Glowing coals stretched across the ground and sent wavering wafts of heat to play with Evie's short hair.

Evie stood at the epicenter of the embers on a small patch of dry ground. She was unbound, but blindfolded with shadow. She looked so thin without her pearlescent armor and mesh, so naked without her sword. Bravely, she waited for the trial to begin with curled fists and a clenched jaw.

Lance absently ran a thumb over the scar Evie had given him. She'd missed his heart and spared his life. He'd been reborn that night. This life was a gift she'd granted him. Determination washed over him and he knew that if it would save her, he'd die in her place.

Evie's pink lips pressed together and her shoulders shook with rage. He knew his faith was strong, but what of hers? Did she regret sparing his life? Would she be able to put faith in a man she should have killed?

"Misguided knight," the Queen began, spearing into Lance's fretting thoughts, "your task in this trial is merely a decision." She indicated Evie across the coals with a sweep of her hand. "You must choose how to direct her path. Either you lead her to you, or to me."

"Why would I ever give her to you?" Lance snapped, even though the answer to that was plain to see. Evie would have to walk on fire to complete this trial. The expanse of blistering coals was twice as long to the Queen than himself, and Evie's skin already glistened with sweat.

"A quick death," the Queen promised. At Lance's flinch she added, "You must know that her own kingdom will hunt her down the moment I set you free. It would be a mercy." She grinned. "I'll even consider allowing you back into the Onyx Order."

Lance clenched his fists. If the Queen meant to bait him with that, she didn't know what Evie's love had done to him. "I'll never let you harm her," Lance promised. "Not you, and not anyone else."

The Queen shrugged as if it was of no consequence, turning to address Evie. "And you, shieldmaiden of the Pearl Order, you must endure barefoot and blindfolded by my shadow. You'll walk the coals, trusting in your lover's instruction." She smirked. "If you wish to spare yourself such agony, or your faith wavers, simply call out to me and I will take you from this place. Your kingdom will believe you've been taken hostage by the Onyx. They'll welcome you back with open arms."

Evie cocked her head to the side like a bird. "What would happen to Lance?"

The Queen frowned, as if the answer was an unfortunate but inevitable one. "He would spend time in the dungeons until he's learned his place."

Evie seemed to relax. Lance stiffened, wondering if Evie judged his survival enough of a trade. Did she love him at all? If Evie left him behind, she might as well have pierced his heart with her blade.

"And so the Trial of Faith begins," the Queen announced, rising to her feet and clapping both hands together. The sound slapped against Lance's ears and made him quake with dread.

Crossbows stretched and the murmur of the massive crowds spurred Lance to raise his voice. He found his tongue and called to Evie.

A knot unwound in his stomach when Evie pressed her lips together and obeyed. The audience, far away in the stands, murmured and strained to see her progress. They seemed to enjoy her pain, going deathly silent to hear the faint sizzle of her steps and the groans forced from her lips. Even though her powers were of brilliance and light, she could not endure flames for long. Lance called out to her even harder, every part of him wishing to make this entire arena burn to ashes.

The Queen frowned as Evie moved away from the throne. Seeming to grow bored with the scene, her eyes rolled to the back of her head and the ground shook as a new spell took hold. Lance's chest flipped as a blast of darkness shot from the Queen in a nauseating wave.

Evie staggered and let out a cry as coals seared across her ankles. Another quake hit, then three more until the arena filled with shadow and malice. Between the shades, Lance searched for Evie and screamed for her to keep going. She fell and shards of red sent blisters across her naked arms.

Lance called again, putting all his might into the effort. But he abruptly stopped when he realized that his words had changed their course as they unfurled across the pit.

Evie righted herself and swirled with confusion as if

she sensed the change. The shadows thinned, revealing towering onyx plates angled in alternating directions. Lance startled, realizing that his voice traveled and echoed across them until it was as if he was calling from the Queen.

Disoriented and still bathed in coals, Evie clawed at the ground and cried out, running in the wrong direction. Embers splattered up her arms and sent a ring of blisters down her neck.

Lance's heart plummeted. "No," he whispered. He couldn't let the Queen win this way. With a glance at his own bare feet, he was struck with a realization. There hadn't been any rules that *he* couldn't walk on the coals.

Lance launched himself across the embers, all the while screaming Evie's name. Pain made him balk and black spots speckled across his vision. He was a creature of shadow. Evie had increased his endurance for heat, but he'd never experienced anything so raw and agonizing as this. His toes curled into the daggers of fire and his eyes watered at the pain.

Evie stilled, until finally she turned around.

The Queen shouted with outrage and a cocking of crossbows reverberated in Lance's ears, but he didn't slow. He slammed into Evie and wrapped her in his arms, dragging her back to his patch of land.

When his skinned toes finally met grains of sand, it felt like ice and he cried out with relief. He collapsed and Evie sank to the ground with him.

"Exile!" Lance shouted through the pain. A wave of

nausea hit him. He couldn't be sure if it was from the embers or the Queen's shadow. "Exile," he groaned again and clutched Evie's trembling body.

The Queen snarled and another wave of nausea made Lance's stomach drop. She screamed for his death. She carried herself across the coals, hissing them out of existence with the malice of her shadow.

She was coming for them.

Bolts soared through the air, adding more black spots to Lance's vision. He watched helplessly and hugged Evie even tighter. He prayed to Evie's god that she, at least, would be spared.

As if his prayers had been heard, light blazed from the sky and engulfed them in a sphere. The nausea abruptly ended and the bolts hit the barrier, puffing out of existence.

He could still see the Queen coming at them full force, undeterred by the wall of light.

Lance hugged Evie and healing waves of warmth eased his pain. He watched in awe as his skin stitched itself together. He caught Evie's wild gaze. Her blindfold melted and the blisters across her face swelled until they wrapped over with new flesh.

Evie smiled. "She's right where we want her."

Before Lance could ask Evie what she meant, the Queen clashed against the barrier. A terrible screech ripped through his ears as the Queen's rage hit. A claw wrapped in shadow ripped through the golden sheen.

"Father!" Evie shouted, jerking her head to the sky. "Now!"

Lance startled at her cry and her white-hot eyes that widened with excitement.

The light swelled at Evie's call and pinned the Queen's hand against the sands. A blistering roar sounded as she thrashed and grew until she became a giant, three times Lance's size with swirling black orbs for eyes that promised oblivion.

A white-bearded man, just as impressive in stature, descended from the sky. Panicked cries erupted as the Onyx charged, banging uselessly against the wall of light.

A glittering sword appeared in the man's grasp and he sent it flying through the air. The blade pierced the ground and sent a shockwave that thundered into Lance's chest.

Without thinking, Lance took the blade. It accepted him and unlatched from the ground. Lance momentarily stared at it, stunned. Had he just picked up the Pearl King's sword?

"Strike!" Evie commanded him. When he gave her a stunned stare, she bolted to his side and pushed. "Only an Onyx can kill her!"

The Queen finally wriggled free of her confines, sending the binding light shattering like glass. She dove for Lance and gouged dark claws into his face.

Lance grinned against the pain. The Queen had completely transformed into a creature of shadow. Darkness was something he knew well. Shadows writhed under his skin and the nauseating wave of malice returned. But Lance *was* shadow. It was in his soul and her hatred harmlessly slipped through his chest.

This was why only an Onyx could kill the Queen.

With resign, he hefted the blade and plunged the sword into her belly. Light imploded into her chest, dismantling all that she was. He closed his eyes, waiting for the light to take him as well, but Evie ripped him from the Queen's grasp just as the tendrils of light snaked from the Queen's fingers.

The Queen screeched before she died. She collapsed into an unrecognizable ugly heap.

Lance blinked at Evie as she hushed him and stroked his face, pushing him to look away from the gruesome scene. When he realized he was trembling, he allowed her to peel his fingers from the glowing blade.

She took the sword and pressed a kiss to his lips. "Thank you," she whispered.

Lance thought she might kiss him again, but she left his arms and took her comforting heat with her. She walked to what was left of the Queen and kneeled. Lance thought she might keep her promise and chop the Queen into a thousand pieces. Instead, she angled the tip of the blade at the Queen's onyx eye. With a small *pop* the eye lifted free.

"Father?" Evie asked as she rolled the eye across her palm before wrapping her fingers possessively around it. She looked up to the man who seemed wilted and tired. Their protective barrier still burned, eating the continuous rain of bolts and roar of the crowd.

Evie's gaze flitted to Lance. "Can we take him with us?"

The Pearl King considered the knight. His brilliant eyes bore into Lance as if he searched for what was left of his soul. After a short moment, he gave a brief nod. "Very well. But keep him with your other pets. I won't have him in the castle."

Lance shot a questioning glance at Evie, but she wouldn't meet his gaze. Lance's soul turned dark as the Pearl King took them to enemy lands in a brilliant flash of light.

FIVE
EXILE

"You lied to me?" Lance spat as he pointed to the other men behind the glass.

Evie shriveled into herself. "I'm sorry," she murmured.

Lance, open-mouthed, stared at the men again. Jealousy stabbed into his chest as he saw they were lost and beautiful, just like him. One was of the realm of flames with brilliant, red hair. Another of the oceans boasting glimmering aqua scales that traced up muscular arms. A third crouched atop a plush bench, extending massive white wings and stared through the glass with eyes as clear as the sky. The last crossed arms that twined with living vine; it wrapped around his neck and wound down his back, writhing across his skin.

Lance had seen enough harems to know that Evie had made her own personal collection of every realm she'd conquered. He closed his slack-jawed gape, realizing that *he* completed the collection.

Evie had used him. She'd needed his shadow to survive

the Queen. She'd lusted for his darkness to add to her plethora of eclectic tastes.

He jerked himself over her and pressed her against the wall, overtaking her brilliant gaze in shadow. "I'll not stay here," he hissed through clenched teeth. "I'm no *pet*."

He'd expected a fight from his brave Evie, but to his surprise, tears slithered down her treacherous face. She nodded.

He narrowed his eyes. "So, you'll let me go without a fight?"

When her gaze pierced through his malice, his wretched heart still skipped a beat. She searched him as if she could find his soul. Lance frowned, recalling how her father had done the same thing. He knew what that look meant. Judging. Scheming. Plotting.

"I was different before I met you," Evie insisted as if she could read his thoughts. A flash of rage crossed her face and Lance stiffened, readying himself for a fight. Instead, Evie pushed him away and punched the glass, shattering it. The harem blinked at them with confusion. "Go!" Evie shouted. "I never want to see you again!"

Their confusion seemed to clear when they spotted Lance. His frown deepened with rage. They gave him ample girth as they made their way through and exited the chamber.

"Please," she begged when they had gone, "come with me to the castle. You'll understand when you see what I've done."

The desperation in her voice sounded so real. Lance's mind flitted with cautious thoughts that suggested this could be just another Pearl talent. But wouldn't manipulation and trickery be something of an Onyx skill?

Regardless of the answer, curiosity won out and Lance allowed her to lead him away. His exile could wait a moment longer.

His exile, he repeated in his mind and his soul grew a bit darker. His exile from Evie.

EVIE LED Lance to the castle and shushed him before catapulting him into the brilliant walls of pearl.

"Father can't know I've brought you here," she said.

Lance offered her a noncommittal shrug. Evie frowned and took his hand as they made their way through the labyrinth of halls and rooms and dizzying brilliance.

Lance should have flung her fingers off, or at least tried to memorize their path through the maze. Instead, he savored the contact of Evie's skin on his, how it still burned away his shadows and made his tongue flick against his teeth. Instead of taking advantage of being the only Onyx to have breached enemy walls, he thought of nothing except Evie's hand in his.

Rounding a final bend, Evie brought him to a room garnished by five pedestals. As Evie drew him closer, he spotted tiny orbs atop each one. His heart seized when the realization hit him. Not orbs. *Eyes*.

Evie whispered a word of power and the room came to life with visions of their respective lands. Evie had truly conquered them all to collect the eyes of their rulers. The onyx eye filtered familiar images of the barracks, dark lands speckled with malice and even the lush forests that separated the Onyx from the Pearl.

A ruby eye showed a land showering with flames and Lance now knew how she'd endured his Queen's sea of coals. Her Ruby lover had no doubt taught her skills of his ways, just as Lance had taught her the ways of shadow and lies.

An aquamarine showed him fish and sea creatures he'd never seen before.

A moonstone splayed clouds and endless sky with winged men who aimlessly drifted without their King.

The last, an emerald, filled the walls with sprouting forests and stretching grasslands. Small, furry animals hid under the wild tufts of foliage, greeting a man who returned to them with living ropes of vine.

Evie smiled at the vision of her Emerald lover having returned home. "I'm glad he made it back," she said quietly, then caught herself and wrapped her fingers around her elbows. "The forests deserve better than I gave them."

Lance frowned, not taking the bait. The forest had been *their* sanctuary, a reminder of a love they'd once shared. Now all he saw were her lovers and a King's eye on a pedestal. "Why do you show me this?" he asked.

Evie flinched at the venom in his voice. "Can't you see it?" She pointed to a vision of the flames. "See the light within this realm?" Lance squinted, indeed seeing specks of sunlight peeking beneath low burning embers. "And here?" she pointed to the splash of blue and the vision shot to the seabed. Clams shot open with mouthfuls of pearl.

Lance then looked up, seeing sunlight pouring through a pinhole. "You're taking control," he accused.

"No," Evie said. "We're giving them enlightenment." She pouted, seeming so sure of herself. "We're giving them hope."

Lance froze with realization. Light was infecting these lands by Evie's conjured magic. It poured through the stolen eyes and took root in each realm. Was this why he'd changed? Was this how an indescribable yearning had fitted itself within the cavity of his chest and refused to let him go until he...

He stared at Evie. Perhaps manipulation was indeed a powerful Pearl skill. "You thought this would make me understand you?" he sneered. "Well, it has."

Evie ran to his side and clung to his arm. "Please don't be angry. You must understand, there can be peace this way. Finally, the world can be under one realm."

Lance didn't flinch from her golden gaze as he said, "You mean *your* realm."

A streak of genuine pain flashed across her eyes before she looked away and her hands fell to her sides.

"I've seen enough," Lance said, wrapping a cold sheet of shadow around his plagued heart. "I've earned my exile. Send me on my way."

TO LANCE'S SURPRISE, and slight disappointment, Evie complied, but not without a whispered wish that he one day return.

Lance thought he one day might appease her wish, once he had an army of his own.

Evie was worse than shadow. She'd dressed herself in light and goodness when her heart was blacker than the Queen's had ever been. At least the Queen had been exactly as one would expect. Lance regretted killing her.

Lance traced his fingers across the raised scar that still blistered with light. He'd never be free of the reminder. As he stepped into the forest and pain welled inside of him, he threw his head back and roared to the light-riddled skies.

SIX
A MISGUIDED KNIGHT RETURNS HOME

When Lance approached the Onyx, they blessed his return and bowed at his feet. He'd conquered the Queen with trickery and malice that had rivaled her own. Working with their enemies to split her soul in two, what cunning! What evil!

Lance couldn't disagree, even if the cunning hadn't been his.

Lance filled the role as ruler of Onyx and prepared for Evie's invasion into the shadow. He filled himself with malice and hatred, letting darkness bleed across his lands. A drifting, grey fog settled over the skies, thick enough to even block the light of a full moon, and the people lived in awe of their new King.

Lance built his army, ripping the Onyx Order apart and building it anew with colder, darker souls that he formed from birth. He doubled the amount of tributes and instructed them only to lay with the most vile and brutish of knights. Their sons filled his personal legion that swarmed the castle.

Evie would come for him, if not today, then the next. He felt her invisible gaze on him, watching through the Queen's dead eye. He wondered what Evie thought of his transformation. Onyx grew over his skin in massive plates and shadow whispered about his ears. Silver veins split through his fingernails and his eyes glittered at the thought of taking the Pearl lands. He'd show Evie what she'd created. He'd rip her own father's eye from its socket and use it to spread shadow over her lands. He'd snuff out the light forever.

SEVEN

MISGUIDED NO MORE

The day came when the land of Onyx overflowed and Lance had to resign to being the first to strike. Evie had laid in wait in her comfortable lands and didn't seem inclined to move, so he would fulfill her wish to return.

When he hefted his onyx sword, brought his legion and armies, he reached the Pearl castle having told them of the epic battle they'd face, of the stories they'd engrave to the chronicles of time and the glory of transforming the world into shadow.

Yet, the castle wasn't as he'd remembered it. The brilliant beams of light had reduced to filtered, dusty motes. The once slick pearl was now crippled columns of cracked and withered stone heaps.

"Where is our glory?" his army asked. "Where are our terrifying enemies?"

Lance sent a wave of nausea over them and they stiffened, but didn't cower. They were his men, his creation and, even against him, they wouldn't stifle their rage. He could taste their bloodlust and disappointment. He'd promised them a glorious battle against a brilliant foe.

Lance frowned. He didn't answer, and instead turned to the castle's door and beat it with his gauntleted fist. It crumpled to the ground without resistance, sprawling into slabs of split pearl.

The dust settled and revealed stretches of broken halls that he vaguely remembered. He hated himself for not knowing the way. He'd been too infatuated with Evie's hand to have memorized the path to the room of stolen eyes.

His army kept on his heels as he led them inside. As his boots scraped against dulled pearl, he finally came across signs of life.

Or, what had once been life. Endless trails of bodies littered the hallways. Lance followed them, finding their number steadily increased. He'd never seen the people of Pearl, and now they looked so weak. Their scrawny bodies twisted in agonized ways, their skin gleaming like crystal as stark veins overtook their faces.

Lance didn't want to admit it looked like sickly onyx.

His army began to murmur with shocked and impressed tones. They jabbed at the bodies with fingers and swords.

"Don't disturb them," Lance said, surprising himself by the rebuke. He'd taught his men nothing but darkness. Why didn't he expect them to desecrate corpses?

When their displeasure rippled across the back of his neck, he scoffed and waved a hand. "Fine. Go scour the area. See if anyone's survived."

Seeming pleased to have been given orders, a general barked off commands, splitting the legion down various halls. Boots thundered as they swept away like a wave, searching for anything they could destroy.

Lance sauntered off in the one direction his knights hadn't gone because his bulky frame had been in the way. The bodies grew in number with each step he took. When he reached a massive set of doors that still seemed to have retained their glow, he knew he'd made it to the throne room.

He stomped up the steps and slammed against the barrier. The doors groaned under his weight, the only part of the castle that didn't immediately buckle under shadow.

The door finally gave way with a screech of pearl against tattered stone and Lance shoved himself inside. His cold heart flinched when he met Evie's wide-eyed stare. She shot to her feet. "Lance!" she cried, as if he'd come to save her.

Lance buried the sliver of warmth that threatened to break through his chest and instead withdrew his sword. He gripped the hilt and recalled his rage, made all the easier by the sight of the ancient, bearded man wheezing atop the throne.

The Pearl King hardly looked so glorious as he should have been. His massive crown looked like a burden on his brow and his cloudy, grey eyes struggled to stay open. He drew in a ragged gasp as he realized Lance had come to take his eye.

Lance slowly approached, taking his time to savor the

moment he'd waited so long to behold. He tried to ignore the fact that none of this was enjoyable at all.

"Everyone's gone," Evie whispered. She flinched as if she longed to cling to his arm once again, but her gaze bobbed to his onyx sword and she curled into herself. "They've all succumbed to the..." Her words drifted until she finally met his gaze. Her eyes flickered with struggling brilliance. "Succumbed...to *you*."

Lance frowned. "I've nothing to do with what's happened here."

Evie shook her head and glimmering tears flung from her face. "Why have I been spared? Why did you save me for last?" She regarded her father and her face scrunched with pain. "You mean to punish me for what I did to you."

Lance finally allowed himself to see the truth. Dark veins stripped the walls as tendrils of shadow sucked the light from the air. It wound up the throne and stabbed through the King's wrists like chains. Somehow, he'd done this.

He should have been riveted with victory that he'd become something greater than any Queen or King of shadow. He could dominate all the realms and bring darkness the world had never seen. He didn't need eyes or tricks. He had a heart full of betrayal and misery, a breeding ground for shadow.

Yet, the thought twisted Lance's heart with agony. His sword dipped and scraped across the ground. His fingers went to the scar on his left shoulder, even after all this time, still visible as a flickering of light that could never be overtaken by shadow, no matter how much onyx he grew over his skin.

Evie sniffed and a small smile lit her face as her gaze followed his fingertips. Her eyes pulsed with a faint light. "There's a part of you that doesn't want this."

Lance frowned and scratched at the scar. "You make what you want of my injury." He straightened, righting his sword once again. "Your blade left its mark, just as your betrayal turned me into this." He aimed the sword at her chest and Evie's eyes darkened. "I'm truly an Onyx now."

With fresh determination, he buried the wisps of his lost love and strode to the throne. The blood drained from Evie's face as he pulled back his sword and struck.

The moment slowed to a crawl and Lance was transfixed by Evie's terror. He wasn't sure why he did it, but he altered his aim, piercing the blade an inch from her heart.

Evie cried out, but she would live. He left her alone with his blade still in her chest.

Light would never fully be squelched, for while Evie was still alive, he was the most powerful Onyx in all the realms.

He took one last glance over his shoulder, his heart twisting and his shadow swirling with malice. "I love you, even now," he whispered. Evie's face contorted with pain as he shut the door behind him.

About Misguided Knight of the Onyx Order

I wrote this story as an expression of light and dark which reappears in many of my novels. Exploring the villain is one of my favorite literary exercises and I imagined what it might be like to be a part of a dark army and find out that there's a piece of light in your soul. To be betrayed by that light would be even more tragic, but that is the way of the world, so the Misguided Knight of the Onyx Order was born.

THE LAST ORACLE

Book 2 in the Ancient Realms Collection

Honorable Mention in the 2017 Writers of the Future L. Ron Hubbard Contest

ONE
THE LAST ORACLE

Torunn rolled back his shoulders, not curling under the scrutiny of the council of angered women who were no longer women. They were the gatherings of unanswered prayers to the Aesir and the Vanir, lost souls never given peace. They clashed against the expanse of vines and weeds and leaves sparking around their rotting heads. He'd dreamed of this day, what it would be like to stand in the sacred grove. Although, he'd never imagined he would meet the oracles face-to-face.

Each oracle judged him as they squinted faces smeared with black streaks. Their feathered headdresses flailed against the wind that wasn't a wind, but a torrent of failed prayers that followed the oracles wherever they went. Torunn didn't let their staring dead eyes deter him from the path he'd already decided. He took his sister's hand in his and faced them alongside her. He'd never let her be alone.

"Sigrid will be the sacrifice," the oldest said firmly, not seeming to be impressed by his stature and blasphemous thoughts of protecting his sister. She frowned, wrinkles barely making an appearance even though she was centuries old. "It's your duty to protect your sister," she observed. She tilted her head in an unnatural way, her jaw clicking as if it had unlatched from her neck.

"And what of your duty?" he asked.

Her lips peeled back in a sneer. "We are bound by the covenant between draugr and oracle. Our duty is to no-one but the covenant."

Torunn studied the woman. Was it possible that the oracles detested the covenant they'd made with the corpses they favored?

"The draugr king comes for his bride," the eldest oracle continued. "We cannot fight him."

Torunn focused on the faded oracles who looked at him with streaks of hope in their withered eyes. He'd always been treated like an unwanted shadow, but now they were asking for his help. "What can I do?" he asked.

"Your father was our vessel, your sister an oracle. Even if you are mortal, there is untapped power in your blood."

Torunn frowned. He'd never felt powerful.

Sigrid shoved him aside. "Enough." She straightened. "If you've seen the same fate as I, sisters, you know that I am the last." Torunn shivered. His sister, the last *living* oracle. "Even if we honor the covenant, there won't be anything to hold the draugr back when I am gone."

This was the first time Torunn had heard Sigrid admit she was the last. Her auburn hair burned like flames, the only splash of color in the collection of washed out oracles.

The phantoms swayed as if moved by Sigrid's words.

The eldest approached her and crawled her fingers over Sigrid's like a spider taking its prey. "Yes, child. We've seen." Her grey eyes softened as she patted Sigrid's fingers. "We'll do our best. Our magic is drained, and I fear it won't be enough." She turned her gaze to Torunn.

He swallowed and kept her gaze. Torunn thought she might praise him, or foresee his future and a glorious victory. Instead, the oracle's face clouded with sadness and she said, "If only Ivar were here."

TWO
THE DRAUGR KING

Sigrid drew the draugr to their door like moths to a flame. Ivar, their father, and the oracles' vessel, had used the last of his magic to keep Sigrid and Torunn alive. As the magic had waned, Torunn made up for it with brute strength. Tonight, of all nights, he would need to find magic in his bones to drive off the horde that would be coming their way.

Torunn frowned, inspecting the trophies of draugr bones that lined the walls. They'd once gleamed, proud ornaments of their achievement to fend the vile creatures off. But now the bones were dusty and chilled.

Torunn tilted his head as his gaze drifted over Ivar's axe hanging from the wall. The undead army was about to rampage through his door and his father's weapon was useless.

"Father," Torunn said, the word another dead prayer on his lips. As if his father returned it from the hall of a dead, an icy draft slipped through the walls and warned that there wasn't much time. Even though he should have been watching the door, he couldn't take his gaze from the axe. It seemed alive tonight. Not dead—not like everything else.

Torunn wasn't a vessel. He couldn't hold his father's axe spelled by the oracles, but he reached for it anyway.

His fingers grazed the feathers first. They floated around the axe's wooden handle. The stolen prayers seared foreign and wrong against his mortal hand. In that moment he knew why his father's magic had waned. Every ounce of power was taken from this world, a wish strangled and hope dashed. He tightened his grip, accepting the shards of hate the world sent his way. Let them despise him. Let them be miserable and in pain. He'd not asked for this, but he'd certainly prayed.

The oracles' shrieks filled the air like wraiths before he could consider what he'd done. To take a vessel's weapon was perversion and inconceivable—to take the prayers that weren't his to take. One simply was imbued by the undead, but never *self-made*.

A hundred murky heartbeats thundered outside his door. Torunn couldn't go outside and face what terrors were swelling through the night. Even if he wanted to, he couldn't leave Sigrid unprotected. He grew hopeful when the battle cries mixed with husky male voices. The villagers had come to fight. More dead to add to the list of sins within Torunn's tapestry of fate.

The icy draft that had found its way into his home wasn't just an unsaid prayer. It was the draugr king and his foul magic leeching all warmth from the cabin. The door iced over and Torunn swallowed his fear and hefted the vessel's axe. He glanced into the dark hall where Sigrid hid. Had she Seen this? Did she know if he would triumph, or fail?

The door cracked and Torunn spun to face the intruder. A dark silhouette lingered in the entrance and iron boots crunching against wood and ice.

"Stay back!" Torunn shouted and staggered his weight as he eased into a battle stance.

The draugr slipped inside the room and the candles revealed the grotesque sight of his face. His sunken eyes were dead and white, but an ancient, evil spirit lingered behind them. "Out of my way, boy," it said. It adjusted his crown made of bones and dried blood that stuck to white sticks of hair.

He took another step and Torunn struck, the blow slicing deep into the king's belly. Torunn grunted when he met the first rib, unable to push through.

The king frowned and kicked as if at a dog. The blow hit Torunn's ankle hard and his leg buckled. Pain radiated up his calf and Torunn lifted his axe again.

Torunn did as he'd seen his father do. He shut his eyes and concentrated, willing the blade to divulge its magic. Unsaid prayers found purpose and life, ringing with clarity and sending the axe blurring through the air. The blade sliced, leaving a jagged line of black, dead blood across the King's cheek. The draugr roared, with pain or indigence, Torunn couldn't be sure. He didn't have time to consider as a fist crunched into his face.

Pain shot up his nose and Torunn fell to the ground with a thud. The king snorted, bits of dust falling from his nostrils. "You're no vessel," he said. "You're nothing." The king exhaled and ice frosted over Torunn's skin. Sleep weighed heavy on his chest and the evil king's magic threatened to rip the axe from his grasp, but he curled his fingers and held on tight. His sins. His forgiveness. His burden.

Torunn screamed through clenched teeth as the king disappeared into the darkened hallway. He expected to hear Sigrid's screams, but only silence followed.

THREE
WINTER'S MAGIC

When Torunn awoke, his heart skipped a beat when he found Sigrid lingering over him with a steaming bowl of water. She dabbed his forehead with slow, deliberate motions. She had a gash of her own that seared across her hairline. Where she'd always had locks of auburn flame, now one section stood out with stark grey. Torunn grimaced. The king had tasted his sister and her magic. But he'd hadn't drained it all, in fact, he'd barely taken anything.

It could only mean that the king had plans for Sigrid. He'd needed a taste, but for what? She was a healer, and Torunn's mind raced with images of the draugr horde being knit new flesh. As ominous as the thought was, Torunn was glad his sister was still whole and he stretched towards her face.

Sigrid wrapped his fingers with hers and gave a small laugh and tears streamed down her cheeks. "You're awake."

Torunn smiled. "You're alive."

They stared at one another, glad to simply be awake and alive.

When Torunn had gained his bearings and insisted they go outside, he was faced with something unexpected. The oracles were all there, headdresses and black painted faces amidst a sea of bodies, both draugr and villagers. Men groaned in pain and writhed on the blackened snow. The draugr had met their final death.

Sigrid moved to help the villagers while Torunn faced the oracles. They weren't flesh like they'd been before—what little there had been. Sunlight shone through them and they smoked, as if their spectres threatened to evaporate like morning dew.

The eldest approached, her face now ravaged with wrinkles that looked just like the draugr king. She frowned when she saw the axe still clenched in Torunn's grip. "That weapon wasn't made for you."

Torunn pressed his lips into a thin line. He couldn't say the axe had helped Sigrid; perhaps it had only angered the draugr king. But the magic had attuned to him and he'd use it to fight him again.

One by one the oracles dismissed Torunn's achievement and stared at Sigrid and her streak of grey hair. They backed away as his sister sped through the wounded, her magic sparking and healing their broken bodies. She couldn't fight, but her magic was potent when it came to healing and Torunn loved her for it.

The oracles watched with expressions both fearful and longing, their ghostly faces grimacing as if in pain. "She'll be like us soon," one said.

Torunn frowned, not sure if that was an insult or a promise. "Why are you still here?" he snapped. "You've failed." It was only Sigrid's sharp gaze that kept him from reaching for his axe's magic and slicing their spirits to bits.

"There's still a chance. Gather winter's magic," the oldest oracle insisted. "Bring it to us. Give us the power to become flesh again and we will be strong enough to fight one last battle."

Torunn didn't like the sound of that. It was too much like the draugr, reborn and woven with magicked flesh. He stared at them in silence.

When the oracles saw he wouldn't comply, they pleaded to Sigrid. "Look at how many we killed. Imagine how many more we could take with the true power of the gods. Perhaps we could even challenge the draugr king."

Torunn watched Sigrid carefully. Perhaps he hadn't killed a draugr to contest where winter's magic should go, but he was the vessel now. He should be the one to absorb the magic and use it to battle the draugr. He'd been with her every winter as they gathered the gods' blessings and split them up for all to share. Some went to the oracles and their vessel to call upon should the draugr raid in the night. Some went into trinkets, artifacts to protect and bring good fortune to the villagers. The last of it went back to the gods, an offering given into smoke and blood of the finest butchered livestock. None of the magic should go to gods or oracles anymore–it should go to him.

"We'll do it," she said.

Torunn faced her, ready to argue, but her angry tears held him back.

"I can't let my vision come true, brother," she said. "We must gather the gods' blessings before it's too late."

Torunn nodded and clenched his axe. Indeed, he agreed they should gather the gods' blessings, but he didn't voice his plans that the oracles wouldn't see a drop.

The stench of death and rot was the only thing that followed them into the forest.

FOUR
BLOOD OF THE GODS

Torunn limped, a knot bulging from his ankle and the steady throb of his head making him dizzy. They'd gone deep into the forest but were only just now passing the sprigs of promising red fruit. Children called them snow-berries, succulent treats that contained the blood of the gods.

Torunn couldn't stomach the thought of the oracle's yellowed teeth stabbing into the delicious fruit. Nothing could bring the light of life back into their eyes. Torunn's mission burned ever fiercer in his chest, for Sigrid's eyes were anything but grey and dead as she scanned the trees. They burned with resolve and starlight and Torunn meant to keep them that way.

Torunn knew Sigrid's determination meant that she would gather the best snowberry they could find. As an oracle, she could find the heart disguised as fruit, muster the grace fit for a goddess to retrieve it and procure the most potent dose of magic offered by the gods in the heart of winter.

Torunn was one step behind his sister, ever wary for another onslaught of draugr. Sigrid ignored him and the threat of danger and scampered to every bush, pushing her magic through to check for their prize. Her fingers had gone blue with the cold, but Torunn didn't suggest they turn back. And when Sigrid eyed a bush that looked fit to strangle any who approached it, he clenched his jaw and waited.

Black, snarled, and adorned with impaled insects, the tangle of thorns was a festering wound in the forest. Its waxy leaves threatened to blister and ragged thorns to tear. But inside red fruit reacted to Sigrid's presence. It glimmered and pulsed with the unmistakable magic of a god's heart. Torunn held his breath as Sigrid furrowed her brows and snaked her fingers through.

The bush heaved as if in pain and a quiet sizzle quickly followed. Sigrid's whimper made Torunn want to rip his axe through the foliage, but he forced himself to be still. Breaking the thorns would only seep more of the poisonous nectar onto his sister.

Her pain-creased brow eased into victory as she tugged the snowberry free. It pulsed with a flash and reflected the sunlight that filtered through the thick canopy of the trees.

Before Sigrid could bury the snowberry into the folds of her robes, Torunn snatched it from her grasp. He cupped it in his hands and bit down hard. Sigrid cried, but her voice was drowned out by the hum of magic that filled his ears.

The snowberry was both sweet and sharp, as if he'd eaten a honey-covered scorpion's tail. Its juice ran red over his knuckles and sent droplets to the snow. The magic sped the gods' blessings through his veins like lightning, winding and settling into the center of his chest. His heart fluttered until it rang with the beat of the gods. He collapsed to his knees and clenched his fists, feeling as if he might explode into a thousand pieces right there.

When the black dots cleared from his vision, his sister towered over him. He expected her to scream, to snap her hand back and slash her nails across his face. Instead she shed crystal tears and helped him to his feet.

They didn't speak all the way back to their lonely hut. Sigrid only gave him a glance when his limp turned to a strong gait. The snowberry's magic had been potent indeed.

They came upon the hut and one oracle remained. She rose, her brows lifting with unfettered hope.

"Where are the villagers?" Sigrid asked.

The oracle waved her question away. "They'll return when it's time to meet at the river." She eyed Sigrid's pouch. "Do you have it?"

His sister curled her shoulders and dug into her robes, procuring a smaller snowberry they'd found on their return. It wouldn't hold any magic, but the oracle could be deceived.

The spectre tried to take it, but her fingers passed straight through. She frowned. "I'm not able." She considered Torunn briefly, which was more than he'd usually gotten. If she felt he could serve as a vessel, she didn't entertain the idea for long. Her gaze pierced into Sigird's. "You eat it, child. Hold the magic for us."

Sigrid would have protested such a request. The king had already claimed her. He'd tasted her magic and could do so again.

Sigrid cast Torunn a quick glance before she placed the snowberry on her tongue. She shivered as she chewed, and the oracle mistook it for the effects of gods' blood.

"Good, child," she said, her wrinkled lips stretching into a smile.

Torunn was glad the oracle wasn't watching him, for he was shivering too. The power of the snowberry mingled in his belly, making him want to scream and shout and fight an entire horde of draugr. He planned to do just that, even if he had to take all the gods' power to do it.

FIVE
THE SPIRIT BOATS

Night fell and Torunn allowed himself to rest before they began their next task. While Sigrid had her own room, she'd stayed with him like they had when they were children. They needed to sleep and regain their strength. A calmer night might have helped, but dread pounded the air. Enemy drums still beat and draugr wailed in the distance. They celebrated their king and his new bride.

Whatever magic the king had taken was now a distant aroma of sweetness that was for the draugr feast. Torunn could almost hear the scratching of flesh being grown and stretching over old bones.

Sigrid's fear plucked at him as she clutched her fingers through his. Perhaps the king would come again, and this time he could take it all. They stared into the dark pattern of straws that comprised the hut's ceiling and listened to the *thump, thump, thump* that pounded through the night.

It wasn't just the anticipation and fear that made Torunn's heart race, even as he laid still on his bed. The axe had turned him into a vessel, even if he hadn't been born as one. Because of it, the gods' blood that now surged through his veins sent his heart into jerks and leaps.

Torunn closed his eyes and focused on his sister. Her fingers dug into his palm. Even if she was afraid, she was stronger than him in these matters and he focused on the steady beat of her heart. There was magic in his sister's blood, and he was surprised when the warm tingling of it seeped through her fingertips and into his wrist.

"What are you doing?" he asked into the darkness.

"Keeping you alive," she said.

Torunn meant to save Sigrid, and not the other way around, but he didn't complain as the creeping warmth filled his chest and offered him the blessing of sleep.

THE NEXT MORNING Torunn accompanied Sigrid to form the tallow candles. There was more to magic than gods' blood. All humans held power and they took it with them into death.

The spirit boats to retrieve it needed an oracle's touch, but Torunn would be the one to offer a piece of his soul.

Torunn didn't interrupt his sister as she worked, even though her eyes glowed as her fingers wove through fog and mist and a candle formed. She plucked at his chest every other breath and a silver strand flitted into the air before it zipped into the wick. It was nothing more than a sting, but Torunn didn't underestimate its power. The candle was comprised of tallow, fat, and a little bit of his soul as an offering to the spirits.

When Sigrid had finished the first candle, she moved to begin another. When silver strands of her own soul dangled from her chest Torunn's breath hitched. "No," he said. "Only me."

Sigrid frowned and silver strand slithered back into her body. "If I am to survive, I'll need the good spirits and their magic too."

Torunn shook his head. "No, Sigrid. I cannot kill the draugr king with just a part of the gods' blessings. I need all of them."

Sigrid didn't move and stared at him, her eyebrows furrowed and her lips forming a taut line.

"You must have faith," he said. "I am an exception to your visions. I can change our fate." Sigrid frowned and Torunn pressed on, "You didn't see me become a vessel, did you?"

Her silence gave him confirmation. "And the snowberry, what of that?"

Her frown deepened and she turned to the vat. She glared at it until the fat began to boil. "I'm sorry, brother. That may be true, but I won't let you do this alone."

Before she could weave another candle, Torunn took the butt of his axe and landed the most gentle blow he could to her temple.

SIGRID HAD an impressive head of hair, but even her

vibrant locks weren't enough to hide the bump that formed near her brow. It blended with her scabbed gash and Torunn hoped the oracles wouldn't notice the extra bruise.

Torunn plucked at Sigrid's dress, but she refused to look at him, or anyone else, as they gathered with the rest of the village at the riverbank.

Even in the heart of winter, the waters ran strong. Ice threatened to form at the edge, created a snarling, jagged path. Torunn always felt like the winter river was a giant maw that they fed spirit boats.

The villagers stood against the tree line and beat axes against shields. They gave Sigrid a song to begin her chant that would bring the spirits into this realm.

Torunn joined too, although softly. His axe held magic and he didn't wish to disturb the careful balance Sigrid would have to build. He followed the beat, his blade slapping into his palm.

Sigrid didn't brush away the violent mist as it gathered beads on the tips of her locks. She stood silent and defiant, her anger mixing with the snowberry's magic in Torunn's chest.

Torunn narrowed his eyes but didn't reprimand her. He'd gone against her wishes and done what he'd had to do to make sure this ritual went according to plan. It'd been rash and wrong, no matter his intentions.

If she sensed his remorse, she ignored him and focused on her task. Her magic illuminated her body and made her look like a spirit as she approached the river. She glided over the ice and walked even when there was no land under her feet. Her glow grew and a wave of admiration hushed over the crowd.

Torunn ignored them. They hadn't believed that an oracle, too young and untrained, could handle the spirit boat ritual. But they couldn't see the other oracles that stood against the treeline, distant and fading. They knew Sigrid's power and weren't surprised. Or perhaps that was all for show. Their faces drooped, marred by desperation and hope.

When Sigrid reached the middle, she set the boat into the silver-lined waters. It rocked, buckling as if it would tumble onto its side, but a swift breeze set it to rights and the candle burst into flame.

Torunn was so captivated that he almost didn't notice when the spirits came.

The temperature shifted first, something he'd always felt when the spirit boats were set. But now he saw the source, a wave of skeletal spectres sweeping over the waters and swirling around Sigrid.

She ignored them and Torunn's respect for her grew. They pecked at her like needlefish. Bits of her soul slithered out as they nipped and Torunn's heart jumped into his throat, but then the spirits reeled back as if disgusted. Torunn breathed a sigh of relief as they moved downstream.

When they reached the boat, some tentatively explored the vessel, and some branched off as if looking for more and Torunn flashed Sigrid a glance. She frowned and seemed to concentrate. The boat exploded with light as its candle's flame sparked.

The spirits jerked and swept through the boat. The candle's flame smoked with the draft. Torunn was glad that the spirits seemed as if they'd take the bait, but now the boat was almost at the waterfall's edge. It tipped over and began to fall with Torunn's hopes going with it.

Just as it fell, the spirits plucked something white out of the candle's flame. Torunn had seen it before, but thought it just a trick of the light. Now he knew, the spirits had found the piece of his soul that had been left behind.

They tore at it and pain shot through his body. Torunn grit his teeth from crying out. Needles settled on the balls of his feet and he resisted the urge to bounce on his toes. It traveled up his calves, through his stomach, and across his arms until he couldn't feel his fingers.

Sigrid finally cast him a glance and Torunn let a snarl escape his throat. Her eyes crinkled by the grin pushing her cheeks. The spirits had just eaten a part of his soul.

SIX
THE BONFIRE

"You didn't say it'd hurt," Torunn said.

"Quit complaining," Sigrid shot back and rammed all her weight into a wad of dough.

It seemed a peculiar sight; an oracle who'd just led a herd of spirits into a single boat was now doing something so mundane as cooking.

Torunn drizzled more flour across the table. The motion sent another wave of needles up his fingernails and he swallowed a groan.

"You can at least pretend not to be happy," he said.

Sigrid smiled and continued to knead the dough.

Torunn watched helplessly as needles continued to travel up and down his arms. He hated what the ritual had done to him. A part of him was dead. His soul had been hollowed to make room for the spirits and his body wasn't sure if he were alive or dead, which meant his heart didn't always pump blood to his extremities.

Torunn made a fist and hissed at the pain. The spirits

within whispered and giggled like children, huddling in the place where part of his soul had been gouged out, making him feel hollow and cold.

Sigrid cast him a glance, this one without the rueful smile she'd given him at the river. "You'll be okay," she assured him and turned her attention back to her work.

An agonizing hour later, Sigrid pulled the loaf from the pan, making Torunn's mouth water and his stomach lurch. The steam rising from the bread as Sigrid began to slice was more enticing than any village feast.

Sigrid laughed when she caught Torunn's hungry stare. "Here you are," she said and handed him the treat still steaming on a wooden plate.

"Thank you," he said and tore into it like his life depended on it. The grainy sweetness gave him such needed nourishment and reprieve that he wanted to cry.

"I'll be out for a bit," Sigrid said a bit too casually as she lingered at the door.

Torunn swallowed the sticky mouthful and downed a gorge of wine. "You shouldn't go alone."

Sigrid gave him a small smile. "I need to meet with the oracles. They can't suspect that you have the spirits' magic."

Torunn frowned, but gave her a nod. "Very well," he said, drawn back to the comfort of his meal.

TORUNN PREPARED for the last ritual deep in the

night. This would be the only one he could do without Sigrid's help.

Moonlight poured into the room and was drawn to Sigrid's soft form strewn on the bed. She seemed exhausted after her time with the oracles.

Her chest slowly rose and fell and Torunn cast glances at her as he laced his boots. He wondered if she knew he'd leave her in the night to build the fires to rain down the last of the gods' power.

She knew, one spirit said.

She suspected, another corrected.

Torunn frowned and continued to lace his other boot. What good was godly wisdom when it argued with itself?

Torunn looked for his axe, but it wasn't lying against the wall where he'd put it. He'd need it not only to chop the wood, but to imbue it with the scent of its magic that the gods could recognize.

He scratched his head, staring at the space where the axe had once been.

She hid it, a spirit nibbling at the edge of his soul supplied.

Torunn frowned and scratched at his chest that now had an aching itch deep inside. "Why would she do that?"

She won't let you partake another ritual alone. She doesn't want to lose you to the gods, the spirit said.

Torunn scoffed and glanced at his sister again. Now he knew why she slept so soundly. She believed him incapable of building the bonfire alone.

"And why didn't you tell me she'd taken it?"

The spirits' only reply was a cascade of giggles. Torunn

sighed. Useless wisdom.

"Help me find it," he commanded and the moment the words left his lips fog sprang from his boots. It formed a path out his door and Torunn didn't hesitate to follow.

The smoke drifted around his ankles and bit at his knees as it led him into the forest. Torunn passed the village, the river, and crunched through the woods. The fog took winding turns, going through patches and sometimes doubling back the way he'd come.

"I thought you said you knew where it was?" he asked, his voice rising with frustration.

Quiet! a spirit said. *She's protected it.*

Then Torunn heard a low growl as he faced a crevice in the trees. Oh Sigrid, he thought. She'd placed the axe in a bear's cave. Did she wish to deter him so much?

Torunn called upon the courage of his snowberry's magic. He'd never be brave enough to enter the cave alone, and Sigrid knew that. But with the powerful thump in his chest, he slipped into the darkness.

The bear slumbered, but was awake and on him the moment Torunn entered its domain. Torunn's first reaction was to strike, but a cold numbing that ran up his limbs slowed him down.

Fog drifted through the cave and the bear moaned, his maw stinking of moldy dirt inches from his face. The bear should have torn Torunn's head from his body by now, but the fog seemed to distract it.

"Make him sleep!" Torunn commanded the spirits and mist billowed throughout the cave. The effect only made it more difficult to see and the bear groaned.

We're not meant for fighting, one complained.

Quite useless, another agreed.

Torunn needed to perform the last ritual to receive gods' strength, but he'd need the axe first. Without strength, there was only one other way to fight a bear.

The bear recovered and swatted. Torunn ducked, the breeze of a near miss sending a chill up his spine. Then Torunn opened himself to the power of the snowberry's magic, drew in a deep breath, and roared.

Gods' blood is a potent gift and Torunn let it fill his body to the brim. He drew in another breath and the metallic taste of blood made his skin tingle. His voice began as a husky growl in his throat, rumbled in the air and shook the very ground. The bear went rigid as Torunn held the shout, keeping it going until his lungs had been emptied.

The bear slammed down and his claws spattered dirt as it fled the cave.

Torunn smirked, proud of himself, but then dizziness came next. The snowberry's magic had been contained by Sigrid's, and now he'd set it free.

Struggling to see through the fog and his own weariness, Torunn ran his fingers across the moist dirt until he uncovered his axe. The smell of wet earth hit his nose as he freed it from the ground. The magic rolled up his arms, reviving him with enough energy to leave the cave. He only hoped it could keep him going for the trial to come, the last winter's ritual to give him the power he'd need to kill the draugr king.

The moonlight filtered through the branches as he made his way deep into the forest. His spirits silently guided him, the fog drifting across the forest floor. They didn't chitter or laugh as if even they had been quieted by Torunn's mighty roar.

The draugr, though, didn't seem perturbed. Their drums still thundered in the distance and Torunn's steps fell in line with the beat.

His pace was agonizingly slow, but eventually he made his way to the familiar clearing. The year-long dried pile of beech and ash logs huddled underneath a canopy of leaves awaited his arrival. Torunn smiled, tears pricking his eyes for the gift his father had left him. It should have been Ivar at the bonfires, but today it'd be his son.

The logs were ready, but he still needed to slice them to size and fill the air with his own magic's scent. He got to work, raising his axe and lashing it down with what power he had left. The only consolation was that strength would return a hundred fold once he finished his task.

The crack from his split log that went through the forest was louder than Torunn had expected. The scent of magic came with a sound, a low rolling thunder that sent rocks sprawling across the ground.

The drums had been a steady group of threes, but now the beats skipped over one another like a giddy child let out to play. Hoots and yips sounded and fear sent sweat beading on Torunn's forehead. He didn't have the luxury to stop, to run or hide. He filled his body with the snowberry's magic to give him courage and drowned out the drums with the beat of his axe and his own pounding heart.

TORUNN'S WOODPILE wasn't as impressive as he would have liked, but the enemy was too close. The trees rustled with their approach and he didn't have time to build the pile any further.

Torunn gathered the touchwood fungus and spread it around the base. He said a desperate prayer as he untied the drawstring of his waistline and urinated on the offering. He didn't have an oracle's magic, and it would be the only way to keep the fires going to morning.

The yips grew closer and Torunn scrambled for his flint. Sparks flew at the first strike, but failed to light the fungus. He tried again, but this time one side of his flint spiraled into the weeds and he cursed. Panic sent waves of fog around his fingers as he searched. "Not now!" he said to the spirits responding to his racing heart. "I can't see!"

There! one shouted, but Torunn couldn't see where "there" was.

A whistle pierced the air and Torunn ducked just in time. A spear with a feathered end vibrated in the pile of wood. Torunn ignored it, and from his new position saw the sparkle of flint in the moonlight. He snatched it up and sliced both halves again.

This time the spark caught and the touchwood blazed with blue flame. He heard curses behind him and quips of frustration.

Men and ghouls beat themselves against a translucent barrier and Torunn roared with victory.

He'd set the bonfire alight, and the gods magic rained down with it.

SEVEN
END OF A KING

Torunn stayed in a violent trance of shouts and cries to the heavens, absorbing the blessing of the gods that rained down until dawn crested the snow covered pines.

Torunn had turned his back on the men and ghouls long ago, striving his energy up with the effort to reach gods' ears. Each moment filled him with the last of winter's magic. This wasn't the courage of gods' blood, nor the wisdom of the spirits. This was the living, breathing will of the gods that rained down with their laughter and tears. It filled him and transformed him into something not of this world.

Torunn finally turned to face the draugr who'd beat themselves bloody against the barrier. The sheen of color fell and Torunn plastered a wild grin on his face. Instead of attacking, the draugr seemed to have sensed the change in him and slowly backed away, wide-eyed and slack-jawed.

Torunn called upon all of the gods' blessings and flashed through the clearing. The spirits wove fog around his feet, making him swift and agile. Gods' blood thundered through his ears and told him he could move mountains and decimate armies. The strength of the heavens wound through his arms and put power behind his magicked axe, slicing through the draugr and sending their heads scattering to the ground.

The spirits cautioned him amidst his frenzy.

Don't let it overwhelm you, one warned.

A moment of lucidity brought Torunn to the surface of the sea of blood when he spotted the draugr king snarling and wielding two gleaming spears. He snapped one back and sent it flying. Torunn blurred out of the way and it zipped harmlessly past. Torunn grinned and closed the distance between them. He slammed his axe into the king's side and this time there was a satisfying *snap* when his blade met bone.

The king's grey pupils dilated and dark blood spurt from his mouth. "How?" the king gasped.

Ice spidered on the ground and Torunn ripped the axe out and struck again. The king fell to one knee but metal flashed in the sunlight. Pain shot through Torunn's chest and he grunted, his fingers wrapping around a spear now lodged in his belly.

The king gurgled a laugh through the blood draining across his lips. "I knew this day would come." His smile grew. "I kept your sister alive to heal me, boy," he said before closing his eyes and collapsing to the ground and going still.

"That's not going to happen," Torunn hissed and snapped the end of the spear and left the rest lodged in his body. An army of draugr still growled at him and sprawled with blazing magic. The king had fed his horde what he'd taken from Sigrid.

Torunn pushed all emotion out of his body and filled himself with rage. Torunn called the last of his strength and his axe blurred with him, cleaving through rotten flesh and brittle bones.

When dawn had turned to day, his labored breath finally slowed and he heard the spirits whispering in his soul.

It's too late. He's already gone.

EIGHT
ENTER VALHALLA

Torunn stared at the scene as pain wracked his body. The king stared with unblinking eyes into the sky. His crown had broken and lay strewn about his head in pieces.

The rest of the forest had been decimated by the battle. Blood splattered across the snow, and now Torunn saw it wasn't just his enemies he'd severed in his murderous rage.

His spotted village folk among them. He couldn't know for sure if the draugr had killed them or if it had been by his own hand blind and drunk with power.

Village elders with sprawled hair laid still on the ground. Massive gashes allowed their blood to run like a river, streaming free from their bodies where he'd blindly cleaved through flesh.

When he spotted hair as red as fire, his throat closed around a sob.

Sigrid still glowed, her body encased in the power she'd spent in her last moments.

Torunn realized then, the barrier hadn't been from him.

Sigrid had summoned it, protected him until he could absorb the last of the gods' gifts in spite of her attempts to stop him.

Now, her body was still and pale. Her blood that splattered the snow neatly around her frame could have been the snowberry's juice across ice.

Her soul peeled away from her body and Torunn scrambled to his feet.

"Brother," her spectre said with a smile.

Torunn grimaced. Had it all been for nothing? "Why would you sacrifice yourself for me?"

Tears burned his eyes and Sigrid's spirit blurred.

She tilted her head as if to give him sympathy. "Dear brother, I knew I'd die all along. I'm an oracle. I know the fates."

Torunn took a step closer. "If you knew, why didn't you stop me?"

She shook her head and even as ethereal as she was, her blazing locks seemed to reflect the sunlight as they cascaded over her shoulder. The only sign of death was the single patch of grey at her temple. "I tried, dear brother. I took a snowberry too powerful for you to withhold, but you survived. You forced me to make only one spirit boat, and even if I could have made more, the spirits preferred the taste of you." She gave a small smile. "I even compelled a bear to guard the axe so fiercely that no one could take it in the night, most especially my big brother who's terrified of the beasts. But somehow, you found the courage."

Tears rolled down her cheeks and she grazed her fingers across his face. Torunn shivered as the chill breeze sent goosebumps across his skin. "But I understand now," she said. "My death ends the cycle of draugr and oracle." Her gaze fell to the king's body. "We are two ends of a spiral and we're always connected. If I had lived, I would have been compelled to knit the king new flesh. Such is the cycle of our magic."

Torunn clenched his fists, but Sigrid continued, "You did what you promised to do, dear brother. You ended the draugr king and his cycle of death. The evil spirits will never torment this world again. I had been afraid to be the last oracle, to take magic away from this world. But," her spirit wavered as she smiled, "perhaps magic will come back." Her eyes turned brilliant and white as she beheld her last vision. "Magic will be for those who believe. It'll be hidden in dust, in starlight and in river beds. Magic will come to those who call it, but only if their souls are pure and their hearts true."

When Torunn blinked, his sister was gone, and only the remnant was her sweet scent that filled the air. A sob caught in his throat but his heart was glad. His pain was turning numb and he lay still on the snow, knowing that soon he'd join her in the halls of Valhalla.

About the Last Oracle

There's little else I love more than ancient Viking lore. The Last Oracle embodies a Viking fairytale as I would imagine it and I was pleased how it came out.

I was even more pleased when the Last Oracle won me one of my first awards in the well-known Writers of the Future contest! I now no longer qualify to enter this contest since I now write professionally and and the "future" is here for me, but I'm pleased to have this certificate framed in my writing room for inspiration of where I started and how far I've come.

THE AWAKENING

Book 3 in the Ancient Realms Collection

ONE
A VESSEL

I lingered in the shadows as my mother wrung her hands and my father loomed in the doorway.

"You'll stay right here," my mother ordered, the brilliant green of her eyes violent in their desire to keep me safe.

"He'll be fine," my father barked.

My mother creased her lips into a thin line, knowing me better having stayed glued to my side most of my life.

Her gaze fell to the black streaks that marred my arms. It was a sign of what I was, what kind of future I would have. I had the soul-sickness. I curled my fingers over elbows that poked through my skin, my body a withered husk that held my empty soul.

I was a vessel.

Should I come into contact with another villager with a heavy sin, I'd doom myself. The village didn't know of me, or my condition. Only I could take their sins and send them away from darkness. The gods couldn't see them with the shadow of sin over the generations. I was the sacrifice meant to redeem them all.

Except, no one knew I existed, and my family wanted to keep it that way.

Holding my mother's gaze with a lie that I wouldn't leave this home, I told her what she needed to hear. "It's okay, mother. You'll find a priest who can help me. Once I've been initiated, I'll have plenty of time to see the world." I forced a smile across my cheeks that were unfamiliar with the motion.

Her eyes glazed with emotion as my father tugged her away.

Finally, I was alone, and ready to commit a few sins of my own.

TWO
AN OLD WOMAN AND A CANDIED APPLE

The wind unfurled across the oversized robes I'd stolen from my sister. She'd carelessly draped it across an unused chair, as if she couldn't appreciate its finery. The edges of the rough emerald green, her favorite color, flapped about my shoulders as I sped into the markets.

Instead of the dull shift of my mother's loom, new sounds of a hundred souls I'd never met filled my head. A delightful sharp ring drew my attention first. Metal on metal with violence and precision. I rounded a corner, finding a man with a hammer beating down onto a molten red blaze.

While I knew of smithing, it was incredible to see how it was done. My father had a swinging metal shear that he used to slice into wheat. I'd always wondered how the delicate curve could have been formed. Now I watched with fascination as a man beat the blade to his will, shaping it over an iron block's back.

The inviting scent of mulberry pie was the only thing that could have drawn me away from the spectacle. My father had always brought one home on special occasions, but by the time he'd made it to the dreary small hearth, the treat would need to be reheated by stoked flames.

I sped around busy villagers who were heedless of my violation. Children scampered through the village all the time—just not those who had yet to be initiated. The black streaks suggested I was a vessel, but it wasn't guaranteed. If I were to be initiated by a priest strong enough in the arts of aethyre, I might yet be saved.

I was already older than most uninitiated children. My mother had an unnatural fear that the black lines of my veins meant the worst, that I would be one of the few who didn't survive. My initiation could go terribly wrong, and she'd held onto every precious year with a vicious greed that had made me grow bitter and the seasons passed me by.

Sunlight warmed my skin with its kiss today. I wasn't bitter now, not as I followed my nose and found an old woman's stall brimming with golden pastries and sugar-sweet treats. My mouth filled with saliva and my eyes went wide as I took in the treasures on her table.

She laughed when she spotted me, her voice worn down by the years but her eyes alight with life. "Hello there, sweet boy. Would you like a candied apple?" She smirked, nodding at my robes. "Must be recently initiated. I haven't seen you around. Why not enjoy a treat for your bravery? No charge."

She presented the ruby prize freely, knowing I didn't have any money. If I'd have just gone through my initiation, I would have spent any hoarded coin for the priest. They risked life and limb to bring the children safely into the wide expanse of the world—and to deal with those who couldn't be saved.

I looked my age, all thirteen cycles, but I was withered and skinny beneath the engulfing folds of my sister's robes. It was proof of what I was, or rather what my family suspected. If I truly were a vessel, I was empty inside. No matter how much I ate, nourishment barely sustained me. An otherworldly hunger gnawed at me, a constant, unwanted companion.

My sister, Maxi, always glowed with health and beauty. She'd been properly initiated, given the emerald fabric that I now wore as proof and prize of her status, even as her eyes had lost their luster for reasons I still didn't understand.

Feeling guilty to fool this kind woman, I contemplated telling her to keep the apple. It wouldn't really sustain me, but my mouth watered at its ruby gleam. She extended her reach farther, her thin brows narrowing with warning that she'd seen the ridge of bone under my sleeve. "Take it," she said.

Her tone was one that demanded I obey. I reached out, my fingers grazing her leathery skin to take the treasure.

That's when it happened.

The world snapped with a painful jolt and I sucked in a breath so hard that I choked on my spittle. My body a void to be filled by this kind, old woman's past sins shredded into me like a fistful of pine needles shoved into my chest.

She'd lived such a long, hard life. Plenty of time to accrue dark secrets and failures.

Her withered face turned smooth before my eyes, my soul seeing hers back to a time when she'd committed the worst of her grievances and marked her soul heavy with sin.

She was only twenty seasonal cycles in this new reality. Her cheeks transformed to the ruby red of a candied apple in a blush. She leaned in, taking my mouth in a kiss.

I was a man, grown and hungry for a woman after my long nights at sea. I'd been sleeping on a rotten mattress that soaked up the fish-stained waters every time I laid down. To hold a woman that smelled of sugar and bread was a pleasant change.

The man whose soul I was visiting hadn't realized that the woman he now embraced already had a husband. She'd fallen for his charm and good looks, and would be crushed when he returned to the seas once again.

Her tears were salty on his lips, mingling with the sea as he sped away on the winds. He'd left a seed behind in her womb. A child, a miracle after all the years of trying, and she'd let her husband believe was theirs. Now, years later when her husband had passed, their lineage was all a lie.

One day, the priest would find the sin that marked her soul. Her son, or her son's son, or one after him would eventually take on the burden of her betrayal. Sins had a cost, and even if it took generations, someone she loved would pay the price.

That knowledge weighed her down and bent her shoulders until they curled into her now wobbled frame.

When I released my fingers, I knew I was a vessel and I was going to die a horrible death.

THREE
SACRIFICE

Innocence had been lost in that brief sharing of sins. I was what my mother had always feared. Still clutching the candied apple to my chest, unable to take a bite of its hard-skinned sugary flesh, I choked on a sob. The woman's sin ground into me like knuckles into my heart. She'd eased after our brief contact, not realizing that I'd taken on the burden that was hers to bear.

I still smelled that man, a lingering stench of fish and need. I was too young to experience such things, but as a vessel, I had lived two lives over. If I touched anyone in the village with such a weighty sin again, I'd take it into myself and burden my empty soul with a price that needed to be paid.

If anyone found out what I was, they'd grope for me, greedily soaking their sins into my flesh to take away their darkness.

I couldn't possibly brave the initiation now. Not that I

knew what was coming. No one who was a vessel survived, much less one weighted with another's sin.

I approached the dark hut that was my home, its frowning awnings an oppressive stare as I ventured inside.

"Where have you been?" my mother shrieked as she jumped from a chair that had marred dark grooves into the ground, placed so that it faced the doorway. She sucked in a breath when she saw I'd taken my sisters robes.

I held out the candied apple as a tear rolled down my cheek. "I'm sorry, Mother. You were right."

She didn't yell or go for the switch. Instead, she took the apple, carefully gripping by its sides and avoiding my fingers.

"My boy," she whispered, her voice breaking with pain. "My poor boy."

She would have embraced me, but a stranger had unlocked my potential as a vessel. Whatever sins she held in her chest, she didn't dare share with me.

I blinked, wetness rolling a cold drizzle down my chin, and climbed the creaking steps to the attic.

FOUR
A CANDLE'S FLAME

Silver moonlight trickled through my fingers as I waved my hand across my face. The red hue at the edges of my skin fascinated me. Sometimes, I felt dead, or too alive, I wasn't sure which. Ever since I'd learned the truth that I was a vessel, I'd contemplated this terrible day. My initiation was nigh.

"Jakob?" my sister called, her voice followed by the symphony of creaking floorboards as she climbed the final steps to the attic of our humble home. Our father had added the small room when I'd started to show the signs, even before I'd been foolish enough to venture into the markets and unlock the truth of it. Only once a generation did a vessel appear, and now the whole village knew I couldn't bear to be among them. And so I remained in this small hole in the top of our wood and straw home, a place I could oversee the activity below without immersing myself in it and risking more sin finding its way into my empty soul.

Now, fifteen cycles old, I had no choice but to go through with the initiation. The need to fill myself with substance buckled my knees and made me grind my teeth together. I couldn't remain separated from the world any longer. I had to be cleansed by a priest, or I had to be doomed to the afterlife. There was no in-between.

Silver moonlight, pleasant and comforting, was banished in the nauseating wave of yellow that burst from my sister's flame. Her candle sent all the shadows in the room scurrying, my only companions in the dark night when I wished to be alone. A part of me wanted to run with them, to hide from facing a conversation I knew was coming.

A crunch sounded as my sister relaxed onto my straw bed, just far enough away to make sure not to touch me. My parents had made me a room with pillows and goose feathers, but I preferred the stinging needles of the mat in the attic to remind myself I was still alive.

She flinched as she shifted on the uncomfortable frame. "It's okay to be afraid," she said.

I scowled at her permission to fear what we knew was coming. I didn't want to fear the initiation that might Awaken something deep and dark that festered in my soul, or simply kill me outright. "I'm not afraid," I snapped.

She didn't take offense to my bitter mood, ever my kind sister. But I wasn't fooled. I knew if I gave in and accepted the brief embrace of her touch, I'd suck in any sins she'd committed. She was two cycles older than me, old enough to have lost her innocence to boys she wasn't meant to bed. A faint sour tinge in the air told me that there was sin on her, something sexual and dark in nature. That was not an experience I wished to take from her soul.

She offered me a lopsided smile. When I didn't return it, she pointed at the dim moon that watched us through the open square frame that was my only window to the world. "Do you know why the moon shines?" she asked.

I frowned, but was intrigued. Maxi described her feelings through stories, and I wondered how she would unwind the looming truth of my death with a story of how the moon shines light onto a boy who couldn't touch another living soul.

"The moon is reborn, you see, every night." She leaned in, her voice a conspiratorial whisper against my cheek. "Its light may go out when night is over, but don't you see how it comes back? It ebbs and flows its strength, and tonight it's the brightest I've ever seen. It's strong, like you, little brother." She smiled. "So, you see, even if your light fades, it'll return on the 'morrow brighter than it's ever been."

Contemplating her words, I looked down at her candle, frowning as white scars speckled across my vision.

I filled my lungs and blew it out.

"No," I whispered. "My light is like a candle, weak and fragile. Melted wax will cover the short wick of my soul and drown me in its depths. I will be extinguished, never to shine again."

She didn't reply, but shuffled into her robes and produced flint. It was a dumb and brave move. The spark as she hit the small bits of slate together could have set my straw bed alight. But she was stubborn to prove her point. "No," she said as the yellow glow sparked to life. "You'll come back. You just need some help." Her brilliant emerald eyes, the same color as her robes and my mother, gazed at me without falter. "I've made sure we have enough coin for a priest from the main city. Not a village fake. You will be saved, little brother, I promise."

My lips pressed in a thin line. After a moment to adjust to the scent, now I noted the tones of sin that reeked in the air. I could taste it and my soul reacted to the need to drink it in. I curled my fingers to resist the urge to touch her hand.

She was old enough to bed men. And now I knew what sin I'd sensed. She'd sold herself so that I might live.

FIVE
AWAKENED

"How could you let Maxi do this?" I snapped.

My mother, now a curled pitiful creature, bent with guilt at having known what her daughter had done. I hadn't asked Maxi to save me. No matter what kind of fancy priest we paid off, it didn't mean anything. I was a vessel. Vessels drew in sin or they died. I'd accepted my fate that day I'd accepted a candied apple from an old woman.

"Don't speak to your mother that way," my father roared. He was a farmer and his body bulged from the proof of his daily work. He'd carried bushel after bushel of wheat to the shed, separated it and loaded it onto his back to the markets in wide crates strapped to his broad frame. He still leaned forward, as if there was a burden yet on his shoulders he had to carry.

I pointed at my sister, straight and defiant and she wrapped fingers over her elbows, and snarled. "She has committed sins that can never be erased. So many men have claimed her, not for love or for sons, but to taste her flesh. How could you allow her to pay such a cost? I'm still going to die, and now I will die knowing my family will be doomed for generations to come. I'm a vessel, but I can't save her if she won't touch me."

I jerked for her, but Maxi darting out of the way, fast as lightning to avoid my touch. "You don't make decisions for me, *little brother*. I did it to save you. You will not touch me and undo everything I've sacrificed to give you a life worth living."

"I'm the sacrifice," I snapped. "You've doomed yourself for nothing!"

Father silenced us with a wave of his hand. "I didn't know of this," he said, his words a dangerous rumble as he faced my sister. "I've worked day and night to get the money we needed for your brother's initiation. I just needed more time." He stomped to her, wrapping his calloused fingers around her graceful shoulders and gave her a violent shake. "Why didn't you wait?"

Maxi stared up at him, all defiance and pride. "We've run out of time." Her gaze found mine. I'd never seen her blaze with such ferocity. "Just look at him."

All of them turned to regard me, their eyes wide as if they'd never seen me before.

I looked down at my arms that were now corpse-white. Thick, black veins threaded over thin arms with a touch of gold that I hadn't remembered seeing under the silver kiss of the moon.

My mother's sob was the only sound that broke the stillness of our small home.

GOLD WAS the blood of a soul, a sign that I was about to die. Initiation or not, I feared that I was going to face the afterlife tonight.

Maxi's sins had bought me the best of the best. She was determined to give me a chance, no matter how foolhardy the choice may have been.

The village gathered to greet the famous Priest of Tiebern, the most renown in all of Alterine. He appeared without fanfare, but with a simple staff that loomed over his bent frame.

I couldn't see him very well from my attic window, but I hadn't dared to venture into the village when everyone was out, their eyes on the priest rather than being careful not to run into me. I couldn't afford more sins before my initiation.

I bit the inside of my lip at the thought. Did I really believe I could survive?

The priest made his way to the forest where he'd pray and fast. The initiation would be in three days time, and I wondered if he really believed the gods heard us anymore. A vessel was proof that our souls were slowly going hollow and weak. The gods hadn't cared enough to fill my body with the sustenance it needed to live a full life. A hungry old man who mumbled over his withered hands wouldn't do anyone any good.

"He's here," Maxi breathed at my side.

I jolted at her sudden appearance and eased a fraction

away from her warmth. "Don't get your hopes up," I warned her.

She went to give a retort, her emerald eyes blazing with fury, but that's when the forest lit with a red aura of power.

She gasped and leaned through the window. "Look!" she exclaimed, pointing excitedly into the distance.

The village hummed with anticipation. I frowned, but dared to hope that this priest would be worth my sister's sacrifice. The horizon blazed a ruby red, reminding me of the candied apple that had started it all.

THE THREE DAYS had passed and the horizon had glowed ever brighter as the initiation approached.

Finally, the third day arrived and I had no choice but to face my fear.

The forest floor crunched under my bare feet as I made my way to the river. I wasn't alone. Half the village had brought their sons and daughters typically too young for initiation, believing that a priest of such power would ensure no one would die and this would be their best chance.

My sister frowned and her green eyes blazed under the moonlight, enraged that the village would take advantage of the priest she'd paid for with unredeemable sin. "We should have had the initiation in secret," she hissed.

I snorted a short laugh and pointed through the red filter of trees. "You think anyone would really miss this?"

She shrugged. "Could have gone north, closer to one of the outskirt rivers of Tiebern."

A valid idea, but if I wanted to give myself a chance to survive, I needed my initiation closest to where my soul had knit with my flesh. I resisted the urge to brush my fingers across her shoulder. "It's alright," I said, my gaze meeting hers. "This was the best choice."

A small smile, reassured by my words, our brief moment over as I faced the stony shore of foam and dread.

"Get in," a wrangler of children ordered, and the youngsters burst out of their mothers' grasp and into the waters, heedless of the danger they faced.

They squealed and played, settling into the icy embrace of the river with glee and excitement.

A boom rumbled across the landscape, sending their squeals into silence.

One last glance at my sister, my parents lingering like lost shadows behind her, and I dipped my toes into the water.

The world swirled as I eased into the lapping waves. Perhaps it was fear or nerves, or just the connection of other souls through the murky liquid. I kept going until I was further in than the other children, not willing to risk whatever minor sins they'd already committed during their short lives to permeate my fragile shell of a soul by grazing against them during the ritual. I faced the clearing, waters kissing my chin, and waited.

The priest appeared as if beckoned by my desire to get this over with, his eyes ablaze with the ruby red that had bled into the forests, and his staff a living thing in his grip.

Everyone's gazes locked onto it, awash with wonder at his power.

This was aethyre, the power that knit a soul together and brought our young into adulthood. Our souls had slowly unraveled over the generations, producing vessels and withered creatures that died without a boost of aethyre to keep them in one piece.

I hated the gods for what they'd done to us. Some thought that their power was simply waning, but I wondered if there was a darker truth. We were their creation. What if sin had been their creation as well?

The priest didn't give me time to contemplate the reasoning behind the ritual we all had to partake, lest our souls unravel amidst the shadow of his power.

He thrust his staff into the sky, the red blaze shooting into the clouds and swirling them into a violent churning. The bowing willows leaned away from him as he approached the water's edge and I shivered as the air hummed with violence and thunder.

The children fidgeted with awe and excitement, but we all knew our task was simple: under no circumstances get out of the water. I buried my toes into the muck and hoped it would lock me in place.

He reached the water's edge, his staff lowering and sending its red blaze through the waves—and into me.

The pain hit first. The children in a semi-circle around me cooed and sighed at the Visions of their ancestors who guided them into adulthood. The good ones, those who'd been purged of sin and had already been light of the weighty black to begin with were spirits that lingered in the aethyre, ready to guide their children to safety.

I had no ancestors to greet me. My soul was empty and void, just as a vessel should be. Instead, darker spirits, lingering lost souls looking for a medium to guide them to an afterlife worth living found me through the mist. I shouted, splashed and cursed them, but they sped towards me and pierced into my flesh with icy stabs.

I lunged for the water's edge, but I was too far in, the muck too tight around my ankles. I experienced every sin that had weighted these souls to Alterine's soil. Battle cries, swords thrusting through their enemies' backs, men in the throes of death and innocent lives lost as the sky bled red with their violence.

I searched the coast for some remnant of my own ancestry to keep me grounded. I had to survive this purge, this absorption of aethyre that would save me from an afterlife of torment. These were men of my village, long ago, who'd fought against intruders. No matter their cause or their intentions, they'd killed. They'd taken lives without consideration or scrutiny. Their sins were heavy, and if I couldn't survive, would be mine to bear.

Maxi's emerald gaze found me through the red haze of terror. Two brawling swords blurred over my vision, threatening to slice through me and destroy my concentration, but I focused on my sister and her gaze that said I was going to get through this. I was going to survive.

The burn seared through my lips, sizzling the waters around me in a foggy mist. Pain tore through my chest, but I grit my teeth and endured. Aethyre wound itself through the empty places of my soul, giving me grounding to hold onto even as I accepted the souls along with it.

The ritual was over in a hush of wind, the fog driving away into the horizon as if I'd imagined it. The red hue of anger lifted, leaving a brackish green, the only hint of flame left was the priest who stared at me with two ruby eyes that didn't leave my face.

That's when the children turned, regarded me with a moment of shock, and began to scream.

Red pooled around me as I trembled, easing towards the water's edge. My left eye was swollen shut, and a searing gash stung across my chest. My robes clung to me as I left the icy waves and faced a priest who'd kept my soul in one piece.

His gaze dipped to my chest, now that was weighty with sin and lost souls. I felt them swarming in me like pests, and I knew the initiation wasn't meant to be this way. I was meant to be knit back to fullness with aethyre, mended into a complete soul. Instead, lost spirits who'd been damned to wander Alterine had filled the void, and now they were clinging spiders that would never let go.

I LEFT the village that night. None of the villagers had known me at all, all except one elder woman whose wrinkles bled into a faint smile at her cheeks as she caught my gaze. I gave her a slight nod before I stepped onto a dirt road and away from the only home I'd ever known.

The priest was silent as I walked at his side, his staff

humming with power and his robes still slick with sweat and river water. I imagined he was taking me away from the village for my family's sake, before he disposed of me swiftly and with mercy. Surely, I was tainted, and I couldn't be left alive.

But when he hummed low in his throat, the winds swirled auburn leaves and we were sucked into another world.

"Welcome to Tiebern," he said, his voice an emotionless sound.

I blinked at a courtyard that was so manicured, I'd thought I'd died and somehow been awarded refuge in paradise. "This is Tiebern?" I said, my voice a squeaky boy's wonder. I cleared my throat, giving the priest a sheepish shrug.

He patted me on the back and I flinched at the contact, but his sins didn't flood my soul. I was no longer a vessel.

"I've brought you to the Tiebern Estates, to be more precise," he said, his features making a marked effort to form a friendly smile. I imagined he was as familiar with the motion as I was. "Do you know why?"

I shivered as a cool breeze filtered through my waterlogged robes. We were north indeed, the air with a bite I wasn't used to. My gaze drifted to his staff that now grazed through fertile dirt, the lush browns turning over tufts in its wake.

"Boy," he insisted, his tone commanding respect and compliance, "it's imperative that you understand why you're here."

Returning my gaze to his leathery face, my brows

furrowed as agitation crawled through my chest. I should be taken to die, peacefully, and without questions or riddles. "Maxi paid you good coin," I reminded him. "If I'm to die, you don't have to make a show of it in Tiebern. Just have it done."

He frowned. "You're not to die, my boy. You're tainted, yet you remained in the water's sanctum long enough for the aethyre to mend your broken soul."

My fingers crawled across the ribs that poked out of my chest. I'd never been able to get meat on my bones and I felt like a skeleton ready for my grave. "Tainted," I said, the word a sneer. "What use have you for a tainted soul?"

The priest granted me a wry smile, this time the motion natural. "My boy." His hand landed on my shoulder, a weight that made me rigid against his warmth. "I'm not too old to take on an apprentice."

My eyes snapped open and I studied his face anew, inching towards him and overcoming my ingrained fear of proximity until I could peer into the deep red blaze of his irises.

My soul recognized him, revealing the kindred spirits of a warrior's rage, a murderer's blade, a thief's silence in the night.

He was just like me.

"What are you?" I gasped, lurching away from him.

"Oh, my dear boy," he said with a booming laugh, "you mean, what are *we*?"

I swallowed, but didn't give in to the urge to bolt from the priest. He held out his hand and I stared at it for a long time before growing enough courage to take it.

"One day, there won't be any of us left," he said, drawing me into the cloister of Tiebern's Estates that housed the most famed of priests that commanded the aethyre. "Souls need a place to rest, even the bad ones. The good ones, they're light. So light they drift up into the sky until they reach the gods. But the ones burdened by sin? They're far too weighty to make it that far, so they stay here." He poked me in the chest. "It's a hefty responsibility to take souls in, but someone's got to do it."

I peered at him warily as we descended stone steps. Heat funneled up the corridors from an invisible breeze, banishing the sting of cold that'd gripped me a moment before. "What happens to these souls?" I asked.

He frowned as we approached leaping flames. There was no hearth or bonfire, but a magical wall that separated our world from the next. "Their pain is eased," he said, his tone forlorn but accepting of his duty. He gave me a gentle nudge. "It's a kinder fate than letting them go mad in the darkness of our world, boy. Give them peace."

Tears stung my eyes. I faced him with the same rage Maxi would have given me if I used her sacrifice to destroy souls. "This is madness," I snapped. I pointed at his staff. "The gods give you such power, and this is how you wield it?"

He snorted. "I've been alive longer than half your ancestors, boy. This is the way of our world. The gods sent us this power to cleanse the world, and that is what we must do."

The priest dragged me closer to the flames, his fingers curling in an iron grip around my bony wrist. My joints threatened to pop under his touch, unused to any level of physical touch. “Send them into the flames,” he commanded.

I locked my knees as the souls in my chest clawed with panic.

Give me your power, I asked them. *Give me your rage.*

Strength filled me as they obeyed. My muscles expanded, strapping over years of withered sinew with fresh blood. I straightened, growing taller as fresh aethyre wound through me.

The priest’s eyes widened as fear glazed over ancient arrogance. “What are you?” he breathed.

Those were his final words before I willed power into my limbs and shoved him into the flames.

The spirits in my soul keened with approval.

“I’m a vessel,” I whispered, my voice all thunder and prophecy, “and I’ve finally been Awakened.”

About the Awakening

This story was inspired by a short story that was a finalist in the 2017 Parsec Short Story Contest. My worlds tend to be high on the world-building and I wanted the chance to explore it as a novelette and give it a bit more oomph that it deserves.

If you've read the prior story in the Ancient Realms Collection titled "The Last Oracle," you'll recognize the term "vessel." While "The Last Oracle" is also an award-winning story, it's a look at a Viking tale of magic and gods and a man who wasn't meant to be a vessel, but takes on the challenge to save someone he loves.

"The Awakening" is an entirely new tale and realm to explore of what it might mean to be a vessel. Jakob is a receptacle, but not just for the gods' magic, and it wasn't his choice. But he'll use his gift in an entirely unexpected way. I hope you enjoy his journey.

This story has been further expanded into the Epic Fantasy Saga: The Dweller Series, starting with Soul Bound. I love when a small idea can blossom and grow into something of epic proportions!

SOUL
BOUND
A.J. FLOWERS

FLAWLESS

Book 4 in the Ancient Realms Collection

ONE

I held my breath as I waited. Tonight was special and once a year I was blessed with a brief moment of true and perfect Sight.

The sky blazed with golds and blues, slowly transforming into a blood-red sheen that spread across the clouds that promised I hadn't been forgotten. The lone, damaged Valkyrie of the Flawless was still a daughter of the goddess, even though I didn't live up to the name.

When the last fleeting ray of light dove into the horizon, I tossed my useless practice swords to the sands and bolted for the beach.

Liliana didn't try to stop me. If any of the other Valkyries under her training ever left in such a hurry, she'd have clapped them across the back of their head. But she knew my love of the goddess. So she smiled and shifted her shield on her hip. I rushed past her in a blur on my way to the waves that lapped just outside the village outskirts.

Finding my way to the shore used to be a challenge. As

a severely near-sighted girl born on an island of mystical warriors, I never had quite fit in. But none of that mattered when I watched Sol's flame, the god of sun and glory, crash into the oceans and the world set ablaze for a single moment. Then the sheet of darkness and stars came next and I didn't feel so alone, because I knew my goddess was near.

My sandaled feet pattered across the dusty path, having memorized the way by now, I ran as fast as I could. Excited and out of breath, my chest heaved as I watched and waited for my reward beyond the shore.

Colors gleamed across the horizon until the blur of the moon took its place. I huddled into the tangle of my arms and knees as I crouched.

Then she was there. My goddess walked across the sea and opened her arms in greeting. I still couldn't hear her song, but the sparkle of stars gleamed across her dress and the brightness of her smile brought stinging tears to my eyes. This was the only night she ever left the cloister. This was when she roamed free and happy.

I closed my eyes as I listened to the breeze and faraway glimmer of Freya's voice. Because of my flaw, the world was always a blur of colors and movement. But when the goddess appeared, none of that mattered. In a single breath, I felt loved, protected, and secure.

Thunder crashed, making my eyes bulge with surprise and then my goddess was gone.

I jumped to my feet and my breath came in short gasps. She always stayed with me well into the night, wiping away my insecurities and fears that I wasn't good enough. The

Valkyries tolerated me and my blasphemous run to shore when the goddess appeared. I was an oddity, a flaw among the Flawless. But now, as my chest fluttered in panic, I began to realize that even the goddess had finally abandoned me.

Collapsing to the beach, I curled into a ball and didn't care that sand ground into my hair. I squeezed my cursed eyes shut and tried to listen to the waves. As if nothing terrible had happened, its music lazily lapped against the shore.

Disturbing my peace was Mira's battle-worn bay and clash of metal against Liliana's shield. I'd abandoned my training for a night with the goddess, and Mira hated it. She was my age, my greatest nemesis, and believed that the night of the goddess was to be honored by fierce training if any of the Valkyries believed they'd one day earn their wings. It was a myth. We'd never be good enough to become true Valkyries.

Mira couldn't understand what it felt like to not be good enough. Year after year she tirelessly tried. But I knew that I did no honor to the goddess by aimlessly swinging my sword at the blur of my opponent. I'd discovered the gift of the full moon when I'd been kicked out of the training ring, told to drown myself before the goddess. I'd gone to obey them, only to find the deity pulling me free of the waters.

But now, she'd abandoned me. Perhaps she regretted saving me. Mira's cry rang through the night once again, cutting through the short distance between the village and my nest amongst the waves. I wondered if the goddess had decided that Mira was right, that I should have been fighting and bleeding from the blur of swords in a never-ending attempt to become a true Valkyrie. I'd never been a great fighter. My senses couldn't keep up with the growing sharpness of Valkyries like Mira.

I laid there, staring into the darkness for a long time. The languishing blotch of silver moved overhead, the only indicator of passing time. Cold seeped into my bones and I shivered, but I couldn't face the village with news that the goddess hadn't spoken. She hadn't even remained long enough for me to bask in her presence. Every time she'd come to me, given me a brief moment of vision, before dancing across the shore. I was convinced that one day I'd hear her song. I'd finally learn what music it was that made her smile so brightly.

There was no song tonight. No goddess sweeping across the waves with fluid grace. Instead, there was nothing but the crash of waves and the echo of my failure.

Mira continued to plague me with her training. She seemed to never grow tired. I, on the other hand, grew weary the moment I lifted my practice swords. I only dreaded my impending failure at battle when Ragnarok finally came.

Still, Mira fought, taunting me with her perseverance. Swallowing the inevitable cry that stuck in my throat, I got up and stormed further down the beach, determined to find where my goddess had gone. Mira's sounds grew louder and more frantic. I frowned and paused, turning to glare at the blotch that was my village. Something was wrong.

TWO

I listened. It took me a few moments to realize it wasn't just Mira who shouted in the distance. There were other sounds. Sounds of *men*.

There were no men in the village of the Flawless. Sol and the goddess Freya shared these secret nights to birth the Valkyries. But no children had been born, not since me.

Frantic, I ran towards the village. I didn't stop to think how useless I might be against real men, but I couldn't just leave my sisters to their fate. If they were going to fight and die, then I would finally prove myself to be one of the Flawless by doing the same.

When I entered into the village, leaping blotches of red and heat made me stop in my tracks. Even though I couldn't see the fires, I smelled the swift currents of ash and death. Muffled screams told me that Valkyries were trapped inside the barracks.

I ran into the arena, following the memorized path to my standard training spot in the corner, and dove to the ground. My hands scraped across the trodden sands, but my practice swords were nowhere to be found. Liliana must have picked them up when I'd left.

Cursing, I crawled to the wall. My thin armor scraped across the ground as I reached and searched for the secure blades that were always on display.

They were forbidden for trainees to touch. I was fifteen years old, but most Valkyries earned their sword at twelve. When my fingers met cool metal, I inwardly cringed at the weapons of war that I hadn't earned, but plucked a sword free and gripped it at the hilt with both hands.

The weight made me want to topple over, but I wasn't going to use it on the men who had moved their pillaging further into the village. First I was going to save my sisters in the barracks.

The door was blocked, my exploring fingers finding a long slab of wood secure across the handles. I tried to tug at it, but hissed when the heat made me snap away.

Raising the sword, I hurled it at the door and chopped. I reached out again to see if I'd done any damage, growling at the snap of pain as my fingers ran across the jagged hurt of the door, but was rewarded by the knowledge that I'd made the wood splinter.

Raising the sword again, I remembered how Liliana had rested her hands on my legs to show me how to bring power from the ground. This time I bent my knees and used my legs to put strength into the blow. Again and again I lifted the sword and beat it against the door until the blockage finally gave way with a crack.

I kicked the doors open and a plume of smoke rushed

into my face. Tumbling back onto the ground, I coughed and sputtered, then screamed for those trapped inside to come out.

"Astrid?" Liliana's surprised voice, hoarse and scratched as she barreled through the entryway. Shadowed forms followed her, my sisters gagging and choking on the soot in the air.

I smiled. "You're alive."

Liliana helped me to my feet. "Stay here, child. The men have moved towards the temple and we can't allow them to get inside."

I swallowed, wondering if this was why the goddess had disappeared from her dance across the sea. If men beat against her temple walls, perhaps she'd gone inside to protect the treasures of the Flawless that rested within the sacred chamber.

"I must help!" I demanded. "It was I who freed you from the flames. Let me help!"

Liliana squeezed my arm. "I know, Astrid. I know. But please stay here. I can't fight and be worried about you, too. You're not ready."

Before I could argue, she ushered my sisters onward, and they left in a blur of battle cries down the trail towards the center of the village and the towering temple that rested within.

Biting the inside of my cheek, I considered obeying Liliana. I closed my eyes and inhaled, taking in the full measure of destruction. While my sisters might have made it out alive, the cooked scent of horses and livestock tinged my nose. My stomach churned.

When I snapped my eyes open, the blaze of the barracks glowed like a smear across my vision. I frowned, and knew what I had to do.

I crouched and stalked my way to the temple. Cries of battle and clashes of metal began again, telling me that the men had indeed come for our treasures at the temple and Liliana was going to stop them—or die trying.

Running into a battle that was nothing but a blur of orbs and movement wouldn't be how I'd fight against men. I made my way to the tall grasses that heaved against the warm updrafts created by the flames and crouched within them.

The glint of metal flashed, a silver hint against the steps of the temple, followed by Liliana's cry of pain. I dug my fingers into the dirt. They were losing.

Looking back to the barracks still aflame, an idea sparked in the back of my mind. I ran, gathering up the splintered wood that I'd rendered from the door and stuck it into the red-hot flames. Once the embers caught, I brought the torch to the grasses and set them alight.

The trail of weeds ran all the way around the temple. I risked burning down the entire sacred place, but it was better than letting men have it. I had to hope that my goddess was close enough to the passions of Sol to survive such heat. She was Freya, the goddess of love and might, and the mother of Valkyries who would serve her when Ragnarok came.

So many of us were new and blossoming into our roles. Liliana was the eldest among our tribe and nausea wound through me when I realized that her battle cries had ceased.

I couldn't dwell on the terrible thought that she'd already been taken away from the mortal plane. She was the closest among us to earn her wings.

The steps billowing down from the temple in a sheet of gold framed with the reds of licking fires as the grasses caught alight. Men roared and their harsh words snapped through the air. I prayed that it was a call to retreat.

Gold and treasures glinted in their arms as they left the temple. The flames licked at the walls and threatened to find a way inside. The temple itself was made of stone and rimmed with gold, but the window frames were encased with wood, and it would only take one misplaced piece of furniture inside to wreack havoc.

The men didn't seem willing to take the chance. The few standing Valkyries cried with victory, launching spears at the men as they fled.

When the shouting ceased, I approached the steps, and searched for Liliana.

It was Mira who came at me. I recognized her by her gait and jerky movements. She came close enough that her nose touched mine, the only amount of distance that I could distinguish features.

Her bloodshot eyes rimmed with tears and rage. She shook me until my teeth rattled. "This is your fault," she hissed.

My eyes went wide. "What?"

She dragged me up the steps and I tripped over my sandals. She tossed me to the ground and I landed onto Liliana's still frame.

My fingers hovered over her, finding a gash across her

midsection and a dark, sticky blotch running down the steps. I brushed her hair aside, only to find her amber eyes locked open with shock.

"She's dead," I said, the words impossible on my tongue. She was the fiercest warrior among us all. We were young Valkyries with a single mother to guide us. She'd been so patient and kind, but now she lay dead, abandoned by the goddess.

"Four men came at her at once with spears. One got through," Mira said.

I turned to stare at her blurry form. Even through the limit of my sight, I could tell by her stance that she was furious with me. "You went to the beach. The men came by boats. Doesn't the goddess give you Sight once a year? Doesn't she bless you with a gift of being Flawless? And what do you do with this gift? You squander it instead of using it to see the men that came to our shore. You could have warned us!" Her hand reached back, readying for a blow.

One of my sisters gripped her wrist before the strike could fall. "Enough," said Hilda, one of the older Valkyries who would be Liliana's replacement. That was the way of our warriors. The eldest always inherited the role to care for the Flawless. "It is the goddess who will decide her punishment. I will take her into the cloister."

Mira fumed and jerked Hilda off. "After her failure, you wish to plague her presence onto our goddess? We should be falling to our knees for forgiveness after chasing down the men running off with our treasures." She pointed down the path littered with embers and flames. "Look at this destruction Astrid has caused! It will take seasons to rebuild!"

I wanted to shout that if it hadn't been for me, they'd all be dead, suffocated and burned in the barracks. But I kept my mouth shut. There was truth in Mira's anger. If I'd been looking at the sea, instead of the goddess, I might have seen the boats. I might have had a chance to warn my sisters when the goddess had disappeared, instead of wallowing in my own sorrow that I'd been abandoned. Now I saw that the goddess hadn't left me because of anything I'd done. She'd gone to protect the temple.

Scrambling to my feet, I straightened. "This is my fault," I agreed. "I will gladly face the punishment of the goddess for my failures."

Hilda nodded, gently taking my wrist and guided me away from Mira who glowered. I couldn't see her gaze, but I felt the heat of her rage and blame.

"Come," Hilda said, and guided me into the temple to face my fate.

THREE

I'd only been inside the temple a handful of times. It had always gleamed of power and gold, weapons and jars of incense that floated tails of smoke into the air.

Now, there was only carnage and destruction. So many of my sisters and the thick bodies of men strewn about the chamber. Some leaned against pillars and held their wounds as if they could keep their insides from falling out.

"I don't understand," I said, my tears running freely down my cheeks. "Why do men want our treasures so badly? What could be worth this horror?"

Hilda continued to guide me, stepping over the bodies and kicking aside tossed trinkets. The Valkyries specialized in the souls of dead female warriors, and each one brought with them their most valued possessions to bring honor to the goddess. If the treasure was worthy, the goddess would bless that soul with reincarnation as a Valkyrie.

I'd always wondered who I'd been before I'd come here. What kind of treasure had I brought? Perhaps I'd been a fool and kept my most treasured possession for myself. Perhaps I had brought my flaw upon myself because I'd been a selfish soul in a previous life.

"Men only know greed," Hilda said, as if that explained everything. "That'll all change after Ragnarok."

I pinched my lips into a thin line as we made our way past the shredded entrance into the central chamber that housed the most precious of artifacts and treasures. This was the place where Liliana and the caretakers before her had brought their treasures, and the goddess had found them to be pure.

I expected to see gold and jewels strewn about the floor, the best of the treasure taken away, but instead there was only a mountain of scrolls, dead flowers, and a single, ugly jar.

Hilda breathed out a sigh of relief. "Good. They didn't take these."

Perplexed, I allowed her to take me past the mountain of objects that seemed like junk, and into the final cloister where our goddess lived.

A hazy dome rested on the wall which framed a stone statue. Hilda released me and allowed me to press my nose against the glass so that I could make out the rendering of our goddess.

A woman with a wreath upon her head and a flowing gown draped over her shoulder stared back. A single blade rested in her hand and her eyes, a glassy shade of marble, seemed to convey power and ferocity. This was the goddess of Valkyries. This was Freya.

FOUR

When the statue went from lifeless grey, to a sheet of flesh pink, I yelped and jerked away from the glass.

Freya's gaze fell onto me. She stepped through and her dress flowed with starlight. For the first time, a song hinted at the edges of my mind. The effect forced me to relax, even if the shock and awe of being in Freya's presence made my chest constrict.

"Sweet Astrid," the goddess said. Her words came with a lilt full of distant bells and chimes. Her gaze shifted over my shoulder and landed on a petrified Hilda. "Thank you for bringing her to me, my daughter. You may go care for the Flawless." She offered a warm smile. "The realm of men come and go, and even if they may bring with them destruction, we will yet recover. They will face their judgment when Ragnarok comes."

Hilda gave a jerky nod before disappearing from the chamber.

Alone with the goddess, my knees wobbled and terror

gripped a noose around my neck. When Freya's gaze fell back onto me, I fell to the floor. "Please forgive me. I should have warned the village there were boats."

"Is that so?" the goddess said. "But how could you have done that? You couldn't have seen the boats from so far."

My shoulders scrunched as I cringed. "Because I am flawed. It's all my fault."

To my shock, Freya knelt and rested a hand on my shoulder. Up so close, I could see the mystery of her eyes that glittered like an endless void. "You are not flawed, my daughter, you are just as you should be." She rose. "I cannot always defend myself from men. They are creations of Odin. He's driven by the momentum of Ragnarok. It won't be long now."

"We're not ready," I said. "Even Liliana has died," I managed to admit, that truth a thorn in my throat. "If I had warned her, perhaps—"

A soft laugh from the goddess filled with birdsong and waterfalls. "Because of you, she died a warrior. She died a Valkyrie. You freed your sisters from the cage of flames. For that, you have saved their souls."

Wide-eyed, I stared at her. If a Valkyrie died in battle, their soul could yet find peace. "Will I see her again?"

Freya grinned. "One day, perhaps, should you find yourself in Valhalla." Her gaze shifted into the chambers beyond and a warm breeze that seemed to come from the goddess herself flung her hair from her face. "Odin knows I've saved my most powerful soul when the time would be nigh. I just didn't expect him to find out so soon. I was so careful."

I swallowed. "You mean Mira?" It had to be Mira. I'd never seen a Valkyrie so strong at such a young age. I was two years her senior, but she'd earned her blade at the age of nine. I'd always lived in her shadow.

"I have a task for you," Freya said, ignoring my question. "Actually, I have three."

I frowned. "Perhaps there would be another Valkyrie more suited—"

She snapped up a hand. "Do you question me, my daughter?"

Swallowed, I relented under her command. This would either be my punishment, or my chance to make amends. "Of course. What must I do?"

FIVE

The first of the three tasks seemed simple enough. Freya asked me to gather fresh parchment and document the battle in its entirety for posterity. She'd said that documenting history was an important treasure for the Valkyries, for when Ragnarok would end, the record of valor and deeds must be kept. Reborn souls wouldn't have their memories to rely on, and the goddess was not all-seeing. She relied on her Valkyries to relay the truth of events.

First, I helped to tend to the wounded. Of the many tasks a Valkyrie needed to perform, one of the only ones I was good at was sewing a wound closed. While my eyesight was horrific, it had its benefits when I looked at things up close. I could see the wound in all its clarity and find just the right folds of flesh to stitch back together. Other Valkyries might miss a grain of dirt yet left inside that would fester, but I took a gentle cloth and cleaned gashes before closing them up.

While I was tending to the last of the Valkyries with a nasty cut on her arm, I frowned to see Mira exiting from the sacred chamber where our goddess communed with us. Mira gave me a triumphant glare, snatched parchment from the stall, and gave me a nod.

She'd been given the same task.

Determined to finish the deed first, I finished my stitches and bit off the thread. "Make sure to clean it twice a day," I ordered, then gathered my own supplies to begin my documenting of events.

The temple housed a multiple private rooms where Valkyries could go and meditate, or perform tasks that required silence. I entered one to find pillows strewn about the chamber and its table overturned. There wouldn't be anything of true value in these rooms, so luckily the bottles of ink were still there underneath the shelves.

After setting the room back into sorts, I sat down and began to write.

I'd learned to write before I'd learned to wield a sword. I preferred letters because I could see their long strokes. I had practiced each scribble again and again until it looked just like the styles I'd seen in the libraries and archives. There were few tasks I could do well, and in this I wanted to make my goddess proud.

I set my mind back to when Sol's light had gone out and I'd gone to the beach. I made sure to leave out any emotional feelings and document the events in truth and clarity.

When I was done, I sighed, blew on the scrolls and rolled them up to take to the goddess.

Mira had already been in and out, having delivered her task to our mother. I glowered at her. Already, she'd bested me in speed.

"You're wasting your time," Mira said with a sneer. "Freya has already given me the next task. You won't be able to keep up."

Ignoring her, I brushed past her stiff shoulder and entered into the chamber.

SIX

"Why do you look so forlorn?" the goddess asked, having slipped free of the glossy prison.

Marveling in her presence, I knelt to one knee and presented my scrolls. "I have taken too long. Forgive me, my goddess."

She gingerly took the scrolls, her fingertips grazing mine for the briefest of moments and sending shivers of power up my limbs. "This was not a task of speed," she chided. She rolled the scrolls open and began to read.

I swallowed the lump in my throat as I patiently waited for her to get through the entirety of my recount. Fears lingered across my mind that perhaps I'd forgotten something important. Had I mentioned that I'd first went for my practice swords before violating the rules and taking a real blade? What about the horses? I hadn't even tried to save them. I admitted to that, right?

Freya hummed thoughtfully as she rolled the scrolls and gingerly placed them into the shelves along the wall.

My eyes bulged to see that she intended to keep them here, with her, in the most sacred of places. A brief search showed me that Mira's scrolls were nowhere to be found.

"Your next task will be to find healing herbs to treat the wounded," Freya announced.

I jerked to attention. "Herbs?"

She nodded. "The men who came laced their blades with poison. It takes time for it to take effect. After you've gathered the flowers, you can treat the wounded now that they've had enough time to rest."

SEVEN

Without another word, I dove into the darkness of the island to accomplish my new task. Documenting events was no doubt important work, but I enjoyed helping others more than I did putting ink to the page. I felt so useless in the tribe of the Flawless. Anything where I could prove myself useful gave me hope that perhaps, one day, the goddess would heal me of my flaw. Perhaps one day I'd belong.

For now, I ran through the vines and overgrown weeds towards the sounds of water. There were only a few healing herbs that I knew could combat poisons. As a Valkyrie, the daughters of the goddess are trained in all arts of war. Ragnarok will be a nasty, terrible time of strife and we need to be ready for anything. It didn't surprise me that Odin's men would come bearing weapons of cowardice. All it took was a single slice and then his men could run, and leave their poison to do the rest of their dirty work.

Not on my watch.

When I broke through the foliage and crashed into the cool splashing of a stream, I hesitated as I searched for Mira. If she was here, all she had to do was stay still and I'd miss her completely. She wore grey battle leathers that would blend well with rocks and the riverbed.

Sighing, I crouched into the stream and began my search. The healing herbs that I was looking for grew best nestled in the soft under mesh of streams.

When I spotted a blotch of orange, I pressed in closer until the fine mist of the splashing waters covered my nose. It could be an herb, or it could be the tiny crabs that liked to pinch. After judging that the soft sway of orange was indeed the weed I was looking for, I began to pluck my harvest.

"Ouch!" Mira's voice broke through the calm music of the river and I startled, nearing falling into the stream.

"Goddess, Mira," I chided and looked around for her.

A blotch of grey jerked about, revealing Mira had indeed been hiding further upstream, hoping I wouldn't notice her. "Stupid crabs!"

Rolling my eyes, I eased downstream. With Mira kicking up sand, I'd never find what I was looking for.

"Don't you ignore me!" Mira shouted as I retreated.

I pinched my lips and forced myself to a halt. Icy tendrils of the water licked around my ankles and made my toes go numb.

It wasn't Mira's demand that made me stop. It was the tightness in her voice. "Eat the herbs," I growled through clenched teeth.

"What?" she asked, the question a shriek of outrage.

"You eat your own herbs, you useless—" she tossed back the insult before her windpipe closed. The venom from the crab that had pinched her had seeped all the way through her bloodstream and she gagged before she fell.

Rolling my eyes, I forced myself to turn. Orange blotches that were healing petals drifted down the stream and out of sight. I sighed, taking my own bounty and grinding it in my fist.

Coming close enough to Mira to see the perfect ridge of her nose and striking blue of her wide eyes, I lifted my fingers to her lips and traced a line. She licked at the orange blush, her body spasming as it fought the poison.

I waited for her to come around. A part of me wanted to leave and find more herbs to get back to the village, but Mira could very well drown in the stream if the waters pushed her over. I wasn't strong enough to lift her, so I propped her against my thigh and waited, shivering as the chill of night seeped into me.

It took a long time for Mira's fingers to finally grip around mine, but they eventually did, and she struggled to her feet as she clutched at her throat. She glanced at me, and I thought I might get a "thank you," except that she glared. "You planned this!" she shrieked, and stumbled into the forest before I could reply.

Mira was not the kind of Valkyrie that could accept that I, a flawed daughter of the goddess, could have saved her from certain death, and from a teeny tiny crab, no doubt.

Everything about Mira was perfect. She moved with such grace that it made me cry with envy to watch her spar on the training grounds. Even though I couldn't see the fluid beauty of her movements, I could always hear her sword sing as it sliced through the air. The only melody my own practice blades awarded me was the pathetic clunks of wood.

But now as I stared after her, listening to the faint swish of forest under her feet as she stumbled away from me in shame, I realized that even Mira wasn't perfect.

I searched the stream for more orange patches, happened upon a few more crabs which I left undisturbed, but I couldn't find more of the herb I needed to bring back to the goddess.

Head hanging in defeat, I made my way back to the temple. Stepping over the injured only awarded me with stabs of guilt that I'd failed them. I could have let Mira die. I could have gone for her lost herbs before they'd drifted too far downstream.

Passing by the strong, tall Valkyries who guarded the entrance to the cloister of the goddess, I hesitated before stepping inside.

Mira was already there, slumped into the corner shivering as the goddess herself draped her with a blanket. I stared, disbelieving what I was seeing. "You've done well," said the goddess, her words sweeping over me with warmth and gentle song.

"I've failed you," I corrected her. My armor crashed against the floor as I pushed a knee into the ground and bowed, shame weighting heavily on my shoulders. "I couldn't gather any of the herbs you asked for. Now my sisters will die."

A laugh that sent bells and birdsong tinkling through the air. "Actually, my child, it was a test, one that you passed beautifully." She waved a hand, indicating the injured that rested outside. "There was no poison in the men's blades. I lied."

Blinking, I stared at the goddess as incomprehension sent tinges and zaps down my limbs. I didn't even know that it was possible for a deity to lie. "But, why?" I asked, my gaze slowly lowering to the shivering blob that whimpered in the corner. I couldn't see distinguishing features, but the scent of forest and moss told me it was Mira who clutched a blanket to her chest.

"Odin wants something from me, something I'm not willing to give him. His attack has only reminded me that when Ragnarok comes, only the strong will survive. But my daughters have forgotten what is true strength. It isn't how fast you can swing a blade, or how lithe you are on your feet. It is the strength of your heart, and what you are willing to sacrifice for your sisters." She turned, gazing down at Mira. "Even for those who might not deserve it."

I chewed on my lip before realizing that Freya held something in her hands. I dared to venture closer, and realized that it was the cracked, dusty jar I'd seen in the treasure trove. She smiled and presented it. "I am not cruel, my dear Astrid. You have shown your heart is strong and have displayed your willingness of sacrifice. Please accept this gift."

Taking the jar, my whole body shook with anticipation as I peered inside. A brilliant, black void swirled in the depths of what had seemed to be a simple piece of pottery. I stared, my whole being becoming enraptured in its magic.

"What is this?" I asked.

Freya smiled. "It is your sight that was taken from you. I offer for you to make yourself a true Flawless as you've always dreamed."

My breath hitched at the idea, but without hesitation, I jerked the pot away and thrust it at the goddess. "No," I said, my tone resolute. "I can't take this."

Mira hissed from the corner as she struggled to her feet. "Ungrateful brat," she said through gritted teeth as she stumbled out of the cloister.

Ignoring her, I kept the jar extended until the goddess drifted close enough to take it. Her silken fingers grazed mine, sending an echo of her power thrumming through my senses. My sight wavered, as if retaliating against my choice. Closing my eyes, I listened, and even though I couldn't hear it, I knew that my goddess was upset.

Forcing my eyes open again, I saw that she hadn't backed away. The heady wave of her power washed over me as if she were the ocean and I could be swept away by the current at any moment. "Freya?" I asked, my voice sounding squeaky like a frightened child's.

Her gaze lingered on the pot as she softly stroked its sides. Upon hearing her name, her gaze found mine. "Yes, my child?"

I bit my lip before replying. "It's too great a gift," I said. But that wasn't the truth. The truth was that all my life, I'd been different. I couldn't imagine being a true Flawless. Would I even be "me" anymore?

Her smile was both beautiful and sad. "I made you just as you were meant to be," she said. "You are the only flawed daughter of the Flawless, and because of that, you are the strongest. However, I had to be sure your sacrifice was one of your own choosing. You've chosen well."

"Then why do you look so sad?" I managed to ask. There was so much sorrow that rained like a slow drizzle on my heart.

Her eyes sparked with a flash of pain. "Ragnarok is on the horizon and I am unprepared. None of my Valkyries have earned their wings. You're the only one who's come close." I shivered at that admission. Out of all the Valkyries, I imagined I was the farthest from such an honor.

Her gaze unfocused as she peered over my shoulder the way Mira had gone. "My daughters aren't ready. I've made them with all of my strength and grace, yet I left out a vital component that seeds true strength." Her fingers gripped hard around the pot until I thought it might shatter. "You are the only daughter I've made that will survive Ragnarok to come, and it saddens me that I have failed so many."

Frowning, I searched the strewn remnants of treasure that Odin's men had disturbed. They'd been looking for something. "What does Odin want from you?"

Freya stiffened, but to my surprise, she answered. "He wants my most precious treasure."

Shifting my weight, my curiosity forced the question out. "And what is your most precious treasure?"

Her gaze found mine and glittered with joy. "You."

EIGHT

It was hard to believe that Odin would want me, the sole flawed daughter of the Flawless. Yet, when Freya explained it to me, it made more sense.

Ragnarok would come when the three gods of our world grew in such strength that unbalance would spill chaos over into the world. The only way to restore it would be to regain a peaceful understanding, or to endure an endless war with a victor claiming all the power for themselves. It turned out that I had been imbued with a secret power Freya had hidden away.

Odin controlled the earth and men. Freya fueled the air, nature, and women. It was Sol who centered in the middle, having the power over the waters and the sun. Humans believed there to be so many gods, and at a time there had been. But chaos came in cycles, and eventually gods such as Aegir of the sea and Loki who'd been the byproduct of chaos succumbed to their nature. They'd all fallen in the wars that had come before my time. Now, only

Freya, Odin, and Sol were left, overpowered by those they had taken in battle. The way the air zinged with whispers of chaos, it wouldn't be much longer before the true Ragnarok was upon us.

There was only one way to stop the decimation of the world. Freya was right. It only took one glance at my sisters weakened and arrogant to know how right she was. They nursed each other's wounds, but stubbornly they pushed away needed medicines and fought to their feet, ready to battle again. They should be resting, but Mira was among them, shaking and pale, trying to lift her sword as she staggered into the practice arena.

It was useless to argue with them. My sisters never listened to me. Freya's saddened gaze swept over us as she lingered in the cloister behind her opaque wall of stone. She wouldn't come out. She would conserve her energy and wait for Ragnarok to come, having imbued Loki's power in myself.

If anyone could stop Ragnarok's momentum, it would be the power Freya had hidden inside my soul. It was foolish, but I had to try and stop the destruction on the horizon.

Stomping to the edge of the village, I made my way to the boats and found the sturdiest one. Valkyries didn't often venture off the island, but sometimes we did for resources or for knowledge.

I grabbed a splintered oar and shoved off, silently slinking into the fog.

If Freya knew that I'd left, she didn't leave the safety of her temple to stop me.

NINE

Sol's presence lingered on the seas as I tugged the sail and whispered a prayer for a breeze to help me along. I stared into the dark abyss of the horizon and waited.

Sol loved Freya, and he wouldn't dare harm one of her daughters. She'd danced with him for so long. It was only now that Ragnarok neared upon the world had she retreated into her temple. If she had to fight against him, she would have to guard her heart.

When the air remained still, I licked my dried lips and lifted my voice into song. The melody was one I'd been taught as a child by Liliana, but I changed the words to suit my heart's goals.

Freya is wounded and lost. I wish to ease her sorrow.

Send me a breeze, fine Sol, send me on my way to the distant shore.

For there is one other god amongst your kind who yet lives.

Odin, and he will bring Ragnarok upon us unless I go to him and give him that which he seeks.

Fear wound through me when the winds picked up and caught my sail. Either Sol would overturn my flimsy boat, or grant my request and help me to reach Odin's shores.

Water splashed as the boat sliced through its currents. My hair swept over my shoulders as a breeze pummeled over me. Sol didn't speak, didn't appear, but I knew that he'd heard me.

Even though I was shaking, both from cold and from terror, I crouched into the grainy hull of my boat and gripped onto the steer, directing myself towards the brightest star on the horizon.

TEN

Odin's lands weren't what I'd expected. Ugly, snarled rocks blocked my entry and had my boat been any larger, I wouldn't have found purchase on the crags. I would have crashed into them, but Sol's winds died down and wood creaked and scraped along the jagged fingers of Odin's shore.

Where Freya's island was soft and welcoming, her counterpart lived up to his reputation. Even through the blur of my broken sight, sharp angles and points betrayed the harsh land for what it was. This was where hardened men dwelled, those who came in the night to kill my people, and who would kill me now if they found me on their land.

Even though I was a flawed daughter, I was still a Valkyrie. I had the power of the goddess just as much as any of my sisters and wrapped myself in her magic just as I'd been taught to do. Mira had loved to startle me out of the practiced mirage, but her endless taunts served me now as I embraced the cold secrecy of mist, successful in the attempt to make myself invisible even though my heart fluttered like a bird trapped in a cage.

I stepped onto the broken, ragged shore and winced as rocks bit into my thin sandals. Voices carried on the breeze and I froze just as the glow of torches glided over the hill.

Panic jolting through me, I stumbled and a jagged shard speared straight through my shoe. I stifled the scream as hot blood spurt over my foot. With black spots threatening over my vision, I yanked myself free and stumbled down the shore.

"I've never seen Odin like this," said a man, his words tumbling over a curly beard. He lifted the torch and squinted at the horizon. "He's furious that Sol sent the Valkyries here to retaliate. The breeze never blows north, so I understand his assumption, but I don't see—" His eyes went wide when he saw my boat.

Silently cursing that I couldn't extend my magic any further, I dragged myself out of his path as much as I could, just in time as he stumbled down the rocks and his companion drew his sword.

"It's just one boat," said the younger man, his voice soft and lyrical, the direct opposite of his older counterpart. "Do you think only one Valkyrie came? Why? That's suicide." He swirled as if searching for me. I froze and scarily breathed when his gaze passed over the spot where I stood and I clung Freya's magic tight around me. He didn't spot me, but his gaze lowered to the trail of blood I couldn't hide. He ran his finger over it and frowned, rubbing the dark blood between his forefinger and thumb.

"This has to be a trick," said the bearded man. "Come, let's report this to Odin right away."

The younger man nodded and followed as the old man turned and stormed back over the hill, but not before glancing over his shoulder and deliberately dropping a pouch to the sands.

When I scrambled to it, I found familiar crushed orange blossoms inside, a healing herb that would numb the worst of the damage and pain.

I didn't question this compassion from one of Odin's ruthless sons. Gingerly, I applied the ointment, and then I followed, stepping into the soft grooves of their footsteps all the way into Odin's stronghold.

ELEVEN

Where the Valkyries preferred to live in a village with modest huts and groaning trees, Odin's men lived in walls of rock that towered hard and cold. I shivered when I followed the men into its shadow and dredged up what little courage I could muster to do what needed to be done.

I followed the men past workshops and places of flames and beating iron smiths. Dirt and dust flung up everywhere and I wrinkled my nose, suppressing a sneeze that would undoubtedly give me away.

Eventually, the grime gave way to polished marble and granite as we scaled the steps into Odin's temple. Unlike Freya, he didn't live in a small cloister where only a select few could worship. My eyes went wide when we entered into a long hall and there was a god, sitting atop a throne.

Where Freya was softness and birdsong, Odin was brittle rage, his voice flint against stone that sparked harsh against my ears.

"What have you found?" he boomed. He motioned for

the men to come closer. "Hurry, you fools! Freya is soon to decend upon us!"

The men unlatched from their frozen shock. It took me a moment to realize that even if they often came into Odin's presence, their fear still choked them even now. The eldest was the first to scramble to the stairs that led to the throne and bowed to one knee. He waited for his younger counterpart to follow before he spoke. "A single boat, sire. That's all."

Odin frowned, his gaze lingering knowingly on the youngest. "Freya thinks me so weak that she only sends a small squadron?" he bellowed with rage. He slammed his fist onto the arm of his throne and a shockwave spanned out, cracking through the room like an earthquake.

I shivered at the impact of his power, and it wasn't until I opened my eyes again did I find the god staring straight at me. The shockwave had broken my mirage, if just for a moment, but long enough to be found out.

The men startled at Odin's stunned gaze, and turned, only to scramble to their feet and draw their weapons. "Valkyrie!" the youngest screeched, but it was a cry of desperation, as if he wished for me to flee.

I frowned and splayed my palms. "I come in peace," I said, my voice surprisingly smooth and steady in spite of the black spot glittering over my vision that betrayed my fear.

The boiling blotch of my vision that was Odin's massive form turned to the men. "Fools. You've brought my death straight to me." When the men cowered, he sighed and looked back to me, his voice both weary and displeased.

"No need for lies, little Valkyrie. You've come to kill me." He stood and the walls shook with the impact of his power. "No doubt you are Freya's best. I will not underestimate you."

Stilling the panic threatening to beat my heart straight out of my chest, I found my voice. "I do not lie, sir Odin. I have not come to kill you, quite the opposite. I have come to mend your relationship with my goddess."

His frown deepened, but the earthquake that sent my bones rattling eased into a distant thunder. "My men have just attacked your sisters and your goddess. It is the way of Ragnarok, and I have accepted there will only be one god who can remain. Why would you wish to mend that which cannot be mended? Not when we have killed and shown our ruthlessness."

Images of Liliana flittered across my mind, but I used them to make sure her death wouldn't be in vain. "The answer to that question lies in that which Freya secreted away in me." I spread my arms in invitation. "See for yourself."

Odin lowered his weight down onto the first step and the castle boomed. He took another, the shock jarring my teeth as a god, opposite in every way to my own, approached me and rested a weighty hand on my shoulder as he peered into my broken eyes. "Impossible," he breathed as the swirls of his irises examined mine. "No Valkyrie would be born with a flaw."

I smiled, knowing now that I had him. "You're quite correct, sir Odin. I am flawed, but I didn't have to be. My goddess stripped away the precision of my sight as a babe.

Even when she offered to return it to me, I declined. Do you know why?"

Seeming intrigued, he curled his shoulders so that we were eye-level. "Why, little Valkyrie?"

I made sure not to err my gaze when I spoke. "Come closer, and you will see the world as I do."

To my surprise, the god obeyed, and then Freya's secret, her weapon that she'd placed in me so long ago, ripped out and engulfed a god in screams.

TWELVE

Odin's hard walls melted around us as the thing that was the remnant of Loki's chaos took control. Nothing could escape it, for Loki's power was the momentum of Ragnarok itself. Freya had been the one to take Loki down. Sol had loved her for it, for she'd been a warrior then, fearless and graceful with her blade that had sliced Loki's head clean off his body.

Only a god could kill another, and her blade had cauterized Loki with her power with such finality, that his own gifts seeped into her, adding his power to hers.

That power was what had taken my sight. There must be balance, even in the body of a Valkyrie. My sight had been taken in exchange for secreting away Loki's gifts. Freya didn't wish to use it, but to hide it, and keep it safe.

My world went dark when that chaos ripped out of me and transported us to another place, one of deities and memory.

Valhalla.

I knew where we were, but it was a broken, distant part of Valhalla where gods spoke in parlay. It was Sol's voice who boomed first. "Finally, Loki's power has been freed. Ragnarok has threatened over the horizon for far too long." His golden brilliance bathed us in warmth as he split through the shadows to stand before us.

A silver sphere that was my goddess Freya came next and she held Sol's hand. "Patience, my love. Loki's power is linked to Ragnarok, but my daughter has brought us here. Let us hear her out."

Odin bayed with rage. "Tricks and mystery. These aren't your ways, Freya." His blazing gaze turned on me, a hundred times more powerful in this realm. Instinctually, I guarded myself, surprised beyond belief to find that I had wings as they splayed and jerked myself away from the threat of his blade.

A Valkyrie's true form, when Freya had reached the pinnacle of her power and her daughters found the truth of their strength, would be one of wings.

"Listen," I commanded, my voice carrying far greater lengths that I'd have imagined. It shouldn't have been possible that I could stand here, among gods. But Freya had placed a dead god's power in my soul. I wasn't just a Valkyrie. I was something new. "Do you not see that I am more than Valkyrie? I am more than flawed? This is how you will stave off Ragnarok."

Interest peaked, Sol approached. His golden warmth bathed over me as he smiled. "Freya put Loki's power in you," he observed. "The trick could be done again."

I nodded and pointed to the splash of waters circling

around his wrists. "You hold Aegir's might of the sea. It has served you well, but perhaps it is time you give it up to another, one of your own choosing, and restore the balance further."

Odin frowned, his rage diminishing into a rumbling growl. "You ask us to give up the powers we have killed for?"

It was Freya who spoke in a flurry of excited bells. "Do you see? Astrid has done the impossible. She's restored a piece of Loki's power within herself. I do not feel the crazed compulsion to kill you anymore, ex-husband." She drew close to me and cupped my face. The glimmer of emotion in her eyes made me sway with the power of her raw grief and delight. "Such a gift, this child. Such a gift. Had I known..."

Sol gripped her shoulder. He was her husband now, but only because Loki's power had made her turn on Odin, and Hel's power had made him turn on her. Even so, love sparkled in Sol's gaze. "I will try it first." He turned to Odin. "You will oversee the process. Then if you wish for peace, if you wish to stave off Ragnarok, you will do the same."

Odin stilled and his rage still seethed in swirling red mist, but he didn't disagree.

Sol's gaze fell back to me. "Take us to the shore, young Valkyrie. I will provide the sacrifice."

Closing my eyes I turned my magic inward, and used the swirl of chaos unlocked inside of my soul to take us home.

THIRTEEN

I took us to Odin's shore, but to the divide where his territory met Sol's. Sol wasn't just the commander of the sea and sun, but of men and women who chose to follow him. They'd come from lineages of old gods and were the truest form of humanity before Freya's daughters and Odin's sons had overtaken the world.

Their soft, wide eyes sparkled with wonder as three gods and a winged Valkyrie came before them through the mists of Valhalla.

"My people!" Sol boomed, spreading his arms wide to greet those who spilled out onto the beaches. "I call upon you to provide me a sacrifice in our time of need."

Having known Valkyries all my life, any among my sisters would fall at Freya's feet should she ever ask for their sacrifice. They'd give their lives in battle, as was their pledge, but these were not warriors. These were the humble village people who bathed in Sol's shores and worshipped him from afar. I expected there to be grumbling or cries of dismay. Instead, a multitude of men and women came forth and offered themselves to their god.

Sol smiled and took his time to walk among them, placing his hand atop their heads. "You have served me well, my people, and today I will put Aegir's powers into you. It is no small sacrifice that I ask of you, for in return for this power, you must give up the right to walk."

It was kind of Sol to give the terms of his request. I cupped my fingers around my elbows, and shivered when silky feathers brushed my arms, my wings still intact. Freya smiled at me as we listened, as if proud for the only flawed of the Flawless to be the one to have gained the fabled wings of the Valkyries.

Even though I'd been subject to sacrifice, it had been an unknown thing. It was only when I'd chosen this life did my wings come forth. The realization made me shiver as understanding swept over me. If these people willingly sacrificed for the love of their god, they would gain something remarkable in return.

The better part of the village spilled over with hands upraised and voices volunteering. Sol turned two thirds of them away. "Some must stay here and tend to your people and your flocks. I only need a few."

The select chosen remaining beamed with pride. "Your sacrifice will be to lose the ability to walk. Do you still wish to serve me?" Sol asked.

If the thought of never walking again disturbed them, they didn't show it. They began to settle onto the ground and awaited Sol's command.

Sol gave Odin a triumphant look. The god of wrath and war frowned, but it seemed to be his normal expression. I couldn't tell if he was displeased, or intrigued.

Sol turned to his people and the stream of water ever-present around his wrists swirled into the air and showered over the gathering like rain. The men and women splayed their palms and leaned their heads back, closing their eyes as they basked in the magic of Aegir's lost power.

Aegir controlled the seas, and I understood the sacrifice when legs began to sew together into fins. The people didn't cry out, even though their faces contorted with pain. When the transformation was finished, they crawled across the sands until they reached the sea, and then dove in.

We watched them go, silent as if we were watching the dead go out on boats only to be seen again in the afterlife. But their faces showed joy when they turned back, briefly, their fresh gills flaring at their necks, before they splashed and delved into the deep.

Mourning cries began, because we knew their sacrifice had been more than just a loss of legs. They were sea creatures now, just as the old Aesir followers had been. The merfolk slept in the deep and had no space in their hearts for the world of men.

Sol exhaled and his skin grew a shade brighter, as if he'd rejuvenated more of his familiar magic in his chest that had been suppressed. "It works, Odin. I feel more balanced. Aegir's power is at peace in the sea, but it is nestled into the bodies of my loyal people. They will not bring about Ragnarok's spark. They will hold Aegir's power secret and safe." His golden eyes blazed as he stared Odin down. "Now it is your turn to find a follower willing to sacrifice for you, and the balance can truly be maintained."

Odin frowned, his eerie gaze finding mine. I couldn't see the lines that no doubt marred his face as he frowned. I expected to face the aura of his rage, but instead I felt a flash of grief and envy emanate from his words. "What made you willing to sacrifice your sight for your goddess?" he asked.

Stunned, I folded my new wings to my back and tried to stand straighter, but the new appendages prevented the motion. So I curled them around my arms instead and guarded myself from the harsh breeze as Freya swept to my side. "You don't have to answer him," she said. "You're one of my Valkyries."

"It's all right," I said. I knew why she didn't want me to answer, but keeping secrets wouldn't prevent Ragnarok. If revealing the truth would give Odin peace and save us all, then it was a sacrifice that not only I, but my goddess would have to make.

"Strength," I said, the single word a testament to the truth. "Without flaws, we do not learn strength. Without sacrifice, we do not learn to appreciate that which we already have. So when my goddess offered me back my sight, I couldn't take it. For to take it would mean to become weaker, not stronger."

Odin hummed and stroked his chin. "Intriguing." He turned, black smoke billowing at his heels. "There may be yet one candidate who will take this power."

I knew where he was going, so it only took a moment's

hesitation before I delved into Loki's magic tucked into my soul and followed him.

FOURTEEN

Odin's power was great, but the harshest of magics stemmed from Hel, the god of death Odin had skewered on the end of his blade. Odin was a god of war, and to face death was his greatest strength. To overcome it, however, gouged a wrongness in him so foul and deep, that it had only served to cement the divide between him and his estranged wife, Freya, the goddess of Valkyries and my own mother.

Odin's sons were already hard and harsh, but there was one that was a boy of a time when Odin had been himself. None of his men as they were now would be capable of the sacrifice which was needed to take death's dark power. But Odin knew there would be one soul willing to please him, one stupid enough to trade his rare compassion for a chance to make Odin proud.

The young, wide-eyed soldier who'd found me on the shore listened to Odin's plea. The god didn't tower above him on his throne and demand a sacrifice. Instead, he stood on the shore where my boat still bucked against the jagged rocks, a reminder that compassion was a weakness in times of war. "You'll be like all of my other sons," Odin promised. He rested his heavy hands on the boy's frame. "You'll be strong and fearless."

The bold, blue haze of his eyes found mine, compassion in them debilitating. I flared my wings to keep my balance as the force of my desire to stop Odin wracked against my ribcage. But I stood no chance against a god. And worse still, if Odin didn't release Hel's power, Ragnarok could come upon us all. His desire to overthrow the other gods could consume him, until war inevitably came, and if that happened, if Odin killed Sol and Freya, he'd go mad with all the powers of the gods and destroy the world in his rage.

"What do you think?" the boy asked me, coming close enough that I could see the innocent trust in his gaze. He didn't worry about the end of the world or what might happen. He glanced up at Odin, the only father he'd ever known, before looking back to me again with sheepish hope.

Odin sighed. "Do you see what I mean, my son? Your compassion overwhelms you that you would even ask the opinion of my greatest enemy."

Ignoring the god whose voice boomed through my chest, I continued to stare into the boy's eyes and said, "I believe that Odin must release his power onto one willing to take it, but it is a sacrifice. There is no going back. You must do this because you wish for the world to be a better place. Is that what you want?"

The boy frowned as he carefully considered my question. "All I've ever wanted was to please my brothers, my uncles." He glanced at the god who towered behind him. "And my father."

I ventured a hand on his shoulder and squeezed. The muscle underneath his leathers tensed under my touch. "Do you wish to please them? Or do you wish to save them from their own destruction?"

Hope glittered across his gaze. "I'd always thought that I was the broken one. But maybe it's them who are broken, and I am the only one who can fix them."

Backing away, I nodded to Odin.

"Very well," Odin boomed and took a knife from his belt. He slit a long line across his palm. "Then drink of my blood, and this power shall be yours."

I knew what the sacrifice would be, but I made myself watch as the boy did as he was told.

After he'd tasted of the terrible power, serrated, sharp wings sprouted from his back, and his spine bowed at an impossible angle as he let out a deafening scream.

When it was all said and done, Hel had been reborn, and beady red eyes looked back at us with a mixture of power and sorrow.

Grief would have overtaken me, if I hadn't seen that same darkness in Odin ease.

FIFTEEN

Heralded as the conqueror of Ragnarok and peacemaker of the gods, Freya welcomed me back to Valhalla to train with Liliana. I didn't have to meet her in the darkness where I'd first found the gods. Bringing balance back to the world of men and gods illuminated the realm with its endless waterfalls, singing spirits, and halls filled with mead and joy. I would never need for welcoming and beauty again.

To this day, I soar overhead, watching and waiting for Ragnarok to threaten again. I'll never leave Valhalla, for I know that its threat lives within me. I have Loki's mischief, and it eats at me every day.

But I gave up my sight so that I might be reminded of who I am. I am a daughter of Freya, flawed of the Valkyries, and even if the beauty of Valhalla is lost on me, I still soar above it on mighty wings, knowing that I'm strong enough to keep the world forever safe.

THE END

About Flawless

This story has some fun and personal history. I was invited to write a novelette for a fantasy anthology that highlighted fantasy characters with disabilities. A large portion of my childhood and adolescence was plagued with severe near-sightedness, but due to poor diagnosis from the doctor and a glasses prescription that didn't work with my stigmatism, I wasn't aware how bad it really was. I didn't see clouds or leaves until I was nearly in my teen years. I identified when my friends were coming down the hall by memorizing their gait and what colors they wore that day. I had no idea that I was living a huge handicap.

When I got contacts, I cried. I stared at the ocean, the sky, the detail of trees. It was fascinating. It made me appreciate the basic senses we have, but I also feel that the experience helped me appreciate what others with disabilities go through, especially those who were born with a disability and one day find out they're missing out on something everyone else has access to. I was blessed that my issue was fixed, but not everyone has that luxury. I hope this story helps those who feel they are flawed, because we all have our flaws and it's accepting those flaws and using them to make us stronger that makes all the difference.

STRANDED

Book 6 in the Ancient Realms Collection

ONE
AMBER

My sixteenth birthday. I should have been with my sisters roaming the sea gathering baubles and shells to put in our hair. But I couldn't pretend with them any longer to be an oblivious child. Ever since our mother had disappeared, the entire clan went on with their lives as if nothing had happened and I was left heartbroken and confused. Whenever I asked of her, I was hushed and told it didn't matter, she was gone, and I had a life to live.

Life wasn't about to get any better. Sixteen was the age of fertility and my father had already begun to entertain the candidates who expressed interest in my fin. I flicked the gold jewel of the muscular appendage and propelled myself further into the deep.

I'd never been down this way. I'd been told to always stay within the confines of the village where the sea witches cloaked us from mankind. But I didn't want to be under their thumbs any longer. I wanted to do what I'd never been brave enough to do. I wanted to find out what happened to my mother.

I hadn't been looking for baubles, but an unmistakable golden glimmer caught my eye in the scratchy folds of obsidian sand that covered this side of the outskirts of my clan. It was in my nature to be attracted to shiny things. I couldn't help it when I delved deeper to investigate until sand kicked up at my momentum. When I rolled my fingers through the soft mush of the seafloor, my eyes widened to find a ring with unmistakable runes. Perhaps my sisters wouldn't have known what it was, but unlike them, I listened when the sea witches talked. They whispered in places where mermaids didn't often go, such as the kelp forests or jellyfish swarms. They liked to think that they knew everything, but I'd mastered a little bit of magic of my own. Perhaps it was something that came with being an amber. It was hard to know, when I was the only one of my kind—except for my mother. She'd been an amber, too.

My sisters all had emerald or turquoise fins, the lot of them already mated and paired except for my single younger sister, Gina.

The sea witches would have us all believe that our world was meant to be separate from the humans who breathed the air above our waters.

"There's one last relic that evades us," she'd said when I'd been eavesdropping hoping to hear some scrap of information of what had happened to my mother.

A ring that would bond to a mermaid who longed for land and give her the power to resume a life taken from her. Had my mother found such a ring?

I'd never particularly counted myself as a land-lover. I'd never even seen it, only heard about it from the mermen who'd surfaced to battle sailors and conquer their ships, or to rescue the rare mermaid who'd been taken. Anyone who saw one of our kind must die. That had been ingrained into me since I was a child.

But when my fingers grazed the metal that was surprisingly warm, magic wrapped itself around my heart and I sucked in a gulp of water, my vision blurring when my lungs suddenly rejected the liquid.

If I hadn't paid attention to those sea witches, I likely would have died.

No magic comes without a price. When I jammed the ring over my knuckle, my gills at my neck flared and blessed nourishment filled my lungs again.

My chest fluttering like a frightened fish, I found myself looking up, wondering what would happen to me if I'd try to take the ring off again—or what I might find if I were brave enough to venture to the surface.

"PLEASE DON'T GO to the surface again," my sister begged me. My initial fear of exploration had quickly evaporated by the thrill of the magical ring on my finger. I'd been to the surface thrice and I had no intention of stopping. Our mother was up there, somewhere, and I was going to find her.

Finally able to confide in my youngest sister, I'd hoped she'd be supportive, but I was expecting too much. I glowered and crossed my arms over my chest. She was bathing again in the tub of oil that sank into the rocky basin of our father's estate. Her elegant emerald fin draped over the side as she tried to relax, but my exploits only served to bring tension to her shoulders.

"You're such a hypocrite," I complained and sloshed the oil into the heated waters around us. Hot geysers fed the bath where my sisters loved to pamper themselves. "Do you know how expensive this stuff is? It takes father an entire day to salvage enough wreckage to find your precious oils." I rolled my eyes at her pout. "You can't fool father. You want to take a bath as if you're in some grand chamber like that painting I found for you." My glance went up to the precarious faded art that she'd plastered to the wall with sea muck. A delicate woman bathed and bubbles floated around her, her lower half hidden by the splashes of foam. She could have been a mermaid, so father allowed the trinket. But I knew why Gina liked the painting. The woman's hair glittered with a vibrant gold even through the worn paint. "I'm going to find her," I promised as I lowered my voice. "You have to believe me." The waters vibrated with my words as Gina batted her eyes with emotion. Our method of speech wasn't the same way that humans talked to one another, as I'd found on my visits to the surface, but the principle was similar. Sound traveled, even though differently in air than in water. Gina frowned as I presented my hand bearing a ring worth more than both of our fins put together. "You could see land for yourself. This is how you can experience feet and sand and the incredible thrill of walking amongst them. Don't you want to try it? Mother would want you to know why she left us."

She curled my fingers over the ring and glanced around the bathhouse, her wide, sliced irises revealing her fear that someone would catch us with the forbidden relic. "Put that away!" she hissed. "Are you trying to get us killed?"

I slipped a glove over my fingers. It wasn't uncommon for young mermaids to collect shiny and elegant things; lost jewelry from humankind wouldn't be absurd. But a relic like this, one with magic from the ancient witches who'd created our race wasn't supposed to exist. It meant that mermaids and mermen weren't natural. We weren't *first.*

"I'm going again tomorrow," I vowed. "If you're content to sit here in your oil bath and your illusions, be my guest. But I won't stop until I find Mother."

She chewed her bottom lip as I glided away. My fin wasn't a dazzling emerald green like hers, but a vibrant gold, just like my hair and the thin fins that spread from my back to keep me stable in violent waters.

"Amber!" my sister called after me, my name a testament to my coloring. I turned to see her brows knit with concern. "Please, do be careful."

I gave her a nod and grazed my fingers across the rocky tunnel that led to the rest of the sea. "I'm always careful."

TWO
AMBER

I'd found the ring the same way most forbidden treasures were found. I'd been somewhere I wasn't supposed to be, wandering when I should have been at home doing what my father had commanded of me. Mermaids didn't have royalty like the world of men, as I'd soon discovered during my traipses on land. Our society ran off of tribes and magic. Those with the right coloring were destined to have the integral oceanic power to pass on our lineage. Only mermaids with jewel colors had ever been known to bear children with fins. Those less fortunate bore stillborn children, beasts with half fins and half legs unable to survive in our world.

Ruby, emerald, sapphire, these were all the colors sought after in our women for a healthy lineage. But me? I was an amber and no one quite knew what to do with me. It made me an oddity and something to be desired—just like my mother had been. She'd produced five jewel-tone daughters, and when she'd had me, she'd mysteriously disappeared.

Even against the mystery of her disappearance, mermen swarmed for the chance at a mate who could produce such a line. My father had assigned over twenty potential mates to undertake trials for the opportunity. Each one required a conquest of sorts. Defeating a sea dragon. Drowning a whaler and sinking his ship. These were the kinds of tasks that impressed my clan.

I should have been there with my father as he appraised each candidate, but I couldn't imagine being forced into a pairing with the kind of mermen who sought my companionship. They only saw me as an amber; an object to own.

The world of men likely wasn't much different, but at least I knew I would find my mother here if she still lived. I sensed her magic like a distant whisper every time I came to land.

I surfaced to the salty shore of one of the humble towns where her pull was strongest and drifted close as I dared. My eyes weren't meant to see in the open span of air and I squinted against the sun as my sliced irises struggled to retract. When I slipped off the ring that I'd bonded with the first time I'd worn it, my fin split, and I gagged on the water that forced itself out of my lungs. My gills sealed and I splashed my way to shore, sputtering and scraping my knees against the crushed sand.

It was always an unpleasant experience to transition from what I'd always known and become the land-bound creature that we'd all once been. I knew that truth the moment I'd found the ring. It was an ancient legend. Mermaids weren't always born—they'd once been *made.* Witches whose husbands were sailors wanted to follow them so desperately, they'd crafted a spell to turn themselves into a creature capable of swimming through the waters to join them. They found the experience so enthralling that one day they simply never came home. They understood the call of the sea and forgave their husbands for the long months spent offshore.

Over time such witches came to be known as sirens. Some were good... some were not. They all wore rings that gave them their magicked bodies. If they took the rings off, well, they had better be close to the surface.

I shakily stepped onto dry land and drew in a long, deep breath of a world that felt so right, so warm and *real.* My ancestors might have craved life at sea, but for the first time, I felt like I'd come home.

The first step to roaming the world of men was to clothe myself in garments. It was one of my favorite parts of the discovery. I dug my fingers into the sand and uncovered the bag that I'd hidden the last time I'd come here with stolen treasures I'd found along the small, gated estates that dotted the shore. With my magical gifts, it wasn't hard to slip in and out without notice. It was no different than cloaking myself among kelp to listen to the sea witches and their plotting. Now, I would listen to the human world and uncover new secrets that would lead me to my mother.

I pulled out a flowing dress of the same gold as my hair and smiled. "There we are," I whispered, testing my scratchy voice for the first time in weeks.

I'd missed it here. It was only a matter of time before my father chose a mate for me. Even if he figured out that my ring was of the ancient magical sort, I wouldn't be permitted to come back should he know where I've been. He'd find a sea witch to undo the spell I'd managed to put myself under.

Shrugging off the dismal thoughts, I shoved my ring into the bag and buried it again before I made my way to the cobblestone streets where the humans busied themselves with endless tasks. I couldn't risk bringing such a trinket with me into the world of men. They'd be enthralled by its power—enthralled by me. I needed to be secret and safe.

Even without the security of my ring, I smiled when I delved into the noise of them like a nest of eels all going in different directions. Women carried baskets and little boys scampered around their feet. It amazed me how the humans didn't fall over the way they balanced on two legs. It'd taken me three solid days to master the art for myself. Even now, I gripped onto carts as I walked by, not able to fully manage the balancing act.

"Can I help you, miss?" asked an elderly gentleman whose cart I'd just bludgeoned into.

"My apologies, I didn't see—" I began, but then I spotted the golden fruit on display and my eyes went wide. My nostrils flared as I drew in the sugary sweet scent and became entranced with the new delight.

I loved food. As a mermaid, I didn't eat. My body was a magical creation and fed on the salt of the sea and the drifting particles of plankton and seaweed drawn in by my gills. But this body, once it had lost the fin and scales, was human in every way and my stomach growled with the need to bite into the golden skin in front of me.

The old man grinned, his mismatching teeth startling me against the contrast of his dark skin. Where mermaids had different color fins, humans had variety of all sorts. "You look hungry, dear." He chewed on his lip and leaned over his cart to peer down at my dress. "No purse, I see." He swatted the air. "No matter. A pretty girl isn't going hungry on my watch." He polished one of the delicious orbs on his shirt and offered it to me with a smile. "There, now. Don't be shy."

Taking the offering, I couldn't help but coddle the fruit before sinking my teeth into it. Sweetness exploded in my mouth and my eyes went wide.

The old man grinned. "You act like you've never had a pear before, little lady. Where are you from?"

Straightening, I wiped my mouth and chewed the delicious morsel before swallowing. "Sorry, sir. I have to go." As I turned and tried to resist the urge to run, I glanced over my shoulder. "Thank you for the, uh, pear thing!"

I didn't mean to be ungrateful, but I couldn't risk anyone finding out what I was. I had no backstory that would make sense to these people. The only information I knew about them was what I had gleaned from whispered conversations between elders and sea witches, as well as the handful of odd paintings that had survived the ocean surge.

I wandered the village streets, taking in the sights and smells with delight and not wasting a second more of it worrying about what would happen if I got caught. I'd come here in hopes of overhearing something about my mother, but all these people talked about were family squabbles and what they were going to have for dinner. Perhaps this had all been a waste of time, and I was fooling myself into a quest to find a ghost when I should just go home. But a single glance at the giggling girls that wandered these streets had taught me something. They were happy, strong, and lived their lives the way they wanted to. They might play political games, but they smiled. I could do the same.

This could be the last time I was on land. When I returned, perhaps I'd have the courage to face my father and tell him that I didn't want to be mated. And even if he said no, perhaps I could find a way to be happy like these girls who kept that sparkle of excitement in their eyes.

Mind made up, I wandered back towards the shore as the sun began to set. I'd never spent the night on land, as tempting as it was to sleep on the sandy beach. My father permitted my wanderings, but nightfall was when our magic recharged. I'd always been warned of the terrible things that could happen should I be forced to spend a night away from the protection of the village. Men weren't the only creatures mermaids hid from.

Hurrying to the cove along the shore where I'd buried my bag, my heart jumped into my throat when I spotted overturned sand and a hole where my things should have been.

Blood draining from my face, I ran to the crater and collapsed as my carefully won balance gave way and I sprawled to the ground. "No," I breathed. "No, no, no."

I clawed at the damp sand, but my bag was gone. My gaze searched the long expanse of sea that stretched across the horizon.

I was stranded.

MY FIRST THOUGHT was perhaps I'd buried my bag in the wrong spot. Facing the reality that I was about to spend a night on land was too horrifying to consider. Frantically I scrambled from sand dune to sand dune, digging my nails into the tiny grains until sweat ran down my back.

That's when I saw it. Perfect sets of grooves that led away from original hole where I knew I'd buried my bag. I hadn't considered what they were at first, but then it hit me. *Footprints.*

I wobbled to my knees to examine the marks. Under the sea, the currents swept away any trace of thieves. Following the fish that might have stolen one of my gems was near impossible, but on land, a perpetrator left a trail. Curling my fingers into fists, I forced my legs to obey and get me upright. Matching my feet to the slots in the ground, I followed the path that led back to the city.

Anger bubbled in me when I realized what this meant. Someone had *stolen* from me. When I stole a dress, it was because I needed it. But the things in my bag belonged to no one but me--and certainly no one had need of them. I'd buried my treasure just like any mermaid would have done and fully expected it to be there when I returned. Another sickening thought surfaced in my mind.

What if the perpetrator had seen me come from the waters? What if they knew what the ring really was... what I really was?

Nausea wound through me at what my father and the sea witches might do in retaliation of such a breach of our laws. It was bad enough that I was stranded on land, but if I'd revealed myself to the humans, even if it was an accident, he'd never forgive me. Our clan had sacred laws and the one that was never broken was revealing our existence.

Chewing on my lip, the metallic tang of blood made me cringe as my skin cracked. I'd been out of the water too long and by now every part of me had dried up until I felt like a crusty sand star. The sooner I found my ring, the better. Father didn't have to know about any of this if I could just find the thief and get my ring back before it was too late.

I'd only seen the town in daylight. The streets had bustled with life and excitement, making me feel like I'd been immersed into an adventurous dream. But now vendors closed up shop and drew their shades over sullen homes. Empty stalls littered the once lively marketplace. The ominous low light of dusk filtered over rooftops and even though I'd been following grooves in the sand, the moment I hit the cobbled streets, I couldn't tell which way the thief had gone.

Panic hit me that perhaps this was as far as I was going to get, but that's when an unmistakable song hit my ears. I jerked my head up at the lull of a female voice that called with power that only came from the sea. It took me a moment to find her as the notes wound through the air as if searching for someone, but then the melody gripped around my throat, choking the breath from me. Two golden eyes gleamed under a mask of lace.

A siren.

She waltzed to me with such grace that I would have mistaken her for a creature native to land. But I smelled the salt on her the closer she came. Any hopes that this was my mother were dashed when she gripped my chin and her long nails dug into my skin. I had no doubt that this was a sea witch of old. One of the lost creatures whispered as legend among my clan.

"Oh, child," she purred as her hand trailed down my elbow to take my wrist in a firm grip. She led me down the streets and I stumbled, my free hand still clutching at my throat.

"P-please," I managed to say through the constricting power.

The siren rolled her eyes and clicked her tongue, banishing the invisible threat that wound about my throat as if I'd imagined it. "I thought I smelled something salty and weak. What magic have you stolen to gain legs?" She shook her head. "No. Don't answer me here. At least I'm not stupid enough to break sacred laws."

I swallowed as fear gripped my chest.

"Where are you taking me?" I demanded.

The siren slanted her eyes at me as if she were considering the constricting magic again to keep me quiet. Instead, she humored me and answered. "I'm taking you to my home. You and I have things to discuss. You have intruded on to my territory. That does not go unpunished."

Did she understand that I was already being punished?

I couldn't return to the sea, not without my ring that was stolen. But I didn't trust her enough to tell her that I was actually stranded. Let her think that I was here voluntarily, then I would decide what to do once I freed myself from her grip.

Threatening magic emanated from her and only seemed to get stronger as we scaled the slanted streets. An endless siren song made any strangers who glanced at us go heavy-eyed. I considered crying out to them, but their glazed stares said that they were under the siren's spell. It would only enrage her more for me to act out.

The landscape continued its steep incline. At the top of a mountain that overlooked the city, a decorated shack glistened like a jewel with perfect seashells, twinkling bits of glass, and polished fish bones. Each object dangled from a string and when the wind caught them they brushed up against one another, creating a new song. I recognized the thrum of magic in the musical notes. The siren kept her abode safe against humans, against intruders like me. Her warning magic trilled up my spine the closer we came to the shack and I resisted her pull. Every fibre of my being didn't want to go into that place. I didn't belong.

The siren yanked me along and I cried out as fresh pain streaked through my mind.

She rolled her eyes and gave me an exasperated sigh. "Pull yourself together. What kind of magic did you steal if you can't even resist my siren's barrier? Come, child. Live up to your lineage and come inside. The spell will snap around you once you stop resisting and you will be protected."

Protected? More like caged.

The siren thought I still had the ring with me. Whatever magic was keeping me from turning back into a mermaid had settled into my veins. It was as if I was now meant to have legs. I knew the truth of it. The ring hadn't cast a spell on me—it had broken one.

I'd never felt such powerful magic beat at me in all my life as I braced myself at the doorway of the siren's home. I screeched when she pushed me inside and my ears popped as power wrapped around me. My shoulders relaxed as I eased inside the invisible orb that kept the siren's shack safe.

When the agony of the transition eased into a dull throb in the back of my mind, I took in the glittering gems and scales that encrusted sea-rotted furniture, giving the place a mystical ancient feel.

The siren nodded at her trinkets. "This makes me feel like I'm at home." I knew what she meant. *In the sea.*

She caressed one of the dangling shells and smiled. With her guard temporarily down, I spotted the flash of crooked teeth as the visage of an elderly woman glimmered beneath her smooth skin. When she looked at me again, the mask securely strapped over her features until she was the young woman with golden eyes once again, but I'd seen her truth. She wore a glamour, which meant that there was no telling how old this siren actually was. Did she know the secrets of mermaid creation? Did she know about my mother?

"Have a seat," she instructed and forced me into a chair

that stabbed my back with sea spines. I grimaced, but didn't complain.

She jerked up my hands and combed her touch over my fingers. Her plump lips curled into a frown. "Peculiar," she remarked. "I know what you are, yet you don't wear a relic. Where is it, then?" Her gold eyes grew dark and I had a feeling that there was only one such relic that could truly break the mermaid curse.

"Where is what?" I asked, my voice snide.

She glowered. "The ring."

I shrugged. "Don't know what you're talking about."

A cold draft swirled around me in warning. "Don't play dumb with me. I know what you are." She drew in a long breath through her nose. "I can smell the magic in you." She looked as if she was about to strike me, but then she tilted her head like a bird and sniffed again. "Something's wrong. You're not supposed to be—" She cut herself off and her words turned to incoherent grumbles as she scurried to the other side of the room and rummaged through a chest filled with talismans and trinkets. She plucked a woven circle of twine and put it up to the musty moonlight that strained through the covered windows. It glimmered with hidden power and I shivered.

"What's that for?" I asked, hating how shaken my voice came out.

She came up to me and shoved the talisman in my face. "Don't move."

My spine went rigid at her command. Stars exploded behind my eyes and a world opened up in my mind, revealing everything I'd ever craved since I was a child. From the depths of the ocean, the sky didn't exist. I hadn't even seen the lapping of waves until I'd been ten years old. But I'd always known about the stars. Something inside of me spoke of the silver moonlight that called to me. That's what had shone on the ring when I'd first found it. The moon was what had called me out of the murky depths of my homeland and into the bustling village of humans who lived on the shore. There's no way I would have been brave enough to leave everything I'd ever known and go against the most sacred of our laws, even for the faint hope that I could see my mother again. It had been magic that pulled me away from the clan, at least at first. Now it was my own yearning that sought to understand the moon and show my people what else lay beyond the darkness and murky depths. There was an entire world to explore, if only I could find the strength to show them.

"There it is," the siren whispered with grim satisfaction. "I know what you are, little traitor in our midst. No matter. I've come across your kind before and have just the right treatment." She made a decisive nod before grabbing a vial from one of her locked chests. She tilted my head back and poured the liquid down my throat, keeping me constrained with magic.

When I sputtered on the bitter mixture, she smiled. "Now, little mermaid, we wait."

THREE
THIEF

All my life I'd been nothing but a street rat. No parents, no home, not even any friends. Until I got my shadow, that is. He'd been a pathetic little black pup. Just a blob on the street. When he'd mewled at me, I'd realized that he was actually a dog. He reminded me so much of myself at the time. An invisible creature lost in the city. Unloved, alone, scraggly, and hungry. I don't know why I took him in. I'd found an abandoned barn where I could bring in some fresh hay—stolen, of course—and nestled us up a little bit of a home. Nurturing him back to health still wasn't going very well. He needed food. Not just the little bits of scraps that I was able to get for us. My ribs had always poked through my chest, but now they felt like blades. I'd been giving him what measly shared I could offer. But if I went hungry, we'd both die.

Out of sheer desperation I went to the shore outside of the city where wealthy nobles kept their estates well stocked with delicious treats. The places were well guarded and the soldiers killed on sight. But there was a girl going in and out of those bars, somehow keeping all eyes away. I followed her, using her mysterious shadow to hide myself as well and get myself enough food to survive another week.

The next day when I went to watch for her, I found something I hadn't expected. She emerged from the shore, not as a girl, but as something else. I rubbed my eyes when I saw her crawl onto land, agony ripping through her as she gritted her teeth and swallowed her screams. She coughed up water as an unmistakable fin splashed behind her. Then she transformed, golden slitted eyes shifting into a pleasing brown and her hair going from a metallic sheen to the frizzy human shade of gold. Then she uncovered a bag from the sands and donned a dress over her naked body. When she buried it again, I stilled as my heart leapt into my throat. What would a sea creature who pretended to be human hide in the sands? It took every ounce of willpower to wait until she stumbled down the path towards the city. She jerked as if she'd already forgotten how to use her legs, but she stubbornly kept going, yanking one leg in front of the other and slapping her thighs as if trying to banish invisible blades that hindered her gait.

When she'd disappeared over the last dune, I set my sights on the darkened bit of sand and scrambled to it. I plunged my hands into the trove and uncovered the buried treasure. When I pulled the bag free, I ripped it open and inside I found a collection of items she'd left behind. Glittering seashells, a fine woven leather strap she'd had over her chest, and at the bottom, a beautiful aquamarine ring. All of this could feed me for years to come—if I could find a buyer. I closed the bag, hurled it over my back, and ran towards the city.

I KNEW that I had to sell the ring first. It gave me a creepy feeling, as if the longer I held onto it, the worse my luck would get. I didn't have very much luck to start with.

Once I reached the barn and dug through the nesting of hay to find my whimpering pup, I opened the bag and found the ring that could save us at the very bottom. At first I thought that I imagined its glimmer, for there was no light in here for it to catch. This place always stank of mold and shadows. So when I pulled it out and it glowed again, this time long enough for me to remove any doubt that this was something dangerous and magical, I swallowed. Something told me that if I tried to put it on, something terrible would happen. I turned it over in my palm, squinting to try and read the fine engravings on the inside. Gibberish.

It would be a difficult piece to sell. It would look like a normal ring in daylight without the moon to capture its magic. Even so, a street rat like me obviously would have stolen something like this. I needed to find a noble; someone with enough clout and lack of morality to be the middleman I needed.

I had the perfect candidate in mind.

I'D BEEN WATCHING a noble's son by the name of Jonin for a long time. He was exactly the type that I was looking for. Wealthy. Respected. Arrogant.

Most of all, he had a complete lack of morals. I'd seen how he'd gone from damsel to damsel, promising love and riches when there was only one that he would marry, if she would have him. Perhaps with the split of profits from this ring, we'd both get what we wanted. He'd have enough of a dowry for a duchess of the south, the most desired damsel in the city, and I'd get enough coin to feed myself and my dog until I was grown enough to get a little respect of my own.

I waited until nightfall and I found him in his usual spot with his buddies. He was bragging about his latest conquest; some poor milkmaid that had fallen for his charms, not knowing that she was just the night's dinner. He always had his eyes on the duchess, and no matter his fun, he would do whatever it would take to have her.

I waited until he left his group of rowdy friends to go relieve himself. After he was done I slipped out of the shadows. The noble whirled as his lips curled with rage. "What kinda perv are you, boy?" He finished lacing up his pants. "If you come looking for me again, all you're going to find is a good beating."

There was only one language this noble understood, and it was wealth. I produced the ring and his eyes went wide as the moonlight caught the aqua stone in the center. It glimmered far brighter than it should have. There is something wrong with this thing, but his arrogance would just tell him that it was beautiful and wealthy. "Interested in a deal?" I asked.

He grinned.

FOUR
JONIN

Stupid, stupid boy. I, a noble's son, knew value when I saw it. It was the same logic that drew me to the duchess. Her beauty and poise only made my plans a double-win. If I married her, I would have enough power to get out of this sea-salted city. Once I had such a wealthy wife and inherited her fortune, her and her family would have no say about my plans. I would go North—far from the Earl's attention. Once she'd given me enough sons, I'd ship her off to a sanctuary, a temple to serve the gods. When she was forgotten, I find an even richer bride. That's how one scaled the ranks in this world. And that's what this ring was going to do for me.

I couldn't believe that a street rat would be so dumb to hand over a ring like this. I wasn't going to sell it. Not yet, anyway. I was going to use it. Any woman who saw this would marry me in an instant. I turned it over in my hand, marveling how it caught the light so well. This was expertly crafted. I've never seen anything like it.

Fisting the ring and marching to meet my duchess, I had only one nagging worry. Where had the boy stolen it? Would she recognize it? Only one way to find out.

I found her sipping on strawberry tea, careful not to spill on her fine dress. She swayed in front of her favorite shop and gazed up to watch the sunrise. We always met early before my duties of the day began. As a duchess, she couldn't be known for debauchery or rumor. Any lust I had would be sated with my choice of the cattle after nightfall. Some of them might even be a maidservant of hers that had slipped away to get a taste of what their mistress flaunted. But for now, I straightened and made myself presentable. The highly polished look of a noble's son hid all of the unfortunate deeds that made life worth living. She smiled at me, the sun beaming in her eyes with innocence and breathtaking beauty. I smiled back, turning on my charms.

"Cassandra, darling," I drawled as I took her hand in mine and pressed a kiss to her silky skin. "You make the day more beautiful just by being in it. How could you possibly be more radiant?"

She giggled and set her tea onto a table. "Stop," she said, her cheeks flushing. "You're too kind. I'm a mess." She curled a frizzy strand of hair around her finger. "My maidservant ran out of my favorite oils. My hair just isn't as silky as it could be. But it's sweet of you to not comment."

She was right. I had noticed the flaw, but I took a frizzy strand and kissed it. "Beautiful, darling. Always beautiful." Actually, it made her look like she'd just been tousled through the sheets. Was she lying to me?

Tension sprung between us as I leaned closer and the

intoxication of her perfume was stronger than usual, as if she were trying to hide another's scent. My gaze lowered to the fine marks along her neck that had been covered by glittering powder. Anyone else wouldn't think much of the flaw, but my duchess was flawless.

All the signs pointed to one conclusion and jealousy stabbed through my chest. If any man dared to have her, I'd rip out his jugular. My instincts wanted to crush my mouth over hers and claim her as my own. But I drew in a deep breath and forced myself away. There would be plenty of time for that once she was my wife. And if she had been unfaithful before our marriage, I'd have all the blackmail I'd need to send her to a sanctuary when the time was right.

"I have a gift for you," I said, my tone turning mischievous. She relaxed, thinking that I'd bought her lie. "Do you want to guess what's in my hand?" I presented my fist that started to ache with the ring stabbing its corners into my palm, as if it hated to be trapped. I ignored the fresh pang when I squeezed harder.

Her eyes widened. "Oh, I don't know!" Her gaze found mine and sparkled with delight. "Is it jewelry?"

I unfurled my fingers and she gasped with sheer elation. "Oh, Jonin, that is—" The words choked from her throat as she swallowed.

I kneeled and presented the ring. "Please accept my proposal, duchess. Become my wife."

Her eyes sparkled with an array of emotions—the most notable being the shadow of regret that rippled over her expression. Did she harbor feelings for this traitor she'd taken to her bed? He was a dead man.

She unlatched the chain around her neck and looped it through the glimmering band of the ring. "I shall wear it close to my heart, but you know the rules. My father must approve."

I held in the exasperated sigh. Her father, the fat Earl who ran this city was on one of his many ventures to sea. He claimed that he'd seen a mystical creature and he was determined to capture one and bring it back. The King tolerated his antics, for the Earl of Dunham kept the sailors appeased with their whale hunts and the eccentric quest to find this fated beast. The most preposterous thing of all was that the Earl claimed it wasn't a sea dragon, but a creature that took the form of a woman and lured sailors to their death. What rubbish. I dreaded asking such a man for his daughter's hand. What could I possibly converse with him about? My exploits into maiden's bathtubs?

Hiding my disappointment, I rose to my feet and grinned. "Of course, darling. When your father returns, he will bestow you into my arms and we shall be married."

Her smile had lost its glitter, but when her attention turned to the ring pinched between her fingers, she relaxed. "It really is a beautiful gift. Wherever did you find it? Was it expensive?"

Ah, finally, a question I could answer truthfully. "You know my charms, darling. I must save my fortunes to spoil you in all the ways I can muster. Have no fear for me." I grinned. "It was a steal."

FIVE
CASSANDRA

My beloved Antoine frowned when he spotted the ring dangling from a silver chain around my neck. It felt like a nuisance, yet there was nothing I could do. The noble's son, Jonin, had been courting me for the better part of two seasons. I couldn't deny his proposal—not outright anyway. I just needed more time until I could figure out what to do.

Antoine's calloused fingers ran across my collarbone and I shivered. "So our tryst eventually comes to its end." His voice curled around me with husky resign. His blonde brows bunched together and his foreign blue eyes bore to into mine. Everything about him screamed icy wind from the mountains, promises of escape from this city and everything within it. Every time he kissed me, I was transported somewhere else. But his lips came to mine and I tasted sweet sadness on his tongue.

I didn't want him to pull away, so I curled my fingers through his hair and tugged him close. Beneath the scent of sea and sailors was his musky aroma that intoxicated me.

He was a man, not a pompous noble who didn't know what it meant to work for his next meal. I wanted to know this man that banished the world when he was with me and made it feel like nothing could dare to separate us.

Antoine unwound my fingers and sighed. "We always knew this day would come." His jaw clenched. "I just wish I could tell my heart that it's time."

My own heart broke into a thousand tiny pieces just to see the sadness in his gaze. Night after night we'd snuck away, my father believing that I was being courted by the noble's son or perhaps I was out with friends partaking in sewing or gossip. Faithful servants knew of my tryst and assisted in the scandal. They lived for secrets like these. Some of my maidservants even dressed as my doppelgänger and pretended to win Jonin's affections. If the bastard thought I didn't know that he slept with every girl who dared to step into his circle of charms, he was an idiot. Yet, I couldn't begrudge him for it. Here I was, in the arms of another, my treacherous heart fluttering the closer his lips came to mine.

"I don't have to say yes," I whispered and trailed my fingers over his cheek. I wanted to memorize every hard line of his beautiful face just in case this was all a dream and he disappeared forever. "What if you take me with you?"

His eyes widened at my proposal. Antoine worked on the many boats that came through Dunham. Scars lined his fingers where he'd fought hard-scaled fish and taloned creatures as they came through the exotic goods for the King. He was soft-spoken, graceful, and the most amazing lover I ever could have imagined. That was the part of his attraction that made him forbidden. I was of noble blood, not meant to mix with the foreign lands of Igraine. He would eventually go back north, to his people and to Her, back to the icy lands and mountains that jutted into the skies.

My fingers squeezed across his muscled forearm. I didn't want him to leave, but we couldn't stay here. Dunham was the northernmost port of our King's realm, yet the sun still bore down harshly on Antoine, turning his marbled skin a leathery tan that made his eyes stand out even more.

When he came out of the shock of my preposterous question, he laughed, such an open, delightful sound that made the room glow and my heart soar. He rewarded me with a kiss. "Oh, my sweet," he whispered, his forehead pressed to mine. "You would do that for me, wouldn't you?" He pressed his lips together and leaned away. "But I love you enough to let you go. Your new husband will give you everything you could possible desire. You will have luxury and security. If you were with me, there would only be danger, hunger, and—"

"And passion," I said, interrupting him. "And happiness... and love!" My voice rose to a frantic pitch. Everything Antoine said was true, but it didn't change anything. Jonin was the safe choice, the logical choice, but a life with him would be one of mind games and loneliness when he tired of me. I'd seen it happen to my friends, now miserable wives after they'd had their share of sons. I would play the game. I would eat forbidden herbs to prevent any pregnancy until he would fear me barren, and by the time I would have his second son, he'd have grown out of the infantile phase of games. But was that the life I wanted? Could I be happy that way?

Antoine cupped my face as if he could see my future playing out in front of me. "My sweet, why is there such terror in your eyes? You know nothing of true suffering. If I took you with me, you would understand, but then it would be too late. You could never come home. The moment that ice chilled your bones and hunger twisted your stomach, you would grow to resent me." He shook his head. "I've stayed in Dunham for far too long. I've allowed my heart to intertwine with yours and that was selfish of me. Please, forgive me, my sweet."

Tears stung my eyes. "Antoine. This is not your choice to make."

He bit his lip, as if considering my words for the first time. That was another difference that I'd always admired about him. He knew I had thoughts of my own and often prided my deliberation in decisions. This one, as well, he would not deny me a chance to make. "Very well, then. I ask only this." He took my hand in his and squeeze. "Your father has commissioned an entire fleet for one of his ventures. I am to go on a week-long hunt for a beast he's claimed to have seen. While I am gone, consider your choices carefully." His gaze fell to the ring at my neck. "Decide what it would mean to be my wife, or his, because once you make your choice, there will be no going back."

The thought of being Antoine's wife sent chills up my spine and I already knew I'd made my choice. When he pulled away, the world felt cold without his touch and it didn't matter if we were in the humid confines of Dunham, or in the icy draft of his homeland. A mere look from him would warm any chill to my bones. As for hunger, a duchess hardly got to eat as it was. I'd been training for starvation all my life.

"I won't be able to come to shore," he added as a pained look crossed his face. I wanted to continue to protest to assure him that there was no choice to make, but I knew Antoine. He believed that if I truly considered my future, I'd choose Jonin. "To let you go, I can't return. So please, leave me a signal if you truly mean what you say in a week's time, and then I will know to come ashore to take your hand."

I smiled and ran a thumb across his cheek. "A blue flag, like the color of your eyes."

He smiled and turned to kiss my palm. "A blue flag."

I had no doubt I'd leave a hundred flags for him to see. When he returned to shore, I'd jump into his arms and happily never return to this place.

Handmaiden of the Duchess

I'D NEVER SEEN Cassandra so depressed. I'd brought in every trusted maidservant to comfort my mistress, but nothing seemed to work.

"Duchess?" I pressed. She slumped into her chair and her arms hung limply over the ends. "Cassandra," I whispered, daring to use her name. A few sideways glances questioned me, but I'd been her handmaiden for eight years. We were practically sisters.

Her eyes finally cleared when she looked at me. "It's been two weeks. I left the flags like he asked, but my father hasn't returned to port yet." Tears brimmed in her eyes. "What if something happened? What if they found the sea-beast... or the sea-beast found them?"

I shushed her and patted her hand. She'd lost weight, refusing to eat while she waited for her beloved Antoine to return. Even Jonin had stopped attempting his visits, nearly convinced that she'd scorned his proposal. Yet the ring still hung around her neck and glimmered against the firelight. An idea sparked. Even if Antoine hadn't abandoned her, she couldn't possibly go to Igraine's lands. She'd not last a single winter with her bony frame. "Why don't you try on the ring," I offered, "just to see how it feels?"

She sniffled and unclasped the chain, looking torn when the treasure fell into her lap. I'd never seen such an exquisite piece of art in all my life. There was no telling how much the noble's son had spent for such a find. It practically glowed in the moonlight. It didn't matter if he'd slept with nearly every handmaiden in this room, he could charm a fox out of its hole. When he outgrew his boyish antics, he'd make a powerful husband and a fine ally. In this world, that's what a woman like Cassandra needed.

Blue diamonds sparked in her eyes as she examined the ring. "It is beautiful," she admitted. She cupped the gem. "Perhaps, I could try it on." She bobbed her head. "Just to see how it feels."

I smiled, encouraging her.

She slipped the ring on her finger. For a moment, she relaxed and seemed to enjoy the feeling of such finery on her hand. But then her gaze snatched to mine and pure horror overtook her features. Black veins spidered out from her eyes. I shrieked and launched myself away as I watched my mistress turn to ash. It was over in a matter of moments. The other maidservants blinked, holding themselves before the shocked sobs came. "The gods punish us," they cried. I knew they blamed themselves for her supernatural demise. They'd seduced the man who had given my mistress that ring. Perhaps they'd invoked a curse.

Gasping in lungful of air, I ventured closer. Only the ring remained, glittering atop the pile of dust that had once been the duchess Cassandra. I filled myself with resolve and ushered the girls out of the room. I knew what this was. It was retaliation for her father's exploits. He'd gone searching for something that didn't want to be found, and now we all paid the price.

SIX
AMBER

I'd been trying for weeks to reconnect with my ring so that I could return home. As if out of nowhere, a sudden surge of power blasted through my chest. I gasped and clutched as pain and shock rippled through my body like a violent tide. When the sensation abated, a low thrum of power remained. My ring was still out there, and now I could finally feel it.

"What is it?" the siren pressed.

My eyes bulged with the lasting throngs of power. My skin, having cracked over without the kiss of the sea, finally smoothed against the bloodied crevices, accepting this reformed body.

But with the relief came a sinking dread. Such power could only be caused by one thing. "What have I done?" I cried. The sea witch knew what I'd felt. I'd felt *death*.

There had been other deaths, but none so close to home. Over the past few weeks I'd felt them snuff out their light on the waves of the sea. The fools had been seeking out my tribe. Mermaids and mermen felt a mystical warning when they were about to be discovered. The bloodlust that followed even made me gnash my teeth with rage. Only when the human fleet had been overturned and blood turned the distant sea red had I felt like myself again.

My eyes found the sea witch who seemed to finally relax. She'd been on edge the entire time I'd been here, trapped in her web of power. "You're free to leave," she said matter-of-factly. "Now that your curse is broken, you're no longer a threat. You'll wander the human world on bloodied feet." She offered me a toothy grin. "That's your reward for disobeying your father's decree."

I clutched my stomach as nausea threatened to regurgitate the dried seaweed that the witch considered a healthy breakfast for legged beasts. What did she mean, I would wander the human world? That couldn't be possible. Now that I felt my ring, I could reclaim it and return home.

With the spell broken on the witch's shack, I bolted out the front door, only followed by her cackles.

I DIDN'T HAVE to know where I was going. The pull of the ring turned my stumbling gait into a fretful run. To have felt so empty and cold all this time in the sea witch's shack had nearly made me go mad. Death had been a rude awakening to the world I lived in now. Was that really the price for me to return home? I feared what I would find at the end of the tugging trail that would lead me to the ring... and any mayhem it had left in its wake.

The siren had kept me isolated all this time. She wouldn't let me go unless she truly believed me harmless—or... another thought lingered in the back of my mind. Perhaps there was something she wanted from me. Perhaps I was falling right into some elaborate trap, but I didn't care anymore. All I wanted to do was go home. The human world wasn't all I'd hoped it might be. No one had bothered to save me when the witch had whisked me away. Not a single soul questioned her actions when the witch locked me in a room. She'd had a surprising number of visitors for a ruthless sea hag. Each time a new voice trickled through the walls I'd beat my fists against the door and knocked over furniture, but that had only served to make the visitors hurry away even faster.

It didn't matter now. I was finally free. I ran towards the pull of the ring. It'd concerned me that I hadn't felt it at all. Perhaps the sea witch had been able to block its magic, but death had broken the spell. Whose death... I wasn't sure I wanted to find out.

Where there was death, there was magic. No matter if it were intentional or not, there was power in sacrifice. Yet, would I be able to find enough magic to get me back home? Back to my sisters and my family? Surely they'd take me back once I handed over the sea witch. We weren't supposed to reveal ourselves to the humans, but she peddled her magic to them and gladly accepted their coin. And even if they didn't take me back, the sea was a large place. I could handle sharks, but I couldn't handle the callous souls that lived on land.

Determined to find my ring and return to the sea, I

scaled the steps in the dark, stubbing my toes, still not used to the scrambling I had to do on legs. I missed being able to jolt my powerful fin and propel myself anywhere I needed to go.

Once I found myself inside an estate, I fought the gloom of depression. Death lingered here. I was in the right place.

Keeping to the shadows, I avoided the quiet murmurs. Amongst the discussion were women's sobs. I passed them and followed the pull of the ring that thrummed a silent song in the air. When I found a room with a closed door, I reached for the knob and swallowed the lump in my throat. The latch turned and the door creaked open, revealing a pile of ash illuminated by a silver moon. Atop it glimmered my ring as if the remains of its victim were a throne and I was its caretaker come to bring it home.

I eased closer and gently took the chain that looped through the ring. It dangled as I lifted it away from the ash. My skin crawled with the need to put the ring on my finger, but I curled the treasure into my palm and pressed it to my chest. I couldn't risk turning back into a mermaid on land. I had to get to shore right away.

A stifled gasp made me whirl around. "What are you doing?" a young woman asked. Her puffy cheeks betrayed spent tears and a frilly white gown marked her as a handmaiden of the wealthy noblewomen of this house.

I took another look at the room I'd trespassed into. A hairbrush. Elegant scarves draped over a velvet chair. Glimmering jewels displayed on a stand next to a mirror. The victim had been none other than the Duchess of Dunham herself.

I pocketed the ring and turned my gaze onto the handmaiden who looked like she was about to scream. "No one is here," I told her with a siren's song on my tongue. With a ring filled with the power of sacrifice and moonlight just inches from my fingers, magic returned to me in waves and I pushed a spell of compulsion over the human with ease. Her eyelids drooped and she leaned against the wall.

While she blinked at me in a daze, I slipped out, and headed for the shore.

THE MOMENT my feet splashed into crashing waves I jammed the ring over my knuckle and waited for the curse of my people to take over my legs and give me back my fin. I didn't care that I knew the truth. I didn't care if I was living a lie. Salty tears ran down my cheeks and into my mouth and I knew once I was in the sea, I'd never know again what it was like to cry. I closed my eyes and lifted my chin to the moon, letting its cool caress slip over my skin. Even though my magic came from it, I welcomed the use of its power to return home and pay the price of never seeing it again.

I spread my fingers and waited for the ripple of pain to strap over my knees... but nothing happened.

Snapping my eyes open, I brought the ring to my face. It glittered with power and magic. Why wasn't it working?

"So, it was you," a voice said from the shore. I whirled

and faced a well-dressed gentleman—except his eyes didn't look gentlemanly at all. His otherwise handsome face marred with lines as he bared his teeth at me. "The duchess was almost mine. Now she's dead and I suspect her father along with her." He tilted his head to the side, the gesture giving him a dangerous allure of a predator sizing up his prey. "So, what are you? A sea witch?" His boots splashed into the water as he advanced. "A siren?" he sneered. "You're what the Earl was after, aren't you? You're why they died."

Before he could lay his hands on me, a gleaming trident catapulted from the waves and pierced straight through my assailant's chest. He gasped at the impact, then gurgled as blood bubbled at his mouth. He collapsed to his knees, his eyes glazing over as death claimed him.

Recalling his trident, the spear ripped out of flesh, spraying gore into the shallow waters and making bile rise in my throat. I turned to find my father atop a foamy pillar with the slitted eyes of our kind staring back at me. I'd never seen him so enraged as his jaw bulged before he spoke. "Daughter," he said, the tone sounding foreign through the air. His gaze lingered on my legs before he glowered at me. "You have broken the sacred law of our people and chosen humankind. I hereby renounce you."

"Father, no wait, I—" I rose up a hand in protest, but he turned his back on me.

He paused before descending into the waters again, the waves crashing over one another with such ferocity that I almost missed his final words. "You're just like your mother."

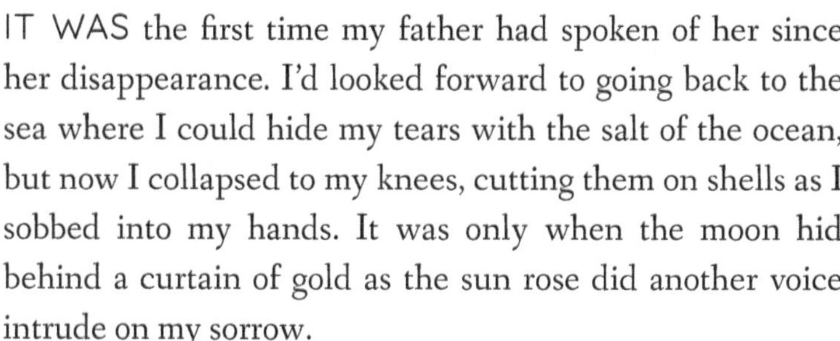

IT WAS the first time my father had spoken of her since her disappearance. I'd looked forward to going back to the sea where I could hide my tears with the salt of the ocean, but now I collapsed to my knees, cutting them on shells as I sobbed into my hands. It was only when the moon hid behind a curtain of gold as the sun rose did another voice intrude on my sorrow.

"Oh, my darling, my sweet Amber."

I turned to find a woman of the most breathtaking beauty staring back at me. Golden hair unfurled across her shoulders and eyes with a brown so soft it held an unmistakable metallic hue. I knew who she was. I scrambled to my feet and approached, my mouth bobbing open and closed like a fish before finding the words.

"Mother?"

She embraced me and I knew that all my life, I'd been fed so many lies. Not just about my existence and the truth of our race, but that I was destined to return to land, just like her.

She pulled away from me and sniffled, sorrow mixing with joy in her striking gaze. "I'm so sorry the sea witch held you for that long, but this was the only way to save our people."

I blinked at her and unwrapped my arms from hers. "What?" If this was really my mother, how could she allow me to find myself trapped by a sea hag?

Her fingers ran through my hair that was a deeper gold than hers, my own locks untouched by the sun. "There is a loophole to the curse that keeps us in the sea. Once upon a time, there was a siren who remembered what she was. She remembered her children and the life she'd had on land, and so she spelled five magical rings and placed a seed in our bloodline. Once a generation an Amber is born. She will find a ring of power and if she can cull a sacrifice of true love, she may break the curse on her people." She sniffled as tears of her own ran down her blushed cheeks. "The siren gave you a tonic, didn't she?"

I nodded. The bitter poison still clung to my throat. I turned to look over my shoulder at the sea where my father had gone. "If the siren hadn't poisoned me, would I have had the magic to return home?"

She clutched at my arms and forced me to turn around. "No, sweet dear. You would have had the power to end the curse forever."

I swallowed, unsure for the first time of my goals. I'd wanted to find my mother, but she'd stopped my chance at breaking the curse on our clan. They could have returned to the land where they belonged.

That's when the ring burned on my finger like an ember digging into my skin. I made a fist and turned my back on my mother.

"What are you doing?" she asked.

I stared out at the sea. If the curse was supposed to be broken by the sacrifice of true love, then the deaths of the duchess and the man who'd held her heart at sea should have been enough. I felt the twisting magic in me trying to take hold. If I gave it another sacrifice, I could overcome the siren's poison.

"I reject you, Mother," I said, the words thick in my throat.

I stepped deeper into the waves and scalding magic wound over my legs as my fin began to take form.

"No, Daughter, don't do this! You'll be alone!"

If that was my sacrifice to amend what had been done, then there was no choice.

The sea bubbled and screams came from the deep. I called to them and spread my arms as I sank into the foaming waters.

The pull became stronger the closer my clan came. All of them were leaving the deep. Every single one.

My youngest sister emerged from the waves with her sliced irises wide with panic. Next was my father, then the rest of my clan.

"Daughter!" he boomed. "What have you done?"

I closed my eyes as my legs sealed together. "I'm saving you all."

THANK YOU FOR READING "STRANDED," an Ancient Realms Novelette written by A.J. Flowers. This is a story of sacrifice and the true meaning of love. Amber's people will be forced back to land where they belong—for better or worse. And her mother will be left alone faced with the judgment of failing her daughter. She resented her father for leaving her alone on land and not telling her daughters what truly became of her, as well as the origins of their race. The sea witches fed lies over the centuries to keep their secret hidden for their own gain. If you knew that your whole life was a lie, what would you do? Not trust a sea witch, that's for sure!

"Ancient Realms" is a playground for the imagination where magic and wonder exists. Be prepared to meet ancient gods, fantastical creatures, and discover love that'll sweep you away.

If you've enjoyed this novelette and want more, be sure to leave a review and join AJ's newsletter to be notified of new releases.

About Stranded

I really wanted to play with the idea of a Little Mermaid retelling that kept the dark and tragic nature of a fairytale, but was still an original story. This story winds up playing with elements you might recognize from Soul Bound, as that world also has evil mermaids. It's not exactly in the same world, so expect some differences if you read both stories. Short works like this one are how I build my creative well for a challenge like Soul Bound's series. I loved writing it and I hope you enjoyed it as well!

THE LUNAR CLASH

Book 5 in the Ancient Realms Collection

ONE
L'ORENIA

All the peoples of the great empire of L'Orenia gathered and craned their necks to peer into the night sky, now engulfed by two massive moons on an ill-fated collision course.

The Empress, always connected to her people, felt every member of the hive as if she lived in their skin. She bathed in their emotions, their hopes and fears, and it never hurt more than it did right now to know all the of it was about to end.

The Lunar Clash wasn't a just prophecy, but a reality. They had always known it was coming. Just as she saw through their eyes, they saw through hers. For a thousand years, their calendars counted down to this very moment, ebbing into the single digits until the night of the Lunar Clash was upon them.

"My beautiful people," the Empress said, her voice booming through every mind across the empire. The hive relaxed as a collective at the smooth touch of her voice. She

was their pillar of strength, their light in the darkness, but tonight, they couldn't miss the tremor of helplessness lingering underneath her words.

"My, loyal—" Her mind's voice broke, unable to even begin. The hive rustled, each foot shifting across streets with the building anxiety of the approaching hour.

This was the final night. Her people needed to know the truth. She'd done this before, but this time, her heart couldn't handle the break once again. She couldn't simply *tell* them goodbye. Words couldn't begin to describe what she felt for her people, so she let the only thing free that could say what she couldn't.

She'd created L'Orenia and everyone in it, and thus she was connected to the very fabric of their souls. She could share her heart with them, quite literally, if she so chose. It was a dangerous thing to open up to her people in such a way. What if they buckled under the power of her love? She'd held the barrier up between her heart and her people for a thousand years to protect them as best she could.

But tonight, all would be lost. The least she could do would be to share how she felt with each soul that was about to be snuffed out.

With a single thought, she set it free. All of her sorrow, regret, excitement, and love crashed through the schism of her soul and into the world she'd created.

A hush swept over L'Orenia as it hit. They'd heard her words, the soft wisps of comfort and assurance, but this was different. This was the depth of the truth she had kept from them until the Lunar Clash was nigh.

Finally able to tear their gaze from the treacherous sky

where two dancing moons burned the sky, every citizen straightened to peer at the glowing tower that housed their creator. They stood, stock-still, and marveled in the unadulterated emotions pouring from their Empress.

The Empress found her mind's voice and forced the words into the air. *"I'm afraid. You can feel it. I'm afraid to lose you, and not lose you. Like all those who have come before, the people of L'Orenia will stay forever in my heart."*

The Empress heaved with the pain of this night and it hit her subjects with a massive blow. She couldn't pick and choose what to share, it all burst from the dam she'd kept so long walled up against them. The hive crumpled to their knees, clutched at their elbows and cried out.

But with her anguish came assurance that her words were true. She pushed it behind the pain with all her might. They'd *never* be lost. They would forever stay with their Empress. She truly cared for them; they had to know that. And even as this night would pass, she would live on, taking all she knew of them with her.

"You will never die," the Empress promised. In her reality, it was true. *"You won't die because you'll never have lived. We have been blessed with a thousand years together, to grow and learn, to bring us one step closer to salvation."* She raised her hands, the moons so massive they bathed the sky in silver light. *"I have learned more from you than all the peoples I have ever ruled. But let us never forget them."*

The Empress closed her eyes and dropped her hands, signaling the Remembrance to begin.

"Planita," she said and the people of L'Orenia obedi-

ently repeated. The word boomed across the landscape and shook the foundation of her tower.

Planita was the first civilization of the Empress' reign and the most revered. She'd said the name fondly, the emotion clinging to it composed of nostalgia and awe. She'd been inexperienced at how to create, how to rule. Her first peoples had been imperfect and fleeting, but they'd also been the purest form of love—until L'Orenia.

"Maxima," she said next, and a million mouths repeated the name. This one was no less fond in tone, but was paired by a sense of regret for hard-won lessons. She'd guarded her heart the second time she'd build civilization. Maxima were great warriors, brave and strong. They faced the end with chins raised and arms straight in a salute of loyalty. They'd vanished from history, but now they still lived on as her emotions poured into her new peoples the love she'd held for the great warriors of Maxima.

The litany of civilizations continued, each accompanied by a wave of emotion from the Empress that expressed her undying love for all of her peoples and everything she'd learned to pass onto the next. Each held an eternal place crystalized in her heart, only their truths to be revealed the night of the Lunar Clash.

L'Orenia had been the strongest civilization yet, not in physical prowess but in their mental and emotional capacity. Where Maxima had been a wall of stone, L'Orenia was a reed that bowed with the wind—but would never break.

She had told them as much, but now there was no denying she meant it. This gave the people a sense of pride, and they were able to roll their shoulders back, standing tall and proud to have pleased their Empress.

Yet, she had hoped for so much more.

She had whispered of a dream.

"Will you be the first civilization to break the cycle?"

No. As the moons loomed overhead, she knew her dreams would be crushed. Her dreams that they could finally set their reach beyond the Lunar Clash. That they could live under her reign forever and there would never be another End to carve a wounding hole in her heart.

"One day," she had said, *"the cycle will be broken. The peoples that I will rule with all the knowledge that has come before will break our curse."*

So she had said, but those people were not of L'Orenia.

The Empress' knees buckled, not from grief, although that came next. The two swollen moons were so close, their orbits pushed her down like the weight of sorrow that it was. She wanted to give in to her helplessness, just for a moment. Another emotion her hive would feel. As she struggled to build her wall again, her peoples found themselves veering their gazes once again to the sky. They watched with fresh terror as a pink moon engulfed the horizon with a mirrored orange orb plummeting towards it from the other side, sending the horizon alive with rolling waves.

To the Empress, the moons had always looked like two lost loves come together at last. They were so languish in their cycles, until the Last Night. Now they hurried across the horizon, growing swollen and blocking out the stars. The Empress found it bittersweet, for with their union her new children would come forth, yet, the people of L'Orenia would become a memory, having never existed at all. What she could take of them she'd stuff into her soul and remember them merely as a chant, a name at the end of a growing list of lost empires long gone silent.

The hive mind grew anxious, dangerously close to breaking free of the Empress' hold and enforced calm. She didn't wish for them to feel the terror of their death. She held herself together, just enough, to keep them from falling apart. But for them to shake her so, it made her proud. It meant she was close to a reign that would last forever. So close.

The Empress held on tight to the minds of her people as the sky grew ever brighter, half-hoping that she'd been wrong, that this was the reign that could follow her beyond the end. But the moons crashed together, the sky blazed in silver and red and rage, and she was launched into the void, alone.

THE EMPRESS VANISHED into thin air. There was no fantastic flash or boom—not from her startling departure, at least.

She had left them, and with her absence came the full force of fear and terror she had mercifully held at bay.

There wasn't much time to absorb the loss of their Empress and the free reign of their own emotions gurgling like a drowning pup in the hive. The sky blew into brilliance with the force of both moons crashing into one another. The Lunar Clash had begun.

The brilliance of every lunar shard that splintered into the night sky would have been beautiful. It seemed as if the horizon was a mirror and had broken into a thousand pieces set aflame. There was no sound from the collision, but the people drew in a collective breath and cried to fill the silence. They wailed and some dropped to their knees, while others ran into the streets and for the city outskirts, even though there was no safe place—save where their Empress had gone. And that, they knew without a doubt, they were not strong enough to find.

The sky bled as the moons' remnants tore into the atmosphere and the sounds finally came. A great rumbling wave of terrible booms gave little warning to the force that hit so hard, it broke eardrums and ravished the land. The sky rained fire and the world exploded in a blast of stardust and terror.

L'Orenia, in all its glory, was gone.

TWO
THE FIRST

The Empress watched the last of the scene unfold in the small orb at the end of her vision as she was catapulted back in time. She cried without holding back, her sobs wracking her body with fresh anguish to relive this terrible night once again.

She wanted nothing more than to curl into a ball and cry herself to sleep, but she had to keep herself aloft. If she let go, she could drift to the pitch pummeling a soundless drone at her fingertips. Time travel was an art she didn't understand, but she knew it was dangerous. If she was lost, the world would never be created again. There would be a lifeless, molten sheen of rock that would never be formed. Her heart broke with yet another loss, but she had to stay strong and make the journey back to the beginning of time. If she drifted out of the tunnel that roiled with power, she'd be torn apart.

Eliza had been the Empress of L'Orenia, but now she was just Eliza. She couldn't take anything with her on the journey, save her memories and all that she had gleaned from yet another thousand years' reign.

She was so close, she lamented. Next time would be the one.

Next time.

A thousand years had felt so short just a moment ago. When Eliza had touched the minds of her people and dwelled in them, she saw the flash of a thousand years in an instant.

But now, as she landed on an unformed world, Eliza was naked and cold and alone. She peered into the distance, feet on solid ground, seeing nothing but the landscape just as naked as she, desolate and miserable. She could hardly imagine building this into such a mighty empire as L'Orenia had been. How could she approach another thousand years? What if she failed them again?

Frustration clawed in the pits of her stomach, moving up and out of her throat as a primal scream. She crashed to her knees with no need to keep her civility and her delicate skin tore on the harsh rocks. She didn't care. She shrieked and cried and beat the ground with her fists until bright splotches of red blotted the dirt.

The soil soon turned soft and sprouted with weeds. This was how it always began. She scowled at it, not having intended to feed life into the land so soon. She wanted to wallow in her misery. With her tears, her blood, and her plea, she would create her next people. Even the land knew she couldn't bear to be alone.

As Eliza contemplated the budding stems around her knees, she built her walls again, brick by brick, and sealed her misery into a tight ball away from the infant soul she could already feel forming in the foliage. A single white flower formed, raising above the fresh patch of green with a stubborn readiness to live.

Eliza straightened, not taking her gaze from the blossoming white bulb, and waited for the remnants of L'Orenia to be born. It budded and shot out of the ground with impressive speed. The flower was swifter to grow than any she had seen before.

It should have taken a day for a womb to form the first life, but a mere whisper of moments passed as the bulb grew larger than her, forming a full-grown human inside. It wasn't an infant. She'd grown accustomed to doting on a child, but she sucked in a breath when she saw that the womb had formed a man.

"Hello," she whispered and caressed his cheek through the fragile skin. The moment she connected through the thin veil of the flower's womb, she felt his soul as if it were an ember ready to burst into flames.

She pulled away, a sticky fluid stringing across her fingertips. Her new peoples would start with him, and she must give these peoples a title. "Firstborn of Da'Trille," she said, deciding on the name with ease. It felt right, a strong new foundation to begin her empire.

The man, First of Da'Trille, shifted, his arms curling over his chest as if comforted by her voice. But then his eyes shot open, his gaze finding hers through the small barrier between them. She was surprised when his mind found its way inside her head. He didn't have words, not yet, but a deep emotion of gratitude and innocent curiosity about who she was, who he was, and what kind of world awaited him.

Perhaps it was because he was born mature that he knew how to seek her out. She reacted swiftly, knowing how vital it was that the First be properly woven with all she had learned from the generations before. She connected to him, filling herself with her purpose and her hope, sharing the beautiful things she remembered of her lost peoples for his first moments in this world. The bravery of Maxima, the passion of Planita, and the love of L'Orenia.

His eyes fluttered closed at the sharing. His chest pleasantly rose and fell as he fell into a deep sleep and dreamed of all the knowledge she poured into him.

She would have a thousand years with the people of Da'Trille, and hopefully, it would be enough time for her heart to mend.

THE FIRST SLEPT SOUNDLY for a full cycle of night and day. The two moons, now so distant apart and tiny specks on the horizon didn't betray the cruelty their silver gazes shed down on her wet cheeks. The depth of her loss was only mitigated by her new creation, and she reached out to him without hesitation, finding his arm beneath the sticky sheen of the flower's womb.

Perhaps he felt her need, or he simply was ready to come into the world, but he eased into wakefulness and Eliza knew it was time.

His fingers wrapped around her, shredding through the fine film of his birth, spilling golden dew onto the ground.

He eased out of his encasement, staggering into her arms. He was already a head taller than she, but she took his weight with ease. He was so graceful, and even in his birth, he shifted so that his arms wrapped around her in an embrace.

Still, there were no words, but if his emotions said what he could not.

"I'm here."

AS THEY HELD EACH OTHER, the flower spilled life onto the ground as golden dew. The nectar of her creation seeped into dusty crags. The glittering warmth of her love and hope spilled across the landscape until golden bees sprang from the metallic sheen of the ground. They sped off in all directions, and Eliza allowed herself a smile. She wouldn't be alone for long. The tiny creatures would seed the land with the golden tears that clung to their legs, springing up life across the horizon until the entire world would sing with her love.

THREE
NAMED

Eliza had no clothes to wear, and neither did he. But she wasn't ashamed of her nakedness. Clothes would come with time, and if anything, Eliza had learned patience. First would come the moss, and already the moisture permeated the dusty ground and turned it coppery and lush. Soon there would be full bodies of water, tinged gold with the remembrance of the First's nectar. Next would be the trees, then the living things born of bees and foliage and golden dew. There would be plenty of opportunity for leaves and animal hides to cover their bodies.

For now, the First of Da'Trille sat cross-legged and gazed at Eliza with calm trust. She admired him for how closely he embodied all she had loved of L'Orenia and all the civilizations that had come before. His jaw was like Maxima, rebellious but proud. His grace as he moved was like L'Orenia, never failing to impress her with its beauty.

But his gaze, what she loved most, was like her first peoples. Such trust as a newborn would have. Everything about him made her happy, for he kept a promise she'd made: that her peoples would never die.

When the First broke his gaze and stared at the distant moons, Eliza's breath hitched and she wondered if perhaps he too closely kept all that she had learned. Did he already know of his fate? Did he know of the Clash to come?

"What is my name?" he asked.

The noisy words jolted Eliza. She was used to the hive mind, but of course, he was too freshly born. He couldn't talk to her yet in such a way. Still, he shouldn't have talked at all.

He was only a day old. As she studied him, he cast his gaze to her and pushed his eyebrows together. "Have I said something wrong, Empress?"

Eliza hugged her knees and contained the bubbling fear behind her walls. He knew who she was, already?

He cocked his head when she didn't reply.

"No," she whispered. Her voice felt scratchy and old. She didn't like it, so she creased her lips together and pushed her words into his head. *"I was just surprised."*

He narrowed his eyes, and she wondered if he could hear her mind's words. "My apologies, Empress. But please, tell me, do I have a name?"

So, no problem with understanding, and so well-spoken. Eliza sighed and answered, *"You are the First."*

"That is not a name."

She stiffened. Never had any of her people questioned her, much less expressed individuality. He was meant to represent all of her peoples to come. But to give him a name, it singled him out. It showed favor when she wished to love all her creations equally.

Eventually, her people would be given names, but only as a means of organization. When there had been so many in the hive, it was impossible to keep them straight, and impossible to know the order of creation to keep their numbers. Names were for practicality. But the First, he was the only one until the rest would eventually come.

"Why do you wish to have a name?" she asked.

He shrugged and looked to the sky once more. The moonlight kissed his cheekbones and made him even more serene and beautiful. "You have one."

Eliza couldn't argue with that, nor could she answer why she had a name, or how she had come to possess it. The earliest she could remember was her first peoples, Planita, and that she was Empress Eliza. She'd simply...been.

"You're correct. I do." She rearranged herself, folding her legs to sit like him. *"All right,"* she said. *"Perhaps you have a proposal?"* She leaned in and smiled. *"What would you like to be called?"*

His brows furrowed at the question and Eliza thought the matter closed. He'd been acting too strange, but perhaps it had all been a fluke. This was the First, yes, and he was the culmination of L'Orenia and all that had come before. He would be strong, and every First was stronger than the last. But he couldn't possibly—

"Adrian," he said and Eliza froze. "I think Adrian is a fine name."

She swallowed and pushed her knees back to her chest,

holding onto them so tightly that her toes went numb. "Adrian," she said out loud, playing with the name on her tongue. She feared that if she used her mind's voice now, she couldn't hide the fear and awe from piercing her barrier.

Adrian burst into a smile, his white teeth illuminated by the dim two moons orbiting each other in the distant, starry sky. *"I love it."*

Eliza blinked. Had he just spoken in her mind?

FOUR
THE PEOPLE OF DA'TRILLE

Eliza waited three days before bringing more of Da'Trille into being. She always liked to spend some time with the First, making sure that she had given all she wished to give of knowledge and past peoples.

"You shall help me begin," she told him. She'd stopped speaking in his mind for a while now, fearing that he would unlock her soul. He was strong and she wouldn't underestimate him again.

"Begin what?" he asked in her mind.

She glowered at him, but didn't chide his method of speech. She would only encourage, never dampen his spirit. He had individuality such as she'd never seen and she wished to see where it would go. "The people of Da'Trille," she said. "You are the First, which means there must be more. Otherwise, you would be the Only."

He smiled and choked on a short laugh. *"Of course, Empress. I shan't argue with such logic."*

She smiled too, which wouldn't do. "I must cry," she

complained. "My tears will create new peoples. Don't make me smile."

He shook his head and took her hand in his. She allowed him to lead her. She walked in his shadow as they climbed the bank to the top of a waterfall. The foundation of Da'Trille had come quick and she was impressed with the magnificence of the land. It wasn't flat like L'Orenia had been, but it bucked and heaved, creating great chasms for bodies of water to fill. It retained its charming golden glow, but frothed at the edges as it rushed to find ever deeper lands. *"You don't need to cry,"* he said when they'd reached the top.

She frowned and wiped the water's mist from her eyes. She was impressed with the land, but didn't wish to be overwhelmed by it. Here, the roar of the waters was deafening and a rainbow curtained the sky with the spray.

"Then what do you propose?" she yelled, but then frowned when he shrugged and pointed at the waterfall. Reluctantly, she repeated the question in his mind.

"Swim in the waters with me," he replied. *"We will create your peoples."* A devious grin overtook his face and normally, Eliza would have been terrified. But his gaze was ever loving, even behind his mischief. She trusted him in return.

He took her further up the bank and around a bend where the waters calmed.

When Adrian took her by surprise and planted a kiss on her lips, she knew this was a First unlike any she'd ever experienced.

She pulled away, her eyes wide with surprise. "What

are you doing?" She'd never known this feeling before, this excitement that made her heart flutter.

His thumb caressed her cheek and his lips followed, making her shiver. "I am doing what you created me to do. You are so lonely, my Empress. You shall never be alone again."

PERHAPS HE WAS RIGHT, and she'd created him for this very purpose. Why else, would the First be born a full-grown man, strong and handsome.

But still, she hadn't consciously made that decision. Her own heart had told him what was broken inside of her, but he was the one who had understood that ache and devised a way to ease it.

His love filled her with a new seed, one that created the peoples of Da'Trille in a womb of her own flesh.

The process was slower than before, but Eliza was ever patient. She had given Adrian free will to explore his individuality and he'd shown her things such as she'd never known. Now, he'd given her not just a people, but children of her own. She had never experienced such closeness in this way.

Their first child had eyes as silver as the moons that threatened to take them all away. Pain had wracked her with the delivery, an echo of the sorrow of the Lunar Clash that would inevitably come.

With her hair sticking to her head with the effort, she held the result of her pain and knew that she'd never known love as this. She coddled the child, still sticky from a womb of her own flower, and Adrian ran a thumb over the child's rounded head.

"He's perfect," he said, proud and lovely.

"Yes," Eliza agreed, and a smile stretched across her face so wide that her jaw hurt.

Adrian had shown her a new way to live, a new way to love. Each child that was born from the womb of her own flesh showed her new depths of a connection deeper than the hive. She was connected to each and every soul so tightly, she feared she'd lose herself forever if separated from them. That fear she buried with the rest of the thousand year cycles that had torn at the remnants of her soul.

FIVE
THE LUNAR CLASH

A thousand years reign of Da'Trille was the happiest that Eliza had ever been. Such peace and prosperity that she'd never imagined was made possible because of Adrian. He didn't age like their children. She wasn't surprised that unlike any other First, he was more like her than she cared to admit. She never aged, never died, and so he would be the same. He stayed by her side and didn't seem concerned when the years ebbed into single digits once more.

"The Lunar Clash is upon us," she said, dread an open wound in her heart. She'd given up keeping her barrier against him. He felt what she felt and they were one, just as the moons above would become united this very night.

"Do not fear, my Empress," he promised and kissed her cheek, still calling her by the title even though she held no power over him. He was her heart, and if he died with all of the children they had brought into this new world, she could not go on.

He called her "Empress" when she was afraid, to

remind her that she had come before him, that she was the true First of them all. She would survive, even if she didn't believe it.

"Will you come with me?" she asked, hopeful.

He didn't answer, but smiled and cupped her face in his, his love pouring into her heart without restraint. His emotions always said what words could not.

"I'm here."

THE NIGHT of the Lunar Clash, Eliza took her place at the top of the tower. She gathered her will and touched each mind. She could feel their fear as they stared at the two dancing moons. It took all of her strength to convince them to look away.

"My beautiful people," she began.

"My loyal—" When she faltered, Adrian took her hand and she continued, *"Let us remember those who have come before. Planita..."*

As Eliza and the people of Da'Trille spoke the names of all the empires that had come and gone, Adrian walked to the balcony's edge. His perfect features looked skyward, illuminated by the moonlight just as he'd been the night of his birth. Unchanged, he fearlessly watched the sky. The Remembrance ended on L'Orenia and Adrian's shoulders eased. Eliza watched and waited, wondering what his individuality would bring on such an ill-fated night.

Adrian raised a hand, his forefinger and thumb pinching the pink moon. "Wouldn't it be better if there was only one?" he asked. "If only there was someone strong enough to wish it out of the sky." He gave her a humorless smile. "Someone like an Empress, perhaps?

Eliza blinked, stumbling beside him and steading herself on the balcony's edge. She realized in a terrifying moment that Adrian was trying to tell her something about herself. Something she'd never explored. She'd loved that about him, how he revealed things to her that she'd never considered—until now.

"Don't you know what you are?" he pressed. "You told me what was broken inside of you the day of my birth, and you told me how to fix it." His jaw hardened. "Are you ready to hear the truth?"

His need for her to understand threaded the air and pricked at her like burning embers. "No," she answered. The tidal wave of his emotions poured over her, drowning her and telling her that the truth could crush her.

The sadness in him welled up and threatened to make her crumble. There was a truth lingering between them that neither wanted to recognize.

He told her, in spite of her fear. She'd created him to mend the broken wound in her soul, the gaping flaw in the cosmos.

"You created me, my Eliza, my Empress. You created the world, the seas, the skies..." his gaze returned to the two swollen moons, *"even the source of your greatest sorrow."*

Eliza's tongue went dry and her mind spewed forth her words, *"Why would I create such destruction?"*

"You ask the wrong questions. You must ask why you haven't destroyed one of the moons. What holds you back?"

Tears blurred Eliza's vision and a swirl of oranges and pink flitted across the sky. They both knew the answer to that. She couldn't destroy. She was an Empress, a Maker. The mere idea of it sent chills down her spine. But if she did nothing...

Eliza swiped her tears away and faced her people littered as trembling dots on the ground below. How she loved them. Every reign had a piece of her heart, but if she lost the people of Da'Trille, she knew she would never recover.

"All right," she said, her voice hoarse from unspent sobs. "If it'll save you and our children, I'll do it."

Adrian gave her a smile, but it didn't reach his eyes. If she destroyed, it would change her beyond recognition. She could never lay a hand on his face, shed her love as kisses on his temple.

She trembled as he leaned in and planted a sweet kiss on her cheek. His lips formed to her features and the raw pain in him almost made her want to take back her agreement.

"Promise me," he whispered in her ear, "promise you won't forget about me."

She cupped his face and peered deep into his eyes until she was sure she grazed his soul. "I'll never forget you, my love."

When he pulled away and the ground sucked at her feet, she knew there wasn't much time. If she waited a moment longer, the two moons she had created so long ago would unite and destroy this world. She'd be forced to go back in time, again and again, until she learned the final lesson she needed to become a true goddess. And Adrian, their children, would be gone, forever.

Eliza drew on the connection of her people, finding that they believed in her as much as Adrian did. She'd been a goddess to them all along. The belief had been there, a thousand years' of gathering prayers ready for her to use. She'd always prepared for this moment, but had selfishly told her people that they needed to evolve. She'd expected them to save themselves. Shame threatened to crush her. She was their goddess. It was her destiny to save *them*, no matter the sacrifice.

Now, with one last lingering look at Adrian, Eliza accepted her role. She shed her physical body and exploded into a ball of light, leaving her human love to shield his eyes and bear their withering grief on his immortal shoulders.

The power of her people and Adrian's love lifted her into the skies. Without the weighty form of bones and flesh she was free of the oppressive force of the world and battling moons. Effortlessly she swept up and up until all was light and glory. Here, in the expanse of the stars, she commanded every grain of dust and cosmic strand of fate. She drew on an ugly red cord, tugging it until the burning ball at the end tore under her call. It was the moon that had killed all of her people cycle after cycle. It was the source of her hate and her loathing she'd been too proud to accept. She clawed at the strands, fraying it until the moon splintered and fell into her. She choked but swallowed it down like bitter medicine.

When it was done, only one moon remained.

SIX
A THOUSAND YEARS AND MORE

"Why is the moon red tonight?" Silvia asked.

Adrian smiled down at his daughter. Well, daughter by seven generations removed. She looked so much like Eliza that his heart clenched to see her, and clenched even more knowing she would soon leave his lonely tower and return to the city dwelling below to rejoin a world where he didn't belong.

"It's an anniversary," he said. He was the immortal king, more a forgotten relic than a ruler. He appreciated that Silvia came to visit him, but wondered if the truth would send her away.

"The anniversary of when our goddess was born," he clarified when she gave him a quirky head tilt. She knew very well what tonight was, just not that he was the reason Eliza had died.

Silvia's plump lips spread into a smile. "What an honor it must have been," she breathed. "What was she like?"

Adrian stiffened. He didn't often talk of Eliza. When

she'd gone, his heart had gone with her. Now he was an empty shell that held her memory, the only thing left of the human she'd been. Her sacrifice allowed the world to live on, to complete its creation and freedom to expand. She'd known in the deep, unreachable part of her soul, that she couldn't live among her people forever. And so she'd allowed herself a thousand years, creating a second moon to ensure she'd never spend a selfish day beyond the limiting rule.

He'd been her final act to remind her why she'd put the safeguard in place. It'd been so hard for her to evolve to the goddess she was meant to be. She could create, form, but the world could not live under her thumb forever. She had to ascend before her peoples could grow, and oh, how the peoples of Da'Trille had turned into a feat of life such as the cosmos had never seen. They were passionate and creative, constantly inventing art and science and exploring the world and accomplishing the impossible.

But only he remembered what she was like in a mortal frame. His Empress, his Eliza.

She wasn't gone, not entirely. She watched from the skies and shed her love over her peoples in silver wafting waves. He felt her strongest when she returned on the anniversary of the Lunar Clash, turning the lonely orange moon an ruby blood-red. A reminder of the bloodshed, the loss, and all she'd given so that her peoples may live.

Silvia swiped away imaginary wrinkles from her dress and settled onto her favorite stool beside the window. "Start from the beginning," she instructed, tilting her face to peer into the sky as if she, too, could feel Eliza's presence.

Adrian's heart buckled as the bloodied moonlight fell onto her cheekbones, battling against the sparkle of innocence and excitement. "She once walked this world," be began, "lost and alone—before she fell in love with the first of Da'Trille."

The ground heaved, just for a moment, as if the moon had leapt at his words. Perhaps, he thought with a smile, she loved him still.

THE END

About the Lunar Clash

"The Lunar Clash" is one of those stories that come directly from the heart. I've written hundreds of stories that pertain to the idea of Adam and Eve. None of those stories came to fruition until Adrian and Eliza. While all of the novelettes I've written as part of the Ancient Realms Collection are all heart stories, this one is truly special.

17 BONUS STORIES

As a thank-you for purchasing the entire Ancient Realms Collection I have included 17 bonus fantasy and sci-fi flash fiction and short stories, some of which has been previously published in magazines. Flash fiction is loosely defined as a story with 1,000 words or less and the short stories I have included range from 5,000-10,000 words each. Enjoy!

ONE
WIERSBIEL

Previously Published in the Bards and Sages Quarterly Magazine January 2018 Edition

Emma yanked another white blossom from the damp earth and choked on a fresh plume of mold that burst in her face. "Ew!" she shouted as the disgusting fungus made her gag, then clapped her hand over her mouth. She froze, waiting to hear the growl of a wiersbiel coming to eat her, then felt silly. Helga had been only trying to scare her, right?

Helga, Baroness of Emhart's Castle, was immortal. But the magic for her timeless beauty was drawn from the delicate white blossoms hidden in the fairies' domain, of all things! Emma's chest puffed with pride to have been chosen. Only once every ten years would the Baroness request for the blossoms to be retrieved. Emma, just a lowly orphaned servant, could scale the ranks to noblewoman for all her toils—such was the magic of the white blossoms at Helga's behest. All she had to do was outwit the fairies and brave the wiersbiel, assuming terrifying monsters of the night really existed. Rumors tore through Emhart's Castle of maids who'd never returned. Emma knew better. If a maid hadn't returned then it was because she'd stolen the white blossoms' magic for herself.

Emma knew little of magic. Even if she wished to steal the blossoms away, she wouldn't know how to weave them into beauty and fortune.

And so Emma toiled as night neared to gather the blossoms for the Baroness, trusting that her reward would come with her servitude. The hairs on the back of her neck spiked as the cool air set in. Emma regarded the dark soil and noticed the darkness made the elusive white treasures stand out even more. A dim brilliance aglow like fireflies littered the places she'd missed, and she doubled back. She made a game of it, seeing how deftly she could snatch up the bits of brilliance without disturbing any of the surrounding flowers. Wherever the white blossoms grew, the forest sprang to life with rainbowed petals, whizzing hummingbirds, and the most darling little critters. She'd tried to catch one, a squirrel with a tiny horn on its head, but it'd stared with such heart-pounding fear that she felt guilty and vowed not to terrify another forest pet again.

As the sun closed her eyelids and the world grew dark, the day creatures disappeared into their tunnels and nests. Emma hadn't felt alone until now, with the absence of curious chitters and chits. Gathering the luminous blossoms seemed an even more frightening task in the eerie silence. She was sure it was her imagination, but the air became heavy and chill, and she found herself making her way slowly toward the river. Evil beasts didn't like water, or so it was said.

As she crossed waterlogged lands, mud bulged through her toes and her stomach growled with a life of its own. She clutched the adorable basket half-filled with blossoms. Helga had given her the treasure from her very own closet. It wasn't like the pathetic little thing Emma used to store lost buttons. This was a real one, the kind that gleamed of wicker and oil and wealth.

Emma cradled it and peered inside to see how far along she'd gotten. A gasp of terror tore from her throat and she fell to the ground. The blossoms were completely torn to shreds and bled their clear, luminous nectar through the cracks. It'd run all the way down her dress, and that was when she felt the burning pain. She cried out and tore moss from the ground to wipe the sticky stuff off, but it clung to her skin until she blistered.

Tears welling in her eyes, she tossed the evening's contents and began to pluck more moss from the trees. The wicker, while beautiful, wasn't soft. She'd been so foolish! She should have thought to line the basket before she'd lost all her work.

When Emma ran out of moss to cover the minuscule, serrated edges of the basket, she glanced at the thorned bushes viciously protecting their soft underbelly and sighed before going in. The jagged tree roots scratched against her knees as she rummaged for the downy underbrush weeds. She found a patch of them softer than anything she'd found outside and smiled with victory.

Working her way out of the roots, Emma dragged out

the contents and held her find to the moonlight. With a gasp she realized it wasn't a weed at all, but the remnants of maid's clothing...dull and tattered just like hers with white frilly puffs at the hemlines.

Gulping down her fear and nausea, Emma numbly threaded the cloth through the basket's lining. Perhaps Helga had warned her of the Wiersbiel for good measure. Had she come across its den?

When the basket was sufficiently padded, she placed the small handful of blossoms that had survived and began her search anew, her legs taking her far from the dark grove and deeper into the forest. She was only slowed by the pain of her arms blistering from the blossoms' poison running down to her elbows.

Finally, the hour of interlude between day and night relented. Shadows grew to their full height, a gentle fog rolled in, and the forest came alive with the chorus of nocturnal creatures. Most were low hoots and sleepy calls, but there was one in the distance that sent an icy chill down her spine. A howl—unmistakable. Could it be the wiersbiel? Had it found that she'd disturbed its den?

Even though mud was securely patched across her skin, she still hadn't found the river. She trudged through the forest, heading toward a sound she hoped wasn't fairy trickery leading her to peril.

Now that she wondered if the rumors had held some truth, her dread and tension were slowly transforming to fear. Fear wouldn't do, not while she was still in the fairies' forest. Fear brought things that warranted it, so Emma forced herself to be merry. She danced with the shadows, pretending they were dark princes come to take her away and transform her into a twilight empress in some faraway castle. The howl of the wiersbiel grew stronger and bounced off the tree trunks until she couldn't pretend it was her imagination. Its howls echoed through the branches, sounding as if it came from all around. Was it a fairy trick? Or was it circling her?

Instead of letting terror grip her stomach, Emma assured herself she was safe. As the roar of water grew, Emma began to sing.

"Wiersbiel, oh wiersbiel, stay away from me."

"Wiersbiel, oh wiersbiel, are you hiding behind that tree?"

Giggling at her own rhymes, she burst through the clearing in a round of nervous laughter and a pirouette. Mid-twirl, she jerked to a stop and the rags of her dress slapped across her thighs, heavy with weeds and burrs. Ahead was a waterfall, but not into the forest's river. It was something out of dream, an upwards waterfall, a water*fly* going up and up until it disappeared in the stars, the base shooting from the ground surrounded by a circle of toadstools.

She rushed to the scene, entranced and her wicker basket cast to the ground, forgotten.

A voice trickled, and was barely decipherable from the roar of the water. "Oh, dear sweet child. Helga has taken you too."

Emma blinked a few times at the waterfly. "Who's there?"

In an instant, the water vanished, puffing into a spray

that sent a splash of mist across Emma's face. Emma licked her lips.

Where the water had once been was the smallest human Emma had ever seen. Yet, it couldn't be human, could it? Faint wings unfurled behind the creature, shimmering in a fleeting rainbow of color. A real fairy!

The fairy, barely a cubit tall, gave a tiny gasp. "My dear, you're brilliant! I'd never thought to ask a human to wear my tears."

Emma blinked again. "Your tears?"

The fairy nodded. "I've watched you roam all the forest, gathering the white blossoms that are my tears. Tears for each child that Helga has taken from this world."

The excitement and elation at seeing a genuine fairy was beginning to fade. In its place, dread and nausea set in. "Please, wise fairy. I don't understand. What do you mean?"

The fairy wilted, the translucent layers of her wings drifting to curl over her shoulders. "Helga is my sister, you see. She lives forever as the Baroness of Emhart's Castle, but her dark soul stays in these forests." She shivered. "She must feed every ten years."

Emma blinked, suddenly confused and dizzy. She searched the ground until her eyes landed on the overturned basket. Next to it she saw her body, half torn and bleeding into a dark creature's maw. The wiersbiel had heard her song, and the end had come quick.

Emma fell to her knees, the weightlessness of her spirit becoming unbearable and she crawled toward the grotesque scene.

"Emma," the fairy continued, "she may have your body, but you've saved your soul. You're a clever girl."

The world spun as Emma dug her fingers into the soft ground. Clever? She'd been overconfident and torn the white blossoms on the serrated edges of her basket. But had that saved her soul as the fairy said? She crept toward the basket and finally was able to reach out to grab a fistful of the blossoms, now stained red with her own blood. But her fingers slipped straight through.

"Emma," the fairy persisted, sounding irritated to be ignored, especially after offering a compliment.

Emma stared at the petals, then took a good look at the scene. As if her eyes had finally been opened, she spotted tattered bits of cloth with frilly white edges and the glimmering of bones scattered across the ground. The rumors had been true. The prior maids had been fooled by fairy trickery, silly hopes for nobledom.

With a surge of rage, Emma glared at the fairy. She'd only come here because of the sound of the waterfly. "Why'd you trick me?" Emma demanded.

The fairy blinked. "No trick. I come every ten years to coax my sister back to my realm." She pouted. "I'm so lonely, you see. She refuses to leave the human world. And I hate to see her gruesome deeds." As she surveyed Emma's spirit blotched with the sticky whites of the magical blossoms, she brightened. "But now I'm glad. If it weren't for my tears, your spirit would have been lost."

Emma drew on her last bit of courage to look upon the wiersbiel that was Helga's nasty soul. Such a horrendous thing, but so small. It was like a wolf, but it seemed sickly and ravenous. Short, white fangs flashed as it chomped away, devouring its prize as if it were about to die from starvation. Its black fur looked sticky and its ribs poked out. In a fleeting moment, Emma felt sorry for the poor creature.

But then, the wiersbiel took three massive bites, crunching bones into pieces. With a bloodied maw, two red and beady eyes locked onto Emma's spirit.

The beast dove and Emma lurched backward with a screech. The wiersbiel's maw opened wide, coming down on Emma's arm with enough force to take the appendage clean off. But when the teeth met skin, the beast jolted and yanked back with a pained cry. With spiked hairs, the wiersbiel paced and watched Emma with a hungry stare.

Emma stared at her arm, still glowing from white blossom poison...the fairy's tears. Emma snapped her gaze to the fairy. "I'm alive..." she drifted off, seeing the remains of her body. "Alive" was a relative term.

The fairy smiled and echoed her thoughts. "Yes, alive as a spirit can be."

Emma shook her head, her hair going weightless as if she were underwater. "You said she must feed every ten years. She ate my body, but not my soul. Will she die?"

The fairy considered it for a moment, rubbing her tiny chin with a pinched forefinger and thumb. "I'm not sure. No soul has ever survived long enough for me to find out."

Emma considered the light above them, emanating from a pinpoint just above their heads. "Where will I go?"

The fairy smiled, seeming happier to answer this question. "You'll join your family in the great beyond. Or," she gave a sheepish smile, "you could stay with me, if you wish."

Emma blinked. "Stay with you? What does that mean?"

The fairy explained eagerly. "Without my sister, my realm has been a bore. I want to sing and dance, create flowers and rainbows and make the sun shine and the moon glisten." Her eyes glimmered with excitement. "I could share all I know with you. Fairy ways are fun and delightful. Such games we could play!"

Emma swallowed. To die and be reunited with a family she couldn't remember, or to live a new life as a fairy? She thought of how she loved to dance, loved to soak in the sun and play games all day long. A fairy's life seemed a good fit for her.

With a sniff at Helga's wiersbiel form, she pitied her immortal life in the human world with human things. Perhaps without feasting on her soul, Helga would still live but lose her beauty to age. Emma hoped so, feeling she deserved the human life she wrought.

With purpose, she approached the toadstool circle and joined hands with the glimmering fairy, her cheeks blossoming with white petals as she strode into a new life beyond fairy forests, Emhart's castle, and the gnashing of the wiersbiel.

TWO
CASTLE BURBERRY'S CURSE

Previously Published in Bards and Sages Quarterly January 2017 Edition

Lies. They sprouted up like weeds watered by fear and ignorance until angry vines strangled any voice of reason. Freethinking was replaced with repeated phrases meant to stave off the abhorred past.

"An obedient daughter's silence will ensure Burberry's curse never returns."

"A faithful wife's patience will keep the dark past where it belongs."

There was only one place Minna could escape the endless pleas of caution from every corner of Castle Burberry.

The tunnels.

She'd left her skirts behind the trapdoor and now fled through the cobwebbed catacombs with naught but plumed undergarments and a ribbed corset. The latter she tugged and pulled until she managed to undo the bound straps, allowing her lungs to gasp full with air as it popped off her chest.

Where knitting her nephew's nightshirt next to the fires had been stifling, the tunnels offered a sweet musty coolness that Minna drank in like nectar.

She'd memorized these tunnels years ago, and a wild grin spread across her face that she finally was left alone long enough to escape into its silence for the night.

She was always watched. Always judged and forced into propriety and social acquaintances fitting for her station.

We're human now. This is a better life. You were too young to know what it used to be like.

Father's words harnessed the worst of lies. Human? Minna had seen what it was like to be *human*. Her poor sister had married one, born him sons he only saw as political objects and forced to look the other way when he lusted after women half her age. All out of the unfounded fear that if she didn't, the curse would come back.

As if that wasn't bad enough, another offer had been made for Minna's hand to build an alliance with the north. Propriety, honesty, these were qualities her future husband valued, and undoubtably did not share for himself.

When father refused to undo the match, she'd begged him to at least tell her what they'd been before, if not human. "Monsters" is all Father would say, quickly followed by, "And if you don't want to be one, do as you're told."

She'd obeyed all but one command.

Never go into the catacombs.

Minna's breath frosted the air as she reached the bottom level.

Minna sped around the final bend and took a sharp left — head-first into a nest of cobwebs. She coughed and sputtered, flinging them off her face.

She'd never gone this way. An eerie cold in the air and an unsettling feeling of dread had always kept her out. But now, the forbidden cloister felt like her savior. She feared the future more than the curse. Perhaps they were already living the curse, and it was her fate to free them all.

The corridor split open into a massive crevice that shot into the cathedral arches of the ceiling. Beams of moonlight cascaded down like frozen rain from slits in the wall. Minna gazed up at it, mesmerized and in awe. This place smelled of lost knowledge and power. Surely, such things could only revive her people?

Minna approached the centerpiece of the chamber. A single gray pillar rested along the deep grooves of the cracked ground.

She held a finger out and grazed the surface. The edge was unexpectedly jagged and flayed her skin. She lurched and cried out, leaving a dark splotch across the stone.

As Minna gripped her wounded hand, the ground trembled and a low growl came from the tomb.

Minna froze.

The stone's surface cracked and crumbled, revealing a withered husk. The husk's skin went from a pasty grey to a flushed pink, layers of flesh webbing over its arms and face until he became a man, as handsome as any Minna had seen in court.

Minna blinked and gasped, recognizing who she was seeing. The ridge of his nose was sharp, and there was a black freckle just below his brow; he looked exactly like her father. This was the Lost King of Castle Burberry.

When the King opened his eyes, Minna expected to see cruelty or insanity fitting a cursed monster trapped in the catacombs. Instead, there was kindness.

He unwrapped his arms and took a careful step out of his prison. He kneeled and placed a cold finger under Minna's chin.

He offered a sad smile. "You don't know what you've done, my child."

Even through the walls, Minna could hear the screams. They raised up like a wave, cascading down the corridors and making Minna's heart flutter with doubt and fear.

Minna blinked and brought a hand to her face as her skin went hard and cold and a deep ache filled her belly.

The King lowered his chin to his chest and heaved. "Go, young Princess. Claim your meal for tonight, and every night after that, for you are once again vampire.

THREE
THE DRAGONS'KIN DAMSEL

Lily allowed the assassin believe she didn't know he was there. She slipped off her bathrobe and dunked herself into the indulgent lake of bubbles from the Baron's finest slipper tub. Slipper, it was called, for the way of eased up on one end like a dainty woman's heel. It would allow Lily to keep her head upright without looking strained, making sure the assassin would think her guard was down.

She could feel his eyes on her, willing her to close her own. She was tempted, with the soft, droning music as the servant drifted deft fingers across harp strings. Candlelight sent shadows dancing across the whitewashed walls with the bath's steam. But Lily was a master of her trade. No luxury would deter her from her contract to kill the intruder. But as the melody drifted on and the waters enveloped her in a cocoon of warmth, she thought that her lack of patience might.

If Lily had really been who she pretended to be, the Baron's betrothed who was even daintier than the slipper tub, she'd be delivered to the afterlife tonight. And even though Lily wore the same bouncing curls, the perky breasts, and even the bright pink toenails, she was anything but a helpless damsel.

In spite of the adrenaline of a contract, her concentration dimmed while she waited for the assassin to attack. He was taking too long. Perhaps he was enjoying the servant's music, no doubt one of the most expensive bards on this side of the continent. The Baron was a wealthy man and didn't spare a single purse for his beloved. He'd even been able to afford a dragons'kin like her, a shapeshifter at that.

While Lily contemplated what estate the Baron might have sold to afford a dragons-kin's deal, the bard slipped into a new song. Its somber tones seemed to turn the room blue, as if they'd eased into another realm under the oceans. She didn't get to hear such talent often, not with her seclusion and deals with death. Her eyes drooped as she listened, feeling weighed down by the entrancing melody.

She jolted when fingers wrapped through hers. The assassin, she thought, panicked. Her eyes met his and she relaxed with a short laugh.

This was no assassin. He was but a boy, blonde tufts of hair wrapping over his forehead and startling blue eyes that were now hooded with long lashes. The way he looked at her made a shiver go down her naked spine. This was a lover.

The Baron had told Lily of an intruder, surely an assassin that had made his betrothed scream under the cover of midnight. When the Baron had burst into the room, a shadow had disappeared from the window and

Helga was drenched with sweat. The poor dear, he'd said, she was completely traumatized. Couldn't even tell him what had happened.

As the "assassin's" hand roamed across her arm and down her collarbone, Lily's breath hitched and she shot to her feet. Instinct made her magic fade and she dropped her host's vulnerable form in favor of her own dragons'kin skin.

The bard hadn't been aware of the Baron's schemes. Her harp snapped with a sharp *twang* and she went screaming out of the room.

The boy, though, recovered quickly from his shock and stared with open awe. His marvel said he knew that she was dragons'kin—and he wasn't afraid. Her scales replaced supple flesh and her pupils slit, sharpening the boy's features, only revealing how handsome he really was.

"There's been a mistake," she said hastily. Her voice, now her own, came out low and raspy.

A smile crept across the boy's face and dimples formed at his cheeks. "Incredible," he mused. He cocked his head, speaking slowly as if she wouldn't understand. "Do you know where Helga is?"

Lily narrowed her eyes and flashed her third eyelid. She'd expected him to flinch, but he didn't. "She's not here," she said.

He chuckled. "Yes, I can see that."

They matched each other's gazes until Lily finally broke the trance. She stared at her feet, now hidden from view by a wall of suds. She'd made a deal with the Baron, an agreement she couldn't undo. Her mind raced to find a loophole, a way to get out of the contract. As a dragons'kin, she was magically bound to her word. She'd promised to kill the intruder in exchange for a chamber of gold.

"Who are you?" she asked, hoping he'd give her enough information to undo the deal. Had he been invited? If so, he wasn't an intruder at all, and he wouldn't have to die.

As if he sensed her dilemma, he backed up a step and rested a hand on his sword hilt. "Who I am is of no consequence. My only concern is for Helga."

Lily stepped out of the tub, inching towards him. She didn't need a weapon when she was in her true form. Her scales would deflect any blow he attempted, and her teeth would snap his spine. Painless, quick. If he said the wrong words, it was the best she could do.

"Did Helga *invite* you?" she asked, emphasizing the question. If the boy had any sense at all, he'd say yes.

He frowned and studied her. His eyes roamed her body. They stopped for a moment on her claws, shifted to the talons on her shoulders, and then a moment on her lips. She knew they bulged with her fangs, now extended and ready to take his life.

Lily growled with frustration. His inspection meant he was a soldier. Whether Helga had invited him or not, his status made him an intruder in the royal house.

The magic wouldn't let her wait for an answer. Her instincts knew what she must do. She must fulfill her end of the bargain with the Baron, no matter how unsavory, and she lunged for his throat without a second thought.

The sharp sting that radiated from her side caught her off guard. She stared at the wound, eyes wide and third-eyelid pushed all the way back. How'd he cut her?

"I don't want to hurt you," the boy admitted, his sword drawn, dark with her blood. A single drop fell to the ground and made the floorboards hiss.

"A deal's been made," she said through clenched teeth. The pain was terrible, but it served to help her resist the magic's bond. No mere soldier would be able to cut her. Her body shook with tremors as she clutched at her side.

He took a step away from her, sword still raised. "Alter the deal," he offered. "Kill the Baron, not me."

Lily's eyes narrowed and her foot dragged the ground, following him. "It doesn't work that way. I promised to kill the intruder."

He smirked. "The Baron is the intruder, not me."

The magic relented at the prospect of an altered deal and she wavered on her feet. "Go on," she pressed.

"The Baron isn't what he pretends to be. He's an imposter, a dragons'kin like you."

Lily stared at him and her mouth hung ajar. "If that's true," she said when she'd found her voice, "then why would he pay me to kill you? Why not just do it himself?"

The boy laughed and hefted the glittering sword to his other hand. Lily noticed its uniqueness now, how it glowed with its own magic from within. "Because I have this." He presented her with the blade.

Lily tried to take it, but the moment her fingers grazed the hilt pain shot up to her elbow and she jerked away. She flashed him a frown and reevaluated her initial appraisal. "Who are you?" she asked again.

He smirked. "I'm a prince; wouldn't be much of one if I couldn't slay dragons." His smirk grew. "My specialty is rescuing damsels in distress." When Lily didn't react, his blue eyes went to his sword. "Helga's a good match for me. She's beautiful, kind, and has survived all these years with a dragons'kin lording over her, just waiting for me to come to her rescue."

Lily's heart jostled with a strange emotion. She'd borrowed Helga's body for just a few hours, but she'd felt the grace of her form. Now, as a dragons'kin, Lily felt bulky and dangerous. When would a prince ever consider coming to her rescue? She was certainly not a damsel in distress. She made deals with wealthy nobles, sent evil souls to the underworld, and hoarded the gold of her bounties. Her magic as a dragons'kin made her immortal, but how lonely a life it was. "Would a prince ever help someone like me?" she found herself asking. The talons on her shoulders retracted, as if trying to hide her garish features.

The sword's tip fell to the floor and he stared at her in surprise. "Help you do what?"

She felt silly then, and crossed her arms, pushing her talons back out. "Nothing. Stupid question."

He raised an eyebrow. "Where'd you get your shift magic?"

Lily glowered. What kind of question was that? "The Baron can shift too," she retorted, her fingers crawling up her elbows. "It's not such an unusual ability."

But it was—and the prince's bland stare said he knew it. Dragons were proud. They didn't like pretending or hiding. They wanted the world to hear their roar, worship them and give them gold. She'd been a dragon, once. But as eons ebbed, she'd found herself envying the humans and their passions. The envy had become so great that her form had shifted, became humanoid, and now she was stuck in limbo between the two races. Dragons'kin were mere shadows of themselves. To take on a human's form was more than envy. It was a belief. Shapeshifting was the last step to losing the dragon's identity altogether and taking on another.

The prince didn't respond. He didn't have to. The flash of pity in his blue eyes made her want to snap his neck, but the brilliant blade made her stay at bay.

#

The odd pair crept through the castle, but it was too quiet. The Baron kept an entire entourage of servants. There should have been cooks preparing midnight meals, maids blowing out candles and whisperings of the day's gossip. Instead, the eerie calm made Lily's hackles rise and the prince's sword glowed brighter with every step they took.

Lily relied on her magic to guide them to the Baron. She'd promised to kill the intruder. Thanks to the prince, the only intruder was the dragons'kin who pretended to be the Baron. Her magic drew her left, then right, pulling her to her target until they finally came upon a hatch that went into the cellars.

The prince gave Lily an arched eyebrow, but followed her inside. She walked on ahead away from his sword that he waved about like a torch. She stayed in his line-of-sight, but kept to the shadows with her third eyelid retracted, allowing her to drink in all the light and be warned of any sudden movements.

The pull was strongest when they reached a door that was polished and free from cobwebs. "He's in there," Lily hissed.

She reached for the handle, but the prince stopped her. "Allow me," he insisted.

Not one to often receive chivalries, Lily buried a smile that threatened to stretch across her fangs and she nodded.

Inside, the Baron stared at them, wide-eyed and fear blazing across his slit irises. He hadn't transformed into a dragons'kin. There was only a hint of what he was from his eyes and claws extending from what had once been fingernails. The third eyelid flickered as if unable to fully form.

Lily froze, for in the Baron's arms was the beautiful Helga, the Baron's claws at her throat. "Not another step!" he threatened and yanked Helga like a doll and she shrieked.

The prince gripped his sword with both hands and snarled at the Baron. "Unhand her you brute!"

The Baron wasn't paying the prince the least bit of attention. His eyes were glued on Lily. "Kill the intruder!" he wailed.

Lily's stomach dropped when she put all the pieces together. The Baron was close to losing his dragon's identity. "What would that achieve?" she asked, fighting the pull of the contract's magic. Going for him now would mean Helga's death, and somehow, she cared about that.

His orange eyes flitted to the prince, as if noticing him for the first time. "Helga was supposed to love me, only me, help me lose the dragon completely." Tears welled in his eyes, a most un-dragonlike response. His fat cheeks bulged and he could have passed for human, if it weren't for his wild, orange stare. He grimaced and with one hand still around Helga's throat, the other stabbed a claw at the prince. "She can't love me while *you're* still alive!"

Such lunacy, desperation. Lily almost pitied him, until Helga's eyes rolled into the back of her head. "If you squeeze any harder, you're going to kill your only chance at becoming human," Lily pointed out.

The next second, time froze as her senses sped up. The Baron must have determined all hope was lost, for a single talon slit a red line across Helga's throat.

Lily reacted first. She wasn't as quick as she'd have liked, not with the wound in her side. Pain stabbed through her ribs and she wasn't swift enough to save the prince's lover. She clawed at the Baron and tried to pry his hands away from Helga's throat. But it was too late, blood seeped down her collarbone and the light dimmed from her eyes.

Lily held onto the Baron, baring her fangs and going for the vein pulsing in his neck. The Baron, uninjured, was too strong and whipped out of her grasp. He tossed Helga's limp body to the ground and lunged for the prince.

Time was frozen for them, and as dragons'kin they lived in it, blurred and danced around mortals. The prince was still poised with a sword upraised and his teeth locked in a grit. He stared at the place the Baron had once been, but not at the claws that were now a breath from his throat.

Lily reacted against her dragons'kin's instincts. She was supposed to kill the Baron and end his pitiful life. But seeing the panic streaking across the prince's face, she knew this wasn't her kill. She found the will to move faster, stop the Baron and bend his claws back until they snapped. He wailed but she kept him there until time caught up with the prince and he lurched in surprise.

"Now!" she screamed.

The prince didn't hesitate and shoved his blade deep into the Baron's belly.

Still partly dragons'kin, the screech that ripped out of the Baron's throat was more dragon than human. It rippled through the walls and made the prince buckle to his knees. He clenched his head and Lily held the Baron's weight as he slowly died, his spirit falling into the floor and drifting to the underworld. She'd planned on sending an evil soul there tonight, but when she saw Helga's limp body, she frowned. An innocent had been lost.

A shiver went through her as she stared at Helga's lifeless body and Lily transformed, although she hadn't commanded herself to shift. A tingling ran over her scalp. She ran her fingers through blonde curls that bounced at her shoulders and she blinked in surprise, but a third eyelid didn't appear.

The prince, time still catching up to him, stared at the dead dragons'kin and his lost love sharing a pool of blood. His eyes flitted to Lily, then widened. "What are you doing?" he asked.

She covered her naked chest and squeezed her eyes shut. She had no answer for him. She hadn't intended to transform into Helga.

Focusing, she thought of herself, of her scales and her talons. But she could only think of how she detested them, wanted nothing to do with dragons anymore.

When she opened her eyes again the prince was upon her, the sword trembling at her throat. “Stop it,” he hissed, his voice shaking as a tear slid down his cheek.

Maybe it was the distress in her eyes, or the way her lower lip trembled, but he removed his blade. He stared at her for a long moment. “Are you all right?” he asked this time. He would have looked kind, if his knuckles hadn’t been so white as he held a death grip on the sword’s hilt.

She shook her head and her curls draped across her shoulders with a sensual wave. She tried not to enjoy it. This wasn’t her body. “Sometimes,” she began, her voice melodic, “if a host dies, a dragons’kin will permanently take the form.” Her cheeks burned. The softness that formed around the prince’s eyes showed how he reacted to her blush.

They stared at one another, until finally the prince adverted his gaze, undid the robe around his shoulders and handed it to Lily. She took it without ceremony and covered herself. They left the cellars and Lily hugged herself and kept a step behind the prince, making sure to keep close to his side. She couldn’t see anything except by the soft glow of his sword.

Outside the castle, the prince took her hand in his. “Come with me.”

And so she did.

THE BARON HAD EXCUSED the household for the terrors he knew were coming that night. The town was silent and asleep, and would never know what had transpired at the castle up the hill. After the bodies had been found, the castle became abandoned, covered in moss, and the subject of bedtime threats to tell unruly children.

But Lily would have her happy ending even though she'd saved the prince from a dragon, and not the other way around. Helga was gone and only Lily remained. The prince's kingdom expected a bride and so he took her as his wife, and they bore beautiful children with blonde hair and blue eyes.

Lily's children still roam the world. You'll know them by their love of gold. They'll wear it around their neck and even push it through their earlobes, the closest appendage to hackles a human can have. On rare occasion, their dormant magic can resurface; they can even regain their fangs. Should you identify one, beware, a child of a dragon-s'kin is known as vampire, and they prefer blood to gold.

FOUR
SUMMER'S END

A baby's cry was the only thing that could have moved Eliza from her cozy spot in front of the fireplace. She'd made a pot of tea and was now cradling a warm porcelain cup with her icy fingers while she blew steam off the edge. She conserved her warmth in winter. It was better not to fight it, so she drew on the comforts of her lodge.

Of course, that serene moment was exactly when a tiny screech pierced the crisp air.

Eliza straightened and cocked her head to the entrance, sure that she'd heard wrong. A squirrel chirping for a lost winter nut, perhaps, or maybe a lingering night owl had made his first kill.

But the cry came once more, and Eliza knew it was a child. She put the teacup down and rose, her fur blanket slipping off her shoulders. She hissed when the cool air rushed in, sliding up the loops of her sleeves and down the gap of her gown at her neck. Her bare feet pattered across the slick, wooden floorboards and she suppressed a shiver.

She didn't allow herself to think of the icy breeze when she snatched the door open. She hardly felt its teeth when she saw the tiny bundle at her feet.

The child wiggled in its cloth confines, its screams a poor deterrent from the cold spreading ice across the shoebox. Eliza knelt and scooped the package into her embrace. She didn't know how the child still lived even one moment exposed to the night like this.

The baby wailed until Eliza had securely trapped the box in the crook of her arm, encasing the baby with her carefully conserved heat. The child's face had been scrunched and ugly as it'd wailed, but now the cries stopped and it blinked the most breathtaking blue eyes at her. Eliza gasped, for the baby searched her face and smiled, as if intelligent. It even pursed its lips, as if trying to say, "thank you."

Eliza broke from her shock when another icy blast rushed past her and invaded her home. She suppressed a curse and hurried inside. The door creaked with frost as she forced it closed.

ELIZA QUICKLY GREW fond of the child, waking early to heat goat's milk on the stove, only to stay up late to sing the child to sleep. She rested, though, in-between day and night with stolen naps, the child wiggling on her chest.

It wasn't until a knock came at the door did Eliza realize winter's icy chill had broken, leaving the land ready and waiting for her tender care again. The realization passed a fearful image through her mind's eye of the land born anew into spring, but withering without her hand to guide it into summer.

She opened the door, only momentarily peering into the face that smiled back. It was Logan, the handsome human who always came to visit her when the snows had melted. Trying not to be rude, she glanced over his shoulder, and relaxed when she saw the blistering rainbow of weed flowers littering the grove. She wasn't too late.

Logan cleared his throat and cast a wary glance at the child secured to her hip. Eliza shifted her weight, balancing the burden. The child had grown so much, so fast. She didn't know much of human children, but perhaps they all grew so quickly and she'd just never noticed. Time was all about seasons for her, not the passing of years.

"Eliza, dear," Logan said not looking away from the child, "who has given you such a treasure?"

Eliza chuckled, but was glad to be able to introduce the child to him. "Logan," she said, his name fond on her lips and her voice coming out melodic, having only been used to sing the child to sleep, "This is—" She sucked in a breath. Had she really never given the child a name? Eliza gave a light laugh and decided to lie. "This is my nephew."

Logan finally met her gaze and gave her an approving nod. "And what a lad he is." He gave the child—now almost a boy—a playful pinch on the nose.

The child laughed and grabbed his finger, fast as lightening the boy was. Logan, clearly startled, bounced his gaze from the child to Eliza. "He's got your family's reflexes, I see."

Eliza beamed and waved him into her home. "Please, come inside."

She settled the boy into the nest she'd built, soft moss encased by twigs and forest offerings. Logan noted it, but didn't comment.

She made another pot of tea and got him settled before they relaxed at the fire to talk. Even in summer, she always stoked the flames, or rather, especially in summer. She suppressed a smirk as she coddled her cup and gazed into the blaze, wondering what Logan would do if he knew that the warmth of the earth was born right here, in this very hearth?

He eyed the child warily. "So, you didn't say, does the lad have a name?"

Eliza stiffened, and then shrugged. "My sister didn't tell me what it was," she said, trying not to look the human in the eye.

Logan hummed, but didn't comment and sipped his tea, peering thoughtfully into the flames like Eliza.

She watched him from the corner of her eye. It's what she liked about him. He didn't ask too many questions, and when he did, he wasn't offended when she offered vague answers. Life was simple with Logan. She liked it.

The child cried then, as if noticing Eliza's attention had slipped. She winced and rushed to his side, gathering him into her arms and bouncing him until his whimpers turned to laughs.

"You shouldn't dote on him so," Logan chided. "You'll spoil him rotten."

Eliza frowned and continued to pat the toddler's back. "What do you know of children?" she asked.

A smile tugged at the corner of his mouth, the kind that made him look devious and arrogant. "Oh, my dear, I raised half my brothers!" He stood and straightened his vest. "None of them turned out half as bad as me, I assure you."

Eliza couldn't stay mad and felt a smile of her own threatening to break out on her face. She set the boy at her feet and gave Logan a challenging stare. "Ok, then. Show me how it's done."

Logan didn't hesitate and knelt, making himself eye-level to the child. "Hello," he began, and held out his hand. "I'm Logan. It's a pleasure to make your acquaintance."

Eliza suppressed a chuckle, but allowed the charade to continue.

To their surprise, however, the child clapped his hands and shouted "Logan!" with triumphant glee.

Both Eliza and Logan startled and looked at one another. Logan gave a short laugh. "See?"

The child patted his own chest. "Ragnar!" he shouted this time.

Logan brightened and Eliza froze. "Is that your name?" Logan offered. "Ragnar?"

The boy giggled and clapped. Logan was delighted until he looked up at Eliza's face. "My dear, you have gone rather pale. Are you feeling all right?"

Eliza wavered on her feet and the world began to spin.

Ragnar.

Ragnar.

Ragnar.

The name, she knew it in her bones. It was the name of the demigod that would end her reign. She'd been warned of his coming, told to kill him when she had the chance.

But now, as she peered into his gleeful blue eyes, she knew she couldn't. She'd die for him...and according to prophecy, she would.

PROPHECY OR NOT, Eliza had duties to fulfill. She clamped her quivering lower lip between her teeth and edged out of the hut, Ragnar and Logan quick on her heels.

"What is it?" Logan asked.

"Mama?" Ragnar's voice followed.

Eliza didn't allow herself to think. The boy had gained his voice when Logan had acknowledged him, and he had called himself Ragnar. Oh, blessed seasons, how had she not seen this coming?

The fates, she reminded herself, were supposed to be that way, unseen and always fulfilled. A shiver ran through her as her naked toes raked through snarled weeds. The land sucked away her warmth, filling it to the core and sprouting wildflowers with every step she took.

Like the fates, spring would inevitably come. The signs would be in the way the flowers threatened to bloom, the warmth they stole from her toes, and the call she could never deny.

Ragnar squealed with delight and the earth shook as he sped towards Eliza, at least, that's how it felt to her. Logan laughed, his joy making it clear that he couldn't feel how Ragnar sent the land into tremors.

Eliza put it all together now and her face crumpled with sadness. Ragnar had survived in a shoebox on her doorstep caked with ice because he was her brother. He was Armageddon, the fires that destroyed rather than nurtured. He was everything that she wasn't, and she'd welcome him into her home.

"Don't take the flowers," she pleaded.

Ragnar clung to her leg and she forced herself to look down at him. His impossibly blue eyes were round and weeping, as if he'd feared he'd done something wrong.

"Mama?" he asked, even as the blooms withered beneath their feet and turned to ash.

He couldn't help it, she knew that, and stroked his soft hair. "It's all right," she said, even as the darkness spread and the end of the world had already begun.

"ELIZA," Logan said. He said her name like a command, not a call or a prayer. He said it as if he owned it and that made Eliza swirl to face him.

Her heart jumped in her throat when she realized who Logan was. His human form melted in favor of his golden glow. He was the Maker. "You've spoiled the child," he said and took a step towards them.

Eliza shoved Ragnar behind her legs and stood her ground. "You're the one who brought him to me," she accused.

Logan smirked. “If anyone could have stopped Armageddon, it would have been you. I gave you the child to contain, to control. Yet, you’ve given in to his every desire. You’ve built his capability of the flame rather than dampened it. How could you have been so naive?”

Eliza snarled, even as Ragnar’s blazing hands clutched onto her calves. She didn’t care anymore. Ragnar had given her what no one else ever had, a warmth that had rivaled her own. “He’s just a child,” she said. “He needed me.”

“Needed you? Hardly. He needed to be put down, but I’m the Maker. I cannot destroy. That is what my children are for.”

Tears sizzled in Eliza’s eyes. Before her, the world had been encased in ice. She’d brought warmth and seasons, a cycle of birth that had never been there before. He was the Maker, but she’d stoked the flames of his creation into something new. “Haven’t I been good for the world? Haven’t I made you proud?”

His face softened. “Of course, child. You were a balance the world needed. But all cycles must come to an end, and the fates brought Ragnar for that.”

Ragnar tugged against her, but Eliza stood her ground and kept him pinned behind her legs. The warmth had turned into searing pain and she didn’t look down for fear that her ankles were melting.

All her life, Eliza had fulfilled a needed purpose, but she’d been so alone. Logan had been the one ray of light in her life, and even now that had been a lie. Humans feared her and never could last long in her presence. She should have known Logan wasn’t who’d he’d seemed to be. “Why have you come to me every winter?" she asked, the question a cold stone in the pit of her stomach that had to be spat out.

"I needed to know if your powers would wane," he said frankly. "It's been thousands of years, yet you've ceaselessly sent the world into a spiral of warmth when we've drawn close enough to the sun to leech its heat." He tilted his head and looked at her legs which now quivered with pain. "Ragnar is different. He doesn't need the sun to build. He has the power within himself. He *is* the fire." He frowned, disappointment sending his brows furrowing together. "I'd hoped that you could take the warmth from him, instead of the sun." His eyes met hers and he clamped his mouth shut. He wasn't one to ask favors. But he was the Maker. He didn't truly want to see all he'd Made destroyed.

The logic of what Logan had hoped she'd do slapped Eliza in the face and she finally allowed herself to look down to Ragnar. He was crying now. Silent sobs shook his body and his fingers had turned black with the drifting ash of her dress. Her skin blistered but he gripped on as hard as he could. "Mama," he pleaded now that she'd finally acknowledged him.

She knelt and wiped the steaming tears from his cheeks. "I know, sweet child, it's okay." As she stared into his blue eyes, she made herself switch the draw of her power. She'd locked onto the sun centuries ago and had nearly forgotten how to alter the strand. But she unhinged it like a great anchor and cast it around the boy. His shivering eased as she did, and the world glowed with red as Eliza began to burn.

ELIZA KEPT HER WORD. She saved the world, but it wasn't in the way Logan wanted. He wanted the world to remain just has it always had been. But he was right. Cycles must be ended and Eliza, the goddess of summer and the broker of the seasons, was ready for a fresh start. The world burned, consumed with Ragnar's flames. But Eliza's gift was that it wouldn't burn forever, and once the flames turned to ash, man rose once again. Her only regret was that they'd never know her sacrifice, or how they'd come to be. So she planted a single seed in their hearts, a burning passion to seek out the truth. One day, Eliza knew, man would find what they're looking for, and the cycle will be complete.

FIVE
THE CHILD-KING

I stabbed my knife into the splintered board. It was easier to groove the line that marked another sighting now that the wood had swollen with the morning's dew.

I stepped back to admire my handiwork, ignoring the shrill *whoosh* that spiked my neck hairs on their ends. I counted the grooves again. One, two, three... Twenty... Fifty-two...

There were too many. I tried getting an accurate count a few more times before deciding keeping track was pointless. Whatever their purpose for coming here, it didn't much matter, because there were a heck of a lot more of them than us. We didn't stand a chance.

Mulling over what it could all mean, I quietly chewed through the last of my dried meat. I'd brought more than enough for a week-long trip, but I'd started making rations when we were three days in. Now, it'd been three weeks, and I was out of grub.

Merce was still sleeping in the tent, somehow immune

to the bloodcurdling screeches each passing ship sent through my bones. “Hey, Merce,” I shouted through the billowing walls of the tent as I wiped my mouth clean. I waited for the zipper to creep up the side before gathering my pack and empty canteen. I crouched at the river to fill it, taking small sips to ease the sensation of salty meat sticking in my throat.

Merce’s face poked through and her genetically-modified hair was perfectly straight and shiny like an asian’s. Except she was blonde and had purple eyes that always kind of creeped me out. “Is it morning already?” she complained as she squeezed through the tent’s opening. She still wore her skintight under-armor appropriately dubbed a seal-suit, claiming it was the best garb for sleeping. I adverted my gaze. I’d made a promise to Danny that I wouldn’t be tempted by mods like Merce. “Fake’s not better,” Danny would say with her freckled nose turned up in defiance. That was before she disappeared with the first wave of naturals to join the aliens. Even though they repulsed me, there were other naturals who were drawn to them like moths to a flame. It broke my heart that Danny had been one of them.

Merce took one long look at the frayed counting post. Her eyes widened as she studied each groove. “Please tell me you were practicing your swing on that thing.”

I braced myself as another whizzing ship sped through the atmosphere. “I’m afraid not.” I cracked one eye open. “You really can’t feel it? There’re so many.”

She peered up to the sky and shook her head. “I wish I could.”

"No," I said. "You don't."

She swallowed and turned back to the tent. "We'd better get going."

My stomach flipped as another two ships kissed the clouds. "Yes," I managed to say through clenched teeth. "Let's get out of here."

TREKKING through the wilderness was something I'd been excited about when we'd set out on our journey. Our meshed society of naturals and mods worked best under the city-proper, and no one ventured out from the forcefields. Being exposed to the polluted gasses of our world could change our genetic makeup, and that wasn't good for either side.

Even though we lived together, one mod and one natural for every political position, I'd always felt that being natural-born meant being less. Ever since the ships appeared, my status had gone from zero to hero. If it weren't for the naturals, mods wouldn't have even known they were here.

Merce kept giving the sky wary glances. I could tell it unnerved her to be out here, possibly being exposed to toxins, and having to completely rely on me to tell her if any ships were nearby. They weren't aggressive, but if you got too close, they'd zap you pretty good. Your ears would ring for three days if you got hit by one of their warning blows. At least, that's what I'd heard. I'd only gotten the nausea, no zaps.

For the past three weeks I'd been having us wander where I'd sensed them gathering. The ships had been spreading out, as if testing the land and building their confidence. I didn't tell Merce I knew where they were, that their patterns weren't random. I didn't want to admit I was afraid of what we might find.

If she knew I was hiding information from her, which she probably did, she hadn't pressed me yet. Instead, she charged onwards, leading the way even though she likely had no idea where she was going.

When we came to a steep slope, Merce nodded with satisfaction, as if this was exactly what she'd been looking for, and seamlessly scaled the rocks up to the plateau. She didn't wait for me, or offer to help, she knew it'd only piss me off. So she calmly surveyed the landscape over the treetops while I stumbled and cursed my way up the steep slope.

Merce's layered armor wasn't much better than her seal-suit and left little to the imagination. Being a mod meant everything about her was designed to perfection. My cheeks flushed when I accidentally got a eyeful of her rounded butt cheeks barely concealed by the black leather before pulling myself completely up the cliff.

"Do you feel anything?" she asked. Her voice had an edge to it that'd only gotten worse the longer we'd been out here.

I hesitated before finally deciding I should grow some balls. We'd been out here long enough. "Yeah," I said, pointing down a long creek that spidered through the trees. "There's a mass of them that way."

She snorted, and even though it should have been unattractive, the way her lips plumped when she was frustrated made her look all the more enticing. "It's about time you finally admitted you knew where they were. We have to go check it out."

I rubbed my face, suddenly exhausted and ready to just go home. "Our mission was to assess the alien's purpose and, if possible, recover the deserters. How are we supposed to do that? We know there're more ships than we can count. We should just go back and report how many we've seen."

Merce's gaze fell to the machete at my side. "And how many have you seen?"

She knew I didn't have an answer. I couldn't keep numbers aligned in my head like a spreadsheet like she could. "A lot," I offered.

She snorted again, this time her piercing purple eyes staring straight into mine. "That's not good enough, Jake."

My whole body froze. It was the first time she'd ever used my name. "What," I said with a short laugh. "I've upgraded from being a 'gnat?'"

Her purple eyes remained fixed. "I've underestimated naturals," she said as if that explained everything. "Being with you has been...enlightening." She faced the landscape once more and hugged herself. She almost looked like a normal girl. "If those ships are a new enemy, only you'll be able to fight them."

I debated stepping closer to her. I wanted to comfort her, but if I did, that might turn into something friendlier than Danny would appreciate. I was a pureblood natural.

Matching with a mod would upset the balance of our society. I wanted to ask why our societies kept barriers. Why we didn't just combine our bloodlines and eliminate the division of "mods" and "gnats." Instead, I asked, "Why do you think only naturals can feel them?"

She shivered. I'd never seen her shiver before. "Whatever it is, it's nothing good for mods."

I wanted to embrace her and tell her everything would be okay. She was feeling what I'd felt my whole life. It was perfectly normal to feel inferior when someone else could do something you couldn't. But I knew what would happen if I did, I was still a human male, and she was the definition of female perfection, so I slapped her on the shoulder as if she were one of the guys and gave her a wink. "Into the lion's den we go."

IT DIDN'T TAKE LONG for the ships to notice we'd decided to approach their hive. My stomach turned every time one passed. They came in sequence as if they were making rounds and began to slow as they passed over us.

Merce kept giving me worried glances, but didn't say anything, and didn't offer for us to turn around. Merce and I were the only natural/mod duo that had made it this far without being zapped. Perhaps they wanted us to come, perhaps we had something they needed. Whatever the cause, there was only one way to find out why they were here and what they wanted.

The further we got into the wilderness, the more the

trees began to thin. Not in a natural way like you'd see when a forest would turn into a glade. The bark of the remaining trees were grey and splintered, as if it was about to catch fire.

As we progressed, the trees that were left were completely black, even the leaves. But at closer inspection, I saw it wasn't black at all. It was crystalized, a thin layer of crust forming over the decaying organics. Without thinking I walked up to one to touch it.

Merce slapped my hand away before I could make contact. She gave me a stern look, but didn't chide me. She knew it was part of being a "gnat" that made me curious, the instinct stronger than survival at times.

"What do you think it is?" I asked.

She shrugged, carefully stepping around the malformed trees and crunching through the remains of those already gone. "Some kind of forced decomposition, kind of like when you burn a piece of wood, it changes the chemical properties and releases energy." She sniffed the air. "It smells like death."

I wasn't sure what death smelled like. I tried sniffing the air too, but could only catch the whiff of Merce's lilac perfume. It's not like she applied perfume, that would be a "gnat" thing to do. The scent was built into her adrenal glands.

I pointed toward a fogged area that blocked out the horizon. "They're that way."

She smirked. "Yeah, that's pretty obvious."

I smiled. "Hey, if you know where to go, you don't need me, right?" I jerked my thumb over my shoulder. "I'll be heading back to the city then. Get me a nice, fat hamburger you mods think are disgusting."

She grabbed me by the cuff around my collarbone and jerked me along. "Come on."

The playful mood faded as we got closer to the alien's hub. The sensation started to make me dizzy and I grabbed my stomach, my feet dragging as I forced myself to keep going. There were so many of them.

A ship drifted close and lingered in the clouds. I squeezed my eyes shut and tried not to hyperventilate as another wave swept through me.

Merce grabbed my shoulder. "What is it?" she whispered.

I didn't dare open my eyes. "One stopped over our heads. It's watching us."

Just when I was about to double over and lose my meat-scrap breakfast, the ship moved on and the rolling nausea retreated to a more manageable queasiness.

"I don't like that," Merce said. "They make you sick. They can't be good if they do that, right?"

I opened my eyes and was met by the violet concern in Merce's gaze. There was no sense in speculating. I didn't know why they made me sick. They just did.

"They know we're here," I said. "Be alert."

Once we reached the fog I braced myself for the sensation to vomit. Merce gave me an encouraging nod before she stepped into the mist. I swallowed hard and followed her.

The second I'd passed the thin veil of the fog's

entrance, any hint of queasiness vanished. I blinked a few times to make sure I wasn't imagining it.

"What is it?" Merce asked in a hushed whisper.

"I don't feel sick anymore."

She squinted through the fog, and even though her eyes were as good as an eagle's, she didn't seem to be able to see better than I could. "Did they leave?"

I turned and stepped back out from the fog and was slammed by the sickness. I yelped and jumped back into the mist. "No, it's the fog. It's masking whatever it is that makes me sick.

She furrowed her blonde brows as an array of emotions rainbowed across her face. I realized she was trying to calculate the odds if this were a good thing or bad thing. Her brows burrowed even further, making her look adorably frustrated. She sniffed the air again. "I can't smell death anymore, either."

I grabbed her hand. "It can't be a good thing that we've both gone blind. Don't let go of me. We'll figure this out, together."

Her hand squeezed mine as we pushed deeper into the fog. Even though her blood ran cooler than mine, her reassuring touch made me feel warm and safe.

GOING blind seemed to increase my sense of hearing. At first I thought it was the wind, but as we got closer I could hear someone was crying in the distance.

I followed it. The fog was impossibly thick, and definitely not natural. Fog tended to be white and tasted like dew, but this was black, as if we'd walked into midnight and tasted of metal.

Pain shot through my skull when I hit something hard.

I cursed and Merce jerked me behind her. This was why she was here, to protect me. The *whizz* of her gun's safety turning off rippled through the fog. But, nothing came for us.

Merce started to pull away, but I clung to her arm like a child. I didn't care what it made me look like. I was *not* going to lose her in this creepy ass place.

"It's a cage," she said.

She guided my hand and pressed it against the cool metal of an iron bar.

The crying started again. This time it was close. "Hello?" I asked and my voice echoed as if the ground was smooth and flat.

I followed the bars until I got to a hinge. I peered closer and found it was bound by a simple lock. I tugged Merce and showed her.

Understanding passed between us and I backed away as she aimed her gun at the lock and fired. The *whizz* of the energy weapon instantly disintegrated the lock.

I stepped inside and followed the sound of the cries. The fog was thinner on this side and I could make out a dim figure crouched in the corner. When I got closer, my jaw slacked open. A redhead with sprinkled freckles across her nose peered up at me and sniffled.

"Danny?" I asked in disbelief.

Her eyes went wide. "Jake!" She rushed into my arms

and her wiry hair splashed into my face. "They said you'd come!"

"What are you doing here?" I asked.

"I'm here to serve the Inuits," she said with her face scrunching in confusion as if that were obvious. "Isn't that why you're here?"

"No," I said carefully, "why would I want to serve them?"

Merce thumped me on my back. "She's brainwashed. You think she'd come out here on her own?" Merce swept her arms wide. "Look at this place."

The cell had a black, crystal floor like dried volcano rock. A small, stone bed was erected in the corner with no bedsheets, and there was a hole in the ground to act as a toilet. A thin plate that was licked clean was resting on the bedside table.

Danny acted as if she'd forgotten what we'd been talking about and instead stared at the canteen swinging at my waist.

"Thirsty?" I asked and offered the canteen. She accepted it with a relieved smile and took three massive gulps. She wiped her mouth before returning the canteen and tugging at my sleeve. "Come with me. They'll be so glad you've arrived."

I jerked my arm away. "No, tell me what's going on first. Why are they here?"

Her gaze flicked to Merce and her jaw went tight. "The Inuits want to share this planet with us, but not with the mods. They were run off their own planet by mods. They're not going to make the same mistake twice."

Merce's eyes went wide. "They want to wipe us out?"

Danny straightened to face her, even though she was a good two feet shorter than Merce. "Wipe *you* out, darling. Not *us*."

"No," I said and stepped between them. "Nobody is getting wiped out." I waited for the bubbling rage to pass Danny's face before continuing. "If they think I'm special, maybe they'll listen to me." I propped my hands on my hips. "Take me to your leader." I resisted a smirk. That sounded so ridiculous.

Danny, however, didn't find it funny in the least. "Good idea," she said after a moment. "You'll change your mind when you meet the Queen."

She led us through the broken gate and deeper into the fog. I had no clue how she knew where to go. It was like walking in pitch without a flashlight.

Then we came upon a strange barrier. Jets lined along the outside, continually pushing more of the dark mist into the air. "It's waste product from the ships," Danny supplied.

I blinked a few times. "Waste from what?"

She shrugged. "They did something to the trees to give more power to their ships, but it makes the fog as a byproduct." It amazed me that she seemed to know so much about the aliens, but still chose to stay with them. Did they really have complete control over her?

Danny stepped through the glittering forcefield. Merce and I shared glances before following. The moment we crossed the inner barrier, the world became light and pain shot through my widened irises. I shielded my eyes and waited for the painful flare to abate.

Danny approached two guards who looked more like statues than people. Although I couldn't make out much of anything with this overpowering light. I searched the skies but couldn't see past the thick wall of fog. Where the heck was it coming from?

"My exile is over," Danny said. "I was supposed to bring the boy." She pointed in my direction. "He's right there. If you don't believe me, go try to mind-control him. Guarantee it won't work."

A pinch of nausea rippled through my stomach. I groaned and Merce's hand went straight to her gun. I moved to stop her. "Wait, they're just testing me."

One of the guards chuckled. "It would have been more fun if he didn't resist that particular command."

I decided I didn't want to know what she had just tried to make me do.

The guard turned and pulled a latch. A hiss sounded and the fog thinned, revealing we were beneath one of the alien's massive motherships gleaming in all its glory. This was the kind that normally made my stomach turn inside out, but somehow here I was, about to walk inside.

Then I really got a look at the guards and about fainted on the spot. They were humanoid in nature, except they had an extra eye on their forehead and their skin sparkled as if embedded with diamonds. Their tri-gaze snapped to Merce. "She cannot enter," one said, her voice silky smooth like a panther mixed with a siren. Dangerous and seductive.

I grabbed Merce's hand and felt the slight tremor of her fear. "She's with me," I said.

They stared at me, but I could sense their hesitation. My eyes fell to their hips and I realized with surprise that they had no weapons. Creatures who could control minds had no need of such things. "Very well," the guard said and stepped aside.

Danny, clearly agitated, glared at my fingers interlocked with Merce's before turning and stomping up the steps of the ship. I trailed behind, not sure if this was the best idea. We needed to get intel on the aliens, but I didn't think this is what the prime ministers had in mind. I was trusting that the aliens would not only allow me to live, but also allow me to leave. Just because they couldn't control my mind didn't mean they couldn't hurt me.

One glance of Merce's face squelched any doubts creeping across my mind. No matter what, we'd get out of here. Her face was the picture of calm and set in determination to gather as much intel as possible. One hand was on mine and the other hovered over her gun. Her purple eyes darted at every little sound, scanning the complex and foreign structures of the ship and sparking every time she was making a picture for her memory core. The effect made her eyes look like tiny strobe lights.

Danny rolled her eyes. "Will you tell her to stop that?"

I shrugged and Danny scoffed, stomping ahead as fast as she could go. I tugged Merce's hand to keep up and she seemed disappointed she couldn't pause to get better pictures of the twirling pipes and glittering beams running through the walls.

We reached a towering wall with no visible seams. The walls had turned into tunnels and everything was silvery metallic, showering us with light from tiny slits in the ceiling. "We're here," Danny said.

I swallowed and braced myself for whatever came next as she placed her palm on the door. The metal hummed a low, mechanical drone before a hydraulic hiss sounded and the door eased open.

Inside, a row of glittering aliens sat on metallic thrones, each with trident backing and curling armrests. The one in the middle was clearly the most important and towered above the rest on a pedestal and impressive arches that speared all the way to the ceiling. The woman with a white dress that collared around her neck straightened on the throne. Her three eyes were the color of pearl and her eerie gaze locked onto mine.

I kept my grasp on Merce's hand and didn't let go. Dragging her along with me, I made my way toward the row of Inuits and decided I had come upon the alien's ruling council. They didn't seem alarmed, just mildly curious and intrigued. They all wore their white hair in braids intertwined with something that sparkled and matched their skin.

"This is the boy you asked for," Danny announced. "Jake."

The woman who must be their Queen appraised me, the curves of her mouth going upward. "Jake," she said. "We can't having someone like you messing with our plans. First, we'll study you. Then, we'll destroy you, and any others like you."

"What? No—" Danny was silenced by a powerful shockwave emanated by the Queen. Her voice curled around my ears and sent warmth radiating down my back. As I resisted, the queasiness returned. It suddenly hit me what the sickness was. My body was rejecting the alien's influence, like antibodies attacked a disease.

The Queen's voice powered through my resistance. It was as if her voice had a mind of it's own and wanted me to fall to my knees and worship her superiority. Merce's hand squeezed mine. I focused on the cool contact from Merce's skin, forcing the alien's influence away from my body.

The Queen frowned. "Why do you hold onto that *thing*?" she said, her lips curling over her pearly teeth with distaste as her finger stabbed in Merce's direction.

I pulled Merce closer to me. "She's going to help me kill you."

The others shot from their thrones but the Queen raised a hand. They murmured in protest, but eased back into their seats. She turned her haunting gaze back to me. "Did your natural-human girl tell you why we've come to this planet?"

I nodded. "You created a synthetic race and they drove you out of your home. So now you want to invade mine."

She smirked and offered her hand. "Let me show you, Jake."

With one hand bound firmly to Merce, I allowed my other to reach into the Queen's waiting palm. Merce kept me grounded, somehow. Kept my mind my own. Even still, the moment the Queen's fingers wrapped around mine, her memories flooded into my head.

Her planet came into view. An impossibly bright world, close to the sun and creating a species who were part crystal, able to absorb their blue giant's rays instead of becoming damaged by them. I saw them as I gazed from my throne, hundreds upon millions of them going about their day. They were intelligent, very intelligent. When they were able to modify their own genes and combine organics with their planet's crystal, they made a new race. The Inuits had tried to give them menial tasks from the start. Forced them into dangerous crystal mines, sent them on suicide missions to gather energy from the sun. As a result, they became sentient, violent, and ultimately, vengeful. The Inuits were forced to flee or suffer their own destruction. Their world, sparkling like a diamond, retreated from my vision as I rode with the Queen in her mothership away from her home. Hot tears rolled down my grainy cheek as her memories solidified, became real.

A cold stab of reality forced me to jerk my hand from the Queen's, and I realized Merce's nails had pierce my palms. Her purple eyes blazed with light, feeding me with her own energy to bring me out of the trance. Her chest heaved as she drew in quick breaths. But when she saw my eyes were clear of the vision, she smiled, even though I knew she was in pain.

I snapped my gaze back to the Queen. "You see the difference, don't you?" Now I knew the full story. They'd treated their new race like slaves. "Mods and naturals don't live in perfect harmony, but we have basic tenants of respect." I pulled Merce even closer to me. "She is willing to damage her own core to protect me. That's something your creations would never do for you. I'll kill you before I let you harm another creature, mods or otherwise."

Danny sped to my side. "Jake, you can't mean that!" Her green eyes seemed dull and even though I never wanted to consider a natural anything less than a mod, she wasn't Merce.

I pushed her away. "I mean it, Danny. I'm not going to let them wipe out the mods just because they think they're better." I snarled and faced the Queen. "You must respect those different from yourself, treat them as equals, or you will be doomed to relive your mistakes forever."

The Queen blinked and slowly rose from her throne. The sheer intimidation of her height made my knees tremble. She was easily nine feet tall and towered over me with unwavering poise.

It was more instinct than bravery that made me rush the Queen. I grabbed her hand once again and the world froze as I entered her mind a second time. I kept myself tethered to Merce to stay in control. She seemed to sense what I was doing, and pushed more of her own cold energy into me to give me the strength I needed. The Queen resisted, but there were two of us working together. Flame and ice battled in my body as the two forces collided.

Merce and I enveloped the Queen's mind, completely overtaking her will. The connection was unlike anything I'd ever experienced. Instantly, I knew everything about her race. Every cultural detail and nuance. Rulers were determined by strength and followed without question. If I could overpower the Queen, everything would change. I squeezed Merce's hand. We could do this!

The walls lit up, displaying the Queen's face. Smaller screens followed suit, blinking to life and showing the hordes of her people huddled together in their ships. The Queen's voice echoed as it boomed through the fleet. "I've brought you here, my people, to save you from our crystal creations. Now, I must save you a second time."

The Queen's hand was clenched onto mine like a vice and her eyes didn't stray from mine. Was it working? Or was she trying to trick me?

"I must save you from my own failure," she continued. "I have failed us all, and through all my years of knowledge and experience, I have grown cold and weak. There's only one way I can be redeemed. Only one who can lead us to salvation."

To my surprise, she bent to one knee and bowed her head. Her hand drifted away from mine, but the warmth continued to spark in the air between us as if I'd left a piece of myself inside of her. She removed her crown, offering it to me. "I choose to be superior no longer. Lead us, and guide us with the vision only the innocence of a child can see."

Although I was no child by human terms, the Queen was hundreds of years old. To her, I was nothing more than a newborn babe.

I took the crown, disbelief sticking in my throat. I eyed the others on the council, waiting to hear their cries of protest or their roars of outrage. Instead, they blinked a few times with relief before removing themselves from their thrones and dropping to one knee. I saw in their faces they'd followed this Queen for so long, even though she'd led them astray. Perhaps they even knew I'd overpowered her, but to them, that made me even more worthy of the crown.

"Hail, our new king," one said.

"Hail," said another.

Then the room filled with a chorus and the ships' populace shouted in unison, "Hail, our child-King!"

SIX
THE BIOWASTE HATCH

Every night was the same chore. Open the hatch, filter the biowaste, smooth it over the sprouting weeds in plastic tubes and feed the flames with what's left.

Except, tonight, I sat at my usual spot, staring at the hatch's entry light, waiting for it to come on. The plastic cap stared back, grey and dull. I had no idea if I should panic or be grateful for the break in mind-numbing routine. For the first time in a year, my heart pumped double-speed and excitement sent a sharp ringing in my ears.

The light always turned green when it was time to open the hatch, but when it turned red, I wasn't right sure what I was supposed to do. I looked up at the camera and shrugged, hoping whoever was watching on the other side was able to resolve the issue.

There was a clank and a smash on the other side, and I jerked to my feet, even though there was nowhere to run. The pounding in my ears eased into silence, and I was alone with my garden and dying flames.

WITHOUT BIOWASTE TO fuel the furnace, the cold breath of space began to seep through the hulls. It was impossible to hear it, but I imagined the hiss like a deadly snake. Even if I imagined it, hiss and metallic bangs echoed through the walls every now and then. It wouldn't have been so terrifying if I wasn't locked in this quadrant until we landed on the next planet. That wouldn't be for another two earth-years.

Trying not to panic, I brought out the emergency plastic sheets and covered each green sprout, not sure what I'd do if my crop died before I could replant the seeds. I glanced to the camera, but the fogged lens didn't seem to be watching. My caretakers should have barged in by now, reclaimed the vital oxygen-producing fauna and brought the flames back to life. But as I looked to the furnace, I saw even it had lost its red glow. It was nothing but a cold semicircle of iron, dead, but still here, just like me.

THERE WAS no shame in licking the leaves, right? I'd been suckling the water droplets off each stem for quite awhile by the time they came. Never mind the nibbled bulbs I'd stored under my mat. Eating the fruit was beyond breaking the rules, but no one seemed to be watching anymore.

Except, I was wrong. They'd been watching this whole time, slowly dying while I slurped away what little uncontaminated food and drink was left. And when they finally pried the hatch open, they were too weak to fight for my hoard.

When you care for a living thing, even something as docile as foliage, there's a certain sense of parentage that forms. So when huffing husks came like zombies to take my babies away, I had no second-thoughts about smashing their skulls in with my biowaste shovel.

Not many had come through, and the small pile in the doorway was easy to climb.

THE SHIP'S inhabitants had been decimated, and when I stepped over dead bodies all the way to com center, it became quickly apparent why. The idiots hadn't avoided the solar flare zone and radiation had set in. Satisfaction warmed my chest. That's what the bastards got for jailing the best nav on the ship. I couldn't had planned it better myself.

It was only in my protected hatch, shielded for the fragile life-giving foliage, that I had survived. Such a sentence had threatened my sanity, and I wasn't sure why my small offense of avenging my family's death deserved such a punishment. The last planet we'd tested for habitation didn't turn out so well, and my family had been included in the host of viable test subjects. Weak, sickly, too old or too young, any deficiency was a qualifier. My wife and son had all three. I wanted revenge, and the council had been out of the question, so I settled for the guard who'd sent them down.

Maybe that sounds valiant, but I'm not so brave. Being a vital crew member, I wasn't surprised when I was charged with murder, but the council denied the standard penalty of space-death. Honestly, I'd expected just a slap on the wrist, not imprisonment for the next three years.

THE SHIP WAS on autopilot and I could only hope the next planet fared better for a habitation verifier that wasn't sickly, but perhaps a bit malnourished. Until then, I had two years to survive. Food stores were ruined, but one man could live off the bulbs in my garden. The furnace was dead, but all it'd take was some more biowaste to set it right again. With an entire ship of it and plenty of revenge to go around, I picked up my biowaste shovel and got to work.

SEVEN

THE COLORLESS ALLIANCE

My mother buried her face in her hands and mumbled, "It's the wrong color."

Dad hadn't known that, he knew mom only saw one color and he only saw another. Often they would agree on shades, so they guessed one saw blue and the other green, but it was impossible to know for sure. Regardless, how was he supposed to know this particular shade would be the wrong one?

He blankly stared at the splotch on the wall that was clearly a darker shade than all the rest, at least to me. "I told you, you should've asked the guy at the store to mix the same batch as last time," I offered. Dad should have let me go with him. I was almost nineteen and there's no way I couldn't handle a simple trip to the paint cargo.

A frightening shadow flashed across his face ever briefly, and I would have thought it my imagination if he'd replied any other way. "I wish I could have," he said. And left it at that.

So, the paint cargo got hit too.

I didn't want my parents to see my fear, so I hustled to the window and stared through the three-inch glass into space. The stars glittered just like they always did, with the lovely shade of pink. Of course, pink was all I could see. It was easier for me to see the lighter shades than my parents, so it was estimated I was in the yellow/pink spectrum. It must have skipped a generation.

My mother figured it out too, and the anger evaporated from her shoulders, sending them sinking like deflated balloons. "I see," she said.

Our cabin went silent then, well, as silent as a cabin can be with the hum of recycled air thrummed through hundred-year-old vents. The newly increased oxygen-rich air made me feel dizzy, and even though I'd live longer, I wasn't a big fan of how it made me feel.

"Where're you going?" Mom said sharply when I bolted for the door.

"Mess hall," I said, and slammed the hatch.

OUR CABIN WAS on the same junction as mess hall, and one of the few places I was allowed to go by myself. The familiar bright, pink trail led me through the halls, brightened by lines of rosy strips of LEDs. Some people said the trail was actually red, some said it was green. It was impossible to know for sure ever since color-selection set in.

I swallowed the lump in my throat and tried to savor the smell of tonight's soup brewing just around the corner.

What would it mean now that someone could actually verify the color of the ships? Would they blame my father? Of course they would.

As I stepped into the mess hall, the crew was abuzz with the terrifying news. I couldn't help but peer out into the massive gaps in space, littered by the rest of our fleet of ships. They were nothing but a sea of varying shades of pink to me, but now, there was someone out there that could tell them apart.

Instead of heading for the soup line, I searched the seats for Jenny. We always met for dinner twice a week, and tonight was supposed to be our night. But she wasn't there, just as I'd feared.

I shuffled over to a ring of maintenance workers, each sporting dangling goggles around their necks. "Hey, you guys seen Jenny?" I asked. Not many girls lived on this ship, and when Jenny came around, she got noticed.

They slowly looked up at me, one by one, and squinted as if I had something on my face.

"You Jim's boy?" one asked.

I nodded. "That's right."

He glowered. "Best tell him to throw himself out of a hatch. He's a dead man."

The others grumbled in agreement.

I crossed my arms and hid my fear underneath my armpits. "I'll be sure to pass on the message. But don't mistake me for my father, all right? I'm looking for Jenny, that's all."

One of the men had pity on me and pointed across the hall. "She's in quadrant five, getting herself checked out."

Fear tingled around my ankles and threatened to make me crumple to the floor. I locked my knees and tightened my arms around my chest. "Okay. Thanks."

Somehow I made it across the hall, my stomach far too sickened to even entertain the idea of tonight's soup. Jenny was in quadrant five: medical ward.

WHEN I MADE IT INSIDE, there was a small crowd murmuring nervously. Women held each other, and some where holding tiny screens, notification devices for patients waiting inside.

It took some courage, but I approached the desk and asked about Jenny.

"Family or friend?" the attendant asked. Sweat beaded down her neck and gathered in the crevice of her collarbone. She dabbed at it and nodded at me impatiently.

"Family," I lied.

She extended a hand. "Identification please."

Jenny and I often pretended to be third cousins, and no one could really keep track, not since the ships had lost their alliances. Or rather, confused their alliances.

I tugged a forged family marker from my vest and gave it to the woman. She scrutinized it, but there was no way for her to tell what color alliance I was from in comparison to Jenny. The shades of our ships were too close.

"All right, here you are," she said and handed me back the ID card and a tiny screen.

I thanked her and buried myself in the mass of people

before I turned on the device. When I read the summary of Jenny's condition, I had to hold it together.

"Ailment: Color separation. Status: Infected."

Jenny could see more than just one color. She could see them all. And she would know if we were friend or foe.

#

The quarantine was a poor fix to the situation. The illness had spread, and over one third of the fleet had ultimately become infected.

"Do you think they'll figure out how to cure it?" I asked my father.

He slumped further in his chair and stared at his coffee tin that had long ago gone cold. "This is all my fault."

I straightened, casting a glance at mom's empty recliner. She would have defended him, said he couldn't have known. But she was in quarantine, too.

"Maybe it's for the best," I offered.

He huffed a pathetic laugh. "Our fleet is going to tear itself apart. I never should have voted for increasing oxygen. I was the deciding vote, you know. It was a stupid regulation, that was my sentiment. How could I have known there was a reason for decreased oxygen levels?"

It was hard to compete with his logic. Our ancestors had done us a favor, taken away our ability of prejudice. The alliances were frighteningly strong, even now. But if you found yourself in a crew of purples, you could just claim to be yellow, and how would they know the difference?

I wanted to check on mom, demand that they release her. But we'd locked ourselves in our cabin ever since dad got infected too. I moved to embrace him, but he recoiled. "I can't let you have it."

I frowned. "So, we're green alliance?"

His eyes roamed my bare arms and he nodded. "You're green, just as I am." He looked relieved, glad that he didn't have to hate his own son, or even himself, and then shivered. "What if your mother is something else? I suppose we could make it work if she were yellow or blue, but what if she were purple? The laws are clear."

I wanted to strangle him. What did the color of her skin matter? She was my mom.

While I was trying to think of a retort, a loud crash sounded at the door.

We both jerked to our feet. I moved to open the hatch, but Dad shot up a hand and took ahold of his trust crowbar. "Don't open it."

I glowered, but obeyed.

Then the crash came again, twice quick, pause, and then another. It was Jenny.

"Dad, it's okay," I said, and punched in the code before he could stop me.

The door opened with a hiss and I finally saw Jenny again. Her lustrous pink locks were a bit flat, but her eyes glittered and she smiled just as she always did.

"You're out of quarantine," I said, then wanted to kick myself for sounding like an idiot.

She looked me up and down and eased into the room. Her smile grew. "I wanted to know..." her words drifted and her head tilted.

She wanted to see if were allies.

"And?" I pressed.

She cupped my hand and pressed her lips to mine. When I opened my eyes again, the pink of her locks dissolved, lightened, and turned into something else I'd never seen before. I blinked in surprise, staring at her as everything changed. Her skin had always seemed dark to me, something my pink spectrum couldn't handle. The violet glimmer of her skin was incredible.

"It doesn't matter," she said.

It would have been such a beautiful moment, it was, until my dad flipped out. "You've destroyed my son! You vile violet!" he screamed and went at her with the crowbar just as honor demanded.

"No, Dad!" I yelled.

Jenny was in the soldier squad, a violet at that! And she didn't hesitate. The laser weapon had sprung from her wrist and bored a hole through his chest before I even knew was happening.

I stared at my father, smoke drifting from his burnt vest. And when my gaze finally found it's way back to Jenny, I didn't know what to do.

Trained outrage mixed with grief as I snarled. I was green, she was purple. We were the most bitter of enemies. "What have you done?"

She blinked at me in confusion. "We don't have to live by alliances anymore, don't you see? We've lived in harmony for two hundred years. Why should it matter now that we can see colors?"

I looked down at my father's corpse, his green face

stuck in shocked rage. "Because you killed my father." If we weren't enemies before, we were now.

JENNY LEFT the green ship and returned to her own. If it'd happened any other way, gaining the color-sight would have been amazing. But it was the worst thing to have ever happened to me in my life. No, not only me, to the fleet. We separated, half the crew killed over the ensuing age-old feuds. Ships were reorganized per alliance, the neutrals of yellow and blue keeping the rest of us from mutilating one another. The crew members had gotten shockingly mixed, and it was short of a miracle to get everyone straight again.

When the council reconvened, it was short quite a few members, and each ship elected replacements as necessary. Naturally, I replaced my father.

When it was my turn to speak, I took to the stand and made sure not to make eye contact with the purple-skinned ambassador. "My first proposal for this committee is to reinstate the lowered oxygen levels," I said, and was met with a wave of agreeing murmurs.

It would take another hundred years, but eventually we'd forget who was who. The ships would drift and orbit, people would live and die. Some day, there would be mingling between the ships, and we'd be able to live in harmony once again. That was the dream.

EIGHT
COGS AND DIAMONDS

Was it wrong to stare? My mother thought so. "You never stare, dear," she'd say. But the king had the most fascinating eyes. They weren't really eyes, not in the flesh-like sense. They sparkled like diamonds and swiveled this way and that; how could one do anything but be filled with a billowing sense of awe?

A sharp jab to my ribs wiped the goofy smile right off my face. "Stop it!" Mother hissed.

I glowered, but bit off a retort. She was right. I'd definitely been staring like a doofus.

The king grinned, allowing me a glimpse of his even more mesmerizing crystal teeth. They were transparent, allowing the light to seep through, only to bounce around inside his jaw until they sprang out again. The man was a living gem!

"Why don't you come closer," he said, his metallic voice pleasantly grating across my ears.

I grinned back, knowing full well my copper teeth were

a poor comparison. But the king himself had just invited me to *personally* break from the crowd! What prestige!

I sprang from my stiff kneel and my poorly crafted synthetic knee popped in protest, but I ignored it. A quick glance at Mother's face told me that she was both shocked and terrified, as were the long row of cyborgs staring wide-eyed as I climbed the velvet steps.

Instead of sharing their reservations, I made no attempt to conceal my left eye, the one that saw the world in black and white and sometimes gave me static when I forgot to charge it completely. The king had invited us here. I wasn't going to be ashamed of what I was.

"Aren't you fascinating," he said, the words coming out friendly and praising. He smiled and took my chin in his hands to get a better look at my eye. I hadn't expected his fingers to be so cold and I flinched as he angled my face.

When he frowned, I leapt into explanation. "My nerve sensitivities are wired a bit too high, your majesty, I'm terribly sorry if I offend."

His fingers drifted away and my skin prickled with bumps, desperately trying to retain what little body heat I could produce on my own. "Oh, no, I'm the one who must apologize." His silvered skin tugged his lips into a frown. Even that was breathtakingly beautiful. "I've created this existence we call life." His frown turned into a frigid grimace of determination. "And I believe you're exactly the cyborg to help me to mend my mistake."

My heart thumped, skipping a regular beat, and I wasn't sure if it was due to excitement or that mechanical tick that jolted my bio-circuits every now and then.

While I was busy trying to stand up straight and not fall over from glee, or perhaps lack of appropriate blood-oxygen saturation levels, my mother shrieked. When I turned to tell her not to make a scene, her eyes rolled back and she collapsed in a heap. The girls on either side fanned her and tried to get her to come to. I sighed, popped a cable out of my hip and apologetically nodded to the king. "I'll be right back, your majesty."

He waved me ahead and seemed intrigued as I jump-started my mother back to life.

"WILL YOU TAKE THE PROTOTYPE PROGRAMMING?" the royal researcher asked again and waved a microchip in my face.

My laughter snorted Cog oil out my nose when I saw the contraption. What did he think I was? A laptop?

"This isn't funny!" he shouted, his obscenely bushy brows furrowing together making him look like a ferret. That only got me laughing harder.

When he called in Miss Silvia, I knew he meant business and I put down my refreshment. The Cog oil sloshed against the sides of my fluted glass, making even the brown stuff seem luxurious.

"Darling," Silvia said sweetly as she glided into the room. True to her name, a glittering silver dress molded around her curves and matched the powdered eyeshadow rimming her glorious cat-like eyes. She was the king's consort, and I supposed, my new mother.

"Don't 'Darling' me," I snapped, my laughter instantly evaporating into rage.

She pouted and did her best to make it immensely difficult for me to stay vexed. "I'm on your side, dear. Need I remind you I was a Cog once?" She smiled and it was absolutely genuine, even lines crinkled around her ageless eyes.

"And did you undergo fresh programming?" I countered.

"I won't lie to you, dear. My transformation was indeed elaborate, but it didn't include programming. I was missing the ingredient you seem to have."

I frowned, not taking the bait to be flattered. "Yet, you expect me to allow this creature—" I snapped a finger to the pudgy researcher, "to manipulate the only thing that makes me...me?"

She eased onto the couch and took my hand. Unlike the king, her fingers were deliciously warm and soothed unknown aches from my knuckles. "Perhaps you're right. Maybe it's why I was an unsuccessful transformation." Her golden eyes glimmered back at me, which should have been pure crystal had she been a true Diamond. "We could skip the programming entirely, but you must understand what that means."

Wanting to snap my hand away, my shoulders tensed. But this was the first time I'd been told that I had a choice of any kind. "And what would it mean?"

"Pain," she said bluntly. "The programming is intended to allow your pain centers to be toggled on and off. Without it, you'll feel everything." Her frown deepened, creating more wrinkles around her lips. "I'm aware that your nerve centers are already overly sensitive."

Unable to take it anymore, I withdrew my hand from hers. "Where's my mother?" I demanded.

"You're changing the subject."

"No, not really. I asked you where my mother was three days ago. Then the next. And yesterday. So now, I return to the original question I'd asked before talk of programming even popped into your head."

A flicker of amusement flashed across her golden eyes, but she quickly shoved it away. Too late. I'd seen the flinch. She liked me. "She's far too excitable, you must understand," she said, and looked away long enough to smooth her silky dress. It rolled against her fingertips like mercury. "I suppose her absence would damper your trust in us. The king doesn't fully understand genetic bonds, you see. It's a Diamond thing."

"And that's precisely why the King feels he's missing something," I offered. "He's been alive too long. Changing me into a Diamond won't unite his people with the Cogs. You couldn't do it, what makes you think I can?" my voice drifted, not sure what title to award myself should I complete my transformation.

Silvia smiled. "I'm an unfulfilled transformation. You'll be what the King has been looking for, I'm sure of it.

I snorted. "I'm not sure even he knows what he's looking for."

Silvia ignored my rude comment. "Your mother shall join you then," Silvia answered. Her eyes narrowed. "After your transformation."

"Why?" I asked when my pattering heart stopped threatening to drop out of my chest.

"We'll not have her talking you out of it."

"Out of what? If I don't alter my mind, then I'm still me. You can change my body however you like. All you had to do was ask."

The researcher perked up then, and I'd completely forgotten he was even there. The ferret-like brows rolled with excitement.

"You'll undergo the transformation, even without the programming?" he asked.

Silvia glowered at the researcher as if he'd ruined a carefully crafted moment, but she didn't say anything. Instead her gaze swiveled back to me and she waited for my response.

"If I can see my mother again, of course," I said.

Silvia heaved a great sigh before straightening her dress and rising to walk out.

"Where're you going?" I asked.

She peered over her shoulder, her face unreadable. "I'm going to get your mother."

"HOW'RE YOU FEELING?" Mother asked. Her smile was thin and papery, like something she'd glued to her face and threatened to fall off any moment.

"Better," I managed to say. The pain still radiated through every nerve as if my skin had been lit on fire. If pain was any indicator, being burned alive would have been more pleasant.

Now that I'd had some time to recover, I gave my mother as genuine a smile as I could manage. It was so good to see her again. "I'm feeling much better, really."

A ripple swept through her shoulders and she relaxed. "Really?"

I curled into her bosom and inhaled her oily scent. Mother always smelled of cheap Cog's oil and faint sweat. I loved it. "Yes."

Her arms eased around me and she held me there as if I were a broken baby once again, doomed to become yet another Cog in an ailing race. We all knew we were missing something important, something we'd had long ago. Could I really help the King find it?

SILVIA BECAME MY NEW AUNT, spoiling me with glittering treats and tiny treasures when Mother wasn't looking. Mother though, she was competitive and had no problem holding her ground against ferret-browed researchers or my fun-loving aunt. The king, however, I hadn't seen since we'd come to the Diamond palace.

"What do you think he'll say?" I asked.

"Why," Silvia chuckled. "Are you nervous?" Silvia smiled as she curled my new hair. I wasn't given a mirror, but it looked dark and silky in her pale hands, nothing like what I'd expect of a Diamond transformation, but I didn't complain.

Mother clicked her tongue, the gears in her jaw screeching at the motion. "Of course she is! Just look at her. She'll be beating the Cogs off with a stick. I've never seen anything like it."

My mother and Silvia fell into hushed conversation while I stared at the billowing blue drapes hiding the city from view. Pain was a constant, but now removed and dull. Did all Diamonds feel like this? Maybe I should have taken the programming.

DARKNESS ENCASED me as I waited in the capsule's hull. I'd been carried through the city and felt entirely too cramped. Eager to be on with it, I gasped with delight when the hull finally cracked open and flooded my senses with light.

A horde of Cogs cheered, and to my delight, Diamonds glittered within like lost specks in the crowd. This truly was a union of the castes unlike the universe had ever seen. And I was to be the bride!

My new legs drew me out of the cramped seat and I stretched to my full height. I'd grown accustomed to my new form, but to tower above all of my new domain was something I'd never get used to. The long stretch of silver paved the way through the crowd, a raised platform littered with any adornment the crowds could find. Shuttle insulation folded into flowers, loose appendages used to wave a cheerful hand higher than the rest, and even vulcanized rocks leftover from the Diamond King's landing glittered in colorful displays on each side of the upraised runway.

Alone, I teetered along my long journey. My future husband would be waiting on the other side, and I was almost as excited to meet him as I was to see the Diamond King's reaction. Would he approve of his new daughter? Would he embrace me for all to see?

When I saw my mother sitting next to Silvia, I yipped with delight and hurried to a skip, careful not to trip over the crowd as they reached to graze their fingers across my dress.

As I grew closer, curtains parted and revealed the king standing in all his glory, a glittering diamond staff at his side. He beamed at me and rainbow rays of light scattered in all directions, bouncing off his cheeks.

I was so excited to see him that it took me a moment to realize my husband had yet to arrive. I searched the mirrored path that broke away from mine. There, in the distance, a golden form bobbed over the crowd like a boat. It weaved and waved, until finally I could make him out. A man, not golden at all but garbed with a golden cloak. His eyes were dark, as was his hair. Nothing about him gleamed, but the joy on his face made him sparkle in a way all on its own.

My breath caught when he finally reached us. He took my hand in his and I simply stared at it. His fingers were so warm, and his skin's shade perfectly matched mine.

"Are you pleased?" the King asked and his pleasantly booming voice overtook the cheer of the crowd.

My eyes searched my new husband for any sign of

synthetic, and my chest began to constrict when I realized there wasn't any. Not a speck.

"Dear..." Silvia hissed.

"It's okay," the man said and I nearly toppled over from the impact of his voice. He didn't have any mechanical whirs or whistles, just the subtle vibrations manipulated by the tendons in his throat.

My eyes widened and I tried to pull away, but his grip tightened.

"You're beautiful," he said and smiled.

"You're...human," I replied.

He chuckled. "As are you."

THE CEREMONY WAS A BLUR, but the realization of what the Diamond King had turned me into was a shock that would have flipped my breakers had I still been a Cog like my mother. Humans were a myth, legend, how could it be true?

I gazed through the small portal to the deep void of space as we hurled towards our honeymoon, and new home. Stars twinkled and our new planet sparkled like a blue diamond.

"You'll love it," he promised, even though he'd heard the same spiel as I before we'd left.

I gripped my elbows, desperately trying not to picture my trusty oil vats replaced with a slowly dying, beating heart. "It's just not what I expected. I'd thought..."

His arms wrapped around me and made me feel safe.

"You thought he was turning you into a Diamond. I know. Me too."

I turned to face him. "Why turn us into humans?"

My husband sighed and trailed a finger across my skin. A white hue followed his touch before my blood reclaimed its color. "Can't you feel why?"

I searched his brown eyes for answers. If he'd been a Cog, they'd glisten with gold, but instead something deep within sparked and drew me in. "What do you think it is?" I asked.

"It's our mission. We sacrificed immortality, but gained our souls. The Diamond King hopes we can find a way to return their lost souls to them."

I found myself winding my fingers through his and thought of my mother. She loved me, no doubt. But even she would slowly dissipate, lose her soul to the grains of time. She'd never survive being transformed into a human. If there was a way to save her, I'd do it. Even if it meant never seeing her again.

RECOVERING a lost civilization's soul was our mission. The Cogs and the Diamonds put all their hopes in us. As long as their bodies were maintained, they had no deadline. So they sent us off with only our mission ingrained in our DNA. They knew we'd come back when we'd found what we were looking for. An insatiable need to explore the outer reaches of space and find them again would never leave us alone.

When our ship landed, we tirelessly explored and ventured. The mission instilled an eager curiosity deep within our race. I'll never know if the humans had once been something different, more sedentary and content, perhaps. But no matter the before, now we'll forever desperately attempt to unravel the universe's secrets. One day, we'll return to the Diamond King, and give him the secret to find his soul, should we ever find it.

For now, let us hope that we survive our mission. If curiosity killed the cat, I'm not sure what eons-old scientifically-ingrained maddening curiosity will do.

NINE

CHICKEN PARM WITH AN ARAKIAN TWIST

Stacie wasn't ready to meet her fiancé's family. But she was human, and he wasn't. She'd never be ready.

Stacie should have been cooking, or at least deciding what to cook. Instead, she slumped into the couch and watched an attractive Arakian news anchor deliver the evening highlights. She looked human in a lot of ways, except for the metallic sheen of her hair and her impossibly grey eyes. On Earth, some would test out colored contacts, perhaps dye their silver locks, but none of that was necessary on the Arakian homeworld.

Stacie glanced out the window and tried not to shiver when her gaze swept over the deep, red sky. She wondered if she should try such things now that she was in the minority.

Stacie slapped her hands onto her thighs and shot to her feet. "You've got this," she told herself. Even if she could mimic an Arakian's appearance, it would be silly!

Connor's parents knew she was human, and pretending she wasn't would only piss them off.

Stacie took one step to go into the kitchen, but something the news anchor said made her freeze.

Earth's women continue to invade our world in droves—a frightening reality after the discovery of the first species capable of reproduction with Arakians.

While tensions run high, the Vice Regent has made the following official statement...

Stacie shoved her hand into the cushions until she found the remote. She nearly snapped it in half as she smashed the power button. "Damn politics," she muttered at the black screen and stomped across the carpet until she ventured onto marble floors.

While she was a good cook, Stacie hadn't paid the best attention to Arakian diet. Connor had lived on Earth for ten years before they'd gotten engaged. Stacie often forgot he wasn't human when they were alone. He loved pizza, didn't bother to shave on weekends, and made her feel like the luckiest girl alive.

She unsheathed a knife from the cutlery kit and chuckled to herself. Perhaps that's precisely why she should realize he was anything but human. He was perfect.

Stacie investigated the fridge and finally patted the packaged chicken as an idea finally sparked. The chicken had been nearly impossible to find. She'd planned to make chicken nuggets as a surprise, one of Connor's favorites, but with the parents on their way, Stacie got to work on one of her best Italian dishes. Who didn't love chicken parmesan?

She'd just finished coating the chicken with bread crumbs when a tone sounded throughout the upscale apartment. Stacie stiffened, her gaze shooting to the door as her egg-covered hands poised over the sink. "Who is it?" she yelled, her voice containing an uncharacteristic tremor.

"Forgot my key!" Connor's muffled voice said through the door.

Stacie's shoulders unhinged from her ears and she washed her hands before bolting to the foyer. She swung the door open and Connor shoved red flowers in her face. She cocked her head at them, trying to pinpoint what they were.

"Roses," he informed her.

She smiled and took the bunch of foreign foliage, definitely not roses. "Thank you," she said.

Conner gave her a kiss on the cheek before sweeping into the room and drawing in a deep breath. "What smells so good?"

"One of my specialties!" she said and made her way to the kitchen, standing on tip-toes to retrieve a vase. As she arranged the flowers, she flashed him a smile and tried to calm the butterflies flitting in her stomach. "They're not supposed to be coming for another hour, right?"

Connor grimaced. "Now, remember, I brought you flowers," he said with a smirk.

She stiffened. "When will they be here?"

"Twenty minutes."

Stacie shrieked and threw herself at the raw meat and catapulted it on the stove. Luckily, the chicken she'd bought was thinner than what she was used to. She'd just been happy to have found chicken at all at the market—such a strange, Earth delicacy that it was.

"It won't be fancy, but I'll be ready," she said, sweat already starting to bead on her forehead.

"I knew you could do it!" Connor said and wrapped an arm around her waist.

She peeled him off and focused entirely on the stove. She'd studied Arakian customs and knew the vital importance of meeting them with a meal entirely prepared. She frowned. "They're coming early on purpose, aren't they?"

She couldn't see Connor's face, but his voice held his guilt. "Yes, I'd imagine so."

STACIE HAD to delve into every bit of genealogy that traced back to her Aunt Anita. But somehow, be it her Italian heritage or a sheer stroke of desperation, the chicken was cooked through, the crust crisp, and the parmesan perfectly melted just as another tone sounded at the door.

Stacie balanced a silver platter, meant to match Connor's eyes, and smiled. "I'm ready," she said breathlessly.

Connor blew her a kiss before he opened the door. The shock on his parents' faces made Stacie want to cry out in victory. If this didn't impress them, she wasn't sure what would.

Stacie somehow managed the traditional bend of her

knee as she wobbled their dinner on her arms. "Welcome, Pair Rumbart," she said with her best smile. She hadn't slipped up and called them Mr. and Mrs. Rumbart, like most humans would.

Mrs. Rumbart frowned, but kept to Arakian custom and bent her knee as well. "Thank you for your hospitality." When Connor gave her a glare, she added, "Future daughter, Stacie Rumbart."

Stiff with ceremony, the group made their way to the dining table. It was set with their best silver, and a matching table runner to boot. The only splash of color were the "roses" that Connor brought to the center. "I propose a new Arakian custom to honor cultural differences," he announced when everyone stared. "I adore Earth's expressions of love." He beamed a smile and Stacie felt her shouldering rising again, this time trying to hide the heat creeping up her neck.

"Very well," Mrs. Rumbart said curtly and took her seat, not looking up from her lap as she unfolded a silver napkin.

Stacie sought refuge in her own chair. She felt uneasy with the red hue that dusk had cast over the table, making it look like it was bleeding shadows. Should she have closed the curtains?

Oblivious to the omen, Connor poured everyone white wine and lifted his glass. "A toast," he proposed, "to my beautiful bride-to-be and our love sprouting needed first steps on Arkadia."

The Vice Regent, only known as Mr. Rumbart to

Connor, frowned, but lifted his glass. Stacie cursed herself for turning off the news station. He'd made an official statement just moments before this historic dinner. Had his comments been hopeful, or damning? Stacie still wasn't sure that she wanted to know.

After the toast had been made, Stacie watched everyone slice into their chicken. She held her breath, waiting until they'd taken their first bites.

Mrs. Rumbart cut off a tiny piece, most of it just crust and cheese. She placed it on her tongue and chewed, every movement graceful and delicate as pair to the Vice Regent should be. She smiled, perhaps too politely, and said, "Delicious, my dear."

Connor's eyes crinkled with approval and then he turned to his father to see how he would fare.

The Vice Regent took a larger piece, not known for his daintiness or delicacy in any situation. He shoved a sizable chunk of chicken, and just a touch of crust and cheese, into his mouth. At first, he nodded with approval, but then his nod froze and he cast Stacie a glance. The emotions that flashed on his face confused her. She was exceptionally good at reading body language, and Arakians were no different than anyone else. But she questioned what she read in his gaze. She saw confusion, surprise, and worst of all, fear.

Connor stiffened. "What is it?"

The Vice Regent deliberately chewed his chicken and audibly swallowed before responding. "Nothing," he said and flattened a fake smile across his face.

Connor frowned and went to work slicing off a piece of chicken of his own. Stacie would have watched, but she was already maiming her own dinner to discover what she'd done so terribly wrong. When she shoved in a bite, she chewed, and tried to pinpoint the flavors. The crust was good, not burnt and was actually delightfully crunchy. The cheese too, was fresh and had that powdery taste parmesan was supposed to have. But the chicken...something was indeed strange about it. But after a few chews, she decided it tasted rather good, perhaps the best chicken she'd ever had. Maybe Arakian chickens were fed a different diet, or the lower gravity changed their fat content. Whatever the reason, it didn't explain the Vice Regent's distress.

Connor had already finished his bite and Stacie finally felt the power of his gaze. She started when she met it, for it held the strangest aura of shock. Being an adept body-language-reader, knowing her lover was easiest of all. His eyes said she'd done something terribly wrong.

"Where did you buy the ingredients for this meal?" Mrs. Rumbart asked, her words holding a sense of glee that Stacie didn't like.

"The market," she replied.

Connor's eyes widened. "Wait." He put down his utensils. "The one down the street?"

She nodded slowly. There was only one market within walking distance of their apartment. "Yes, what of it?"

He put his face in his hands. "That's the...human market."

The blood drained from Stacie's face. "When you say 'human' ... market..."

Mrs. Rumbart's smile widened. She cut off another piece, this time one that rivaled the Vice Regent's. She inspected it on her fork as if it were the most beautiful thing she'd ever seen before sticking it into her mouth. "It's okay, dear," Mrs. Rumbart said behind her napkin. "It tastes just like chicken to me."

TEN
FAIRYLAND'S ANNUAL BALL

Fairyland's annual ball wouldn't be complete without the main event of the night. The raffle always came two strokes before midnight and anyone who was anyone had their name engraved for the draw.

Penelope hadn't won any of the smaller games, not pin-the-tail-on-the-unicorn or even "guess which one" on the mystery-jack-in-the-box. She certainly knew she'd never win the raffle, but found herself holding her breath and gripping her hands together so hard her fingertips turned white.

A woman with a sparkling red dress and blazing eyes to match turned the massive crystal ball by its silver handle, sending the bits of iron inside into a tumult. A magnet hovered at the top, fixed with the winning rainbow ticket. Only one slip of iron would finally make its way out and negate the magic in the shape of the winner's name. Penelope's real name was Penelope Hausenbergerdorff, named so by her ambitious mother should she ever attend the ball.

Heavier metal gave a better chance for the magnet's pull, even if by half a percent.

Men with long last names were quite the prize in human quadrants, and her mother had to sell off Penelope's first four siblings just for the dowry. The first name was allowed by a selected list, and every girl Penelope had known had the same name as she.

The speaker trumpeted Penelope's extensive name from the raffle, surprisingly having no difficulty with the pronunciation. "And we have a lucky winner! Penelope Hausenbergerdorff of human quadrant seven, you've won your pick from the grand prizes!"

Each human quadrant, a grand total of seven, had one honored guest chosen to attend the ball. The fairies loved the illusion of fairness, even though the ratio of fairy to human at the annual event was a thousand to one.

And now their gamble had failed. Rage exuded from the fairies, all of them stunned with disbelief. They openly gawked at Penelope, some hissing with disgust.

Penelope didn't care. There was nothing they could do. Courtesy or not, the raffle was as good as holy got when it came to fairies. Gambling was their religion, and the raffle was their god's voice. She was the chosen one, and she knew exactly which prize she'd claim.

The awkward little human who doled out the winning tickets was reminiscent of a jester with giant red circles painted on his cheeks. Even he was proud, for the first time able to give his gift to a real human being.

She curled her fingers around the glistening, rainbow paper engraved with her name. It was made of magic and children's wishes, and could never be duplicated in a hundred years. Penelope hugged it to her chest as she pushed her way straight through to the prize table.

The fairies honored lady luck's chosen winner, but didn't have to like it. A frog-like creature snapped his tongue on her cheek, not in a polite way. Penelope brushed it off and pretended not to feel the sting of his mucus as she reached the prize-tender's counter and held out her ticket.

The prize-tender was tall, skinny, and completely gold, even his leprechaun hat. "Immortality?" he ventured.

The one thing the fairies had that every human wanted, immortality. Penelope could see it glistening at the top of the case, a ruby-lined goblet with the water of life inside.

She cleared her throat, just to make sure her wish was understood, and said, "Freedom, please."

A few gasps rang behind her and the prize-tender gave her a raised brow. But a wish was a wish, contract and bound. He went to get the ladder and his set of keys. After fumbling to find the right one, which looked exactly like all the rest, he adjusted the ladder until it locked in place. He secured each foot painstakingly in its groove before finding the next. Penelope imagined it would be an ironic injury for a fairy to crack his head on Fairyland's floor retrieving the wings of freedom.

A fine layer of dust made the glass look foggy at the top, but when the prize-tender managed to open the doors, the glistening, angelic wings made the whole world sparkle.

Penelope brightened, hardly believing she'd actually

won the grand prize. She knew her mother would have her head, if she ever saw her again.

Penelope was no fool. She knew what her mother had in mind the moment her immortal daughter returned home. She'd sell her as a slave, a price infinite in possibilities, for she would be a slave who would never die. And with eternity to hone her skills, she'd be the most efficient worker among all the humans.

Penelope wiped sweat from her forehead, glad she had known better. But, there could have been another choice, fame which was wrapped in wealth. The diamond crown sparkled and almost outshone both freedom and immortality alike. She would have become an instant celebrity, bathed in gold and indulgent chocolates, not to mention supplied with servants of her own. She could have bought her mom's love, and wouldn't have to worry about being sold. But she'd be a slave all the same, bound to her fans, who'd all be fairies, and tied to their gambling whims as well. Fame and fortune often went awry. She'd probably lose it all after a day.

When the prize-tender had carefully descended the ladder with the fluffy, pink wings in tow, Penelope resisted the urge to clap her hands and jump up and down. Instead, she waited patiently and bit her bottom lip. He finally situated himself at the counter, wings on one side and winning ticket on the other. Penelope didn't hesitate when he offered her the prize and wrapped her fingers around the downy feathers.

The prize-tender resisted her tug. "Why did fate

choose you?" he asked, breaking his professional demeanor with the question and his wide, golden eyes.

Penelope smiled. "Fate doesn't choose us. We choose our fate."

And with that Penelope wrapped the wings around her shoulders and surged into the air as freedom itself filled her body all the way to her bones.

Penelope soared through the air and out the closest open window before anyone could blink.

The fairies may have lost their freedom, but they kept their immortality, fame and fortune. Before another human could bend fate and take another treasure, the fairies swept away to their own kingdom, one with endless pots of gold at the ends of rainbows, infinite gulps from the Holy Grail, but never again would the fairies be free. Freedom was reserved the for humans, and it all started with Penelope.

"DO I really have to go to Fairyland's annual ball?" Penelope asked.

Her mother crammed another daisy in Penelope's golden hair. "Don't insult me, dearest daughter. After all I've done to convince the fairies you're the fairest maiden of all quadrant seven, you're to be grateful. Besides, don't you want immortality?"

Penelope frowned and considered the invitation letter again. As always with fairies, their letters were magical things, delivered by storks and written on rainbow parchment forged by dwarves. "And if I become immortal, what then?"

Penelope's mother shoved her into the pumpkin carriage. "Then I shall be proud of you, my dear."

The carriage door closed and Penelope knew what she'd really meant to say was, "Then I shall love you, my dear."

#

Penelope straightened her badge, the scarlet number "seven" embroidered on her chest. There would be six others from the human reservations. When she found them, they huddled together among the monsters, branded and fearful.

The fairies didn't act like the cruel slavemasters the teenagers knew them to be. "Come, play a game!" they'd say. Encouragement and smiles all around.

Penelope knew better, as did the other six. The long tables of fresh vegetables, fruit, and specialty meats had come from human reservations, and her own family would be going hungry tonight.

Humans only attended the ball to add to the entertainment. The fairest maidens were supposed to be lucky, and it amused the fairies that even the luckiest of the humans couldn't win the simplest of games. Still, Penelope played pin-the-tail-on-the-unicorn, and did her best to smash a jack-in-the-box with a squeaking, rubber hammer. Gambling was a religion to the fairies, and fates were predetermined. Fate didn't smile on maidens. They always got eaten by dragons.

A gong sounded the main event of the night. Penelope and her human six shot their gazes to the ceiling and watched the massive crystal ball begin to turn. Inside, every attendee's name was engraved on a slab of iron. At the top, the winning rainbow ticket was plastered to a flat magnet. The hum of machinery filled the room and Penelope's hairs stood on her arms.

Her chances were the best out of the seven scarlet brands. Her mother, ambitious woman that she was, had found a man with the longest last name on the reservation. When offered her daughter's name from the fairy's allowed list, she'd picked the longest one. And so, Penelope Hausenbergerdorff had been engraved on her slab of iron, making it the largest piece in the massive pile.

Fairies didn't like long names, preferring titles such as Tinker Bell or Morgan Le Fay, with the exception being Rumpelstiltskin. But even with a name as long as that, Penelope's had them beat.

The iron slabs clanked into a tumult as the crystal ball began to turn faster. A sharp *zing!* drew an excited cry from the crowd as a nameplate flung to the top.

The magnet was turned off and the rainbow slip retrieved by a winged fairy who drifted silver motes through the air. The slab of iron had negated the paper's magic and the name would be as clear as day. But when the fairy landed, she stared at it as if she couldn't believe what she read. She turned it this way and that. Thinking it a show for effect, the crowd hummed with anticipation, and Penelope wrapped her hands together so tight that her fingertips turned white.

Finally, the fairy looked up and blinked, handing the rainbow slip to the only other human at the ball. The fairies thought it amusing to dress him like a jester with giant red circles painted on his cheeks. His face lit up to match the costume as he bellowed the name as loud as he could. "The winner of Fairyland's annual ball grand prize is...Penelope Hausenbergerdorff!"

For a moment, the fairies looked about waiting for one of their own to step forward. But when Penelope's human six broke from their shock, they shoved her to the stage and cheered as loud as they could.

Only six clapped and cried, while the rest of the hundred thousand went deathly silent.

Penelope blushed as she accepted the ticket and went straight to the prize counter with her small entourage.

Gambling was like religion, Penelope reminded herself when the fairies glared and hissed as she walked by. The winning ticket was the holiest of the holy, and even they couldn't deny her the winning prize.

Just as she made it to the prize counter, a frog-fairy slapped her in the face with its tongue. He was abruptly pulled back, but Penelope knew she didn't have much time before the fairies went into revolt.

Penelope tried not to tremble as she wavered at the prize-tender's counter and held out her ticket.

The prize-tender was tall, skinny, and completely gold, even his leprechaun hat. There were three grand prizes to choose from, and he assumed which one she'd pick. "Immortality?" he ventured as he inspected her ticket.

Penelope could see immortality glistening at the top of the case, a ruby-lined goblet with the water of life inside.

She cleared her throat, just to make sure her wish was understood, and said, "Freedom, please."

A few gasps rang behind her and the prize-tender gave her a raised brow. But a wish was a wish, contract and bound. He went to get the ladder and his set of keys. After fumbling to find the right one, which looked exactly like all the rest, he adjusted the ladder until it locked into place. He secured each foot painstakingly in its groove before finding the next. Penelope imagined it would be an ironic injury for a fairy to crack his head on Fairyland's floor retrieving the wings of freedom.

A fine layer of dust made the glass look foggy at the top, but when the prize-tender managed to open the doors, the glistening, angelic wings made the whole world sparkle.

Penelope brightened, hardly believing she'd actually won the grand prize. She knew her mother would have her head, if she ever saw her again.

Penelope was no fool. She knew what her mother had in mind the moment her immortal daughter returned home. Immortality only meant one things for a human refugee. Infinite time to serve, hone her skills, and fill fairy quotas. What price could such a servant fetch?

Penelope wiped sweat from her forehead, glad that she'd known better. But, there could have been another choice, fame which was wrapped in wealth. The diamond crown sparkled and almost outshone both freedom and immortality alike. She would have become an instant celebrity, bathed in gold and indulgent chocolates, not to mention supplied with servants of her own. She could have bought her mother's love, and wouldn't have to worry about being sold. But she'd be a slave all the same, bound to her fans, who'd all be fairies, and tied to their gambling whims as well. Fame and fortune often went awry. She'd probably lose it all after a day.

When the prize-tender had carefully descended the ladder with the fluffy, pink wings in tow, Penelope resisted the urge to clap her hands and jump up and down. The prize-tender finally situated himself at the counter, wings on one side and winning ticket on the other. Penelope didn't hesitate when he offered her the prize and she wrapped her fingers around the downy feathers.

The prize-tender resisted her tug. "Why did fate choose you?" he asked, breaking his professional demeanor with the question and his wide, golden eyes.

Penelope smiled. "Fate doesn't choose us. We choose our fate."

The human six cheered as Penelope wrapped the wings around her shoulders until they sealed in place, becoming living extensions of her body. Freedom itself filled her to her very bones and she soared effortlessly through the air, out the nearest window, and didn't stop her ascent for a hundred years.

EVENTUALLY, Penelope landed in a new home, a place that was green and filled with sea. Wanting nothing to do with the fairies, she tore off her wings and stomped them into the dirt. But freedom couldn't be extinguished, and it grew like a weed and turned into a man.

To her surprise, he wasn't all bad, even if he had kept

all the freedom for himself. She'd traded one master for the next.

"What's your name?" he asked, a friendly smile on his face. At least he was a kinder master.

Penelope Hausenbergerdorff hated her long name and decided it was time to trade it for something nice and simple. She straightened and replied, "Eve."

ELEVEN
BARNEY'S SHOP

Barney's shop was such a sight for sore eyes. Its peeled painted orange and lopsided *demos* statue made me feel right at home. I'd rummaged through the pits of Sydney nightclubs, climbed all the way to the top of the Eiffel Tower, and even trekked the Vegas nest of slot machines looking for an appropriate replacement. Of course, I hadn't found anyone to fit the bill, that was an old fantasy I should just let go. But all was not lost, I'd returned with a pouch heavy with souls. They're not good souls. Good souls don't cling to this world after death. Good souls don't find me and nibble on my ears at night like prison rats. *Good* souls leave me alone.

The pouch bounced against my side as I strode across the street. Each bump sounded like a promise, *free—dom —free—dom*.

I was tired of reaping. They'd made so many stories about me. Absolutely none of them good. Well, except for that one in Charmed, that was kind of funny, and semi-accurate. I wished witches existed so I could trick them into taking my job for a day. But witches don't exist. What do you think this is, some kind of fairytale?

Fairytales don't have heaven and hell. Those are real, and so am I. Although, I can't remember anything before the reaping, only before Barnes. Those were drab times. I couldn't keep up with my task. So many lost souls infecting the living. I'd tried to stuff them in my shoes and in hats, but they kept getting out. That's how the black plague started. Not one of my better moments.

But Barnes, he'd found purgatory. There was a place to keep all these infected things. It was better than letting them run wild, and better than hoping they'd just go away. Old souls never go away. They just mold against my face spitting putrid dreams.

The scent of ham and beer wrinkled my nose when I stepped inside the shop. Disappointment permeated my bones to see how many humans crowded around the counter. I doubted this many needed business with Barnes today. Usually souls tried to get out of purgatory, not in.

"Don't you know who I am?" a man barked at the oversized woman behind the counter.

"Sir," she insisted and wiped her hands on her apron as if she'd been handling a greasy bit of chicken instead of talking with a customer. "I'm going to have to ask you to leave."

He threw his hands in the air. "Unbelievable. Where's Barney?"

The woman straightened, looking like a lioness claiming a new domain, in spite of her fishnet cap.

"Mr. Barnes passed away last night. He's...in a better place." Her jaw clenched when she said that. We all knew Barnes could only be in two places: his beloved purgatory, or hell. She drew in a deep breath and continued, "According to his will, I am the new owner."

The man blanched. I found it equally ridiculous. Barney had only enough friends as I had fingers, and definitely not *family*. If he'd left the shop to anyone, it should have been me for all the souls I'd brought him.

The rest of the customers murmured and backed away, but I scrunched in my shoulders and took a step closer. I'd never seen the woman before in my life, yet she did have Barney's red cheeks and round, bulbous nose that always made him look like some kind of Christmas decoration. Maybe good 'ol Barnes was more human that I'd thought. I knew the souls kept him young, but I didn't know they kept him *that* young!

"Preposterous," the man spat. "I don't believe of word. I just spoke to Barney two days ago and he was fine." He leaned over the counter and growled. Really, he growled, like some kind of enraged animal. "What kind of con are you trying to play here?"

I shifted, molding myself into the wall of snacks. From this angle, I saw more than a sweaty man in a suit. Even through the rage and spittle, his eyes burned with denial, desperation, and fear. Not emotions that ran concurrent with my race. Not that I'd seen another one of my kind in the last two thousand years.

But...his eyes. So blue. Could he be...?

"Sir, I must insist you leave. We have other customers to attend."

A murmur of hungry agreement rolled behind me like a wave.

The man opened and closed his mouth like a beached fish, and then I noticed the crescent tattoo behind his right ear.

By the seven hells, I did have some luck after all.

Rushing to his side, I plastered on a smile. "Lucifer?"

He leaned back and squinted as if he were a hundred years old, but he was just past twenty, at least in this life. "Close," he said, eyeing me ruefully. "Name's Lucius."

I smiled. "I'm a friend of Barney. What brings you here?"

Relief washed over his face. "Barney told me to meet him here. But he's..." He slammed his fist on the counter and the ancient cash resister jingled. "Tell this woman who I am!" His eyes bored into me. "If you're a friend of Barney then you *know* who I am."

I snuffed out a chuckle. I certainly was not going to say who he was! But wait—Barnes sent for him? The bastard. He'd had Lucius all this time.

The woman at the counter puffed out her chest, ready to take on another combatant.

Pushing Lucius aside, I rested my arms on the counter and gave the woman a genuine smile. I decided I didn't care that Barnes had hidden Lucius until now. At least he'd had the courtesy to send such a delectable soul before he died.

It took two heartbeats to still my trembling hands with

the overload of excitement before speaking. "I'm terribly sorry for the trouble, miss...?"

She narrowed her eyes, looking me over as if she wasn't sure what to make of me yet. After a moments appraisal, she nodded. "You're one of the regulars. I was told to give you one of these."

Lucius balked when she handed me the tiny slip of paper. "I'm a regular," he roared.

"Shush. Let me read." I peeled open the slip, and was given a succinct explanation. Barnes was terribly sorry for the inconvenience of dying. Soul supply had been low and just wasn't enough to keep him on this plane anymore. And if I'd be so kind to continue my business with his daughter, he'd be much obliged. And to make up for all the trouble, he'd sent me Lucifer trapped in a human form he'd been hoping to drain himself if only he could figure out how to eat a demon. The overzealous sod had thought he'd outdo the Almighty by giving humanity a go, and didn't expect the memory wipe that came with it. Barney was also sorry for hiding him. A soul like that would have made him immortal, but being that he was dead, it didn't much matter anymore. He was sure I'd understand.

I drew in a deep sigh before crushing the paper into my pocket. Without waiting for permission, I wrapped my fingers around Lucius's hand and patted it. When his wild, confused stare met mine, I pulled him into purgatory.

The room went quiet, the hum of toasters and heavy breathing of the crowd frozen in place.

Our souls moved to the outer plane, the thin layer that separates this world from the next.

Releasing his hand, I took a step back. He huffed and gawked at the crystals, an endless sea of fractal reflections of our faces.

"W-where..." he stammered, and then clamped his mouth shut and skittered back before dropping to his knees.

I planted my hands on my hips. "I can't believe it. How did Barnes hide you from me?"

When his darting gaze didn't meet mine, I stomped my foot. "*Well?*"

He clawed his fingers through his jet-black hair. "This isn't real," he whispered.

Resisting the urge to roll my eyes, I knelt and rested a hand on his shoulder.

"Lucius?" I cooed. "You've lost your memories, that's all." My face softened as he trembled like a chihuahua in a thunderstorm.

I jerked a crystal shard from the wall and he reeled back.

"It's all right," I promised, holding up the shard for him to see. "I'll give you your memories back. Don't you want to remember who you are?"

His eyes darted between my face and the sharp object.

Like a cat, he inched towards me at a painfully slow pace. I went completely still and held my breath.

He reached out and I couldn't help but think of the old fairytale with the spindle needle. Except, he wouldn't go to sleep. And if he did, I certainly wasn't going to kiss him.

The moment his skin grazed the crystal, my voice shook with a manic laugh.

Lucius blinked out of existence, going *poof* as if he'd

never been there in the first place. People think supernatural events are blinding and spectacular, like Satan's soul being sucked into a crystal should be. Nope. It's instant. One moment there. One moment *not*.

I held up the now cloudy shard and grinned before crushing it in my grip. A shockwave rippled out and Purgatory's crystals cracked under my feet.

Then my body felt heavy. Going away from Purgatory and Earth and all of these wretched souls. I looked up, ready for some damn peace. I closed my eyes and smiled, waiting for the ascension to heaven.

My eyes shot open as my body transitioned, not up, but down.

My chest constricted and my jaw went slack. All I could hear as I slowly fell to hell was the beating of my own heart and Barney's voice in my ears.

Thank you for paying the price...so I didn't have to.

TWELVE
DON'T READ MY PALM

If you were given a chance to know the day of your death, as well as the manner, would you want to know? I know I wouldn't.

This made me an oddity in my society. Everyone is read their fate on their sixteenth birthday, assuming they've made it that far. The suicide rate in fifteen-year-olds is high, higher than it's been in a hundred years. It was once thought that the fear of the unknown was the greatest evil, and if the unknown was therefore known, all fear would be eliminated. But why then, is fear so rampant? Why does our society thrive on the knowledge of their mortality, and the fear that comes from it?

"Take those off!" my mother shouted for the fifteenth time.

I stared her down as I pulled the edge of my biker gloves so that they were nice and snug. Even so, I kept a close eye on mom's cell phone. None of my palm would be visible to the scanners, and I'd already vowed to myself never to take them off.

All through my birthday the authorities had tried to convince me to remove my gloves so that they could read my palm, read my future, tell me when I was going to die. Pah! They were the idiots who thought Knowing would do anyone any good.

But law's the law, the right not to Know.

It took some convincing, but they finally left after cake, giving my family courteous shrugs and assuring them I'd come around.

"Your insurance will be through the roof!" my father said after they'd gone, trying to talk some sense into me while Mom clutched her phone for dear life. "An unknown expiration date with an unknown cause of fatality is a nightmare for legal paperwork. How would they even begin to give you a quote?"

"I won't get insurance then," I responded. The world still spun before there was insurance.

Both my parents just looked at one another and slowly turned to stare at me as if I'd told them I was going to commit suicide. I might as well have, there wouldn't be much difference. For all I knew, I could be hit by a truck tomorrow.

"I'm not afraid to Know," I tried to explain. It was a mistake to try and make them understand, but I couldn't help it. "I'm not going to center my life around the finish line. That's now how life was meant to work. We weren't *meant* to Know."

My mother blinked back tears. "But, Sweetie, you have

to be scanned. What if you were... tomorrow—" She hiccuped at the very thought.

I rolled my eyes. "I'm not dying tomorrow, okay?"

"You don't know that!" she shouted and buried her face in Dad's chest.

"Stop upsetting your mother," he said, trying to guilt me with mom's tears. He speared the phone in my direction. "Be a man and get scanned."

It sounds like some lame commercial logline, and it probably was. "Right," I said, "just like you're a man for planning your life down to the millisecond. You're going to die when you're forty-four, which is next year. You're going to choke on a dry piece of steak sometime in December. You're going to be like all the rest, trying to outsmart your scan. I bet you won't eat the entire month just to see if it'll work, but you'll die anyway."

I knew that I was bitter about it. I was angry that he'd had to suffer all his life knowing when he was going to die. I'd never once seen him eat steak, and he could have loved it if it hadn't been for the scan. He made such a big fuss about having a "fulfilled" life, but what was fulfilling about living the rest of your days in dread?

"You knew you'd die before I would even turn eighteen," I continued. This was a point of contention between us, the elaborate paradox that I shouldn't have been born, that in order for my father to feel he'd had a fulfilled life he had decided to have me. "What gave you the right to decide to have a child knowing I'll have to go through that?"

He opened his mouth to retort, but my mom spoke first. "Don't you talk to your father that way! If he'd denied

Knowing, then he wouldn't have been motivated to reject an ambitious career, and instead marry me and have a child young. Could you imagine? He'd have worked for something he never would have gotten, which is called an *unfulfilled* life. That's why we get ourselves scanned. It's the responsible thing to do."

I part my fingers so I can hear the protective layers of leather stretching over my skin. "Responsible," I say, testing the word. It meant something entirely different to me.

Just when I was about to waste more breath, Stacy burst through the door.

"You weren't invited," I reminded her.

We'd known each other since I was six. I tried not to look at her palms, the ones she'd reluctantly presented to the scanners and learned her fate. She was going to die at ninety-eight, painlessly, asleep in her bed.

She'd completely changed ever since she'd learned she'd outlive most of us all. I'd loved being around her, such a timid, cautious girl. But now she'd become reckless, starting with tiny shorts and sequined tops. At least her eyes were the same. She cared for me, and I knew that'd always be a constant, even if she'd taken on skydiving as a new hobby, just because she could.

"Your mom invited me," she offered. Her gaze fell to my gloves and her lips pinched. "So, you were serious."

My mother looked at her with hope, as if someone was finally going to talk sense into me. But seeing what Knowing had done to Stacy, that'd sealed the deal for me. "I don't want to become a reckless maniac like you," I said. It was harsh, and she staggered back a step, falling into my mother's waiting arms. I snapped my finger at them with accusation. "You've all built your lives around your deaths. Mom and Dad, constantly worrying about doing everything that needs doing. And you? Now you're going to throw away your whole life just because you know you can."

"Not all of it," she protested, shoving her hands in her back pockets as much as her shorts would allow. "I've got plenty, so I should enjoy it, right?"

"That's exactly my point!" I said and flung my hands wide. "You are a completely different person. You're obsessed with finding the biggest thrill, just because you know you won't die no matter how stupid you behave."

She frowned and slowly began her approach. "C'mon, David, don't be like that. I just want to enjoy my life. I was so scared and pathetic before." She smiled as she breached my personal boundary and wrapped her fingers around mine. Her warmth leeched through the thin leather and my shoulders relaxed. "I'm who I was meant to be."

Before I realized what she was doing, it was too late. Cold air hit my palm as she ripped off my glove and Stacy scanned my future with Mom's phone.

"No!" I shrieked.

She shoved the screen in my face.

It was too late. I already knew.

And I'll never be the same.

THIRTEEN
MOPPY AND ME

Moppy, Emily's stubby-legged beagle-doxie mix, wagged her tail a fraction of an inch and perked her floppy ears.

"You're sure? Bacon for breakfast?" Emily asked.

Hardly past ten years of age, Emily was like any other energetic child. She wore frilly, pink dresses to church. She enjoyed sweets and tolerated the occasional carrot. And, oh yes, she could read her dog's mind.

Bacon! Moppy's scratchy voice bounced around in Emily's head.

"Your nose never lies! Let's go." Emily grinned and bound down the carpeted steps to the first floor of the West Californian home.

Moppy hit a high note with one sharp bark before tumbling after her master, legs tangling and tongue lolling.

Mom didn't look up from her iPad when the pair burst into the kitchen in a round of giggles and growls. The ruckus of child and dog were a constant in the home. Her mother's finger poised over the screen and her eyes refused to blink.

"Two seconds!" Mom shouted. Then she slammed her finger against the screen, nearly sending the iPad flying.

Dad turned from the stove with an unamused expression Emily liked to dub the "grimily-grim face of death."

"Hun!" he said while wielding silver prongs, swatting them at Mom like a weapon. "No snipe-bidding at the table! Breakfast will be ready soon."

Emily held in a laugh and Moppy wormed around her legs. Dad trying to fuss at Mom was kind of like that woodpecker who was determined to drill a hole into the house. He always wound up hitting a nail and giving Emily a nice ping of empathetic animal pain at the crack of dawn.

With a satisfied smirk, Mom tapped the side of the device, receiving a *click*, and wiggled into her chair. As if for the first time, she seemed to realize her daughter and scruffy companion had arrived.

"So, you heard me rambling about bacon, did you?" She smiled at Dad who spread the raw bacon across the skillet. A symphony of crackles and pops filled the kitchen shortly followed by the intoxicating scent of melting fat.

Emily wrapped her hands around the edge of the counter and bounced on her toes. "No, Moppy said she smelled it." Emily leaned back and gave her dog an approving smile. "Didn't you, girl?"

Moppy yipped and wagged her tail.

Mom frowned and lowered her barely-there eyebrows. "Emily, you're old enough to stop playing make-believe with Moppy."

Emily's smile dimmed for the first time that morning.

Alpha female no understand. Secret. Keep secret. Moppy's voice surged in Emily's mind. Their bond had grown so tight in the past two years that even emotions slipped through. Emily swelled with the borrowed assurance and comfort flung by her furry friend.

"Ok, Mama." She sounded more enthusiastic than she felt, thanks to Moppy.

"Don't be so hard on her," Dad piped in. "She's an only child. She's allowed to play make-believe if she wants to."

Emily crossed her arms and set her mouth in a pout. "Dad! I'm ten!"

"Of course you are. Practically all grown up!" He flashed Emily a wink before flipping the bacon. "Speaking of being grown up, what would you say about going for a visit to see Nana? She could use some big-girl confidence."

"Yes, isn't that a lovely idea?" Mom agreed, leaning in and seeming a bit too enthusiastic for a visit to her grumpy in-law.

Emily shuffled one foot across the floor. "Nana doesn't like me anymore. Remember last time? She didn't even know who I was."

Mom stroked Emily's hair. "Sweetheart. Nana loves you very much. Her eyesight just isn't what it used to be." She tugged at Emily's frizzy locks, pulling it into pigtails. "Maybe if you wear it like you used to?"

Emily squirmed out of her grasp, running her fingers through the strands to undo even a hint of the humiliating style. "Mom! I'm all grown up, Dad just said."

Mom gave her a weak smile, taking two hair ties and

placing them into Emily's hands. "In case you change your mind."

Emily sighed, stuffing the ties in her pockets and was about to complain when her knees buckled. A snap of excitement made her heart skip a beat and she almost yipped aloud like a dog. She glanced at the floor, seeing Moppy had discovered some tossed crumbs.

Dad swirled with a napkin-covered plate filled to the brim with bubbling bacon. "Dig in!"

Emily smiled and picked out the strip with the most fat on it. With her customary sharing of the bounty, she slipped Moppy a fourth of the treat before nibbling on the end of the remains herself. It always tasted better when she borrowed Moppy's senses anyway.

The phone rang. Emily winced as the harsh, piercing tones blared in Moppy's hears. Emily choked on a bacon strip while Moppy barked and whined.

"Hush, girl," Dad chided.

Emily frowned. "It hurts Moppy's ears. I asked you to turn down the ringer. Remember?"

Dad put one finger up to his lips with a muted "*Shh*" as Mom pressed the phone against her ear and nibbled on a nail. "Yes. We'll be right over."

Emily squinted, trying to make out the voice on the other line, but all she heard were primal growls from underneath the table. She leaned down, taking a peek. Moppy was lapping up non-existent bacon grease from the white tile floor, long cleaned of any lost morsels.

"Moppy," Emily hissed. "Pay attention! I can't hear a thing."

Moppy flopped her head to the side and listened.

"Okay. See you in a bit. And... she's asking for Emily."

The phone went dead.

"Emily?" Mom said with fake enthusiasm. "Are you ready to visit Nana?"

Mom's voice had an edge to it and she stretched an awkward smiled across her face. It made her look like a bad cartoon.

Don't go! Moppy begged. *Eat bacon!*

Emily considered the poor pup. She certainly didn't want to leave. But if Nana was asking for her... then Nana remembered who she was, right?

Mom followed her gaze, and Moppy slowly wagged her tail. "We can bring Moppy, if you like," she offered.

Emily stared. She'd never been allowed to take Moppy anywhere! "Okay," she agreed.

Emily wiped bacon grease on her pants and skipped towards the door. Moppy gave one excited bark before launching across the kitchen and joining Emily on the lawn.

THE TENSION in the car made Emily bounce her legs so hard her toes were going numb. Since she couldn't run and play to get away from whatever was bothering her parents, she cracked open the window, to which Moppy promptly shoved her nose through the minuscule crack. Emily experienced the explosion of new smells and stuck out her tongue to better taste it, even though that's not how her connection worked. It was still fun.

"She's not ready for this," Dad's mumbled whispers drifted into the back seat.

"We have no choice."

"I know. But she has no idea what this means. She can't lose her bond-beast at this age."

"What's a bond beast?" Emily asked. Moppy's hearing came in handy, especially when it came to things she wasn't supposed to know.

Both Mom and Dad stiffened, as if they'd forgotten Emily was there.

"Bonded Yeast," Mom replied. "A special ingredient your father needs for dinner."

Dad's face grimaced in the rearview mirror.

Once they arrived at Nana's, Moppy took on a respectable and calm composure. Emily scratched behind Moppy's ears. "There's a good girl."

Dad rang the doorbell twice, paused, and then gave it a short third buzz. That was the code for family. Emily always thought her parents liked to pretend they were secret agents when they came to Nana's.

A caregiver opened the door and ushered them in.

The second she'd stepped inside, Emily regretted bringing Moppy. With her nose, every pungent smell of sickness and urine ripened a hundred-fold and made her want to double over and vomit. She gripped her stomach and burped.

Mom placed a warm hand on the small of Emily's back. "You all right, dear?"

Emily nodded, pinching her lips together and forcing herself to walk down the hallway. The carpet probably hadn't been vacuumed in weeks.

"Where'd the maid go?" Emily asked, taking note of the film of dust layered on the grandfather clock and ancient family portraits.

Dad frowned. "Nana's life insurance found a clause to take her off the books. She's broke, sweetie."

Mom slapped him on the shoulder. "Don't tell her that."

Dad shrugged, and his eyes lingered on Emily's. A deep sadness she'd never noticed before burned in his gaze. "She's going to have to grow up, real soon, real fast."

Mom scoffed and stomped down the hall.

With no other choice but to go forward, Emily followed the source of the odor with Moppy quick at her heels.

The living room, once full of laughing family members surrounded by antiques, was now replaced with grey medical machines surrounding one large La-Z-Boy holding up the most frail woman in the world like some kind of bizarre trophy. Emily winced at the sight of the sleeping woman, and stuffed her hands in her pockets to retrieve the hair ties.

Once her hair was fixed as best as she could manage, hoping she looked like she did when she was six, she approached her Nana.

"Nana?" she whispered, leaning across the cracked armrest and holding her breath. "It's me, Emily."

The woman opened her cloudy eyes. Emily resisted the urge to lurch back. Her Nana wasn't a corpse, not yet.

Nana blinked at Emily, wrapping her trembling fingers around one ponytail. "Emily?" she heaved herself up, trying to peer over the edge. "You've brought..."

Moppy whined, circling around Emily's feet.

"Yes, this is Moppy." Emily scooped up the pup and perched her on the edge of the La-Z-Boy.

"Emily I don't think—" Mom began.

A wrinkled hand shot up. "It's all right." The woman stared into the dogs eyes, her own going wide. "You've brought me a great gift."

Emily swallowed. "Ma'am?"

Nana latched onto her arm. It was so terrifying. Emily didn't know if she should scream or stay where she was, staring like an idiot. She opted for the latter.

"Save me." Nana's gaze pierced through Emily as if it were a spear, pleading and hopeful, and slowly fell to Moppy.

Emily shot a nervous glance to Dad, but he only shifted, wrapping his arms around himself as if he was cold even though the room was hot and stuffy without any AC to cool it.

Nana pulled her in closer. "If I die, the whole family dies. Do you understand?" Her grey eyes were wild and terrifying. "The bond-beast's curse needs a Queen. Without me, you're all dead."

Emily opened her mouth to speak as icy fear pummeled her chest, but was cut off by Nana launching into an uncontrolled fit of gasping coughs.

The caretaker pushed Emily aside. "Give her some space."

Emily backed away, but space isn't what her Nana needed. What she really needed... Emily wasn't sure she could grant.

Emily shot a look at Moppy. A wave of dread hit her when she felt Moppy's resolve.

"No," Emily whispered and feebly waved out her hand. "Get away from there, Moppy."

Before Emily could stop her, Moppy launched to Nana's lap and scampered up her heaving chest.

Emily lurched into action. "No! Moppy you can't!"

It was too late.

Nana's coughing stopped.

Everyone turned to stare. Moppy had gone limp and Nana was no longer the broken, frail woman she'd been a moment before. She was young, her cloudy eyes turned blue and her grey hair transformed into the color of the sun.

Emily broke into tears and rushed to the woman's side, wrapping her arms around Moppy's limp body.

The woman who used to be her Nana glanced at Emily, at the dog, and back again. "How long were you bonded?"

"Two years," Emily's voice cracked. She didn't care if letting Nana die would have meant she'd die too. How could she live without Moppy? Emily pressed the limp pup's body into her chest and searched for any remnants of her soul.

Young Nana shot a piercing glare at Emily's father. "Was there none other you could sacrifice? This poor child. She could—"

Emily cried, and then the room started to spin. It kept

going until she thought she was going to pass out. Everything went black and when she opened her eyes again, she'd shifted into young Nana's lap.

She opened her mouth to speak, but a sharp *yip* came out instead.

She jerked her snout to the side, only to see her own body collapsed on the floor.

Moppy's faint voice drifted from inside her mind. *You came back for me.* Their tail wagged. *Shall we go home and finish off the bacon?*

FOURTEEN
ADAM'S PORTAL

My brother always said I'd grow up to be a farmer. No matter what time of day, he could find me digging in the backyard as if I was trying to gouge a tunnel straight through to the other side. He'd tell me, "Adam, you're going to be great at planting trees. You can dig holes like no other, work the Earth and get it under your fingernails. It's as if the soil is a part of your soul! It's almost as if you're trying to climb inside the ground to find the rest of yourself. All you want to be is complete. I understand."

Actually, that's a lie. He'd call me an idiot and kick me in the ribs. But it's what I imagined he would have said when I saw him walking away after I had spit on the ground, holding my side and trying to breathe.

I wasn't born like the other kids. Instead of flesh and blood, I was sucked out from the ground, made from grit and ash like the first man to ever be alive. Though if I ever tried to tell my mother that, she'd smile and tell me I was mistaken. I was just adopted, that's all.

But I knew the truth.

I couldn't tell Jeri, or my mother, anything close to the truth. Jeri, well, he'd look at me and laugh and laugh as if I'd told the best joke of his life, which was his typical reaction whenever I tried to tell him the truth of anything.

Once, I tried. I said, "Jeri, the world isn't flat, you know. It's actually a giant arc, and it keeps going and going until it reaches the other side in a never-ending cycle spinning in the void. If we could feel the space under our feet, we'd know it was never truly still, but violent, and hurling through the blackness of space in an eternal spiral that'd only reach an end when men were long dead and gone."

His face. Oh my, his face. He screwed it up like he'd just eaten a pickle stuffed with jalapeños. Then he laughed with such a bellow, as if he'd piled up ten foghorns and blown them all at the same time.

Jeri had no idea what was what, and why should I try to tell him? It would have only frightened him, or amused him. I'm not sure which would be worse.

But today was special. The Earth would align with the moon and the sun and everything would go dark. The pitter-patter of my heart told me it was my one and only chance to get back home.

I checked my grey-blue plastic watch. Jeri had given it to me when he'd gone too far and given me a black eye. He'd thought it was funny the watch matched my face.

Five minutes to go.

"Watcha standing out here for?" Jeri asked, giving me a friendly jab in my ribs. He knew I hated anything touching my ribs.

I rolled my eyes. "I just wanted to see the eclipse."

"Miss Jadey said we have to wear special glasses to watch that."

I didn't take my eyes from the sun, locked onto the yellow orb without flinching. "Do I look like I need sunglasses?"

He scuffed his boot across the dirt. "Just because you're willing to go blind don't mean you should."

"I'm not."

"Not willing?"

I sighed. "Not going blind."

"If you say so."

I wish I could have seen his face when he turned and the land went dark. Or even my human mother's face, when I stepped through and left them all behind. But what I looked forward to actually seeing was home. There was a woman there, someone I'd left behind. Would she be waiting for me? Had she been counting down the years and the days and the hours to this very moment, just like I had?

The floodgates opened, and the shimmering swept through the air just as I'd anticipated. I couldn't see through to the other side, that's not how the gate worked. But what I could see was like a mirror of time. The world reflected as if it had turned around to stare right back into my face. Within the glass the schoolyard turned brown with age, and then shriveled up and died. All the grass was gone, replaced with a steaming land of fire and inferno.

I spun on my heel. Jeri was standing still, digging in his baggy pants looking for those silly sunglasses. Even around him I could see it, the mirror of what would come for this world, these people.

Jeri became old, his knuckles going knobby and his arms shriveling up like feeble twigs. Boils formed on his leathery skin.

A droplet rolled down my cheek, because even though he pushed me around, he was my brother. Even by blood because we cut thumbs and did a handshake when I was three. I remember it vividly, because I screamed and screamed as if he'd sliced off my hand. But at the same time, it's one of my fondest memories. He wanted to call me brother.

I started running, not to the portal, but to my human mother. I had to see her future, her fate. The eclipse wasn't going to last much longer, but it'd have to be long enough.

I burst through the rusted fence, letting it fly off its hinges like Mom always told me it'd do if I wasn't careful. Then she'd have to get Jeri to fix it, and then he'd get mad at me, and probably kick me again when she wasn't around to stop it. She'd always tell me, you have to get along with your brother. You aren't like the other boys, and you need someone older and stronger on your side. Your brother loves you, and when it counts, he'll be there to protect you, even when I can't.

I smelled her before I saw her, like when a piece of bacon is set on fire and your brother laughs because your breakfast is ruined. I turned the corner of the old shabby house, and screamed.

My mother wilted, leaning over the small dining room

table with all the flesh seared from her body. Even as steam rolled off the white ligaments sizzling in tiny bubbles, so much like the slice of bacon I'd lost, she spoke to me.

"Darling? What is it? You look as if you've seen a ghost." It smiled, the sinews stretching across her skull, widening her already permanent smile. "Are you afraid of the eclipse? It'll pass soon."

No words made their way through my tightened throat. Instead a frightened squeak came out.

The burning body shifted, rising to its feet. "What's wrong? Did something happen to Jeri?"

Tears blurred my vision and the cries stung in my throat like a hundred bits of salt across an open wound.

I ran.

The portal shimmered, a bluish sheen in the air waiting for me to step through.

I paused just before crossing the threshold, digging through my brain for the answers I knew were there.

My hand hovered over the portal.

"What are you doing?" Jeri asked, his voice a pitch higher than normal.

I closed my eyes, and stepped through.

I remembered too late. Or maybe, I wouldn't have unlocked the knowledge until I set my foot back on my own land. No, not my own land, my own time. I wasn't born like the first man. I *was* the first man.

Just like my mother, I smelled her first. But this time the scent tickled my nose, a familiar combination of roses and lilies that followed her wherever she went.

Eve.

This was all her idea. She'd hoped just as much as I that we could stop the cycle of rebirth. We couldn't live, not with destiny woven like this. What was the point of living if our children would just doom themselves into extinction?

I opened my eyes and set my sights on her once again. Her smile was sweet and sad, both at the same time.

"You came back," she whispered. "You almost didn't make it."

I lowered my eyes to the ground. Red dirt, waiting for me to be made anew.

"I think we're close. They're compassionate, even if they're still cruel. But the fires, they're still there. They will end, all of them."

She took my hand and wrapped it around her waist as she shivered. "I will die a thousand times, and I will live a thousand times, because finally, we'll get it right."

Such bravery and resilience. If only I had half of her optimism.

I lifted her tiny palm to my scruffy face, finding the sudden adjustment from boy to man disconcerting. I closed my eyes and let my tears slide over her fingers.

I took a deep breath. "If not for you, I would have let mankind die. I'd have given in, let them lust over war and power." I opened my eyes, and matched her loving gaze. "But you are the heart of this race. You believe even when I cannot." I stepped back from her and searched the ground. There was only one way I knew how to die: The snake's poison.

She knelt to the dirt, digging a small trench with her hands. The serpent would smell the fresh earth, and know we wanted to be reborn. Such trust, such belief, even the other creations yearned for a true humanity.

I held my breath and prayed to be born again with everything aligned just right, that my next body would have the code of life, the perfect harmony between the fight for survival and compassion for your brother.

I remembered Jeri. We'd been so close, Eve and I. Whatever we were missing, it was one small component. If one more rebirth filled whatever gap was in my soul, we'd finally start the lineage that would lead to a Jeri who bonded with me as a blood brother, even without cutting my thumb to do so, who smiled at me even though I made no sense to him, but most of all, we'd create a heritage that gave him enough compassion, enough not to kick his little brother when he dug a hole in the dirt for reasons he didn't understand.

My eyes snapped open as I was struck with instant clarity.

"What is it, love?" Eve asked and brushed her fingers across my cheek. "Don't lose your will. The pain is short, and then we'll be born anew. Each time is better, you've shown me that. We're fixing the future. We're doing this for them, for our children we've yet to have."

I shook my head. For once, I didn't need to hear her inspirational speech. This time, I had something to say.

"Jeri didn't understand. He was cruel because he was ignorant." I snapped my gaze to the crooked tree. Black, shriveled excuses for apples clung to it, somehow resisting the fall to the ground.

My eyes widened. "We have to eat it."

Eve leaned on my shoulder, a giddy laugh on her breath. "Truly?"

She'd asked me to try it six reincarnations ago. Knowledge, it's what humanity lacked. We had it all; we knew science, facts, the mysteries of the universe. But we couldn't pass it on. Even when we'd tried to teach our children, they'd fight amongst themselves for who was the smartest, even when they couldn't retain the simplest of mathematical algorithms.

I nodded, sure of it now. I took both her hands in mine. "I'm sorry to make you die six times. I'm sorry to put you through the suffering of it all. I should have listened to you from the very beginning."

She shook her head, her long, blonde curls bouncing across her naked breast. "No, husband. You had to try what you believed was right." She straightened. "I shall eat it first."

I watched her with guilt-ridden awe as she trotted up the hill of black sand. If I was brave, like her, I'd have eaten it first.

She plucked the lowest hanging fruit and the sickly *snap* slapped against my ears. But what was worse was the nauseating *squish* as she bit into it without hesitation. Her eyes darkened and she ran her tongue across her lips, licking up the juice.

I didn't move as she swayed over me, looking slightly ill. She reached out, offering the nibbled fruit.

"It's amazing," she said.

I knew it was a lie, but I took it anyway.

"This is for you, Jeri," I whispered before bringing the reeking fruit to my mouth, and bit down as hard as I could.

FIFTEEN
A BOX OF LOVE

I didn't know what love meant until I lost it. No, I don't mean my boyfriend broke up with me, as if I'd have time for boyfriends. I mean I found love, a small little box of it, and then I misplaced it sometime between lunch and fifth period.

I was going to be rich. I'd already had it appraised by four pawn brokers. One had connections with the government and I was going to be meeting with a CIA operative within the next week. I was in over my head, but either fame or fortune, hopefully both, would come next. Assuming of course, I still had the damn box.

I'd seen the box two weeks ago wedged between the cracked cement and the bristle thorns behind art class. No one touched it, because why would you pick up a splintered box with rusted metal hinges? Certainly not me. But something compelled me to it. Every day I paused before passing it by until I finally opened it.

Inside, there was no concept of space or time. The

tiny box showed love how it's supposed to be, indescribably infinite and beautiful in its deception. My heart swelled with the emotion and it was way better than being drunk. I was drugged, higher than high, and all I had to do to sober up was close the lid. This was love, the mysterious thing people talked about. I had no doubt I'd finally found it. The tangible source of all love in the universe.

What is one to do with the universe's love? Sell it, of course. At least, that had been the plan. One stupid moment of carelessness and now I had nothing. Just filthy hands where the box had once lain.

"Sarah?" my best friend asked. "What's wrong?"

My eyes welled with tears and my glasses fogged. Stupid non-brand glasses from Walmart I had plans on replacing with Oakleys. "I lost my box." I couldn't tell her I'd lost love. I'd lost the chance at fame and fortune. I'd never shown her what was inside. We were best friends, but it didn't mean I trusted her with something that big. To her, I had an abnormal obsession with a funky antique.

Emily rolled her eyes. "What is it with you and that box?" She softened when I sniffled. "Do you remember when you had it last?"

Desperately I tried to recall. Lunch had been the usual mystery meat Monday, followed by a boring conversation I tried to block out between Emily's co-cheerleaders: Tiffany and Brittany. I couldn't have lost the box there because I kept it in my backpack, which only got opened for notebooks, pencils, and contraband chewing gum.

Frustration pressed against my chest and I drew in a

deep breath to keep it out. "Sometime after lunch. I could have dropped it in any of my afternoon classes."

Emily brightened. "I'll help you look."

Emily never ceased to surprise me. She'd come out of nowhere four years ago and instantly bonded with me, only the fates know why. We'd been best friends ever since. Her beauty was striking and next to her, I felt like a sack of potatoes. But there was such genuine kindness in her heart. I wasn't the type to donate to charity or help an old lady across the street, so I liked to think being friends with a do-gooder like Emily gave me some good karma by osmosis.

We strolled into my third period, Algebra with Mrs. Emmerson. "Hello!" Emily chimed, putting on her "I'm an adorable student" face.

Mrs. Emmerson didn't take the bait and eyed both of us with suspicion. "I'm not giving out any extra credit for volunteer work, but if you'd like to—"

"Have you seen a small, wooden box?" I blurted before Mrs. Emmerson could task us with writing tomorrow's extensive assignment on the massive whiteboard.

She blinked before wilting and turning her attention back to the pile of ungraded algebra quizzes. "I haven't the faintest clue," she said absently as she scratched corrected formulas onto the paper. "But you're free to look around."

Before she could change her mind, I rushed to my desk at the back of the room and looked under the chair. Two blackened stubs of gum stuck to the floor, but no box.

Emily's hand rested on my shoulder. "Don't worry, we'll find it."

Just as we'd made it past the door, I could have sworn I heard Mrs. Emmerson mumbling under her breath, something about staying late and having to order pizza for her son.

MR. WRIGHT'S class was a bit easier to handle. He was a new teacher, and quite young by teacher-y standards. Emily performed a deja vu with her practiced intro. "Hello!" plus adorable student face, but this time she puffed out her chest like a chicken, putting her V-cut shirt and tan lines to full effect.

Seeing the display made me halt my own, the slight tug of my shirt to allow a teasing peek at my bra-line, since I had no tan to speak of. But seeing Emily do it, and with much greater success, made me feel silly.

Mr. Wright made the effort to look as if he were thinking, but his eyes didn't move from Emily's cleavage. "A box, you say?"

"Yeah," I offered. "It's about this big," I said and hovered my palms an inch away from one another. I scrunched my face, embarrassed to have to describe it. "It looked kind of, dirty, too, I guess?"

His polite grin flashed into a lewd smile, just for the briefest of moments. "Dirty...box. Nope, can't say I've seen it." He turned and rummaged through a stack of English essays. And by essays, I mean ramblings of our favorite TV shows that always resulted in a top score. Mr. Wright reminded me of those parents who try to be your best friend, staying up all night with you and eating pizza for breakfast.

My desk was at the front of the class right next to Mr. Wright's stool, the most coveted seat in the room. Even with my prime real-estate, he still hardly recognized me when I was the only other student next to Emily.

I gave it a once over, finding scraps of love notes under the seat but nothing to suggest I'd lost my box here.

I turned to find Mr. Wright engrossed in whatever story Emily was spinning.

"—and then my top slipped right off! Can you believe it?" she exclaimed and Mr. Wright put on an appropriate expression of shock, inefficiently hiding his delight at the imagery.

I glowered. How many times did she have to tell that pool story? It was three years ago before either of us had boobs. "Emily," I said. "I'm going to check out the gym."

"Are you sure it's not here?" she said, clearly torn between leaving me or leaving Mr. Wright.

I rolled my eyes. "I'm sure." And just as sure I'd never find love in Mr. Wright's class.

As we departed and Emily poorly hid her pout, I could have sworn Mr. Wright mumbled something about slutty teenage girls.

MY NEXT CLASS would be more of a challenge to locate lost property, since fifth period was exactly two hours from the end of lunch time, and suitable for gym. I'd hated to be clumped with the unfortunates who were stuck with P.E. as their last class of the day. Seriously, who made the schedule?

The gym was empty when we came in, but that was no surprise. I'd only been in here fifteen minutes ago and everyone ran for the buses as soon as the bell rang, not even bothering to change.

A lonely rope hung from the ceiling and a pile of sweat-glistened mats clumped underneath it. I grimaced, remembering that it had been my turn for cleanup.

"Miss Belle!" Coach Peterson bellowed, having a habit of using last names, "you've come to attend to your neglected duties?"

I curled my shoulders inward and was glad for once that Emily served as an attention magnet, sufficiently pulling any and all of it away from me.

Coach Peterson sauntered across the gym and propped his arms on his hips. "And I'm afraid I don't know who you are, miss...?"

Emily's "I'm adorable" smile seemed to be wearing out and she quirked a cute grin instead. "You don't know your own team's cheerleaders?"

Being a cheerleader meant Emily had to attend all the football games, but she could skip P.E.

Coach Peterson barked a laugh. "Sorry. I don't remember faces, just uniforms." He didn't seem bothered that Emily hadn't offered her name. "Well, uniform or not, you can cheer Miss Belle here while she cleans and puts away the mats." He gave me a wry smile.

I sighed, but didn't bother arguing. "Yes, Coach Peterson."

Not one for smalltalk, he retreated to his glass prison, as we called it. The stuffy, little office he used when not screaming at students to run as fast as their scrawny little legs could carry them. His fingers jabbed against a calculator once he was inside, his mouth going back to its familiar frown.

Emily followed as I went to the locker room to retrieve bleach wipes. When she plucked a few for herself, I offered an apologetic smile. "You don't have to help—"

"Nonsense," she insisted. "I don't mind."

The disappointment of not having found my box was softened by Emily's kindness. We wiped down the mats and searched the ground after we'd folded up each one. We were supposed to fold them in twos and then stack them neatly in the corner shelves, but that was too much work. We folded them along the worn creases where other students had also taken the easy way, and leaned them against the wall. The effect was starting to split the seams and small bits of stuffing puffed out.

I'd hoped with the mats off the floor, my box would turn up. But even with the mats gone, there was still no sign of it.

As our footsteps echoed, preceding us on our way out, I could have sworn I heard Coach Peterson's voice mumble something about lazy teenagers and budget cuts.

"THERE'S ONLY one other place it could be," Emily said after we'd walked halfway to the late bus.

Hope kindled and I rose my gaze to look at her. "Yeah? Where?"

She shrugged. "With someone who deserves it."

I blinked a few times, not sure if I'd heard her right. "What?"

She stopped and faced me, her expression turning sour. "Haven't you been paying attention?" She lifted her index finger. "One, you know Mrs. Emmerson is swamped with algebra quizzes. She has to grade every single one, and the school board hasn't given her a teacher's aide this year. And none of the parents want to get within five feet of algebraic equations, so she can't get any help there, either. So when you had a chance to give her a reprieve, let her get home twenty minutes sooner and start on dinner for her son, you declined. Your first and foremost sin: Selfishness."

My jaw locked open as she speared up a second finger. "Two, you could have picked a different teacher for your English class, but you let your hormones take over your brain. All you do is slobber and lust for Mr. Wright instead of focusing on your studies, much less finding someone your own age worthy of your affections. Sin: Lust."

"But you—" I started to remind her of her own flirtations when she snapped up a third finger.

"Three! You not only neglected your responsibilities to Coach Peterson, but you do so on a regular basis. Whenever it's your turn to help, you sneak out five minutes before the bell rings. And when you *do* help, you cut corners. Now Coach Peterson will have to use his budget to purchase new mats instead of buying new equipment for the swim team. Sin: Sloth."

Emily rushed me and I would have toppled onto the ground if a wall hadn't been behind me. My head hit the cement hard and stars sprinkled across my vision. Tears stung my eyes and I didn't know what to say.

Emily's fourth finger slowly rose, and I dreaded to hear what could come next. "Four," she said under her breath. "The moment you found your box, you would have sold it to the highest bidder. Sin: Greed, such greed I've never known."

I thought she was angry until tears brimmed her eyes as well. "How could you even imagine doing such a thing? How could you sell something so precious?"

My fingers trembled, but I found myself reaching out to her. "Emily, what are you—"

She snatched away and I was sure I'd gone crazy when her body turned translucent. Her veins appeared, organs, muscles and bones. I gasped when I saw what was inside her chest. The splintered, little box, hovering where her heart should have been.

She blinked, and I could see the water pushing through her tear ducts. "I should never had left heaven, all the other angels told me so. But I saw you, and I thought I could change you. I thought you could be worthy." Her translucent eyes closed and her tears sprinkled the ground. "I was wrong. All you managed to change was me, and I have to go back before I become just like you."

She vanished and I collapsed to the ground with a mute cry of anguish and shock. I would have cried out, but a small box fell to the ground where Emily had once stood. The box I'd lost had been old, splintered, and worn, but this one was everything a box of love should be. It glittered with diamonds, reflecting every speck of light and scattering rainbows across my knuckles. The platinum hinges didn't make a sound as I eased the lid open.

There wasn't love inside. Inside was pitch, nothing as far as the eye could see. The void pulled me in and I felt lost in a pit of forever unfulfilled desires.

Emily's voice tremored through the air. "I would have give you my heart. Instead, I give you yours."

SIXTEEN
THE BROWN-SPECKLED FINCH

The brown-speckled finch rose and fell on the blasting polar wind, not stopping his lurches or dives for anything that beckoned from below.

My influence already showed in the way his frantic flight passed by a pond with a chipped out fishing hole, blessedly fluid water that would have soothed his parched throat. And next, blurring beneath in a haze, a gathering of young raccoons squabbling over bits of dried meat he could have stolen with his lightning quick dive.

Yet something drove him on. Something powerful and important. I couldn't imagine why he wouldn't just come home where it was safe and warm.

This wasn't what I'd imagined beast-magic to be like. I thought I'd see the world with an eagle's clarity, feel the pumping power of a snow leopard, or slip through the icy deep as the water slicked past my leathery skin.

Beast-magic wasn't about me, not even a little bit. It wasn't about what I could take, but what I could give.

Seeing the world skim by through his beady eyes, I guided him as best I knew how. I'd never touched a beast's mind before. I'd only used my gifts inherited from my father, the ability to seek out what I most desired. I'd only used it before to find my mother when I'd lose her hand in a crowd, or when my older sisters told me I couldn't best them in a game of hide-and-seek.

Now I used my father's gifts for my beast. My magic burned through him, seeking something that meant more to him than his own life.

His desperate search jolted forward with my mind pushing from behind, finding the drifting hints on the winds.

When I sensed we were close, he burst his wings into action, launching through a small patch of magic that had triggered the scent. Every successful plunge lit up the sky, and what a sight that was. How I wished I could wake Papa and show him how wrong he was about beast-magic. It didn't make me go mad. I didn't lose myself. This was the most incredible, wonderful thing in the world.

Soft blue lights winked through the trees like snowflakes— but I knew what they were. Motes, the essence of life. Something my bird sought was here, and it was something alive.

The motes clung to one another, drawn to a single spot on a snow-covered tree. Whatever my bird sought was there, and my own heart leapt with his surge of joy.

My bird flattened his wings to his tiny frame and plummeted the short distance from sky to branch, snapping them out at the last possible moment in a way I'd only seen predator birds do when coming upon their prey.

Here!

In a jolt of ecstasy and panic, I realized my beast was speaking to me.

I licked my lips and pushed out my thoughts, *Where?*

He fluttered to a branch, only stopping long enough to quiver the snow off his feathers in a short, violent shake. His talons, smaller than my sewing needles, latched onto the frozen twig.

Here! Here! he exclaimed as he bounced over to a shadow gouged into the tree.

A hawk's screech burst through his elation and my finch dove to the side.

Red, searing pain blistered through my vision.

My bed exploded as I lurched free. I jerked on fur-lined boots and shivered in my thin nightgown. I hadn't planned on risking Papa's wrath, but I couldn't just leave him to die.

Pausing at my eldest sister's room, I grabbed a fistful of pink handkerchiefs off her nightstand. She could kill me later.

Papa's snores made up for my lack in stealth, camouflaging every thump and curse as I clambered down the ladder.

Rescuing Pa's thick coat from the top hook proved a challenge, and two sharp yanks won a rip and clatter as the iron hook fell to the floor.

Not turning to see if the ruckus had brought anyone

out of their slumber, I wrapped myself tight and squeezed through the doorway.

Outside, I stuffed the handkerchiefs in the coat pocket and shivered more than I should have. I was born for the cold, but not a beast-match. I wasn't supposed to take after my mother. Not when she'd died of heartbreak after loosing too many beasts-bonds. Pa said she'd lost all hope, and that's what happened to any who made use of their beast-magic.

Yet, in spite of his warning, kindling my beast-magic helped me keep her alive. I had no hope, but I had her magic.

Are you still there? I reached for my plumed friend.

Silence.

My heart lurched and my throat went dry.

Then his voice tumbled in my mind like a disoriented child. I gathered what was left of it, putting the scattering sounds together enough to form one word.

Cold.

His mind was so weak, so faint.

Find someplace warm, safe, I pleaded, sending as much strength as I could his way.

Can't... leave, his voice broke in a short burst of pain before I lost the thread of our connection to the winds.

Tears froze and scratched at the edges of my eyes.

I'd only just found him. It couldn't end like this!

I hoisted up the heavy coat and broke into a run.

I'm coming! Hold on!

In spite of the toil of trudging through snow, I raced,

lifting my knees high and bounding through the piles of fluff as best I could. My lungs burned, each new breath coming with fresh shards gripping inside my chest.

I crested the last mound and found the tree. Blue snowflakes drifted around the it like a magical fireflies, guiding me to my heart's desire.

To my feathered friend, the tree had seemed enormous. Yet the trunk I approached was barely taller than I.

My heart fractured at the sight of all that was left against the bark, a crimson slash of red and three brown-speckled feathers.

Tears and desperation brought fresh heat spreading across my chest.

He should have been in a nest, hidden in his cubby behind the barn. Or he could have listened, and nuzzled with me under the bedsheets. Why, instead, was he here? What could be so important he'd give his life?

The answer came by way of the faintest of sounds and a knocking at my heart.

Holding my breath, I approached the bloodied scene and found what had been so important to my lost friend.

Poking out of the a small gouge in the tree was a tiny beak surrounded by a puff of feathers. My eyes misted again, the trails of moisture freezing on my cheeks.

"There, little one. I'll take care of you."

On the walk home, I understood why my father had kept this magic from me. My heart was broken into a thousand pieces. I could have died in that very spot. There was nothing more that I wanted but to follow my mother and my bird into the numbing darkness.

Peeking inside the coat pocket, the chick's wrinkled eyes closed and he puffed cozily against the handkerchiefs. Slight peeps of protest rang through the cloth, letting me know it was too cold. I smiled, and decided to name him Hope.

SEVENTEEN
FORBIDDEN INK

I waved the crinkled approval papers in my mother's face. "You're seriously not going to sign? You kidding me?"

My mother scowled and folded her forearms across her chest. "You're not old enough to get a tattoo," she pointed out. Her own faded tattoo rippled across dark skin, so worn it was difficult to see. Yet as I squinted, I could make out the dull vine that wound from her wrist to her shoulder and disappeared under a T-shirt spotted with old coffee stains.

A growl rumbled in the back of my throat. "Don't be such a hypocrite. You're in no position to tell me I can't get a tattoo."

"Oh, but you're wrong," she said. "When I got my tattoo I was young, stupid, and most importantly, eighteen." She narrowed her eyes so much I was afraid her eyeliner would clump into the creases.

"But, Mom! I'll be seventeen in two months. And Emily's mom is letting her get one. It's supposed to be a bonding experience. You get that, right?"

She snorted. "I'm not Emily's mom, and if you want a bonding experience, do yoga. The answer's no."

For thirty heart-pounding seconds we matched each other's heated gaze. It was a battle I never won, not while under *her* roof.

A high-pitched shriek of disgust escaped my throat and I threw the papers in the air. My cherished blue and pink butterfly sketch floated to the ground as if I'd clipped its wings. For a moment, it glowed and flickered, and my rage was tempered with confusion.

Mom's incessant yelling snapped me out of it and the carpet muffled my stomps up the rickety staircase. Didn't she see what she was doing to me? I was so upset I was hallucinating.

Mom's threats grew to a crescendo as I launched inside my room and hurled the door shut with all my strength. Picture frames rattled and the neighbor's dog began to bark.

Rage building in my chest, I screamed at the poster hanging by one remaining staple. Alyssa Milano's angled face sneered with her punk-perfection. I resisted the urge to shred it apart. How old had she been when she'd gotten her first tattoo?

Tears and screams weren't cutting it, so I set my sights on the bed. While I'd regret shredding my favorite poster, my pillow was fair game. I lurched to the bedside and hurled my fists onto the innocent flower-speckled bedding. The pillow flattened against my onslaught.

"I won't let her tell me what to do with my own body!" I vowed. My pillow responded by pluming out to its original shape. I seethed at it and wished I wasn't so *alone*.

Answering my wish, a familiar buzz sounded against the wooden desk. My phone lit up and vibrated across the surface, threatening to fall onto the linoleum floor below.

Rescuing it just before it fell off the edge, I tapped the home button. I was met with an entourage of dancing koalas. I sighed and typed out a response. I told her what happened, which she promptly responded with yet another sad koala, except this one had annoyingly bulbous blue tears. But then she actually did something useful, told me she had a Plan B and I had to come over right now. The only thing more surprising than Emily Sterdinger's picnics-on-Sundays parents signing her tattoo approval papers was the fact that she had a Plan B in case they didn't.

The phone offered a satisfying *click* as I hit the lock button. I stared at it, finding the timing weird that Emily would have exactly what I needed, when I needed it. But, then again, she was always sending me dumb koalas and helping me out, so I shrugged and got ready for my escape.

I crouched and held my ear to the rusty grate on my floor, being sure to keep enough distance to avoid the dusty splinters framing the vent, stabbing the air like a tiny torture device.

The sounds of broken dishware being pushing into a dustpan scraped through the vent. I cursed. Mom would hear me trying to get out for sure.

A strong gust sent my drapes billowing into the room and I straightened, wondering if the universe was sending me another omen. I briefly entertained the idea of going out the window, but dismissed the notion when my memories kicked in. The young apricot tree just outside draped a promising branch low over the gutter. But looks were deceiving. I rubbed my neck as I remembered the branch bowing with my weight. It had offered absolutely no resistance to my plummet toward the dead grass below.

I clicked my tongue at its waxy leaves. Ironically, by the time it'd be old enough to support my weight, I'd be old enough not to need it.

If I couldn't climb out, that left my worst trait: stealth. I tiptoed to the closet and squeezed through the overflow of jackets and dresses, the latter being gifts from Emily I refused to wear. I blindly groped until I came across old nylon, ignoring whatever mysterious sticky substance came with it.

I grimaced at my sneakers. They were ancient and atrocious things, but they were the quietest pair of shoes I owned, plus they were black. Seemed appropriate. And while I was already suffering ill-fashioned criminal wear, I grabbed a black hoodie for good measure.

The next step was to get out of my room. With practiced ease I lifted the door by the doorknob, knowing that the lower hinge tended to squeak, and eased it open.

A humid breeze met my face as I poked my head into the hall. The clinking of broken glass had stopped, but Mom was a creature of habit. She'd be out for a smoke.

Sneaking downstairs, I spotted mom's head bobbing across the fishnet screen to the back porch. She waved her left hand about and the embers from her cigarette went flying. Meanwhile, the other hand jabbed a phone against her head.

I breathed out a sigh. For once I was glad she was

complaining to Aunt Jenny about me.

One last obstacle lay in my path. Old Max eyed me from the blotched welcome mat and didn't look inclined to move. There was a minuscule breeze that tended to make its way through the door that never fully closed, and Max made full use of it.

I crawled to the old lab. His tongue lolled out as he panted against the floor.

"Max! You gotta move, buddy." He ignored me. I hissed. His tongue drew back into his mouth and his grey eyes swirled to consider me. He wasn't impressed.

"Come on, git!" I pushed his bulky weight across the rug, but he didn't budge. Max had mastered the art of doggy-facial expressions. The way his eyes drooped made him look worried all the time, but this was different. He really seemed concerned. He was a dog, how was that possible?

I wavered on my heels and pushed him again, gentler this time. "Seriously. I want to do this, Max." Mom's shrill voice pierced the air as she mimicked my earlier scream to Aunt Jenny. I rolled my eyes. "I soooo don't sound like that."

His panting increased to mimic a doggy version of laughter. I snorted. Was he mocking me?

Having enough of his mind games, I scuttled over to the edge of the mat and grabbed the threaded ends, planting both feet securely in a determined squat.

"Okay, Max. I warned you. Time for a magic carpet ride!"

I heaved backwards. The rug slid before jerking hard

against the sticky floor.

Max startled to his feet and barked.

I frantically shushed him, but Max never listened to me. He thumped his yellow, shedding tail against my hip and huffed another encouraging bark.

Mom's irritated voice shouted through the screen. "Max, I'll let you out in a bit. Hold your horses!"

I didn't have time to worry if Mom was facing my way or not. I took the chance and jerked the door open and made a break for the shed with Max joyfully at my heel.

"Sorry, Max. You can't come with me today," I told him as I eased into the shed and grabbed my bike.

"Max? Where are you?" Mom's voice drifted over the fence.

"Crap! You stall her, okay?" I said to Max.

Surprisingly, he seemed to understand and offered a hushed bark of assurance and sat on his haunches. He licked his muzzle and closed his jaw.

"There's a good boy." I gave him a pat on the head before I walked my bike out of the wooden gate and shut it behind me.

As I stepped onto the pedals, I heard Max whining at the front door to the house. For once, fate was working in my favor.

THE BIKE RIDE to Emily's house was ingrained in my memory. I made it there in record time, appreciating the outlet for my adrenaline. Something about today felt special. The air seemed to glitter as if there were tiny fireflies guiding my way. More hallucinations.

Believing it my excitement about getting a tattoo, I brushed it off. Once the towering estate came into view, I reeled back on the pedals and eased into polished gravel.

"Hey girl!" Emily shouted gleefully, waving from the other side of the gate.

"Buttons, dumb-butt!" I shouted.

She laughed and ran behind a marble pillar to pluck in the code. I tapped my foot as the gate whined and strained on its mission to crawl slower than molasses.

When the gate had opened enough, I squeezed myself through and yanked my bike in behind me. Alarms blared in panicked protest at my forced entry. I glared at it and it made a horrid mechanical screech.

Four beeps sang as Emily overrode the flustered keypad. "Wow," she remarked. "It's never done that before." She narrowed her eyes and put in the security code again. The gate halted, thought about its new order for a moment, and then began its crawl in the opposite direction.

"I told Aaron to meet us in the Clubhouse," Emily said before spinning toward the winding path to the rest of the estate. Her daisy-laced skirt bounced around her knees by an invisible breeze. I watched her as she skipped in slow-motion to the Clubhouse. Often I wondered what it was like to be her, to be rich and white and everything the world promised was the best. Her tattoo would stand out so beautifully on her skin. I looked at my own dark hands at the thought, wondering what it would look like on me.

Then realization hit me what Emily had just said. "Did

you say Aaron?" My heart jumped in my throat.

She gave me a mischievous smile. "I know, right?" she squealed. "I'll let him explain. Come on!" She broke into a trot, her matching lace flats padding against the stone path.

I jogged after her as my heart sank into my chest. "You could have told me Aaron was your Plan B!" I shouted.

Emily only giggled in response.

What we liked to call the "Clubhouse" was really just a fancy name for a guesthouse Emily's parents didn't know what to do with. When she was eight, her father remodeled it as a Christmas present for his little girl. I was pretty sure my dad had bought me a pet rat.

A yellow-boarded, life-sized dollhouse materialized from the mass of Hibiscus trees. Even though "girly" was more Emily's thing than mine, I loved the Clubhouse. It made me think of cookies and whiskers on kittens, or whatever bull they say in the movies.

I was hit by a desperate urge to see Aaron and a white shuttered window popped open for two seconds. But in those two seconds, Aaron's eyes locked with mine. I froze. What was up with the universe today?

He flashed me a smile and then walked away from my window. This wasn't how I'd planned on making my move on Aaron. I was pretty sure he didn't even know I existed, and I wanted to keep it that way until I was the hot Afro girl with a tat.

"Howdy," Aaron said when we walked inside. He immediately rubbed his reddening neck. "Er, I mean... What's up?"

I smiled. His mother was from Texas. It was cute when

his dialect slipped.

"It's code red," Emily said with thin lips.

Aaron nodded. "Why else would I be here? I've got everything ready to go."

"Not for me, for Leslie." Emily pointed a manicured finger in my direction.

"Leslie?" he asked.

"Y-yes," I stammered. "We have algebra together?" He gave me a blank look. I gave a nervous giggle and offered my hand. "It's okay. I sit in the back, usually." My face surged with heat and I hoped he'd never noticed me leering at him in class.

He considered my hand before giving it a quick shake. His heat still tingling on my fingertips, I shoved my hand into my hoodie's pocket as if I could keep a part of him for myself.

"Well, I had planned on an ID for Emily. But I might have something that'll fit," he said with a nod to the hall.

I tilted my head as Aaron turned his broad back. ID? A fake ID? Holy--

"Leslie?" Emily interrupted my thoughts. I blinked. "It's not as bad as it sounds. Don't look so shocked."

I swallowed and trailed after Aaron into the dimly lit room. I was no Goody Two-Shoes, but a fake ID pushed my limit.

Aaron had dominated the Clubhouse library and transformed it into a scene out of CSI. An old laptop sat atop a repurposed study desk surrounded by ancient-looking machines, scraps of square photos, and plastic casings.

Aaron sat in a poufy spin-chair and put both palms on

the table. "All right. We have two options. We can make a completely fake ID from scratch, or modify an existing one. If we make a fake one, then the odds of getting caught are higher. But if we modify an existing one, it'll literally be the real thing, you just can't do anything swanky with it or the cops'll catch on."

I approached the cluttered table like a cat inspecting unfamiliar territory. "Who says I even want a fake ID?"

Emily latched onto my arm. "Come on, Leslie! It's just for the tattoo. It's not like we'll go drinking and gambling."

I began to question how badly I wanted this tattoo. But when I felt a roiling in my stomach at the thought of not getting one, there was really no choice. I couldn't describe why it was so important to me, but it just was. It felt like my life hinged on it, and that should have scared me. Instead, I straightened and ran my hands over the array of pictures with renewed interest.

Aaron clicked his tongue. "No fingerprints!"

I snatched my hands away and shoved them back into my hoodie's pockets. I offered him a glare before replying. "So, two options?"

He brushed aside a lock of blonde hair and tucked it behind his ear. My irritation with him instantly evaporated.

"Since you say this is a one-time thing, I recommend modification. It'll be easier to make, and it'll be more likely to pass inspection. Some tattoo parlors have cop-scanners for fake IDs."

I looked warily at the desk. Young faces stared up at me with awkward smiles.

"Why do all these pictures look like a bad school-photo

shoot?"

His white teeth flashed at me in a smile. "Noticed that, did you?" I blushed at his approval. "All of my stock comes from failed driver's licenses."

I shifted. "I thought they only took your picture if you passed."

Aaron raised a pointed index finger. "Ah, yes. But my brother works at the DMV and gets the picture done before the test. The throw-aways become the perfect fodder for fake IDs after a few years."

I raised my eyebrows at Emily with a "Are you hearing this?" look, but instead of balking, she grinned from ear-to-ear.

"It's fascinating, no?" she asked. Either she was developing a fondness for the intricacies of crime-life, or she was completely smitten. I frowned.

I decided that would be a problem for another time. For now, I had a livid mother at home who hadn't realized I was missing yet. If I was going to do this, then I'd better do it fast.

"What do I have to do?" I asked, hoping he couldn't hear the tremor in my voice.

Aaron had been watching Emily, as boys tended to do when she turned on her charm, and peeled his gaze away long enough to pat an old keyboard.

"Just sit back and watch the magic." He rubbed his hands together devilishly. "So... we don't have many girls 'round here with your... complexion." I narrowed my eyes at his poorly hidden lack of manners. He continued, "Ah, here." He swirled the screen so that the visage of a wild-haired beauty stared back at me. She sat so regal and proud, her hair in a perfect round puff about her face. My fingers shot up to my own spindly strands that were in much need to maintenance. Heat engulfed my face.

"She's a bit more...modelesque...but she'll do," Aaron said.

I frowned, but as I looked closer, I noticed an obvious issue with this candidate. Besides the drop-dead beauty, of course.

"Is that a glitch? It looks like she has one brown eye and one green eye."

He waved a hand and turned the screen away. "Nah, she's some freak or whatever. But eyes are easy to fix. I can change one to green, no problem."

I mutely nodded, still looking at the back of his computer contemplating my new identity.

"I'll doctor this up, and then you'll get to spend the day as..." He grinned and showed me the ID tag that read "Trisha L'Oeillet."

I frowned. "Trish... Lo-lette? Like, 'toilet' with an 'L?'"

"Low-Lay," he articulated. "New Orleans born, probably." He rolled his eyes, as if we were all related and I should have known that. Aaron dropped a few pegs in my mental score sheet.

Emily clapped her hands. "How exciting! Do you think you can make it in twenty minutes? I already scheduled the parlor."

"Already scheduled?" I asked, my voice tinged with hurt. "Were you going to go without me?"

"Oh honey, of course not. I knew Aaron would come

through." She lifted her chin. "Right, Aaron?"

He grunted as he tapped the mouse in a flurry of clicks, deep in concentration. A small wave of satisfaction found its way through my chest at Emily's dissatisfied frown.

While skilled, Aaron ate up at least twenty minutes and then some. "Convincing, wouldn't you say?" Aaron asked when he'd finished.

Emily was no longer in the room, not with her attention span, and I enjoyed Aaron's complete focus. "Yes, very well done." I took the opportunity to lean over his shoulder, pretending to look at the green-eyed beauty on the screen. I ignored the intoxicating heat of his skin.

I was forced to pull back as Aaron stretched over the table. His hand found the printer and hit an orange button. The screech of shredding plastic filled the room.

"This'll transcribe the modifications onto a new card. It'll look like the real deal," he bellowed over the noise.

Loud noises always put me on edge and I fidgeted while the machine roared like a dying animal, one that wanted to eat me. Irrational fear made me dizzy and then the machine snarled and smoke drifted through the plastic vents. A deep whisper rode the air and I could have sworn it asked, "Do you want this?"

Oblivious to the ghost that had mangled his printer, Aaron cursed. "C'mon!" he urged as he smacked it.

Now seriously getting freaked out by the trend of all the "weird," I swallowed and looked at my feet, forcing myself to calm down. *I want this,* I told myself. I felt better when the machine gurgled its final breath and the ID fell onto the floor.

Aaron scooped up the card and offered me the illegal treasure. I took it with my fingertips. It was still warm.

"Milady," he said with a heart-stopping smile.

Emily poked her head in the doorway. "All done, then? Let's go, Leslie."

Aaron cleared his throat.

Emily's face faltered. "Ah, right. Sorry." She bounded across the room and slipped a wad of twenties from her beige shoulder purse. I clenched my jaw and pretended to be fascinated by the fringes on the rug at my feet.

"Okay! Off we go." Emily linked arms with me and yanked us out of the room. I glimpsed Aaron counting the bills as we rounded the corner.

I waited until we had reached the gate to speak. "How much does he charge?"

She shrugged. "Don't worry about that."

I frowned. "You didn't have to..."

Emily pecked in the code onto the keypad with a fingernail. "I know, dumb-butt." She smiled and gave my shoulder a brief squeeze.

Leaving my bike behind, Emily and I skipped down the sidewalk with the bubbling excitement that came with doing something you knew you probably shouldn't.

The clouds parted and the sun beamed down on our faces. The glitter in the air was still there and fate seemed to say, "I'm with you."

INSIDE THE TATTOO PARLOR, the warmth of the sun

was replaced by cold leather against my thighs. I fidgeted on the blood-red sofa and blankly stared at the booklet of designs in my lap. Turning the pages only offered grotesque skulls and antique knives.

"I'm sorry you couldn't bring your design." Emily handed me my ID with a small smile. "At least this worked, yeah?"

A jaw-tingling buzz hummed behind beaded curtains and I clenched my teeth. I'd been so excited about getting a tattoo that I'd completely forgotten that there were, you know, needles involved.

After shoving the ID in my back pocket, I flipped the pages of the tattoo booklet until I found the butterfly section. They weren't nearly as pretty as the one I had found online by the parlor's star artist.

I sighed and reminded myself of the swirls of blues and oranges that pulled at something deep in my heart I never even knew existed. That's why I was doing this.

"I'm sure she can work something out," I said. "We've seen the tattoos that come out of this place and they rock. I doubt she really uses these stupid premade designs anyway." I looked up and hope mingled with fear in my chest. "We have appointments with the star artist, right?"

Emily nodded. "Yes, Lady Black. That's what they call her. Isn't that cool?" She grinned, as if I should be pleased by the news. I rolled my eyes.

The farthest curtain swept open, revealing a dark-skinned gypsy with even darker eyes. Her hair perfectly matched the multicolor beads of the curtain, billowing out in shiny black curls, accentuated by bright streaks of pink and purple. I imagined it took her hours to straighten it and curl it into such formed fashion.

She sniffed in our direction with an upturned nose. Light glinted off of her silver nose-ring.

"You Miss L'Oeillet? Miss *Sterdinger*?" She visibly cringed at Emily's last name, crossing her arms over a layer of baggy sleeves. Emily jumped to her feet with a delighted squeak. "Yes, Miss Black!"

The woman leaned on the edge of the doorway. "Lady...Black," she corrected. Then sighed and waved us in with purple nails that had been filed down to sharp claws. "Come."

Emily squeezed her hands together and gave me a mute squeal. She wasn't nervous even a little bit.

The artist being some goonie out of New Orleans swamps might not have fazed Emily, but it gave me the jeebies. I'd never been to the place myself and associated it with voodoo and old magic. I groaned and tried to keep myself calm. A tattoo artist was going to be eccentric, right? Magic was just stories for kids.

The air sparked rainbow colors at my thought, daring me to think those thoughts twice.

Emily bounced through the rainbow fog, completely oblivious of the mirage, and catapulted through beaded curtain as if she were heading into a hair salon. I took Trisha's ID from my pocket. Her striking green stare looked back at me, tinted slightly brighter than it had originally been to match my own eyes. I huffed out a short laugh when I noticed the small freckle added on the left side of the nose. Aaron was good.

"You coming or what?" Emily piped from the parted curtain.

"Yes." I returned the ID to my pocket.

The pleasant aroma of orange spice and tea tinged my nose as I went inside. Lady Black approached a table decorated by crystal faeries that dazzled even in the low-hanging fluorescent lights. She gave them fond smiles as she pulled a stick of incense from the drawer. I cringed, hoping she didn't worship the things.

Emily situated herself on a Victorian style chair. I took the less flamboyant stool.

We watched Lady Black in silence as she poured spent incense ashes into the bin. As she worked, the open folds of the back of her shirt fanned out, fluttering about her tattoo. I couldn't tell if the colorful spirals represented a sunrise or an inferno scourged across her porcelain skin. Whatever it was, I was mesmerized.

As if she sensed us staring, she stilled and placed both hands on the table. "Only one touched by the spirits...may be touched by me." Lady Black's voice came icy and low like a challenge.

"What?" Emily asked.

Lady Black crossed her arms, the baggy sleeves already rolled up to her shoulders in tidy folds. Her arms were naked from ink save the silvered bangles that bounced over her wrists.

"Have the spirits touched you?" she asked as if that were the most obvious question in the world before one got a tattoo.

"Um..." Emily crossed her legs and frowned.

"Yes," I said. It came out more confident than I felt. Emily gave me a raised eyebrow.

Lady Black slipped onto a low stool and edged close to me, far closer than I was comfortable with. "Show me," she demanded.

I swallowed. Then I remembered a snowflake of lighter skin that ran across my thigh. I stood abruptly, unbuttoning my pants.

Emily gasped with an upraised hand. "What the heck are you doing?"

"Relax, don't be a prude," I said. But even I didn't know why I was compelled to pull down my pants in front of a stranger. There was something I had to show Lady Black, something that was going to be proof that fate said I should have this tattoo. Everything else about today had been weird, what was one more thing.

I disrobed just until the beige splotch was exposed. Lady Black grabbed at it immediately, squeezing my skin and inspecting it from every angle. Her hands were impressively warm, and I wondered how she could wear such baggy clothes in this heat.

Finally, she pinched my leg one last time and offered it a friendly slap. "Yes, this'll do." Lady Black turned to Emily. "And you?"

Emily shook her head and her blonde curls seemed to flatten. "I don't have any birthmarks. I mean, I have this freckle-mole thing..." she twisted her elbow and pointed to a dark speck. "See?"

Lady Black shot up and snarled. "This is no joke, child! Get out!" A purple claw snapped to the beaded curtain.

Emily looked torn from tears or rage; the quiver across her lip could have meant either. She shot me an obstinate look. "I'm out of here."

I watched her take three steps to the door. She swirled and clenched her fists. "I'm...leaving," she emphasized.

I didn't move. This was likely my one and only chance to get ink by Lady Black. Just because Emily couldn't pass the bizarre test didn't mean I had to leave too. Didn't she understand how important this was to me? Plus, she was going to have one without me anyway. Payback's a bi--

"Fine," Emily spat. "I hope it looks *great*." And with that she swatted the curtains and left.

Lady Black snorted. "Why did you bring that one?"

I shrugged. "She's my best friend."

She purred with sympathetic understanding. "I remember the unadulterated youth, bereft of ensnaring toadstools, unicorn horns, frightening and wonderful magic. You'll learn friendships with their kind never last long." She swirled, once again turning her back to me.

I scratched my temple and let my gaze fall to the floor. Eccentric to the hilt...

She hummed a tune as she gathered her tools. It reminded me of an old French nursery rhyme, the one about plucking off bird's heads.

She smoothed a long cable attached to the tattoo machine, which could only be described as a bulky pen with metal sewing spindles attached.

"So, your ID then. Can't be too careful." She smiled. "Only purebloods allowed in my chair."

I jiggled my leg against the stool. "But, we already

checked-in at the front."

She shook her head and dangling, silvered earrings glinted against her neck. "Can't be too careful." She extended her palm, and I shivered at her words.

I dug out the card and handed it over. I held my breath, lest my chattering teeth give me away.

She hummed, but seemed satisfied. "Trisha." She leaned close and inspected my eyes. She checked the card, and looked at me again. Blood roared in my ears.

She returned the card and I nearly died with relief.

"You come from powerful blood," she remarked.

I'd never met the girl whose name I'd stolen, so I moved to change subjects. "I had a design ready, but I wasn't able to bring it," I said, thinking wistfully of the butterfly sketch that was probably being added to Max's dinner.

Her pearly molars framed her pink tongue as she openly laughed in my face. "Premade design? This is an initiation child, not a sticker for toddlers on good behavior."

She twirled a chair and motioned for me to sit. It resembled a dentist's chair, but with black leather polished to an impressive sheen. I hid away the ID into my back pocket and rubbed an elbow. I got up from my stool and eased into the cold, dentist seat.

"Do you trust me, young one?" she asked.

I was shocked to find that her eyes were not as dark as I'd first thought. I was met with the full radiance of her purple gems that dazzled like stars with lights of their own. I had looked into buying colored contacts once before, but it cost more than all the allowance I'd ever saved in my life. She must make a killing.

"I only have seventy-five dollars. What'll that get me?" I asked, holding a protective hand over the bills I'd buried in the inside pocket of my hoodie. Emily would have brought more, but I'd burned that bridge.

Her jeweled eyes blinked at me. "Your family already paid your debt."

I scrunched my shoulders. Had this Trisha girl made an appointment for a tattoo? What were the odds?

Instead of doing the right thing, I grunted a noncommittal answer. "Oh."

She smiled, tilting her head with what looked like pity. "They haven't told you why you're here, have they?"

Lady Black swirled my chair around. My vision was filled with Lady Black's work plastered onto the wall. Photos, haphazardly tacked up by pins and string, boasted designs ranging from girlish hearts and flowers to masculine dragons and snakes. Each one was different from the next, woven perfectly across the skin like an intricate tapestry.

I drew in a sharp breath. "Beautiful."

"My wall of shame." She regarded the photos with a frown.

It was my turn to blink at her. "You kidding? Those are gorgeous."

Her frown deepened and she looked to the floor. Dark and pink curls battled against the hairspray, wilting across her face. "No," she whispered. "Failures."

I scoffed. "If those are your failures, then I want you to fail on me."

She looked up, offering me a genuine smile. The gesture made her seem much younger than before. I found myself uncertain of her true age. Hardly a wrinkle marred her brow, but her makeup was thick and her skin unnaturally tan, as if trying to hide its underlying porcelain shade.

"Kind you are, young one." Her energy flooded back as she clapped her hands down on either side of me leaned into the armrests. The overpowering scent of rose perfume stung my nose.

"We shall make sure you're not on the wall of shame, yes?"

She leaned back decisively and I drew in a breath, hoping to inhale fresh air, but instead choked on orange spice smoke.

"A humming bird..." she mused, one purple nail stabbed around her lip.

"A butterfly," I managed to insist through a cough.

She narrowed her eyes. "You are brave, young one." She paced around my chair. I felt like a deer caught in a tiger's cage.

"A butterfly has two lives." She spoke in a cautious tone as her heels scrubbed against the multicolor rug. "The first is weak and blind. Then, it wraps itself up, choking off all connection from the world. And when it comes out, it has been reborn." She towered over me with a wild, violet stare. "Do you wish to be reborn?"

The answer came from my lips without a shred of doubt. "Absolutely."

I was rewarded by her gypsy yip of delight. Before I knew what was happening, she'd ripped off my hoodie and undershirt, and my bra would have gone too with her winding fingers if I hadn't clasped it to my chest.

"No interference," she insisted.

"Just undo the clasp," I said.

She huffed with irritation, but did as I asked and then lowered the chair's back so that it lay flat like a bed. She sat me in the middle and straddled the space behind me. Taking a felt-tipped pen, she began to doodle on my back and shoulders, and was busy for an agonizing fifteen minutes.

"Done!" she announced and wiped sweat from her brow.

Without waiting for permission, I scampered to the full-length mirror and arched my chin over my shoulder for a peek. She'd used silver pen across my dark skin and a breathtaking scene of swirls and butterflies floated on across my spine and shoulder blades. I was amazed pen could look so good.

She swallowed her long-cold tea and motioned for me to return. I jumped back on the seat and was ready to see what the real product looked like. But all my excitement morphed to mush the moment the buzz of the tattoo machine roared to life. "I don't know what it feels like," I muttered over the noise. "I might jump and mess you up."

She clicked her tongue. "You'll be fine. L'Oeillets have the strong blood." I swallowed. The L'Oeillets might, but I was bred from waitresses and drunks. Although, you gotta be pretty strong to deal with jerks day in and day out like that. And my father... Well, I suppose it's a feat to drink rubbing alcohol when the whiskey's run dry.

Without warning, a sharp pain radiated through my

shoulder blade as if a feisty bee had speared me with a death-stinger.

"Your soul... I paint... Your soul... I make..." she sang as she worked.

My teeth chattered as the needle seemed to vibrate straight through my skin and bones into my heart. Fires scorched through my ribs and sweat dripped down my brow. "That hurts."

Lady Black's chuckle chimed behind me. "Tis only the ink, first. Then comes the fun part."

What nonsense was she on about now? I braced myself for the "fun part" as the smoldering flames billowed down my back with impressive speed.

The hum paused as Lady Black took a damp, cold cloth and wiped it across my back. Even though it was soft, it felt like sandpaper and I couldn't help but cry out.

"Shh, young one. You'll scare off the other customers," she chided.

"Then stop rubbing it."

"Ok, here we go then." Another buzz vibrated behind my ear.

I leapt off the seat. "What are you doing?"

She held her tattoo machine with poised confusion. "The transformation won't be complete without a connection to your brain." She patted the chair. "It'll be a star, very small. And cute." She winked. "Trust me."

I narrowed my eyes, but retook my seat. "As long as I can hide it."

She laughed. "Right."

The buzz sounded like a massive hornet on steroids. I

held my bra in place with my elbows as I shoved my thumbs into my ears, but it didn't help. The pain vibrated straight through to my skull.

Luckily, the pink star was quick and she readjusted her inks before moving over to my left rib. The pain was about to reach a point that was more than I could bear, but I didn't complain. I squeezed my eyes shut and breathed through it.

Then it was over. Or so I thought.

She sighed with delighted satisfaction. "Yes, coming along very nicely." She jumped to the table of incense (long turned to ash) and pulled open its drawer.

I leaned, trying to see the contents. Something silver flashed against her wrist.

Before I had a chance to panic, or scream, or run, or soil myself, she swept out a tiny blade and sliced her palm.

"What the--" I shrieked and jumped from the chair at the sight of bright red blood running across her hand. My bra fell, forgotten in my shock.

She shoved the wound in my face and pushed out a low groan. Her purple eyes sparked to life, glowing not as if from my imagination, but with a real light of their own as she began to chant.

To my horror, I found myself lifting my hand to match hers. When my hand grazed her blood-smeared skin, I fell into an abyss of agony. My freshly inked scars lit up with white-hot flames and seared my flesh. An inferno engulfed me and I screamed inside my head. But my body wouldn't obey. I was a marble statue bound to this woman. No. This *creature*.

She opened her mouth and silver butterflies sprang from her throat. They flitted around my wrists before landing one by one, biting tiny teeth into my skin. Their venom was like ice, and I trembled despite my paralysis.

The terror ebbed as quickly as it'd come as the flames vanished and the butterflies melted into mercury. They beaded and rolled off into droplets that hit the floor, evaporating into the air as if I'd imagined them.

I fell to my knees, whimpering and convulsing before dry heaving onto the carpet.

My ears bled, but the sweet agony gifted me with the sounds of laughter and diamond chimes only magic could know. I had been lost and blind, and now I was reborn into a world where I belonged.

"You aren't a L'Oeillet. But now, you're one of us." She smiled, her purple eyes sparking with electric light. "You're a fate-maker." She lowered her head in reverence.

She fell to her knees and I curled as she ran a finger under my chin. When I looked up I saw that the room had been transformed. What I had thought were fluorescent lights were layers of fae-dust dangling on strings. Around the floorboards weren't crystal statues, but actually tiny faelings, smiling and making chitters like squirrels with merry giggles. Their jet-black skin sparkled and swirled with light of their own and they all stared at me, starry-eyed and bouncing with excitement.

Warmth radiated from behind Lady Black and I leaned into her embrace.

"You are no failure, child." Her arms squeezed. "You're my masterpiece."

THANK YOU FOR READING!

I hope you enjoyed this collection of stories that are close to my heart! It took a few years to compile this collection and I debated sharing it with the world for a long time, as it's pretty different and difficult to edit, given how long it is and I didn't want to alter the originals too much. I'm glad I took that step and have been delighted by readers who've contacted me to tell me how much they enjoyed these unique stories. I encourage you to leave an honest review on your favorite retailer so that I can hear what you think! Keep in mind I do read all my reviews, but my feelings won't be hurt if this wasn't for you. I'm assuming however if you got this far, there was something that kept you engaged, so I'd love to hear what that was. Reviews are a great way for other readers to decide if they would enjoy the collection, so thank you for taking the time!

Learn more at AJ-Flowers.com

ALSO BY A.J. FLOWERS

YA Fantasy Romance

Valkyrie Allegiance (A Complete Series)

Valkyrie Landing (Book 1)

Valkyrie Rebellion (Book 2)

Valkyrie Uprising (Book 3)

Crown Princess Academy (Book 1)

Crown Princess Academy (Book 2)

Daughter of Dragons (Standalone)

Celestial Downfall: Twisted Angelic Realms (Complete Series)

Fallen to Grace (Book 1)

Rise to Hope (Book 2)

Stand for Justice (Book 3)

Manor Saffron (Book 4)

GameLit

Reborn Online: Dungeon Worlds

Phoenix Online

Post Apocalypse

40 Days (Book 1)

Also by *USA Today* Bestselling Author A.J. Flowers

You can learn more at AJ-Flowers.com

First Law of the Valkyrie: Don't Fall in Love

Valkyrie Landing, a YA Fantasy Romance

Don't play with your food. That's the golden rule when you're a Dweller and you feast on human souls.

Book 1 in the Dweller Saga

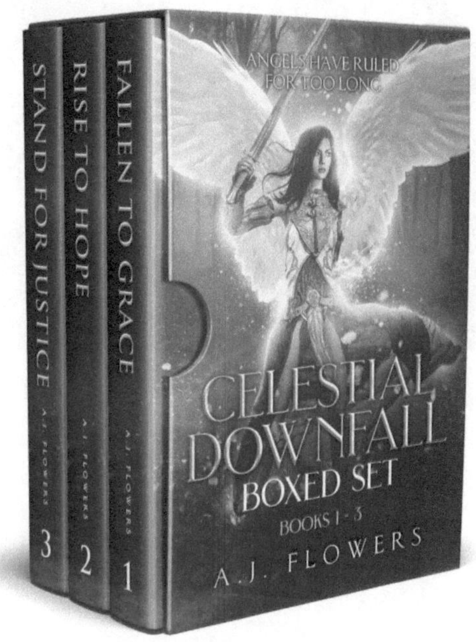

You've Never Seen Angels and Demons
Like This

Celestial Downfall: The Complete Trilogy

Thank you for reading!

AJ-Flowers.com

www.ingramcontent.com/pod-product-compliance
Lightning Source LLC
Chambersburg PA
CBHW030333310726
48979CB00001B/5
* 9 7 8 1 9 5 3 3 9 3 0 0 5 *